PUTNEY'S LAW

THE TRIAL OF DEIDRE O'NEILL

BOOK FOUR IN THE NAHUM PUTNEY SERIES

D. PRESTON DAVIDSON

For my brothers, Ed and Charles and my sister Mary.

Contents

Foreword

I thought it only fair to advise the reader that this book, in the series, makes a big time leap of fourteen years. The reason for this is the first two books of the series ended with cliffhangers. My editor, at the time, advised that I needed to present the readers with some sort of conclusion to tie up loose ends. In order to do that, in the first, Putney's War, I added an epilogue to give closure to the events at Crying Rock. But I couldn't help myself, I ended that with a cliffhanger, also. In order to wrap up that ending, I added another epilogue to the end of the second book, Putney's Secret, which also ended with a mystery.

It had occurred to me to continue in that manner, but after the third book, it simply did not make sense anymore. Besides, I had people clamoring to know what happened to Deidre O'Neill. My wife, who is always my guiding light said I should make the epilogues the beginning of another book. Like most sensible husbands, I realized my wife would have to work at being wrong, so Putney's Law was born.

Instead of making the epilogues the first two chapters though, I decided to squeeze a chapter between them. So, if you read the first two books, you will find something familiar about the first and third chapters. I did take the liberty to make a few small changes which you may not notice, unless you go back and read the epilogues in the first two.

In case you are wondering, Putney will be time traveling back to 1871, where he will be involved with a sinister group called "The Knights of the Rising Sun". No he will not be battling Samurai. That would take me out of the world of historical fiction and into the world of Fantasy Adventure, which I will leave to my friend, Bill McCurry.

Chapter One

There had been a dramatic change in Fort Worth since the first time Nahum Putney had been there, in 1871. At that time the town was just emerging from a depression caused by the Civil War. Even though it was the county seat it had still been a small, grubby, nasty place. Now as he rode down Main Street, he had to dodge the traffic of wagons, carriages, and carts of various sizes. Fort Worth had become a major stop for cattle herds, on the Chisolm Trail. A place where cattle companies could pick up supplies and cowboys could get in a little fun. When the railroad came in 1876 the town started its real boom. Now in 1884, it was a city still growing on the crest of that boom. On the south side of town, an area called Hell's Half Acre had blossomed into a twenty-four-hour sinkhole of corruption. The north side held the opposite image as the hoity-toity section of town where high-end restaurants like the Planters House and the Commercial were located. There were also saloons and gaming houses such as the Cattle Exchange Saloon and the newly renovated White Elephant Saloon. None of these were more popular than the hotel and restaurant Putney now rode past. The sign outside had gold lettering that was outlined in red and simply said O'NEILL's.

Putney had received a letter from Mary Johnson at his apartment in Austin asking for the deputy marshal's help, something Deidre O'Neill would never have done. Putney thought to himself, *"It was good Deidre had people like Mary and the Shakespeare twins to look after her because her streak of independence could often get her in tight situations."* Mary had written that a man, with a reputation with a gun, named Jim Courtright, was bullying Deidre into paying protection money. Courtright was a former city marshal who had just returned from El Paso and started a detective agency in Fort Worth. It was under the guise of this detective agency that Courtright was running his extortion venture. Mary had said the current city marshal, W. M. Rea was doing little to nothing about Courtright's racket. Mary had also written that Courtright had been running his protection scheme in Hell's Half Acre and after four owners of saloons, a bawdy house, and a dance hall had been found murdered, Courtright's business flourished. So much so that he had stepped up his endeavors to the northside establishments.

Putney knew of Courtright's reputation and, though he had never met him, Putney didn't like him. The previous year Courtright and Jim McIntire were working as deputies for U. S. Marshal A.L. Morrison in New Mexico. At the time there was one of the regular cattle disputes occurring in New Mexico and Courtright and McIntire had been part of a posse sent to arrest some cattle rustlers. The posse had stopped overnight at a line camp. The next day part of the posse went to look for rustlers but all they found were two squatters. The so-called posse took the squatters out to a ravine and executed the men. Each posse member shot into the bodies of the two Mexicans so that they would all be equally culpable. Some people said that Courtright and McIntire were part of the gang of murderers, but the deputy marshals claimed they had not been there. Thinking to cover themselves, Courtright and McIntire arrested some of the gang for the murders. Their plan backfired when those men started claiming the two deputy marshals had indeed been among the murderers. The two fled to Mexico and then returned to the United States at El Paso where they sought protection from some Texas Ranger friends. The two former lawmen managed to successfully defend themselves against extradition to New Mexico.

Nahum Putney was still working as a Deputy U. S. Marshal, but Fort Worth was no longer in the Western U. S. Court District. It was under the Northern district that had been created in 1879. So, Putney had taken some time off and wasn't in Fort Worth on official business.

Nahum decided his first stop would be the much ballyhooed, White Elephant. In the few months it had reopened, the saloon and gaming house had become the foremost jewel in Fort Worth's gaming establishments. Its reputation had already gained it a place on the West's famous gambling circuit. A big reason for its success had been the addition of Luke Short as a part owner. Short was a well-known gambler and shootist whose reputation had spread from Dodge City to Denver to Tombstone and Fort Worth. Putney wanted to see what all the puffery was about, and he figured he might find Courtright there. There was no hitching rail

3

in front of the saloon which meant Putney had to tie his horse and mule up across the street.

After dismounting Putney needed to stretch to get the kinks out. At forty-two years old riding in the saddle, days at a time, tended to knot up his muscles. Putney checked the traffic and then hurriedly crossed the street. There were two doormen on the boardwalk in front of the entrance. One stepped in front of Nahum, preventing him from entering, saying. "Don't you know there's a law against sporting that hardware openly?" Putney's pistols were plainly visible below the short vaquero-style jacket he wore.

Putney pulled back the lapel of his coat, displaying the badge, "That law doesn't apply to me." Putney told the man. The doorman looked to his partner who indicated he should let the deputy pass. The inside was everything it was purported to be, spacious and ornate. There was a long bar on one side, in the back were several pool tables, the center was filled with dining tables, and along the wall, opposite the bar were nooks where people could dine more privately. Between the pool tables and the nooks was a door with a sign that said "GAMING" and an arrow indicating the gambling hall was upstairs. Putney approached the tobacco counter located just past the entrance and asked for a pack of Kinney's. He paid for the cigarettes and hung his sombrero on a rack just inside the main hall. He walked past the men at the bar and stood at the end. Nearly every eye in the place watched the tall redhead as he strode down the bar. Putney ordered a bourbon from the barman, who readily obliged, and then Putney turned to survey the room. It wasn't but a moment when a diminutive man exited the door that led to the gambling hall. The man was wearing a tailored suit with a double-breasted vest, and a top hat. He was carrying a cane with a gold pommel, and was sporting a luxurious and dense mustache. The man walked directly to Putney and the boisterous room fell silent. The bantamweight stuck out his right hand to Putney. "Luke Short," he announced in the way of an introduction.

Putney shook the hand Short had extended and noted that the man had a firm but not hard grip. Putney also noticed that Short had the soft hands of a gambler. Someone unused to any sort of hard labor. Nahum Putney smiled and stated his own name. With

4

the tension broken, everyone in the room let out a collective sigh and went back to their business.

"Mr. Putney, we don't usually allow patrons to make such a conspicuous demonstration in the White Elephant," Short pointed to the pistols.

Putney was lighting a Kinney as he said, "There will be no trouble." and displayed the badge under his lapel. "I won't be long, Mr. Short. I was hoping to find someone and have a word with him, and then I will leave." Nahum shook out the match and put it in a brass ashtray on the bar.

"Maybe I can be of assistance," offered Short. "Who exactly are you looking for?"

"Jim Courtright," Putney's reply was short and to the point.

Luke Short flinched slightly. Most people wouldn't have noticed it, but Putney did. "Ahem. I see," Short said, "Well you can look around and observe he is not here and I can assure you Longhaired Jim is not upstairs."

"I wouldn't know. I've never seen the man," returned Putney. "But I do need to have a word with him."

Short didn't need to ask Putney why he wanted to speak with Courtright. He knew it wouldn't be a pleasant conversation. "I tell you what, Mr. Putney, I will have one of the boys scour Jim's usual haunts and give him a message that you would like to speak to him. Where should he tell Jim you will be?" Short hoped his not-so-subtle hint would encourage Putney to go elsewhere.

"Mind if I finish my cigarette and drink before you hustle me out of here?"

"Not at all Mr. Putney, in fact, I will have a drink with you," Luke Short smiled and ordered a whiskey from the barman and another for Putney. "You know I've heard of you before, Mr. Putney."

"That so?" asked Nahum "I never heard of you. Are you famous for anything?" Putney knew Short was associated with the likes of Bat Masterson, Wyatt Earp, and John Holliday, but still, he couldn't help needling the peacock of a man.

"No. Not really," said Short, realizing Putney was having a jest at his expense, so he followed up brusquely with, "Where did you say you would be?"

5

Nahum finished his drink and stubbed out his cigarette. "Anybody that wants me, can find me at O'Neill's." Putney walked out, retrieving his hat as he went.

"Give Miss O'Neill my compliments," Luke Short called after Putney, not willing to let the tall marshal have the last word.

Putney untied his animals and led them down the block to O'Neill's. It had been three years since Deidre and crew had left Austin to relocate to Fort Worth. Deidre had been wounded in a fracas at Crying Rock when Putney had been hunted down by a gang of killers led by Sherif Buck Oberman. After recuperating in Austin, Diedre returned to Llano where she and Mary testified against Buck Oberman, and she continued to run her hotel for a few years. She and Nahum would often rendezvous in Fredericksburg when he wasn't out hunting bad men, but that got tedious. Also, Llano was on the decline and so was her business, so she sold out to Bill Slocumb and moved to Austin and opened operations there. It also gave her more time to be with Putney. Business was steady with people coming to the state capital to conduct political commerce, but Austin was too prim and proper for Deidre. She sought the adventure of a boom town which had led her to Fort Worth. Putney and Deidre corresponded regularly and sometimes Putney had business in Fort Worth, but they hadn't seen each other in quite a while. Though Nahum would never admit it to anyone else, his heart began beating a little quicker as he approached the entrance.

The first person to see Putney was Mary Johnson who was working at the reception counter. When she spotted him she let out with a shriek, ran around the counter and literally jumped into Nahum's arms. She hugged his neck so strongly that he thought she might choke him to death. The staid customers entering and exiting were a bit shocked by this show of affection. Nahum gently unlocked her grasp, held her at arm's length, and looked her up and down. "Just as pretty as always, Mary," Nahum said, and he meant it.

"Wait until the boys know you're here!" Mary exclaimed. "They will be thrilled! They are in the main dining room. I'll go tell them you are here."

"Nah, let me surprise them," Nahum requested.

"All right, but I have to tell Diedre or she will skin me alive," Mary told him, then in a whisper, "Don't tell her I wrote you."

Nahum simply held his finger to his lips and gave out a quiet, "Shhh."

Nahum walked through the doors to the main dining room and waited. The diners stopped what they were doing and gawked at the tall man wearing the Mexican jacket and sombrero. He hardly had the look of O'Neill's normal customers. Theparalyzation of the customers caused the Shakespeare twins to look around. Upon seeing the deputy marshal they both hurried to greet him. "Marshal!" They both shouted as they shook his hand and patted him on the back. Then they alternated, "It's great to see you. Where you been? How long you staying?"

Putney held up his hand. "Whoa, boys. I'll be here for a couple of days. I have some business to attend to. Don't you two look stunning?"

The ebony twins were dressed in evening clothes, except their coats were the color of red wine and the lapels and cuffs were embroidered with gold. One's coat had a "B" in gold embroidery and the other a "C", an obvious attempt to distinguish the twins. Their nominal job was to greet customers and ensure they were being well looked after, but everyone knew what their real job was. From time-to-time rowdies from Hell's Half Acre would stumble in and insist on eating with the posh crowd. It was the job of the twin giants to convince them to go elsewhere. And they were very good at their jobs.

As they were winding down their greetings the double doors to the private dining room opened and loud enough for all to hear Deidre O'Neill announced, "Well! If it's not himself, the high and mighty Marshal Nahum Putney! He has come down from the mountain to grace us all with his magnificence!" Deidre took great pleasure in trying to embarrass Nahum and she was usually successful. This time was not an exception, though he tried not to show it. Instead, he walked directly to her looking her in the eyes, then with a flourish of his hat and a deep bend at the waist he announced, "I have come to bask in the radiance of Deidre O'Neill!" Deidre wasn't embarrassed at all. She simply took him by the arm and escorted him to her office, behind the hotel reception desk.

Once they were alone, Deidre threw her arms around Nahum's neck and kissed him, passionately. Their embrace and kisses lasted an eternity. When they both returned to earth Nahum held the beautiful Irish woman out to look at her. As always, she was stunning! Her red hair still blazed and seemed more red for the brilliant white streak that ran across one side. She was dressed in an elegant ball gown whose hem still touched his boots even when she was held at arm's length. It was made from emerald green taffeta that was embroidered with gold vines and red flowers. The shoulders were oversized puffs that poured into a sweet heart shaped bodice. Deidre was ageless.

Deidre was also measuring Nahum's dress and asked, "Why are you dressed like a Mexican caballero?"

"Functionality," replied Nahum. "The jacket makes it easier to get to my pistols and the hat is just better in all kinds of weather. Besides, I think it gives me a certain flair."

"There's no doubt of that," Deidre agreed, teasingly, as she walked to the door. "Mary, have the chef prepare something for me and Nahum and have it brought here. And have someone bring some champagne! Oh, and be a dear and take care of the private diners for me. I shan't be available for the rest of the night. And one last thing, Mary, Putney probably has a horse and, if I know him, a mule tied up out front. See they get taken care of, dear. Thank you," She returned to Nahum and gave him another long kiss after which she had him sit in the settee. She walked to the bar tray poured two glasses of whiskey and handed one to Nahum as she sat. "I'm finally able to get Irish here. Now tell me why you've come and why didn't you let me know."

"Business," his answer on that subject was short. "And I wanted to surprise you."

"Well, you accomplished that! I hope your business has nothing to do with Montague Russell. I saw him just the other day. He was working as a shill for Soapy Smith. How the mighty have fallen!"

"I thought Smith was in Denver," responded Nahum.

"Oh, he was, but it seems that the reopening of the White Elephant drew him back. I doubt he will stay long. What about Russell?"

"No, I'm not here for him. I reckon his time in Huntsville took the wind out of those sails," answered Nahum, remembering when he had arrested his former captain. "But enough of that. Let me look at you again."

Nahum and Deidre had been catching up for about half an hour when there was a knock on the door. Without waiting for an answer Caesar and Brutus brought in a tray of food and a magnum of chilled champagne. After they ate and drank the champagne, Deidre led Nahum down a hallway to her private apartment at the back of the hotel. They weren't seen again until noon the next day.

That morning Deidre found a tray of breakfast food and coffee on her desk. Next to her desk was a bundle that she assumed was Putney's personal items. She brought the food into her sitting room. The two had breakfast and relaxed, smoking panatelas and Kinneys. Nahum broke their silence by saying, "It looks like Mary is doing well."

"She practically runs the whole place by herself. Sometimes I think the place is mine in name only," Deidre laughed. Then in a more somber tone, she said, "Every year Mary takes the stage to Fredericksburg to visit Charlie's grave," Deidre said, referring to the fugitive Putney had been hunting near Llano and who had been killed by outlaws at Crying Rock. "She has never gotten over him. I'm sure she never will. Every time she returns, she always goes on about the beautiful marker you had made for Charlie."

"It was the least I could do for the man. And her. I wish things would have turned out differently." Nahum sincerely meant what he said.

A little after noon there was a knock on the inner office door that led to Deidre's private apartment. Deidre answered the door and returned with an envelope marked "*Private for Nahum Putney*". "I suppose this has to do with your business," said Deidre as she handed him the envelope.

Putney took a long wallet from inside his jacket and placed the envelope inside. "It can wait," he said calmly.

Deidre swiveled on him and said excitedly. "I want to promenade and shop on Main Street. You go eat some lunch or something while I get ready."

Nahum excused himself and went out into the reception area. There was a different woman, instead of Mary, at the desk, that giggled when Putney walked by and said hello. The dining room was about half full when Putney entered. He found a table, sat down, and took the envelope from his wallet. He paused until a waiter had taken his order, and then he opened the envelope. The note inside read: "I understand you want to meet with me. If that is so, I will be at the Emerald Saloon at six this evening." It was signed, "Jim Courtright."

The breakfast he and Deidre had was sufficient, so Nahum wasn't hungry and had only ordered a cup of coffee. He had just finished when Deidre came into the dining room. "How do I look?" she asked and gave herself a twirl. She looked magnificent, dressed in a tea gown of blue silk taffeta and burgundy wool. It was high-collared, long-sleeved, and had no bustle. There was gold braid that ran down the front panels of the burgundy and it was belted with a matching burgundy and gold braid belt. The blue was in the center so that there was the appearance of a burgundy coat over a blue gown. Her hair was piled high on her head which was topped by a hat filled with blue and burgundy feathers. To finish it off she carried a matching blue purse and parasol.

"You look perfect," Nahum gushed, "Much too wonderful to be seen with an old trail rider like me."

"Don't worry dear, we are going to remedy that," Deidre advised him.

They created quite the scene, walking down Main Street toward Fourth, the fashionably dressed metropolitan woman and the tall man looking like a Mexican cowboy. At the corner of Main and Fourth was a men's store and Deidre guided Nahum inside. There were the fashionable clothes such as the ones worn by the gambler, Luke Short, but Deidre knew it would be a vain attempt to get Nahum into such outfits. Instead, she looked around until she found a green sporting blazer the color of sage. It was perfect for Nahum. It had short lapels and buttoned from the center of the chest to the center of the abdomen. From there it cut away which would leave his pistols accessible. It came with a matching waistcoat that would cover the center. Deidre knew Nahum's contempt for ties and cravats, so she picked out a collarless shirt that was striped white and dark green. She found some wool pants that were already hemmed and fit Nahum

10

perfectly. The pants matched the green stripe in the shirt and went perfect with the rest of the outfit. She wanted to select a high-topped bowler which was in high fashion for men, but again she knew it wouldn't suit Nahum. Rather, she selected a dusty-colored Stetson with a wide brim that turned slightly up on the sides and dipped slightly in the front and back. The crown had a single crease that was high in the back and low in the front. She insisted that he wear the new clothes from the store and had the salesman package up Nahum's trail clothes and told him to deliver them to the O'Neill.

Next, the couple strolled over to Houston Street and back north. There was a confectioner's on Houston Street and it sold ice cream in a bowl that could be topped with syrups of different flavors. Deidre asked Nahum if he had ever eaten ice cream and he told her he hadn't, so she insisted they buy two bowls. They sat at a counter, and she ordered one with strawberry syrup and one with chocolate. Nahum agreed he had never eaten anything like it. Deidre said she might buy an ice cream machine and put it in the restaurant, a remark that made the proprietor scowl.

After leaving the candy shop, they walked arm in arm up and down the streets with Deidre looking in the windows of the various shops they passed. Often during their day, Deidre could be caught laughing like a schoolgirl. She could not remember when she had such a wonderful day. They had been gone a few hours when Nahum looked at his watch. It was five o'clock. He told Deidre that they must return as he had an appointment at six. Deidre playfully pouted but finally acquiesced. They turned back toward Main Street on Second and were passing an alley. Nahum casually looked down the alley as they passed. A man with a bandana pulled up over his face emerged behind a stack of crates, with pistol in hand. Putney swirled, pulling his own pistols. Shots rang out in the streets of Fort Worth. The only thing that could be heard over the sound of gunshots was the screaming of Deidre O'Neill.

Chapter Two

In the dim lamplight of the little room at the back room of the Emerald Saloon that served as his unofficial office, Jim Courtwright stared into a dark corner. Jim McIntire understood that this was an ill omen. McIntire and Courtwright had been off and on partners for many years and McIntire was familiar with Courtwright's moods. In this instance, Courtwright's mood was darker than the room where they sat. McIntire knew that the fuse had been lit and Courtwright might explode at any time. The other four men in the room were just as aware as McIntire that Courtwright might erupt into a tirade or just as easily pull a gun a shoot somebody, just for the hell of it. Courtwright slowly swiveled his head until his gaze fell on Montague Russell, immediately causing sweat to suddenly break out on the former captain's brow. Years earlier Russell would never have been intimidated by the likes of Courtwright, but that was before he spent ten years in prison at Huntsville. Now Russell was a shell of the man he had been.

Instead of exploding Courtwright adjusted his hat to the jaunty way he liked. When he spoke, it was more like the buzzing sound a rattlesnake makes before striking. Still looking at Russell, he asked, "Who told Blakey to shoot Putney?"

Russell shivered when Courtwright posed the question to him, implying Russell had given the command. "Not me Jim, I swear," Now sweat was running down Russell's face. "I would not overstep like that Jim. Upon my honor."

"Who would have more reason than you, Captain?" Courtwright continued his interrogation. "And you and Blakely were thick as thieves."

"Listen, Jim," Russell was pleading. "I understood your order about hands off of Putney and the O'Neill woman, at least until after you had your conference with him."

Little placated, Courtwright turned to look at McIntire. Courtwright didn't intimidate McIntire and Courtwright knew it. "James," Courtright always called his old partner by his formal name. "What do you think?"

"I'm pretty sure nobody told Blakey to shoot the deputy. You know how he felt about Putney," said McIntire. "He was drinking pretty strong yesterday. He probably took it on himself to revenge his grudge against Putney."

Courtwright mused to himself, and the dark visage slowly faded from his face. "You're probably right, James. He was dumber than hair on a barber's floor."

Everyone around the table chanced a chuckle at the remark, each one hoping it didn't set Courtwright back into a black mood. Looking around the room, it came to Courtwright that somebody was missing. "Where's Clint?"

Each man looked to the other and they all shrugged. Martin Caine, the youngest of the men in the room spoke out. "I saw him yesterday, down at a livery, grooming his horse. You know how he cares about that horse."

"Maybe he went to see his mother in Decatur. He told me she had been ill of late," this remark came from Max Poe, a big brawler who had once been a good boxer but had been punched in the head, too many times. Courtwright kept him around as a leg breaker, to help collect gambling debts.

"Possible, I suppose," agreed Courtwright. "But from now on I don't won't anyone leaving town unless they check with me or James, first. If anyone sees Clint tell him I want to see him pronto."

Courtright uncorked a bottle of whiskey that had been sitting on one corner of the table. McIntire understood the signal and went to a table on one side of the room and picked up a tray of glasses. He sat the tray down on the table as Courtwright said, "Have a drink, boys," McIntire and the other four men around the table simultaneously exhaled in relief. Catching the attention of the fifth man at the table, Bob Forney, Courtwright said, "Bob, I want you to take Max and Marty around the Acre and check on things. Collect any insurance money that's owed us and generally keep a lid on things. We don't need any attention down here for at least a couple of days." Forney nodded that he understood, quaffed down his drink, and signaled for the other two men to follow him. Courtwright then ordered Russell to go keep an eye on Soapy Smith, "I want to keep informed on what that slippery bastard is up to. You understand me, Monty?" Courtwright enjoyed calling the once proud Confederate Captain by the shortened name because he knew it ate at Russell's craw and to make sure Russell always knew who was in charge. "James, you stay here with me, we have a guest coming to visit."

The night before the meeting at the Emerald Saloon, Clint Doby made it to his mother's home outside of Decatur just after midnight. He barely had the strength to take the saddle off his buckskin mare. He had lost a lot of blood, he was sure. He had bandaged his wound the best he could, with some rags he had found in the livery barn. Luckily, the bullet had passed through the fleshy part below his right shoulder joint. Even with strength ebbing from his body, he took the time to put his horse, Molly, away in the pole barn behind the house. He had ridden her hard, getting away from Fort Worth and he didn't want to leave her lathered up in the open night air. He found a dry horse blanket and began wiping down Molly. He had always heeded his father's advice to never put a horse away wet. A man's voice came across the yard to the pole barn.

"Who's out there? Answer up. I've got a shotgun and I'll blast you to kingdom come if you don't answer up," called the man's voice.

"Don't shoot, Barney. It's me, Clint," The young man called out to his stepfather. "I'm hurt, Barney. I could use some help."

Barny Stegall arrived at the pole barn, shotgun in one hand and lantern in the other just in time to see Clint Doby slump to the ground.

Marshal Bill Rea marched through the Emerald Saloon, with the confidence of a wolf walking through a herd of sheep. Rough men and wild cowboys turned away as he strode past them, not daring to look into the eyes of the stern lawman. The soiled doves glided away from him knowing he was not a man to be approached by the likes of them. When he reached the end of the bar he stopped, hailed the barman over, and said, "Bottle of O. Z. Tyler, Jake." The barman went to the center of the bar and reached into a

14

cabinet where they kept the good bourbons, Irish and Scotch whiskies. "Bring it to the back room, Jack," said the marshal.

Bill Rea entered the room which was more well lit than it had been half an hour earlier. Jake the barman entered behind him and placed the Tyler on the table. Rea fished in his vest pocket extracted two silver dollars and gave it to the barman.

Jim Courtwright cheerfully said, "You know Bill, you didn't need to buy that bottle. I have one right here." He waved his hand at a twin bottle sitting on the table.

"I bought this bottle out front, so everyone knows I'm not beholden to you for a mere two-bit shot of whiskey," replied Rea.

"Well, sit then and we'll drink your whiskey," Cartwright smiled and pushed a clean glass toward the marshal.

Rea sat down, broke the seal on the bottle of whiskey, poured himself a healthy drink, and pushed the bottle at the two men sitting opposite him. "What's on your mind, Jim?" Rea asked Courtwright. He knew this conversation was between him and the former city marshal and that McIntire was just there as a show of strength.

"What's on my mind is that shooting yesterday," Courtwright said.

"Which one," Asked Rea.

Courtwright laughed and said to McIntire, "You see James that's what I like about old Bill. A sense of humor." Then turning to the city marshal, "Nahum Putney, of course."

"Deputy U. S. Marshal Putney was shot and nearly killed by Ned Blakely, a man of whom I think you are familiar. In turn, Blakely did wind up dead, himself."

"Did Putney kill him?"

"I doubt it. As far as I can tell, Putney fired only once. Then it seems that the woman who runs the hotel and restaurant, O'Neill's, emptied the deputy's pistol."

"So, she killed the back shooter?"

"It's hard to say right now. I'm waiting for the coroner's report. I should have it tomorrow."

"Just to let you know, Bill, it wouldn't hurt my feelings if O'Neill went to jail over this."

"What's your business in all this?"

"I would like to own her enterprise. If she were to go to jail, I figure I could buy it, cheap."

"And what do you suppose that would be worth, Jim?"

"A hell of a lot more than a two-bit shot of whiskey. Let me know when you have that coroner's report, would you, Bill." Jim McIntire picked up the marshal's bottle of whiskey, placed a fifty-dollar bill on the table, and set the bottle on top of it. Jim Court right pushed the bottle of whiskey with the fifty across the table.

Bill Rea finished his drink, pulled the bill out from under the bottle, and rose from the table. "You can keep the bottle, Jim."

Chapter Three

Nahum Putney woke and had to blink his eyes several times to get them to focus. The first thing he saw was only a blank white wall in front of him. Thinking he still hadn't focused he blinked several more times, shut his eyes hard and this time looked above himself. He saw only a blank white ceiling. Nahum was confused and wondering what had happened to him. He attempted to rise, then the pain in his chest reminded him what had happened. He had been shot. Things were starting to make sense. He must be in a hospital. He attempted another look, but this time only raised his head. Now he could see a doorway that led to a hall, but he saw nobody. Suddenly Nahum was very thirsty. He decided to call out to see if he could get someone's attention, but his voice was hoarse and croaky. He could barely hear himself, let alone make anyone else hear him. He laid his head back down in futility. He would try again in a moment.

Nahum must have fallen asleep because the next thing he knew there was a sharp pain in his chest that brought him to immediate consciousness. Opening his eyes he saw a man about his age, wearing a white smock of some kind. This man had his hands on Putney's chest and seemed to be probing around, trying to cause Nahum pain. "Stop it," Putney croaked.

The man in the white coat jerked his hands back, but gathered his wits quickly, then said, "Oh, I see you're awake, Mr. Putney."

"Water," Nahum said in little more than a whisper.

"Certainly," said the man, who by now Nahum had figured out was a doctor of some sort. Speaking to someone Putney could not see the doctor said, "Nurse, get Mr. Putney a glass of water. Maybe crank up the bed a bit first, so he can drink."

Past his feet, Nahum saw a starched white hat set on a head of dark brown hair and he heard a groan from the same direction. Nahum felt the upper portion of his body rise a little and he felt the pain in his chest again. When the nurse had him positioned where she thought he could drink she disappeared from his sight but soon returned to his side. She lifted his head slightly with one

17

hand as she placed the rim of a glass on his lips. Nahum took a few sips then she let his head back down on the pillow.

Nahum watched as the doctor replaced the nurse in his vision. "There," he said, "is that better?" Nahum nodded. "I'm Doctor Adams. I guess you're wondering why you're here."

"Somebody shot me," said Nahum as if it were an everyday occurrence.

"Yes, and they nearly killed you," Adams made it sound as if it were Putney's fault. "The bullet passed very close to your heart. You're a fortunate man to have survived. But the bullet did puncture your left lung, collapsing it. You will be here sometime until that lung heals and you can breathe well."

"What about Deidre?" Putney was less concerned about his lung than what had happened to Deidre.

"Miss O'Neill? She's well, but I think she could do with some rest," Adams said. "I asked her to step out while I examined you. She will be pleased to know you're awake. I'm about through here, anyway," Then speaking to the nurse the doctor said, "Miss Carter, be sure that someone changes this bandage every six hours until the wound stops seeping. I don't want an infection setting in and causing more problems than we need."

"Yes, doctor," said Miss Carter.

Returning his focus to Putney Adams said, "Mr. Putney, you are going to be restricted to soft foods for a while, soup, porridge, that kind of thing. We will take a look in a few days and see how you are progressing. And please don't try to get out of bed, you need to heal."

The doctor didn't need to tell him not to get out of bed. Nahum felt like he couldn't get out of bed if he tried. It wasn't a few minutes after the doctor left that Deidre came into the room. "There you are, then," she said, trying to sound cheerful. "I saw the doctor and he said you were on the mend."

"Yeah, that's his story," Nahum was not feeling Deidre's cheerfulness.

"Well, I know you, you'll be up and around in no time," Deidre said to him.

"Sure," said Nahum. "That's me. Nothing stops me." He did not believe his own words and it showed. "What happened? Who shot me? Was It Courtwright or Russell?"

18

"Neither it was some cowboy by the name of Ned Blakley is what they said," There was something in Deidre's voice that made Putney think she was holding something back. Deidre continued, "Have you ever heard of him?"

Nahum started to laugh, but it caused a coughing fit. Deidre got some water and let Nahum have several sips. When the coughing calmed Nahum said. "I know him. Remember, years ago, when I told you about Jack Callahan?"

"Yes."

"Blakely was the Missouri Bushwhacker I left nearly naked on top of that mountain," Nahum told her.

"Oh," said Deidre, "Just one of the many enemies you've made in your life."

"I guess some people can't let go of a grudge. What happened to him?" Nahum asked

"He's dead," Deidre didn't offer anything else. "I thought you were going to die too. And you would have if it hadn't been for an Indian."

"Who was he?" Nahum asked.

Deidre shrugged her shoulders. "I don't know. An Indian, tall and dressed like a white man. He saw everything that happened. When he saw you on the ground, he rushed over, picked you up, and took you to a wagon that was across the street. From what I have been told he drove those two horses like the devil was after you, to get you here. I haven't seen him since. But he most likely saved your life."

"I guess I'll have to thank him, one day," Nahum posed. "Surely somebody knows him."

"No matter, all that," Deidre told him. "The important thing is you're going to be alright. I was afraid I had lost you."

"You can't lose me. I'm like a bad penny. I always show back up," Nahum joked.

"You could turn in that badge and live here, in Fort Worth, with me," Deidre knew her plea would fall on deaf ears. She had tried before to get Nahum to give up being a lawman and settle down, but he always refused. To him, it was like a religious calling, to atone for his prior sins.

Nahum gave Deidre a look as if saying, "Please don't go there, again." But instead, he said, "I'm tired. I think I'm going to sleep a little. You go on back to your place. You can bring me up some soup later. I'm sure it will be better than what they have here." This was Nahum's way of avoiding the conversation about him taking up residence with Deidre.

"Sure, darling," Deidre knew Nahum's looks and how to read what he meant, rather than what he said. "I'll have the cook make up some beef broth with barley."

"Thank you," Nahum said and closed his eyes. He really was tired and in pain. Nahum just wanted to rest. Before leaving Deidre bent over the bed and kissed him on his forehead.

The next time Nahum woke, he was startled by what he saw. Standing at the foot of his bed was an Indian, almost as tall as he. The man was wearing a brown tailored suit and a hat with a tall round crown and wide brim. "I see you managed to live again Eka Toyatuku. I thought maybe this time you might die." Quanah Parker had a grin on his face.

"You could have let me. I guess it was you that brought me here." Said Nahum.

"I did bring you here. I was surprised to see you on the street and I was going to come speak with you when you were attacked. I needed for you to live so you could see my prophecies come true. So, I rushed you here, to the railroad hospital," Quanah said.

"What are you talking about? What prophecy?" Nahum queried.

"I told you one day I would be a great chief among my people, and you didn't believe me. You also said my mother was famous, but I was not." said Parker. "Do you remember that?"

"It took you a while, but I guess you finally made it." Said Nahum, "but not before I kept you from buying guns from Joaquin Doyle."

"Yes, our paths have crossed often and sometimes I hated you," Parker was blunt. "But I have read about you, and I have come to respect you."

"I have read about you, too, and I see that you too are famous and have done well for yourself and your people. And I want to say thank you for saving my life," Nahum was being his most sincere.

20

"That was to fulfill the second prophecy," Quanah said.

"I don't follow," Nahum said.

"Remember, I told you one day I would hold your life in my hands," Parker reminded Nahum.

"At the time, I don't think you meant it quite that way," Nahum in turn reminded Parker.

"Prophesies are funny that way, they don't always occur as you believe they will. We live in a strange world. Things happen for a reason, but who are we to question the ways of the Great Spirit?" Parker said. "But now you owe me a life and someday I will collect."

"And I will gladly pay," Nahum said. "That is my word, and you know I have never lied to you."

"This is good Eka Toyotuku," replied Quanah. "And that woman with the fiery hair. She is fierce. You should do right by her."

"Now what are you talking about," Nahum was getting tired, and Parker's ways were wearing on him.

"When that man came from the alley and shot you, you fired at him once," Quanah told Nahum. "You hit him; I think because he fell also. But I don't know if you killed him. The woman you were with. She picked up your gun and shot five times. I think maybe she wanted to make sure he was dead."

"Thanks for telling me that. I don't remember anything after I was shot," Nahum said.

"You do right by her, Nahum Putney. Like you did for that little girl so many years ago." With that Quanah Parker left the room. There was no goodbye. He was just gone.

Nahum thought to himself that it was indeed a strange world.

Two days after he had wakened Nahum was feeling much better. He was staying awake longer and even passed the time reading the local paper. It was in the paper, where he read, that another Comanche chief named Yellow Bear, who was visiting Fort Worth along with Parker, had died because of a faulty gas lamp in his hotel room. Nahum was saddened over reading about Yellow Bear, but he was glad it hadn't been Quanah.

Deidre had been visiting but had gone back to her business, and Putney was secretly glad. He loved it when she came but Deidre always made such a fuss over him that sometimes it tired him out. It had been the same with Mary Johnson when she came to visit. Mary was always fluffing his pillows and filling his water glass, which he then felt obliged to drink, and then she would refill it again. It reminded him of the time at Fort Laramie when Sue Landon and her whores had cared for him after he was shot there. He guessed it was the way with women regardless of their station in life. Women flourished when they believed a man needed to be cared for like a child.

It was different when the Shakespeare twins came to visit. Brutus and Caesar enjoyed heckling him about getting shot in the first place. He always liked seeing the twin giants, they were good company. Their good-natured joshing would lift his spirits more than the women's fussing over him. Once they brought a bottle of whiskey and Putney enjoyed a few sips until the nurse busted in. Miss Carter's original purpose was to reprimand the twins for their boisterous laughter but when she saw the bottle of liquor, she had a real fit. She ordered the twins out and told them to take the bottle of "Satan's brew" with them. Putney chuckled at the sight of the two giants slinking out of the room, hats in hand, with the short, chubby woman upbraiding them like a hen herding her chicks.

The next day nurse Carter entered the room to check on her ward. She fluffed his pillow and took his temperature and pulse before telling him there was a lady outside who wanted to see him, She asked Putney if the woman should be admitted. Nahum was tired and he couldn't think of who it would be. The last time he had been in Fort Worth he, Everett Jackson, and Margaret Swenson had arrested five members of the Knights of the Rising Sun, one of which was Captain Montague Russell. The others had been up-and-comers in Fort Worth politics, so he hadn't left Fort Worth with a lot of friends. As far as Nahum knew Meg was living in Paris, Texas with a lawyer she had married. That had been fourteen years ago, and he couldn't think why Meg would even know he was in Fort Worth. Curious, Putney said to bring the woman in.

The nurse admitted a young woman. She was a striking beauty in a very well-tailored traveling suit. The jacket was light brown tweed with a fur collar and cuffs. The skirt was a darker brown tweed that matched the fur trim of the jacket and was a newer fashion that had no bustle. It was long and fit tightly to the mid-thigh then flared out slightly to give a long bell appearance. The hem of the skirt was also trimmed in brown fur and swept a mere two inches above the floor. The lady's hair was blond and hung down to the center of her back and was topped with a fur hat that matched the rest of the fur trim. It had been a long time since Nahum had seen the woman who now must be in her mid-thirties, though she looked ten years younger. Nahum was pleasantly surprised that he should be visited by Imogene Foster.

"Well," Imogene started. "We don't see each other often and it seems when we do there's trouble. Now look at you."

Nahum took Imogene's admonishment as a good-natured jab, then said, "It is wonderful to see you again, Imogene. I have to say you look stunning. Much better than the first time we met."

"Thanks to you, of course," Imogene replied. "I dread to think about what I would have become if you hadn't rescued me. But now here I am to look in on the famous Nahum Putney. How are you, Nahum? What happened? Why aren't you in Austin or San Antonio or something, instead of Fort Worth?"

"The doctor says I'll mend alright," Nahum told his young friend. "You know I always mend. I have a little pain still, but I'm ready to get out of this place. All the nuns running around make me uncomfortable."

"I imagine so," Imogene said. "From what I read, you're lucky you don't need a priest. So, why are you here? What happened?"

"You know I've told you about Deidre O'Neill," started Nahum.

Imogene interrupted, "Oh, her," she said. "I should have known that the infamous Miss O'Neill would be involved."

"Don't start that, Imogene," said Nahum. "I've just been shot, and I shouldn't have to listen to your opinion of Deidre,"

"I'll let it pass this time," Imogene relented. "But only because you're an invalid, so go on. What happened?"

Nahum started again. "She and I were just taking an afternoon stroll around town when I was ambushed. You remember, before Quanah captured me, I told you about the Missouri Bushwhacker I had left on that hill. It was him. Evidently, he has been carrying the grudge all these years. He saw me somewhere. And true to his back-shooting nature, took advantage at my most vulnerable time. How did you know I was here?"

"Do you think something like you getting shot wouldn't make the Dallas paper?" asked Imogene. "Hell, you're as famous as Wyatt Earp or Bat Masterson. Didn't you know that?"

"I don't pay much attention to the newspapers. Most of what they write is fiction anyway," said Nahum. "I mean all the stories about Luke Short would have you believe he's ten feet tall. I met him a few nights ago and he's not as tall as you."

Imogene was about to say something when the door opened, and Deidre swept in like she owned the place. At first, she ignored the other woman in the room as she went directly to Nahum and kissed him long and passionately. It wasn't until Imogene cleared her throat that Deidre looked up and saw her. "I see, Mr. Putney, another one of your many women has come to visit."

"Hardly that, Miss O'Neill," Imogene said, truthfully although she would give almost anything if it weren't so.

"Excuse me, have we met before? I don't remember if we have," Deidre was getting ready to bare her teeth.

"No, Miss O'Neill," said Imogene. "I've just heard a lot about you from Nahum."

"All good, I'm sure, Miss…"

"Imogene Foster,"

"Oh," said Deidre. "I've heard about you, too. It's nice we finally meet. I mean we are the two most important women in Nahum's life. It would seem. He's always bragging about you and how well you've done. And how prim and proper you are," the words prim and proper were soaked in sarcasm. "But I must say I do respect your accomplishments. Especially being one of the only women to graduate from the Saint Louis School of Law."

"Thank you, Miss O'Neill and I too have heard a great deal about you," Imogene could barely hide her disapproval. "You are quite a successful woman yourself, in your way."

Nahum could see that things were about to go upside down and he was in no condition to stop a catfight. "Deidre! Imogene! Stop, both of you," he demanded. "You are both special in my life, in different ways. I will not put up with either of you sniping each other." Both the ladies took seats on either side of Nahum's bed.

24

To Putney, it was like two boxers going to their respective corners. Resting, but prepared to come to the middle of the ring as soon as the referee signaled.

Deidre took Nahum's hand and said, "You're right dear. After all, it is you, we both worry about."

Not to be outdone, Imogene took Nahum's other hand and was about to speak when there was a loud knock and a tall young man walked in, bold as brass. He didn't look to be more than twenty years old. He was wearing a six-pointed star of a sheriff on his coat lapel, and he was carrying a gun.

To Nahum, the entrance was rude, and he made a point of it, saying, "Do you always barge into rooms unannounced, boy?" Nahum asked. "And wearing your hat and all. Does this look like a barn or a saloon to you?"

The young man jerked the hat from his head and stood turning it in his hands by the brim. "No, sir, Mr. Putney. Excuse me."

"Don't excuse yourself to me, son," Nahum was intent on his lesson in manners. "There are two ladies present here, you should be apologizing to them and introduce yourself as well." Even severely wounded and lying in a hospital bed, Putney was still an imposing figure.

"Yes, sir," The young deputy sheriff was nervous in the presence of such a notorious lawman. Addressing the women in the room the deputy said, "My name is Hubert Forsythe. Excuse me ladies for bursting in and for my ungentlemanly manners." Both Deidre and Imogene nodded that they accepted his apology.

"Now, Deputy Forsythe," said Nahum. "I suppose you have business here."

"Well, uh, yes, sir," stammered the young lawman. "You see Sheriff Maddox sent me over here with a warrant for murder."

"Why did he send you and not come himself?" Putney quizzed the youngster.

"The sheriff said you might have pistols in your room, and you would be less likely to shoot a novice, like myself, than an older man," said the young deputy.

So, somebody had the gall to swear out a warrant on me for shooting a bushwhacker, thought Putney. "Well, since I'm not likely to get out of this bed, at the moment, go ahead and read your warrant. I promise when the doc allows me, I'll come over to the jail and turn myself in."

"Oh, no, sir," said Hubert. "You don't understand, the warrant isn't for you."

"Well, son, then why are you here?" Putney demanded to know.

Gathering up all his courage Deputy Hubert Forsythe announced, "Miss Deidre O'Neill, I'm here to arrest you for the murder of Ned Blakely."

Chapter Four

Had Nahum Putney been at his full health, he would have taken young Deputy Sheriff Forsyth by the ear and marched him to the Sheriff's office and told Sheriff Maddox that he could come to arrest Deidre O'Neill himself if he had the cojones. But, at best, he could only make a feeble attempt to rise from his hospital bed to protest as he watched the deputy sheriff lead Deidre out of the room.

Imogene was stunned for a moment but regained herself quickly and left to catch up to the deputy and his charge. Putney could hear her questioning the deputy, who seemed to be non-responsive, as Putney could not discern any comments from him. Imogene returned to the hospital room and showed her frustration by stomping one foot and crossing her arms. "He told me to get her an attorney," her face was turning red as she spoke. "When I told him I am an attorney he chuckled. He chuckled!" she emphasized.

Putney felt impotent. He was impotent. And he was angry. After several moments he finally said, "You must help her Imogene. I'm sure many people in this town remember me from years ago when I sent several leading citizens to prison. There is nobody here I can trust."

"But I'm not admitted to the bar here," Imogene protested. "And you have no idea how difficult it is for a woman to get admitted to the bar in a jurisdiction like this."

Putney ignored her remonstration, "Then I want you to go to O'Neill's Hotel. Talk to Mary Johnson and get a room. Tell her I sent you and she will give you the best they have. Then get over to the jail, and make sure Deidre is alright. She may balk a bit at you being her lawyer but tell her I am insisting on it. Tell her not to speak to anyone."

"But Nahum, I have my work in Dallas. I'm not making that great of a living and this would cost me clients."

"Do you have any court appearances scheduled in Dallas?"

"No…."

"Well then," Putney cut her off, "What sort of work do you have on your schedule?"

"Some wills and other civil documents that need to be filed."

"Then stay here until Deidre's preliminary hearing and she pleads not guilty. That ought to be tomorrow. Try to get a bond set."

"They're not going to set a bond on a murder case," Imogene advised Putney.

"I know that, but they should set a date for a bond hearing. That would give you a couple of days to go back to Dallas, get your cases in order, and get back here."

"But Nahum," Imogene continued her protest. "I must make a living."

"I'll pay all your fees and expenses. That will add up to more than you will make in half a year filing wills. If you need to, I will pay for another attorney to take your cases off your hands. Believe me, Sweetie, once you win this case, you will be so famous, that people will be beating down your door to hire you."

"But...." Imogene tried to continue.

"Listen, Imogene," Putney had a card to play, even though he didn't want to. "You and I have experienced more in our life than most people will in five lifetimes. When I was at my lowest, you and your family took me in and saved my life, at least from ruin. I have always been grateful for that. Because of that and your early childhood events, I set up a fund for your college and later your law school. I never wanted a thing from you other than your success and happiness. But now I'm begging you to do this for me."

Imogene's face flushed red, partly because of embarrassment, but partly due to anger. She knew Nahum understood how much she had appreciated his help. She had told him often enough, in her letters. Now he had the gall to throw this in her face. Then she looked at the ailing lawman. He lay in bed looking more pitiful than the time she and her uncle had rescued him outside a bar in McKinney, Texas on a cold winter day. Her heart softened toward him and Deidre O'Neill. "I will do my best, Nahum," she said. "But I meant to return to Dallas on the evening train. I don't have any fresh clothes, nothing that ladies need."

Putney hadn't thought of those needs, but he was glad she had made him aware. "There is a satchel in the hotel's safe. At the bottom, there is a buttoned-down pocket. In it there are five one-hundred dollar bills. Take that and get what you need. I'm sure Mary will take you to the good shops. What you don't spend, keep in the hotel's safe," Putney was starting to weaken from the excitement. Stopping to take a few breaths he gathered himself, then said, "Tell the Shakespeare twins to come see me as quick as they can."

"Shakespeare twins?" Imogene looked confused.

"I know the name sounds queer. Just tell them to come see me."

"Nahum, I don't know if I should stay in that hotel. It has a reputation."

"Forget about that. When you show up in court to represent her, you're going to gain a reputation anyway. But when you beat this charge, you will be the most famous lawyer in Texas."

Looking once again at the man who had saved her from a life of captivity with the Comanche, Imogene pitied Nahum. Probably more than the time she had discovered him outside of that saloon in McKinney. How could she refuse the man that meant so much to her? The only man she had ever loved. She bent over his bed and kissed him on the forehead. "I will do what I can, Nahum. You rest now. I will return this evening."

"Thank you, Sweetie,"

Putney was tiring quickly now and needed the rest. Imogene slipped quietly out of the room. When she was gone, Putney's mind swirled with the event of the morning. He knew he needed to rest. But how could he with so much at stake? It was an impossible situation. The doctor had told him he would have to stay in the hospital for at least another two weeks to ensure his lung capacity had returned. Even when he got released, he still wouldn't be at full strength. He would have to depend on others. The thought irritated him. He worked best on his own. The story told to him by the Apache philosopher, Jimmy Two Feathers, about the blue whale came back to him. *I got it, Jimmy.* The thought comforted him. *That's just the way it is.*

29

Putney had no idea what time it was when he was shaken awake by a nurse. He wiped the sleep from his eyes and tried concentrating. For a moment, in that time between sleeping and waking, he thought he was still dreaming and was seeing dual Colossus of Rhodes standing at the end of his bed. Blinking several times, Putney finally realized that it was the giant Shakespeare brothers. This day they were not being their usual jovial selves. Putney read the looks on their faces. "Well, I guess I don't need to tell you boys the news," he said.

"No," said Caesar. "Miss Foster told us everything."

"I don't know how this could be happening," Putney said. "But I know there is little I can do about it from this bed. "As soon as I am up and about," he let the words trail off. "I need y'all to take care of things while I'm laid up."

"Whatever you need, Marshal, we will handle it," said Caesar.

"I know you will," said Putney. "Is there anybody else in town, that you know and can trust?"

The twins exchanged looks, "There's a couple," said Caesar. "Depends on what you need."

"I need someone that can ferret out information without it getting around they are doing it for me," Putney told him.

"What do you think, Caesar?" his brother asked.

"I'm thinking Tommie Fogg, the shine boy," Julius said.

"Yeah, that's exactly who I was thinking. Nahum, Tommie gets all over town. Uptown as well as down in the Acre. People talk to him without giving it much mind. He ain't but fifteen, but he's smart as a whip and knows how to keep his mouth shut," Caesar informed Putney.

"He'll do fine, I'm sure," Putney said. "Talk to him and tell him it's important and he should be careful. "I think Courtwright may have had something to do with this, but I want to know for sure."

The twins looked to one another then Brutus asked, "What makes you think Jim Courtwright would have anything to do with any of this?"

"Because he's why I'm here. Mary wrote me about his efforts to shake down Deidre for protection money. I was supposed to meet with him the evening I was shot," Putney told him.

"Whooee," exclaimed Brutus. "I wouldn't want to be in Miss Mary's shoes when Miss Deidre finds that out."

"She's not going to, because the two of you aren't going to tell her," Putney's voice was stern.

"Not us," said Caesar. "No sir, no way."

"Good, y'all get with this Tommie Fogg. Tell him not to ask too many questions, Just keep his eyes and ears open. Tell him to get the information to one of you. You can relay the information to me."

"Consider it done," Caesar said.

"Now," Putney continued, "The second thing I need is for one of you to be with Mary and the other with Imogene all the time. Even when Imogene needs to go to Dallas. I don't want either of them moving around unprotected. Imogene has access to my money, and she can pay all expenses."

"You ain't got to pay us nothing," said Caesar. "No, sir. And we will make sure they are both safe, all the time."

"Good, that takes a weight off my mind," Putney told them. "The doctor said I could expect to be here another two weeks. Even when I get out of here, I'll be pretty weak, but I need to investigate this thing. You two are going to be busy watching the women. I need someone that can come here. Someone who can move around freely and ask questions, then report back to me. I need to know what in the world all this is about. Most importantly someone we can trust."

"I think the man for this job is Henry Morgan," Brutus said. "He's one of the daytime barmen. But I think the other barman can take up the slack. Henry's trustworthy, too. I know Miss Deidre trusts him.

Do y'all have any idea what happened with my belongings after I was shot?"

"Miss Deidre collected your clothes and the like. One of the town deputy marshals confiscated your guns.," Caesar told him.

"Alright, it may be a long time before I get them back. Tell Imogene to give Henry money to buy me a new Schofield. Two of them if possible. As soon as I have at least one under my pillow, I want to see Courtwright. Henry can get the word to him."

"Do you think he would try something, here in the hospital?" asked Brutus.

31

"I don't know. What I know of the man, he's smarter than that," Putney tried to take a deep breath, but the pain was too much. "But if he is involved, I wouldn't put it past the bastard to send an assassin to finish the job."

"What else do you need?" Caesar asked.

"I can't think of anything right now. I'm too damned tired," Putney attempted another deep breath and the pain hit him like a black smith's hammer. "I know, send someone from the restaurant with some food. The nurse will tell you what I can have."

The twins said they would take care of it and would make sure he got meals from the restaurant every day until he was ready to leave.

"Good," Putney had one last thought. "Y'all stay safe out there."

Chapter Five

Imogene had gone to O'Neill's and introduced herself to Mary Johnson explained her relationship to Nahum Putney and told Mary the two of them needed to talk. Mary had to first find Janet Maybury, the restaurant hostess who also helped at the hotel front desk. Mary told Janet to bring some coffee to Deidre's office and to watch the front desk. In the office, Mary and Imogene seated themselves in comfortable plush chairs and waited for the coffee. After Janet left Imogene began to explain the conversation Putney and she had at the hospital.

"Oh, my," Mary was impressed by Imogene. "A lady lawyer. I cannot imagine. Well, I will arrange a room for you. There is one right next to my room. It will be perfect for you. It has a wash basin with running water, but you will still need to use the common water closet at the end of the hall. When you need to bathe, I will have a copper tub brought to your room, so you can have privacy."

As impressed as Mary had been with her, Imogene was as equally impressed with Mary's hospitality and kindness. "I need to go to the jail and speak with Miss O'Neill. I'm afraid she will not be very responsive to my offer to defend her."

"Tish tosh," said Mary. "I will go with you and together we will make her understand it makes sense."

"I would so appreciate it, Mary. I fear there is some animosity between Miss O'Neill and myself."

"We will take care of it, Imogene. She can be stubborn, that is true, but she will come around."

"Thank you. Nahum also told me to send the Shakespeare brothers to see him."

"Of course. I am so glad you are here, Imogene. I was so scared for Deidre, but now I feel there is hope and it will be so nice to have another woman around to spend some time with."

"I hate to put off going to the jail, but I think I should send a telegram to Judge Willis in Dallas asking if he will send a telegram confirming that I am admitted to the bar there and that I practice law in his court. I'm afraid the sheriff here will try to prevent me from seeing Deidre unless I can prove I am indeed an attorney. I didn't bring any documentation with me, as I had just come to see Nahum."

"We have a telegram pad here. You can fill it out and I will send a bellman over to the telegraph office. In the meantime, what about clothes and other necessities?"

"You read my mind, Mary. Nahum said he has a satchel in your safe with some money in it. I will need to go shopping."

Mary clapped her hands. "That's excellent. We will go shopping while we are waiting for a response from your Judge Willis."

Imogene could tell that Mary and she would become fast friends. She was happy because she thought a friend would be something she would need in this town that was part city, part frontier town, and part cattle depot.

Mary retrieved Putney's case from the safe and brought it and a telegram pad to Imogene. "You take care of what you need," she told Imogene. "I will go tell Brutus and Caesar to go see Nahum."

Deidre O'Neill was livid and as usual, when her temper was up, her Irish brogue became more pronounced. "I will not have it," she announced to Sheriff Maddox. "I will not submit to being put on the same floor as men."

Maddox was a large affable man who was more a politician than a lawman. However, he was beginning to tire of the wild woman with the blazing hair and temper to match. He calmly removed the wire spectacles from his nose and rubbed his eyes, then looking at the woman seated in front of him, he started again as calmly as he could. "Miss O'Neill, I told you. I have directed the jailers to move the male prisoners to the cells at the far end from where you will be."

"Oh, I'm sure you have," Deidre spat the words from her mouth. "But this jail isn't known for its security. Sure and it will no be long before the guards are selling peep shows to the men. And what will stop those savages then? No, you must move all the men to a separate floor. You have three floors in this monstrous looking dungeon. You may put me on the top floor and move all the men to the first two."

Maddox exhaled with a deep sigh of exasperation. "That will not happen. I want you on the first floor where you will be safer. I keep the misdemeanors there. You will be safe."

"Oh, I see now you want to put me in with all the drunk cowboys from the stockyard bars and Hell's Half Acre. If Nahum were well, he would put you straight so quick your head would spin."

This remark was the last straw for Sheriff Maddox. "I don't give a hoot owl's damn about Nahum Putney, ill or well. I'm sheriff and his word holds no sway here. He's not even a deputy marshal in this jurisdiction so he can go piss up a rope. As for you, you will go where I tell you, else I will have Deputy Forsythe go get four or five jailers and they will haul you there, bodily if they must."

This made the young deputy sheriff very uncomfortable, and he shifted his weight from one foot to the other. "Miss O'Neill, I wish you would do like the sheriff says. I would be terribly upset if was to have to force you to a jail cell."

"You would be upset? Well, the Good Lord forbid I should upset you," Deidre's sarcasm was not lost on either the sheriff or his deputy.

"Look, Miss O'Neill," pleaded Maddox. "This is my last offer. I will send for some wagon tarps and have them strung up to separate you from any men's cells. And I will hire jailers' wives as matrons, so you won't have to deal with the men prisoners or the men jailers. That is the best I can or will do. If you don't accept that, I am done and anything that happens will be on your head."

Seeing that she had pushed the sheriff as far as he would be pushed, Deidre finally acquiesced. "Well then," she said. "I suppose that must do. But I will not go until those accommodations are in place."

"Fine," said the sheriff, though he felt far from fine. "Forsythe sit Miss O'Neill down on that bench behind the clerks. And don't leave her for nothing. I will send one of the jailers for the tarps and get some of the wives in here."

"Yes sir," Forsythe was relieved he wasn't going to be ordered to wrestle Deidre to a jail cell. "Come with me, Miss O'Neill."

Deidre allowed Hubert Forsythe to escort her to her designated spot. Sitting on the hard bench she could see over the high counter where three clerks were perched on stools. In front of one clerk stood Marshal Bill Rea. She wondered why he was there, but then she thought it wouldn't be unusual for the city marshal to be doing business at the sheriff's office.

On the third floor of the Dean Mercantile building was a suite of offices. As Bill Rea trudged up the stairs, he recalled his visit to Chicago a few months back. He had gone to the Burley and Company building and ridden an elevator to the sixth floor. It had taken less than three minutes. He hoped that buildings in Fort Worth would soon have elevators. On the third floor, he walked directly to the office of T.I.C. Commercial Detective Agency. Even having to climb three flights, he much preferred it to that seedy room behind the Emerald Saloon. He opened the door with gold lettering announcing the name of the agency. Except for a desk and a few chairs, the anteroom was empty. Rea passed through the dreary quarters, opened the door to a connecting room, and stepped into the main office. In contrast to the anteroom, the office was well appointed with a large oak desk, a small bar, four chairs, and a couch covered with leather dyed the color of blood. Behind the desk, sitting in a highbacked rocker that matched the other furniture was Jim Courtwright, feet on the desk, smiling and smoking a fat cigar.

Saying nothing to the occupant, Rea removed his hat, hung it on a coat rack, and moved directly to the bar. He mixed himself a drink of Gilbey's Gin, a dash of bitters and tonic water. There being no lemon he took his drink to the couch where he sprawled out lengthwise and took a sip. "Help yourself to a drink," Courtwright tried to make his comment cheerful, but it was soaked in sarcasm.

"Don't mind if I do," Rea returned the sarcasm. "You know Jim it wouldn't hurt you to buy a few lemons or limes once in a while," Rea needled at Courtwright. The disdain the two men had for one another hung in the room like a cow's fart. Neither Rea nor Courtwright liked the other, but theirs was a mutually beneficial relationship. Rea kept policing in Hell's Half Acre to only the most necessary and Courtwright was willing to pay handsomely for the service.

Ignoring Rea's remark, Courtwright asked, "Did you get the coroner's report?"

Rea returned with a simple, "No."

Courtwright dropped his feet to the floor, squared himself, and slammed both hands on the desk. "Why the hell not?"

"Because Sheriff Maddox got to it first. A young Deputy named Hubert Forsythe picked it up and took it to the sheriff's office."

"Damn it.

"That's not the worst of it."

"What do mean?"

"I stepped over there and got a clerk to let me have a gander at the report. A half decent lawyer would get that O'Neill woman off in a heart beat."

"How could that be? There were witnesses." Courtwright was fuming.

"Well," Rea stretched out the word.

"Come on, damn it. Quit drawing this thing out,"

"You see, Jim, I'm enjoying watching you get all itchy. This is becoming the best part of my day."

"God damn it, Bill, you don't want me to come over this desk."

"Jim, we both know that's not going to happen," Marshal Rea was serious about not being threatened by the likes of Courtwright, but he had tired of the game of taunting the former marshal. "Seems Ned Blakely was shot twice. One bullet, a forty-five caliber, hit him in the hip area and lodged up against the hip bone. It was not a mortal wound. That was most likely Putney's shot. "But," Rea paused for effect. "The second wound was in the back...."

"That don't mean anything," Courtwright jumped in, "That first bullet caused him to turn around and O'Neill picked up Putney's gun and shot Ned in the back. That's better than I could have hoped for. Murder, plain and simple."

"Not unless O'Neill is some sort of wizard, Jim. You see the second bullet lodged in Blakely's heart and it was a thirty-eight. We have both of Putney's guns and they are locked up in my office and both are Schofield's and they use the Smith and Wesson forty-five."

"That's impossible," exclaimed Courtwright. "The coroner must have made a mistake."

"You can hardly mistake a thirty-eight for a forty-five."

"Crap, you're right that calls the whole thing into question,"

Rea stood up from the couch and walked back to the bar to make himself another drink. Mixing the ingredients he said, "That would be true, unless you have an extra two hundred dollars."

"How is two hundred dollars going to fix the problem?" Courtwright was eager to know the answer."

"I'm not the only one in this town that likes a little bonus. There's a boy who works down at the coroner's office, cleaning up and such. Now, people think negroes are dumber than rocks, but that just isn't true. For a price he can be persuaded to change out the report, with the coroner's signature, mind you." Rea took a sip of his drink, then reached into his vest pocket, pulled out a small object, and tossed it at Courtwright. The object hit Courtwright's desk and bounced onto the floor. Courtwright bent over and picked up a forty-five slug. Rea continued, "And for a little more money, I can get the sheriff's clerk to replace the report and switch out the thirty-eight slug for that."

"That's brilliant," Courtwright nearly shouted. "How much is it going to cost me?"

"I already told you, Jim. Two hundred dollars. I will take care of the negro and the clerk out of that money."

Courtwright stood, smiling. "Fix me a drink, Bill. You've got a deal."

Chapter Six

Before Imogene and Mary went shopping, Mary sent a bell boy to the jail to find out when visiting ours were. He returned quickly and advised that visiting time was over at six. It was seven o'clock before a telegram arrived from Judge Willis. Mary convinced Imogene to eat a good dinner, while she had a bathtub sent to Imogene's room. The tub would be filled when Imogene was ready. She could take the night to arrange her new clothes and get anything in order she needed before they went to see Deidre the next day.

Mary knew that the previous day had been long for Imogene and let her sleep in until nine. They had a good breakfast then Imogene and Mary, accompanied by their twin bodyguards walked north on Houston Street until they came to the corner of Houston and Belknap. Across stood the county jail. Imogene was impressed by the three-story building, even while considering it a monstrosity. There was a tower that jutted out from the rest of the building. The entrance next to it looked like an afterthought. The tower was topped with a high gabled roof and to one side there were two similar towers with less high gables. On the other side, there was only one gabled spire. The building looked lopsided. Running along all three stories of the building were eight double windows, all barred. Imogene thought it looked like the castle of an evil king from a fairy book story. Imogene and Mary entered the jail, while the Shakespeare twins opted to remain outside, neither feeling comfortable being inside a jail building, even if they weren't prisoners.

As they passed through the large double oaken doors there was a set of double glass doors with Tarrant County Sheriff's Office in gold letters on one door and Walter T. Maddox, Sheriff on the other. Inside was a long counter much like that of a bank. From little barred windows built into the otherwise solid wall, clerks were conducting business. Imogene and Mary approached the only one where no other person was. A bald man with long bushy sideburns and wearing a banker's green visor asked their business.

As officially as she could, Imogene announced, "My name is Imogene Foster. I am an attorney representing Deidre O'Neill. This is my assistant; Mary Johnson and we are here to see Miss O'Neill."

The clerk chuckled, turned to one of the other clerks, and said, "Hey, Bob, get this. There's a woman here claiming to be the lawyer for the O'Neill woman." Then looking back at Imogene said. "Lady, I don't know what you are trying to pull here but the only person getting into see O'Neill will be her real attorney." He emphasized the word "real".

Imogene knew this would be the reaction. Reaching in her satchel she pulled out a yellow telegram envelope, slapped it on the counter, and with steel in her voice said, "I suggest you read this and cease giving me a difficult time."

The clerk opened the envelope and read, "To Whom It May Concern STOP this wire is to Miss Imogene Foster STOP She is an attorney admitted to the Dallas County Bar STOP She practices law in my court STOP Please provide her with all legal accommodations STOP Signed Judge John T Willis 2nd District County Court"

"Wait just a minute," the clerk said, turning to face a man sitting at a desk in the center of the room. "Tobias, come here and take a gander at this."

Tobias, a slender man with spectacles hanging on the end of his nose rose and came to the clerk. He read the telegram, then said, "Wait a moment." Tobias turned on his heels and walked out of sight through an adjacent door. It wasn't long before a large man with dark receding hair, wearing a dark suit and a string tie entered the foyer. As he approached he retrieved a case from the inside breast pocket of his coat and extracted a pair of round rimless eyeglasses. He took the telegram and studied it carefully.

Looking at the two women he asked, "Which of you is Mrs. Foster?"

Imogene raised one gloved hand, "It is Miss Foster."

"Well then, Miss Foster, my name is Walter Maddox. I am the sheriff of Tarrant County."

Imogene was impressed that her notice had gotten to the high sheriff so quickly. She had expected much stronger opposition to her request. "Very nice to make your acquaintance, Sheriff

40

Maddox. This is my assistant, Mrs. Mary Johnson and as I told this gentleman, I represent Miss O'Neill and I need to speak with her."

This being the first time he knew of Imogene's request; Sheriff Maddox was caught off guard which caused him to linger a second before deciding what to say. "Miss Foster, I know you must be fully aware that this is not Dallas County, and this request by, uh," Maddox paused to look down at the telegram, "Judge Willis just doesn't hold water here in Fort Worth, even if it is real."

Imogene was incensed. "Are you saying I am trying to fool you by showing you a fraudulent telegram?"

"It wouldn't be the first time somebody tried to use a ruse to gain access to a prisoner."

"I assure you, were I to use a ruse to gain admittance to your jail, I would have simply brought a man to say he was an attorney, and I was his assistant. You would have admitted us with no question."

The statement made more sense than Maddox wanted to admit. "What you say may be true, but I still can't accept this as prima facia evidence you are a lawyer." He could see Imogene was about to burst into a fit of anger and he had already had enough of one angry woman today, so before she could retort he said, "But I tell you what. I will let the two of you in as friends of Miss O'Neill, but only if you agree to not take anything in the cell with you, such as that bag and you submit to being searched by a matron."

Imogene crossed her arms and began tapping her foot as she was formulating another verbal attack on the sheriff when Mary tugged on her sleeve and pulled Imogen's ear down so she could whisper, "What difference does it make right now as long as we get into see Deidre?" she said, "We can come up with another strategy later, but right now this will do."

Imogene was glad she had brought Mary along with her and was thankful for the older woman's sage advice. "Thank you, Sheriff, that will suit for the time being."

"Tobias," said Maddox, "Go get Tildy to escort these two ladies to see Miss O'Neill."

Deidre leaped to her feet when she saw Mary standing on the opposite side of the bars. As soon as Tildy opened the cell door and allowed Mary in, Deidre rushed and took the smaller woman in a long embrace. "Oh, Mary I am so glad to see you." It was only after a second embrace that she noticed Imogene Foster. She looked up and down at the younger woman and greeted her with a simple, "Imogene." Deidre continued with Mary, "Oh, Mary look what they have made me wear." She stood back and twirled slowly. She was wearing a too-big, straight shift that hung on her like the wash behind the Chinese laundry. It was a dingy gray with wide black stripes that ran horizontally. Her once luxurious, fiery red hair with the white streak hung limply from her head having been gone through by matrons searching for contraband.

Mary assessed her boss acknowledging to herself that Deidre looked a pitiful mess, but in an effort to cheer her said, "There certainly is nobody who could make it look as good as you do." Continuing in that vein she excitedly said, "Look, Imogene has come to represent you as your lawyer."

Deidre took a step back and the other women saw the look of astonishment on her face. "What? Sorry dear, but I need someone who can help me win this case. I'm sure you're a good attorney and all, but I need a man lawyer, with some prominence here in Fort Worth."

Imogene had expected the rebuff and shot back, "Oh yes, and who might that be? The afternoon paper already has you half-hanged. You have a certain reputation. Deserved or not. What so-called respectable woman is going to let her husband represent you?"

"I have plenty of gentlemen friends," started Deidre.

"That's the problem," Imogene cut her off.

"I have done nothing here in Fort Worth to be ashamed of."

"I'm certain you haven't but gossip will be what it will be. And this charge of murder doesn't help that."

"Besides," Mary interjected. "It's what Nahum wants. He believes his enemies will take this opportunity to get at him through you. Deidre, Imogene is your best hope. And you must trust her and Nahum."

Deidre put her hands on her hips, stamped her right foot, and turned her back on the other two women. She didn't want them to

42

see her pout. She relaxed her shoulders and walked to her bunk, "Sure, and there are two stools by that little table there. The two of you should sit." With the last of the wind gone from her sails, she turned and sat on the edge of the bunk.

Chapter Seven

With some help from a dose of laudanum, Putney managed to sleep through the night. When he woke, he was confused and suffered from a headache and nausea. He also itched for no reason he could discern. When Doctor Adams came around that morning, Putney told him how he was feeling. "That is not uncommon for someone who isn't used to tincture of morphine," Adams said.

"Well, don't give me anymore," Putney instructed. "I can stand the pain better than this. I feel wretched."

"Certainly, Mr. Putney, but if you change your mind, all you need to do is tell the nurses," After examining him, Adams told Putney, "You seem to be healing well. I may allow you to be taken to the veranda, in the afternoons, weather allowing. But no smoking until you are much improved."

Putney said he would welcome the opportunity to get some fresh air. He was tired of smelling starched sheets and uniforms and antiseptics. The nurses and nuns in the Railroad hospital were staunch adherents of Florence Nightingale and Joseph Lister. "A nurse will bring you something to eat, soon, Mr. Putney. In the meantime, try and rest. I've been told there has been a steady stream of visitors. I would discourage you from over vigorous activity."

"Sure doctor," Putney said, knowing full well he was not planning to follow the doctor's instructions concerning visitors. There were important things that needed to be done and since he was laid up, the only way he could accomplish what he must was by having people report to him. "And no need for the nurses to worry about feeding me. I have meals coming from O'Neills."

"Just have them clear the meals with a nurse, first," Doctor Adams said as he was leaving the room.

Not long after the doctor had left there was a knock on the door and a teenage girl with long mouse-colored hair poked her head in the room. "I have brought you some breakfast, Mr. Putney," a squeaky voice that matched her hair announced. "And Mr. Morgan is with me."

Putney waved her in. She carried a tray topped with two covered bowls and a glass of milk. On her heels was a short but fit man with an unruly mop of blond hair. The girl looked around the room until she spotted a table where the tray could be placed. "Miss Johnson sent over some oatmeal and soft scrambled eggs. The nurse said it was all right." Putney nodded his approval. "Do you want the oatmeal or eggs first?" the girl asked.

"Let's hold off on that while I speak with Mr. Morgan. You don't mind waiting in the hall for a few minutes, do you?" Putney's voice was very kind to the girl. She nodded and stepped out. "You got the guns, Mr. Morgan?"

"Sure did Marshal. I was able to find one new Schofield, but the other is used. I took the liberty of running a few rounds through it to check it out first. Shoots good as new," Henry Morgan told him. The barman opened up a package wrapped in brown paper and produced the two guns.

Putney checked the weapons to make sure they were loaded. He slid one under his bed sheet, next to his right leg, and the other under his pillow. "Thanks, that was good thinking. Any news?"

"No. Nothing more than what's in the papers and what the twins told me."

"Fine," said Putney. "Do you know where the shooting took place?"

"It would be hard to miss. Soapy Smith has already started running tours to see it. He reads a lot from one of those dime novels about you."

"I haven't seen a one of them that wasn't a pack of lies," said Putney. "Anyway, here's what I want you to do. Go down there and look around. From what you say, it's probably been trounced all over, but I want you to look for anything unusual. Were those brick buildings lining the alley or wood? I don't recall."

"They're both brick, 'ceptin one has a wooden second floor," said Morgan.

"Alright, look for any scars that may have been made by bullets and see if there are any bullets lodged in the wood wall. I know Deidre's a good shot, but in the heat of things, bullets often go awry. Come back and let me know. Then I want you to find Jim Courtwright. Tell him I want to see him at six this evening," Putney thought it would be ironic to set the time the same as he

45

was supposed to meet Courtwright before. "By the way, have you got a gun, yourself?"

Morgan pulled back his jacket lapel to show a short-barreled thirty-two caliber pistol in a shoulder rig, then produced a forty-four Derringer from his vest pocket. "That's good. Go ahead and send the girl in. And be careful."

The girl entered and gave a small curtsy and walked to the tray. "What's your name, young lady?" Putney asked.

The girl blushed at being called a young lady. "Elizabeth, sir, but people call me Betsy," Putney discerned a slight downturn of her mouth when she mentioned the moniker. "What's it going to be first, Mr. Putney, eggs or oatmeal?"

"Well, Elizabeth, it all depends. Is that oatmeal sweetened?"

"Oh, yes sir," Elizabeth beamed when he called her by her name proper.

"Then let's have the eggs first. That will make the oatmeal kind of like dessert."

Elizabeth brought the tray to the bed, but it sat kind of awkward with Putney almost lying flat.

"There's a crank at the end of the bed. Think you can manage it?" asked Putney.

"I think so," Elizabeth found the crank and started twisting until Putney was in a seated position. She came over and took the cover off the eggs, reached in her apron, and pulled out salt and pepper shakers, placing them on the tray.

"Thank you, Elizabeth," Putney said. "Will you stay and keep me company while I eat?"

"Oh, yes sir," Elizabeth beamed again.

"And Elizabeth, if it's alright with you, tell Miss Johnson that only you are to bring my meals," Putney was concerned that too many people involved would present a leak of information and that was not preferable. "Unless there is a reason not or if you don't want to."

"Oh, no. I would love to bring you all your meals, Mr. Putney."

After Elizabeth had left, a nun brought Putney a copy of the Fort Worth Daily Gazette. He read a reporter's story detailing the arrest of Deidre O'Neill. The story had gone into depth about the shooting of the deputy marshal and what witnesses had said about the aftermath. Putney did not remember the details, so he had no way of judging the accuracy of the report. He read up on some other local stories, then looked up the baseball scores. The major sports stories were on the games between the Boston Beaneaters and the St. Louis Maroons in the National League and in the American League the game between the Baltimore Orioles and the Brooklyn Grays. When he got to the editorial section his blood began to boil as he read an opinion piece by Buckley B. Paddock, one of the editors of the newspaper. Paddock disparaged O'Neill's Hotel and Restaurant by calling it an "establishment of dubious reputation". Paddock listed some of Putney's past exploits and referenced two dime novels that had been written about Putney. Novels that were totally fictional having no relationship to any truth. But worse of all Paddock had the gall to refer to Deidre O'Neill as "a woman with a colored past". Paddock had all but convicted Deidre of murder. Putney threw the paper to the floor, seething with anger and thinking to himself, *As soon as I am well, my first visit may be to Buckley B. Paddock, himself.*

Putney was still fuming when there was another knock on the door. "Who the hell is it?" Putney shouted.

The door swung open about halfway and a diminutive man with a luxurious mustache peeked around the edge. "Maybe this isn't a good time," a cautious Luke Short said.

Placing his hand under the cover, Putney felt the grip of the Schofield pistol and said, "No, you may as well come in. Unless you're friends with that maggot Buckley B. Paddock."

Short looked at the paper on the floor and guessed Putney had read the editorial. "No," he said. "I can't say that I ever met the gentleman."

I am certain he is no gentleman," said Putney, "At least not a person men like us would think of as a gentleman."

"Aha," Short said proudly. "So you have heard of me."

"Sure, I have. Just getting your goat the other night. Come on in and state your business."

"I read the article by Paddock this morning and thought you could use a friendly face."

"I haven't yet decided whether your face is friendly or not."

"Believe me Putney, it is. I have no animus toward you. Especially considering what I believe to be true about your feelings concerning Long Hair Jim Courtwright."

"What do you imagine I think about Courtwright?"

"Since it's no great secret that Courtwright has been offering his detective agency to help protect businesses, especially down in the Acre, I imagine he was trying to muscle in on Miss O'Neill's place. I also imagine you came here to dissuade him of that notion."

"Assuming your imaginings are correct, why make it your concern?"

"I don't like Courtwright. It's as simple as that. He gives lawmen and shootists, alike a bad name. having had a foot in both endeavors, I take umbrage to the likes of a Cretin such as Courtwright."

"An opinion shared by many an honest man, I am sure."

"I am sure," agreed Luke Short. "But that is only one reason I have come to see you. Have you ever heard of William McLaury?"

"I can't say I have," admitted Putney.

"Maybe you have heard of the gun battle between the Earp brothers and John Holliday against the gang known as the Cowboys, in Tombstone, Arizona?"

"I expect I have, as well as most Americans."

"Two of The Cowboys killed were Tom and Frank McLaury."

"I'm guessing William is related to them in some manner."

"Brother," Short told Putney. "But more. At the time William was an attorney here in Fort Worth. He received a telegram shortly after the killings. He immediately hopped a train west and was in Tombstone three days later. Once there he joined the team of prosecutors against the Earps and Holliday."

"And what does all this mean to me?" Putney wanted to know.

"Judge Spicer held that the Earls and Holliday were all duly sworn peace officers, and all had acted within the scope of their duties."

"I'm still wondering what this has to do with either Deidre or me," Putney pushed.

"William McLaury has been appointed to prosecute your friend, Miss O'Neill. Ever since Tombstone he has a dislike

48

toward marshals. After Wyatt's appointment to Deputy U. S. Marshal, McLaury's dislike is particularly hot against federal marshals and their deputies. I think you can figure out where this is going."

Removing his hand from the butt of the pistol, Putney rubbed his temples with both hands. "What you are saying is that McLaury might try to come down heavy on Deidre because of her relationship with me.'

"No," said Short. "What I am saying is that he is going to come down heavy on her. He said as much on the courthouse steps this morning. And take a wild guess which person is the only marshal that McLaury was and is a friend to."

The pain was returning to Putney's chest and his head was now pounding. "Long Hair Jim Courtright."

"There you go."

"What is your interest in all of this?" Putney asked.

"The Earps are friends of mine. Wyatt always thought that William McLaury put up the money to pay for the assassination of Morgan and the attempted murder of Virgil. There never was any proof, but it is what Wyatt believes. I hate to think Miss O'Neill may suffer at McLaury's hands due to a vendetta against the Earps. She doesn't deserve it. And neither do you."

"Mr. Short," began Putney.

"Call me Luke, please."

"Luke, I appreciate you telling me this, but right now I am in no condition to investigate everything you have told me. But as soon as I am able it will have my full attention."

Luke Short rose from his chair and placed his Derby hat on his head. "If I can help in any way, you know where I can be found."

Putney nodded his head as Short left the room. Then he winced from pain. But this time not the pain in his chest or his head, but rather the pain in his heart.

Chapter Eight

Clint Doby lay on the bed in an upstairs room in the home of his mother and stepfather. He had hardly stirred for three days. His mother, Emma Lou had wanted to send for the doctor in Decatur, but her husband had talked her out of it. "You bring the doctor in and he will tell the sheriff," Barney Stegall had said. "The bullet went clean through, doesn't seem to have hit any bones or vitals. Blood loss, mostly. If we just keep the wound clean and feed him plenty of beef broth, he'll heal up in time. No need to bring the law into our business."

Not knowing why her son had been shot, Emma Lou saw sense in what her husband said. She prayed every morning and every night that her son would heal and not be in any trouble. Her prayers were only half answered.

On the fourth day, Emma Lou was in the kitchen cooking up some bacon and biscuits for her husband, before he went off to open up their store in town. Barney had not missed a day since Clint had ridden in on that late night. He didn't want to give people any reason to be suspicious or start gossiping. Barney was on the back porch washing up when Emma Lou heard a noise coming from the room above the kitchen. She moved the frying pan off the wood stove and called out for Barney to watch the biscuits as she headed upstairs.

Doby was sitting on the edge of the bed feeling dizzy when Emma Lou came in. "Lord, what are you doing?" She rushed to the bed.

"I gotta pee," he mumbled.

"Wait," she ordered and brought a chamber pot from under the bed. She started to pull his drawers down so he could take care of business.

"What are you doing?" Clint was nearly shocked into full consciousness.

"It ain't like I never seen you naked before," his mother told him.[9]

"Well, I ain't no baby anymore. I can take care of it from here."

50

Emma Lou sighed, exited the room, closed the door, and waited, listening for water to hit the porcelain covered pot. When the noise stopped, she waited a few seconds and then reentered the room. She found Clint struggling to get his drawers up. She went and helped him. She got no complaints this time. Clint hurt too much to complain anymore.

"How long have I been here?" he feebly asked.

"Four days now," said Emma Lou.

"Anybody come looking for me?"

"No. Nobody knows you're here. Are you in trouble son?'

"Dunno."

Emma Lou's voice was trembling when she asked, "What have you done son?"

"I don't want to talk about it right now, Ma. I'm hungry. Is there anything to eat."

"I'll bring up some bacon and biscuits with gravy."

"And some coffee, Ma. Please?"

She brushed a lock of black hair out of his eyes. "Sure son," Emma Lou kissed him on the forehead and left the room.

"Well, what did he say?" asked Barney Stegall.

"Said he was hungry," Emma Lou said.

"No. I mean about how he got shot?"

"He didn't."

"Do we need to worry about the law coming after him?"

"Damn it, Barney. I don't know. You go on to work. I'll try and get something out of him after he eats." Emma Lou seldom cussed, except when Barney started getting on her nerves, which he was right now.

"Alright, alright," Barney said. "I'll be home for lunch as usual. We can talk about it then."

Emma Lou was filling a cup with black coffee. She nodded her head as Barney walked out the back door with a biscuit and bacon sandwich.

Clint ate some of his breakfast and drank most of the coffee, but he tired quickly and went back to sleep. When Barney came home there was a lunch of warmed-over ham and fried potatoes waiting for him on the kitchen table. Emma Lou, sitting at the table, was shelling black-eyed peas for dinner. Saying nothing, Barney laid a copy of the Fort Worth Daily Gazette on the table, with the headline up, and went out back to wash up. Emma Lou gasped as she read the headline, "Deputy Marshal Shot in Fort Worth". She picked up the paper and read the first line. "A Deputy U. S. Marshal was shot on the streets of Fort Worth yesterday. Nahum Putney was taken to the Railroad Hospital and his current condition is unknown." Emma Lou gasped and dropped the paper as Barney was entering the kitchen, drying his hands. "I see you read the news," he said.

"Oh, my God," exclaimed Emma Lou. "You don't think…"

"I don't know what to think," said Barney. "Don't know how far you got, but it says another man was killed. Some cowboy named, Blakely."

"Well, that must mean Clint wasn't involved. What else does it say?"

"Not much. Some woman named Deidre O'Neill was with Putney when he was shot and an Indian hijacked a wagon to rush Putney to the hospital."

"I think we need to talk to Clint," said Emma Lou.

"I think we do," agreed her husband.

The couple climbed the stairs and opened the door to Clint's room. Doby stirred and read the look on his mother's face. "What's wrong, Ma?" he asked.

Saying nothing, Emma Lou handed her son the paper. He glanced at the headline, laid the paper down, and said, "I was going to tell you."

Emma Lou burst out in loud sobs. Barney embraced his wife, patting her on the back, saying, "There, there, Em." Looking over his wife's shoulder he asked Doby, "What does this have to do with you?"

Clint Doby let his chin sink down on his chest. Without looking up he said, "I think I killed him."

Emma Lou broke the grasp of her husband, spun around, and with eyes blazing said, "What in the Billy Blue Blazes were you thinking?"

"I did it for Pa," said Doby. "Putney killed him. I shot Putney." Then with conviction, he said, "I hope he's dead."

"Why would you do such a thing?" his mother questioned, her ire not yet spent.

Defiantly Doby said, "I told you I shot him for killing Pa."

52

Emma Lou reached out and slapped her son. Hard. "You stupid, stupid boy," she said.

Tears welled up in Doby's eyes. "I thought you would understand," The tears were slowly trickling down his cheek.

"Your father was no hero to be honored and avenged," said Emma Lou. "He was an outlaw and a sorry excuse for a man. He killed that soldier from Fort McKavett for no other reason than he could. Then ran back to our measly ranch to hide out. Marshal Putney tracked him there and gave him every chance to surrender. But nooooo. Your father wasn't having any of that. He wanted to be a famous badman. He snuck out the back and around the house and tried to shoot Marshal Putney in the back. Now you've done it for him. And for what? A drunk, that lost all our money gambling, and fell into cattle thieving?" She turned around, stomped out of the room, and slammed the door.

Barney Stegall stood in the center of the room; slump shouldered. "I'll try to calm her down. She loves you, boy, and now she's afraid for you. We'll work something out," he said. Barney walked slowly down the stairs knowing he would find his wife crying in the kitchen. As he had known, she was sitting with her head in her hands, her chest heaving heavily from the sobs. Barney pulled a chair up next to her and put an arm around her shoulder. "We will figure something out, Em. I don't know what it will be, but I'm sure we will."

Emma Lou raised her head, looking at her husband, "You're too good Barney. You've never done anything to deserve this."

Elizabeth had brought Putney his lunch and was sitting watching him eat the bean soup the cook had prepared. There was also a slice of fresh bread. Elizabeth told Putney that the nurse had said he could only eat the bread if he let it soak in the soup. Putney finished off the soup and soggy bread with a drink of coffee. "I would give just about anything for a steak and some potatoes," said Putney. Elizabeth smiled. "Have you heard anything from Mary or Imogene?"

"No, sir," she said. "They went to the jail this morning and hadn't come back when I came over here."

"I'll bet Deidre is chewing the bars off that jail by now."

This made Elizabeth laugh. "Don't you know she's at least trying," Elizabeth chuckled.

Just then there was a light rap on the door and Mary Johnson entered without being invited. Elizabeth stood. "Keep your seat, Betsy," Mary said. "Nahum, how are you feeling today?"

"Elizabeth is good medicine for me, Mary," he said. "I feel much improved." He motioned to Elizabeth. "Take this on back and I will see you at dinner time."

"Yes, sir," Elizabeth said and scooped up the tray and dishes.

"And Elizabeth, have the cook send me some peaches this evening. I need some peaches." Elizabeth said yes, sir again, and swept out of the room. "Alright, Mary. Tell me, how is Deidre? And where is Imogene?"

"Deidre is spitting mad. And Imogene has gone back to Dallas," Mary told him.

"What? Did Deidre make her that mad?"

"No, it's nothing like that. At first, Deidre didn't want Imogene to defend her, but Imogene set her right. Of course, I had to smooth things over a bit."

"Then why has Imogene gone to Dallas?"

Mary told Nahum about the run in with the sheriff and his clerks. "This being Saturday, the judge said he wasn't going to have a preliminary hearing until Monday. Imogene went to Dallas to see if she could convince Judge Willis to come over here tomorrow and appear in court to get her admitted to the bar here."

"Good thinking," said Putney. "Anything else?"

"Why, yes," said Mary. "It's quite a mystery. Deidre said she never shot at that man. What's his name? Oh yeah, Ned Blakely."

"Then what happened?" Nahum was interested and half sat forward until the pain hit him and he rested back again.

"Yes. Deidre said there was another man in the alley, and he was shooting also. Deidre said he fired a few times then turned and ran. That's who Deidre was shooting at. She thinks she hit him also."

"So, my shot must have killed Blakely. Why did they arrest Deidre?" Nahum queried, mostly to himself.

"Deidre said she told the sheriff, but he didn't believe her, because Blakely was shot twice."

"Maybe Deidre hit him as she was shooting at the other fellow."

"Not according to Deidre. She said Blakely was already on the ground by the time she picked up your gun and started shooting at the other man."

"I suppose the sheriff didn't believe that, either," said Putney.

"No, he thinks Deidre just made up the second man."

"I see," said Putney. "When you go back to the hotel, ask Henry Morgan to come over here."

"I will," said Mary.

"Anything else?" Putney wanted to know.

"No that's it. Except you should see the way they have Deidre dressed. I'm not certain that's not what she is angriest about."

"I have no doubt," agreed Putney.

Chapter Nine

Saturday evening Elizabeth was once again escorted to the hospital by Henry Morgan. When Elizabeth uncovered one of the dishes, Putney saw a brown creamy bowl of something. From the frown that formed on Putney's face, Elizabeth could tell he didn't find it all that appetizing. "I know," she said. "It doesn't look that good, but you should try it. I told the cook you were yearning for steak and potatoes, so he made up this steak and potato soup. I tried some. It really is good." Putney dipped a spoon in and tried a taste and found it was better than good. He woofed it down. In the other dish was a bowl of sliced canned peaches in syrup. Putney devoured the peaches and drank down the syrup. Seeing the young Elizabeth watching him, he was reminded of when canned peach syrup had been the only thing Imogene and he had to drink when they were stranded out on the Llano Estacado. That had been twenty years ago. Elizabeth wasn't even born at the time. Putney was glad that no young girl like Elizabeth would ever again have to endure the trials that Imogene had to experience.

Putney wiped the sticky syrup from his beard. "Elizabeth," he said, "I need a wet cloth to get this stickiness off me. Reckon you could find one?"

Elizabeth hopped up from her chair. "I'll be right back," she said.

Putney stopped her. "Wait until Henry and I have finished talking before you come back in. I can stand sticky for a bit." Elizabeth curtseyed and left the room.

"She's a good girl," Morgan said when Elizabeth had left.

"Yes, she is," Putney agreed. "So, tell me, what did you find?"

"I looked around pretty good," Morgan started. "First, I found what looked like ricochet marks on one brick wall. Thing is they looked like the bullets that had made the marks came from two different directions. The ones that looked like they went from south to north seemed smaller than the marks that went north to south." Putney closed his eyes trying to picture what Morgan was describing. He signaled with his hand for Morgan to continue. "I saw a pockmark in the wood wall. I stacked some empty crates in the alley so I could get a closer look. The bullet was still in the wood."

"Did you take it out," Putney asked.

"No, I didn't know if I should."

"That's fine. Go ahead," said Putney.

"I decided to look around some more. Across the street was another mark. I couldn't tell if it was made by a bullet, though."

"Good work," Putney was glad he had Morgan working for him. "is there a good photographer in town? One you can trust?"

"There's several good ones, but they're mostly studio-type fellers. But there is a new guy, from New York, who just opened up a shop on Seventh, a little west of the town central," Morgan told him. "Before all this started, I had gone over there and looked around. Turns out this feller has a new kind of camera that he can carry around with him. He called it an Eastman-Strong camera. He explained all of it to me, but he lost me with all the jargon. But he's new in town. He ain't beholden to no one. I think he would be worth a try."

"He sounds promising," agreed Putney. "I want you to hire him. Have him take photographs of all the bullet marks you found. Do you think he could get a ruler in the photographs?"

"I don't know why he couldn't."

"That would be good," Putney said. "Then I want you to dig that bullet out of the wood side of that building but have this photographer take photographs of you doing it. Be careful not to scratch up that bullet, any more than you have to."

"I'll make sure it gets taken care of."

"Now, one more thing. Poke around and see if you can find out if anybody else around town has been shot. They may not be dead, but there may be someone around who was wounded. See if you can find out something," Putney thought about what else could be done then he snapped his fingers. "Get with that shine boy, Tommie Fogg. Tell him to keep on his toes and try to pick up any of the same sort of information."

"You got it, Marshal," said Morgan. "Anything else?"

"I can't think of what, right now. may as well tell Elizabeth to come on in. I can't stand this sticky on my beard anymore."

Elizabeth had a pan of water with a wash towel. The water and towel had been warm when she got to the room but now, they were tepid. Putney said it would do."

"Mr. Putney, I want to ask you something, if you don't mind," Elizabeth told him.

"Not at all, Elizabeth," Putney almost called her sweetie but stopped because it was what he called Imogene, when they had escaped from the Comanche.

"Why do I have to stand in the hall when you're talking to Mr. Morgan or Mrs. Johnson? Do you not trust me?"

Putney felt a lump in his throat. "It's not that at all, honey," He had decided to replace sweetie with honey. "The first thing is, you're still young and you don't need to be burdened with what we discuss. The next thing is that nobody can make you tell what you don't know. The truth is that if I weren't in this condition, I wouldn't be talking to hardly anyone about all this. I would just do it all myself, but here I am stuck in this hospital. I find it hard to trust anyone, but it's what I have to cope with right now. But do you want to know a secret?"

Elizabeth brightened and said, "Oh yes. What."

"There may be a day when I need something special and the person I would trust to do it is you. I trust you most. Right alongside Deidre, Mary, and Imogene."

Chapter Ten

It was a warm Sunday afternoon and Nahum Putney was sitting in a bath wheelchair on the downstairs veranda of the Railroad Hospital. There were three other men at the other end of the porch smoking and playing cards. Putney guessed they were railroad men, but he didn't know for sure. He was uncomfortable and antsy in a cotton shift. Fortunately, a nun had seen him and brought a shawl for his shoulders and a blanket to hide his knees. It was an improvement, but he wished he was wearing trousers. He also wished he had a cigarette and a glass of whiskey, but the doctor had forbidden both.

Putney watched as a man exited a carriage that had stopped at the gate of the rail fence that surrounded the hospital. He was stylishly dressed in the mode of a city dweller, wearing a light brown vested suit with darker brown pinstripes, a starched collared white shirt with a small bow tie, brown oxford low quarter shoes, and a tan fedora topping his graying hair. The man was about six feet tall and starting to lean toward portliness.

He walked up the steps and came directly to Putney who closed his fingers around the butt of a Schofield. The man stopped, doffed his hat, and fanned his face a few times before speaking. "A might warm today," he said in a languid, deep south accent.

"A bit," responded Putney who tensed slightly upon seeing the butt of a pistol that was in a shoulder holster under the man's jacket.

"I'm going to make an assumption, since you are the only person here with long red hair and a red beard, that you are one Nahum Putney."

Putney's finger slid around the trigger guard of his pistol. "I am," he said.

"Let me introduce myself," the man said reaching toward his left side where the pistol sat, with his right hand.

Suddenly the man was looking down the barrel of a forty-five Smith and Wesson. He stepped back, looked to where his hand had been going, stopped the movement, and held both hands palms out. "I may have miscommunicated my intentions. If you will permit, I was simply going to extract a calling card."

"Go ahead. Slowly," said Putney.

The man retrieved a card from his vest pocket and held it so Putney could see. It read William S. Cabell, United States Marshal, Northern Judicial District of Texas.

"Oh," said Putney. "I guess I can put this away." Covering his pistol with the blanket and saying, "Sorry."

"No need," said Cabell. "I suppose I might be a tad skittish were I in your position. Do you mind if I pull over one of those wicker chairs and sit where we may converse?"

"Of course not, sir. Please do."

Cabell pulled a chair over so that it was forty-five degrees to Putney. A comfortable angle for both men to converse and still look out on the lawn. He sat and pulled a cigar from his breast pocket. "Mind?" he asked.

"Not as long as you let some of that smoke drift my way."

Cabell laughed. "Not allowing the demon weed in the hospital, are they?"

"Maybe for some, but since I had a collapsed lung, the doctor said he would prefer I not smoke."

"I see," Cabell said as he struck a match and rolled the cigar around in the flame until it was burning evenly. "I suppose you are wondering about my visit."

"I guess Marshal Jackson may have asked you to check on me," said Putney who would be surprised if it were true. Marshals liked his abilities but did not commonly like him.

"As a matter of fact, yes, but that is only part of it," Cabell exhaled a large cloud of smoke aimed in Putney's direction, but high, so as not to be directly in his face. "To tell you the truth, I'm a bit strapped for deputies. This damn district takes in nearly everything west of Dallas all the way to the panhandle and down to San Angelo and back across to Waco. It's a lot of country."

"Not as big as the Western district used to be," said Putney.

"Ah, that is true, but big enough, still. Bigger than most states. So, I was wondering if you would like to come work for me. Full-time, same salary as you have from Jackson."

"It sounds like a proposition worth considering. How much court would I need to sit in?"

"We only have one judge. Judge McCormick and he sits in Graham, which is a pain in the ass for me, but that's a different problem. No, I have part-time deputies that take care of that. Instead, I need a man hunter and an investigator. In short, I need a man of your skills."

Putney combed his fingers through his hair and thought. "I'm not at the top of my game right now," he said. "And I have a lot of personal business to take care of here in Fort Worth."

Cabell blew more smoke. "That won't be a problem because I want you to man an office right here. I believe you have some experience in that."

"Some," Putney said.

"Then why so hesitant? It sounds like an opportunity you might jump at," said Cabell.

"Like I said, I have this personal business," Putney said.

"Of course. And of course, if you came on, you would have to set that aside."

"There's the rub. I don't think I can do that right now."

"That's a shame because I have a major case that needs investigating, and you are just the man for it."

Putney's curiosity had been piqued and he said, "If you don't mind my asking, what would that be?"

Cabell smiled. He had his fish hooked. Now all he had to do was dip the net and haul it in. "I need someone to investigate the attempted assassination of a Deputy United States Marshal."

Putney smiled and thought, *You're a crafty old buzzard.* Then said, "I'll have to send for some of my things and later have some time to move my household goods."

"That shan't be any problem," Cabell said. "Judge McCormick is to meet me here tomorrow. We will come out and he will swear you in. I will start looking for a good location for an office. Now, do you suppose they have a room at this place O'Neill's I've heard so much about?"

"Just tell them I sent you."

Cabell stood, bent down, and shook Putney's hand, "Good man, Deputy Putney."

The hospital was quiet at night. Elizabeth and Morgan had come and gone. Putney had eaten the stew and cornbread that Elizabeth had brought, and it was good, but he still looked forward to eating more solid food. Morgan didn't have any particular news, except that he had scheduled with the photographer and the two of them would be taking care of that chore in the morning. Putney had asked Elizabeth to bring him some britches and a shirt in the morning. He was tired of the nightshirt the hospital had him wearing. In fact, he was tired of the whole experience and was antsy to be out of his confinement.

There being nothing left to hold his attention, Putney had decided to try to sleep when there was a rap on the door. *Who the hell could this be at this time of night*, thought Putney. The door opened slowly and a head poked through the opening. It belonged to a man with longish curly brown hair, not as long as Putney's. The face was hard with close-set eyes and a nose that looked like a hawk's beak. A thin droopy mustache with a tuft of hair beneath the lower lip finished off the look. Putney's hand instinctively touched the grip of the pistol that lay under the blanket.

"Got a minute?" the voice asked.

Tension set in Putney's jaw as he answered, "Depends."

The door opened more allowing the whole body to step into the door frame. The man was tall. Maybe an inch shorter than Putney. Otherwise, there was nothing remarkable about him. "Courtwright. Jim Courtwright," the man said as a way of introduction. "Heard you wanted to see me."

"You always do your visiting, creeping around at night?" Putney asked.

"Times are busy. Got a lot of work. Gotta make my visits when I can. Mind if I step in?"

"You're here. Might as well," Putney's grip on the pistol tightened.

Courtwright fully entered the room and closed the door turning his back to Putney as he did so. Putney slid the Schofield out from under the blanket. "My bet is you have a hide-away pistol under your jacket," said Putney. "I would recommend you keep your hands where I can see them."

Courtwright turned to face Putney squarely, "Trusting soul, ain't you?"

62

"I trust God and myself. Take a seat," Putney motioned with his gun barrel.

Courtwright moved warily, mindful of his circumstances. He removed his Homburg hat and placed it in one chair, sat easily in the other, and made sure his hands stayed on the chair's arms. "I talk easier when circumstances aren't quite so edgy."

"My room, my rules."

"Good enough. You asked to meet, so here I am. What can I do for you?"

"The last time I asked to meet with you I nearly ended up dead."

"An unfortunate incident for sure. One, in which, I had no hand."

"So, you say."

"Since we aren't going to come to agreement on that point, and I'm here now, what can I do for you?"

"It's plain and simple. I want you to keep your hands out of this situation with Deidre O'Neill. It could be unhealthy to do otherwise."

I wonder what he knows, or thinks he knows, thought Courtwright, then feigning innocence, said, "I have no idea what you're talking about."

"What I'm talking about is you trying to push your extortion racket on Deidre. Stay away from her and the restaurant. And keep any of your so-called detectives away, as well."

"Extortion? You harm my esteem, Nahum. May I call you Nahum? That is a harsh word, extortion. I simply offered a security service to help prevent any bad thing from happening to Miss O'Neill, her employees, or her establishment."

"Call it what you want. We both know what it is. You've been warned. I suggest you heed it."

"I'm not certain a man in your condition can enforce any such warning. But, as I am, generally speaking, a peaceable man, I will take your advice. Call it professional courtesy. One lawman to another."

"You may have been a lawman, but you aren't anymore."

"Well, since you aren't in your jurisdiction, that means you ain't a lawman, here, either. So, I guess the point is moot."

63

"Only until tomorrow afternoon," The cryptic look on Putney's face concerned Courtwright.

☒

Putney wasn't sleeping well. He was normally a light sleeper, but this was different. The atmosphere was filled with danger. Courtwright's visit had only heightened his sense of wariness. These nuns and nurses were no match for clever outlaws that inhabited a bustling boom town like Fort Worth. Putney felt sleep coming to him and he was ready to drift off when his eyes suddenly snapped open. The only light in the room wafted through the half-open door, from a gas fixture somewhere in the hall. Putney's eyes were well adjusted to the lack of light, and they immediately picked up a shadow crossing the door frame. Putney's hand automatically gripped the gun under his blanket as the shape of a hatted head began to take form, blocking the dim light. "Your best option is to stop there," the growl in Putney's voice was fiercely commanding.

"You wouldn't shoot me, would you Nahum," the words came from a cheery and familiar voice.

"Is that you Jefferson?"

"Nahum, I appreciate it when you use my real name instead of that awful sobriquet of Soapy," The man known as Soapy Smith gingerly stepped into the room.

Putney grimaced, "There's a lamp on the table to your left. Light it."

A match flared up revealing the dark bearded face of the gangster as he found the lamp and lit it. Smith adjusted the wick until the room was lighter, but not fully so. "You don't look near as bad as I thought you would," he said.

"I don't feel near as bad as what you and others may hope."

"Now that's not nice, Nahum. I mean we're friends."

"There's a difference between being friendly and being friends, which we have never been."

"I suppose you're right Nahum, but I never wished you any harm." Smith was correct. So was Putney. The two had a connection some years back and Smith had helped Putney with information on the Knights of the Rising Sun.

Switching the gun to his left hand, Putney reached out to the side table with his right and picked up his watch. "Damn it Jefferson, it's four in the morning. What the hell are you doing here at this time?"

"You know Nahum. In my occupation, it's not good business practice to let my competitors know I'm meeting with a lawman."

"I reckon you have a point."

"Look Nahum, I'm catching a train out of here tomorrow. Headed back to Denver. I can't stay away too long, or my brother might start getting ideas he runs my operation."

"So, you just wanted to stop by and say adios."

"Yeah, sort of, and to see how you are making it."

"I'm making it just fine, so I guess you can leave Fort Worth without losing sleep over me." Putney's snide remark wasn't lost on Smith.

"There was another reason I stopped by and that is to warn you that you arc in danger."

Putney tapped the healing wound on his chest. "I never would have figured it out."

"No, I mean it's more than you think. I'm sure you know a man named William Dawson."

"Bull Dawson?"

"The very same. He just got out of the Walls down in Huntsville. Despite his looks and demeanor, it seems he can actually read, and he read about your, er, mishap. He showed up at the Emerald Saloon last night. He ran into another old friend of yours. Captain Montague Russell."

"An employee of yours, I think."

"Nah. Russell's more of a free agent, you might say. Looking for any old job. He's not near as haughty as when you put him in jail those years ago."

"Anything else I should know."

"I watched earlier when Long Hair Jim came down here. Don't trust him or Marshal Rea."

"What else?"

"That's it, Nahum. I'm out of good news."

"Thanks for the heads up. And Jefferson."

"What?"

"Leave that lamp on. Have a good trip and don't come back to Fort Worth."

Smith gave a tip of his hat. "All the good pickings are gone from here." Then he slipped quietly into the hallway.

Chapter Eleven

The door behind the judge's bench opened and out stepped a small man, wearing a dapper suit. Behind him stood the judge in his black robe. He was a tall, handsome man with graying hair. The little man in the dapper suit loudly announced, "Oy ye, Oy ye, Oy ye. Court is now in session. The Honorable Robert Emmet Beckham presiding for Tarrant and Parker Counties in the State of Texas. Let us pray. God bless these United States, the great State of Texas, and this Honorable Court."

Judge Beckham ascended the three steps to his bench and stood before his high-back, leather-covered chair. He scanned the crowded courtroom. The first thing that caught his attention were two very large black men, sitting on the back benches. One on either side of the double doors. He didn't know them personally but considering who had been charged he easily guessed who they were and they had quite the reputation in Fort Worth. The judge glanced at the table where the prosecutor, William McLaury stood with Sheriff Maddox and City Marshal Rea. He then looked at the defense table. Standing alongside a woman with fiery red hair, dressed in a jail smock, was a younger woman who was wearing a very professional dark blue serge suit with a high-necked frilly blouse. But the man standing next to the younger woman was his only surprise of the morning. Judge Beckham blandly said, "You may be seated." Then sitting himself he directed his attention to the man next to the younger woman and said, "Judge Willis, it is a pleasant surprise to see you have come all the way from Dallas to join us. But are you the attorney for Miss O'Neill?" It would have been unusual for an active judge to be representing any defendant, much less the defendant in a murder trial.

Judge Willis stood. "No Judge. I am here as a friend of the court and to introduce an attorney who practices in Dallas, is a member of the Dallas Bar, and one I am proposing you accept in this court, to represent Miss O'Neill."

"We would be very pleased to consider a recommendation from an esteemed juror such as yourself," Judge Beckham interlocked his fingers, held his hands in front of him, making a steeple with the index fingers, held against his chin. "But I would think that a letter from you would have sufficed and that you needn't have come this distance to personally introduce him."

"In usual circumstances, this may be true, judge. But this attorney has already been presented with difficulties at the sheriff's office and I felt that were I to present myself directly to you it would make things easier. I would also request that you direct the sheriff, the prosecutor, and other officers of the court to cooperate fully with this attorney, within the confines of the law."

Judge Beckham had a confused look which, as he turned to look at Sheriff Maddox, quickly turned to a scowl. "Please proceed, Judge Willis, and introduce the man."

Judge Willis cleared his throat and said, "This may be the problem, your honor." He signaled for Imogene to stand. "If it pleases your honor, I would like to introduce Miss Imogene Foster. Miss Foster graduated from the prestigious St. Louis School of Law, in 1881, ranking number five in her class. Miss Foster was admitted to the Dallas County Bar in 1882 and has been practicing in my court ever since. Miss Foster has an excellent reputation in the community, and I highly recommend her to this court, to be admitted to the bar."

Judge Beckham's eyes had opened wide when Imogene had stood, and he had managed to get them down to normal by the end of Judge Willis's presentation. "Judge, I respect your recommendation, But Miss Foster seems young. Are you certain she is capable of taking on what may turn out to be a very difficult case?"

"I have no doubt, Judge. However, in the unlikely event that she has trouble, she can always depend on my advice, which I will welcomely provide."

"I see," said Judge Beckham then turned his remarks to Imogene. "Miss Foster," he began. "Do you understand that if I accept Judge Willis's recommendation and admit you to the bar of Tarrant and Parker Counties, that you will receive no special treatment, simply because you are a member of the fairer sex?"

Imogene stood very straight with her chin out and said, "I do Your Honor."

"And do you further understand that you will get no preferential treatment, simply because of the recommendation of Judge Willis, whom I consider a friend?"

"I do Your Honor."

"Very well. Miss O'Neill, please stand."

Deidre stood self-assured next to Imogene. She had the weekend to consider her situation and had come to the decision that she was honored to be represented by Imogene and was proud to be represented by a woman.

"Miss O'Neill," Judge Beckham said. "Do you understand the gravity of selecting the proper lawyer for your defense and that Miss Foster may not have the experience that some more, ahem, traditional lawyers may have?"

"Aye, I do Your Honor," replied Deidre.

"And do you further understand that by choosing Miss Foster as your council, you cannot then use her experience, or lack thereof, as a basis for an appeal, should you be convicted?"

"Aye, I do Your Honor."

"Even more, do you understand that Miss Foster will receive no special accommodations from this court simply by virtue of her sex and the recommendation by Judge Willis?"

"Aye, I do Your Honor."

Judge Beckham then turned his attention to William McLaury. "Mr. Prosecutor, do you have any objections?"

McLaury looked at Maddox and Rea, gave a little smile, and returned his attention to the Judge. Still smiling, he said, "No objections here, Your Honor."

"Mr. McLaury," said the judge. "You should know by now that I never miss anything in my court. If you think I did not see that smirk, you are sadly mistaken. If I accept Miss Foster's application, I will not tolerate any disrespect toward her by yourself or by any other officer of this court. Do you fully understand?"

Blushing under the judge's admonishment McLaury gulped and quietly said. "Yes, Your Honor."

"Sheriff Maddox," the judge had turned his attention.

Maddox stood hoping he was not the next target of the judge's ire and said, "Yes, Your Honor."

"If I accept Miss Foster's application, I would expect that you and all your deputies, guards, clerks, and whomever else will afford Miss Foster with every courtesy and respect you would give to any other attorney. Do you fully understand that?" the judge had emphasized you when speaking to the sheriff.

"I do and I will, Your Honor."

Judge Beckham leaned back in his rocker putting his steepled fingers to his chin once more and thought for a moment. He leaned forward. "Very well," he said. "Having heard the application by Judge Willis, and having satisfied myself that Miss Foster is competent and that Miss O'Neill is pleased with her representation and there being no objection, I will admit Miss Foster to this court. You may all be seated, except you Miss Foster." When everyone else had taken their seats. Judge Beckham swore Imogene in and directed her to sit. Breathing a heavy sigh Judge Beckham said, "I can see this is going to be an interesting case. Before we go any further, we are going to take a fifteen-minute recess. Judge Willis, I would like to see you in my chambers." He stood to walk toward the door where he had earlier exited. The clerk announced, "All Rise." And the judge exited the court.

Ten minutes after the judge had recessed, Judge Willis exited Judge Beckham's chambers and walked directly to the defense table, where Mary Johnson had joined the other women. "What did the judge say?" Imogene asked.

"Nothing much. Just catching up a little. We haven't seen each other in some time," said Willis. "Miss O'Neill I'm going to leave you in the very capable hands of Imogene here." Deidre nodded. "I hope you will listen to what she tells you and follow her instructions. She has your best interest at heart."

"I will, Judge," Deidre told him.

"Imogene," he said. "I'm going to catch the next train back to Dallas. If you need anything at all let me know."

"I will, Judge and thank you very much," Imogene and Judge Willis hugged before he left.

A short time later Judge Beckham and his clerk re-entered the court. The clerk told everyone to rise and when the judge had seated said, "Be seated."

70

"I see we have another lady sitting at the defense table," said the judge. "I suppose she is a lawyer, also."

Imogene stood and said, "No Your Honor. This is Mrs. Mary Johnson; she will be acting as my assistant and secretary during the proceedings."

"Very well," he said. "Miss O'Neill, please rise." Deidre stood. "Miss O'Neill," he began again. "I want you to understand, today's hearing is a preliminary hearing. We are not here to determine guilt or innocence, but rather to see if there is enough evidence to hold you over for trial. Do you understand?"

"Aye, Your Honor. I understand."

"Alright, Mr. McLaury, please provide your evidence."

McLaury nudged Hubert Forsythe who had replaced Sheriff Maddox. Forsythe looked oddly at the document in his hand, then handed it to McLaury. "Judge, I would like to present, for purposes of this hearing, the coroner's report and I ask it be labeled as Prosecution Number One."

"Objections, Miss Foster?"

May I see it, Your Honor?" The judge nodded to McLaury, indicating he should let Imogene see the document. After perusing it Imogene said. "Solely for the purposes of this hearing, there are no objections, Your Honor."

"Very well, so entered." McLaury retrieved the report and took it to the clerk. "Anything else?"

"Yes, your honor. I would like to call Marshal Rea to the stand."

Beckham told Rea to take the stand and the clerk swore the marshal in. McLaury took the coroner's report from the clerk and handed it to Rea. "Marshal, do you recognize this document?" Rea said he did. "Would you please tell the court what it says?"

"Yes sir. It says that the deceased, a Mister Ned Blakley, was shot twice before he died."

"And did the coroner offer an opinion as to the caliber of bullets that made the wounds?"

"Objection, Your Honor," said Imogene, standing. The judge looked at her. "It seems to me that the coroner should be here testifying to the contents of the report. Not second-hand testimony from the marshal."

"Since this is just the preliminary hearing, I think the marshal is capable of reading what the report says. If we go to trial the coroner will be here to authenticate his report. Overruled. Continue, Mr. McLaury."

"Go ahead, Marshal," said McLaury.

"It says there were two wounds, both consistent with a forty-five caliber bullet," Rea told the court. McLaury took the report and handed it back to the clerk. He looked over to Forsythe who looked confused. McLaury wished that Maddox had assigned a more experienced deputy to the task. Forsythe snapped out of his confusion, reached under the table took two Smith and Wesson pistols from a box, and handed them to the prosecutor.

"Judge I have tags on these pistols, and I would like to present them as exhibits two and three."

"Without objection, they are entered," said the judge. Imogene had no objection. After they had been labeled, McLaury handed the guns to Rea and asked if he recognized them.

"I do. Here on the butt of the grips I marked the wood with R, using a pocketknife," said Rea.

"What else? asked McLaury.

"These are the pistols we recovered at the scene. We determined one had been fired six times and the other had not been fired."

"Did you figure out who these guns belong to?"

"We did. They belong to a man named Nahum Putney."

"And why is that important?"

"Putney was the other man shot at the scene."

"Thank you. Now, I have some more documents," McLaury picked up some papers off his table. "Judge I would like these marked as exhibits four through eight."

"May I see them, Judge?" asked Imogene.

"Certainly," said the judge.

Imogene stood and was reading the documents for a few minutes when the judge asked, "Miss Foster, is there a problem?"

"Your Honor, as Judge Willis alluded, no one from the Sheriff's office or the prosecutor's office has cooperated with me and this is the first time I have seen these documents."

"Is this correct, Mr. McLaury," the judge asked.

"Your Honor, I didn't know until you did that Miss Foster would be representing Miss O'Neill, so how could I have let her see these?"

"Didn't you have fifteen minutes while I was in chambers that you could have let Miss Foster see them?" asked Beckham then waving for the prosecutor to go back to his table. "Miss Foster, I will allow you five minutes to read the documents."

"Thank you, Judge," Imogene said and sat at the table and huddled over the papers. When she had finished, she said, "No objections," while handing the papers to McLaury.

After the papers had been marked, McLaury handed them to Rea and asked if he recognized them. Rea said he did and that they were statements from persons who had witnessed the shooting, including that of Quanah Parker.

"Do all the statements say virtually the same thing?" McLaury asked.

"Yes, sir."

"Please summarize what the witnesses said."

"They all said they heard shooting coming from the alley. Then they said they saw Putney draw his pistols but only shot once. Everyone said Putney was hit and some thought he had been killed because he fell to the ground. Then Miss O'Neill picked up one of the guns and started shooting down the alley."

"Thank you, Marshal," McLaury told him, then to the judge, "That's all I have, for now."

"Would you like to cross-examine the witness, Miss Foster?" asked the judge.

"I would your honor." Picking up the coroner's report she handed it to Rea who looked at it. "Just to be sure, Marshal Rea, you did not have anything to do with writing this report."

"Of course not, it's the coroner's report."

"So, you can only testify to what it says, but not as to the truthfulness of the report."

"I've known the coroner for a good long time. And if he says it's the truth, that's good enough for me."

"But the coroner is not here to say whether it is the truth. You are, so I ask again, can you testify that this report is one hundred percent true, and correct?"

"Well, no, but…"

73

"That's good enough Marshal."

Now, I would like to ask you. When you arrived at the scene, was either Miss O'Neill or Mister Putney there?"

"No, they weren't."

"But several other people were hanging around?"

"Well, yeah."

"Could any of those people have touched or tampered with the guns you say belonged to Mister Putney?"

"Well, I suppose they could have."

"Is it possible that neither of these guns belonged to Mister Putney?"

"I don't think so," Rea's voice was starting to show some stress.

"Have you interviewed Mister Putney?"

"No, he's been laid up in the hospital."

"Have you gone to the hospital to see if Mister Putney could have visitors and to see if the guns, in fact, belonged to him?"

"Well, no, but…"

Imogene cut him off again. "That's good, Marshal, further explanation isn't necessary. Now let's get to those witness statements. When I read over the statements, I saw where they all said Miss O'Neill shot toward the alley, but I didn't see anywhere that anyone said they had actually seen Miss O'Neill shoot Mister Blakely. Did I miss something?"

"Well, no, but there wasn't anybody else in the alley."

"There wasn't anybody else in the alley when you got there. Is that correct?"

"That is correct."

"Judge," Imogene said. "May I take one more minute to look at the statements?"

The judge allowed it. After she had taken a second look at the statements she asked if she could hand them back to the marshal and the judge granted permission.

"Marshal," she said. "Please take a close look at each statement, then tell me what time each witness said the shooting took place."

Marshal Rea took his time looking at the statements and then said, "They all say the shooting happened around five in the afternoon, give or take a few minutes."

"Thank you. Now, what was the first time when either you or one of your deputies arrived where the shooting had occurred?"

"About five-fifteen or five-twenty."

"Which? Five-fifteen or five-twenty."

McLaury interrupted. "Objection, your Honor what difference can it make?"

"Miss Foster?" asked the judge.

"Judge a lot can happen at the scene of a crime in five minutes. I'm trying to establish that there is a possibility that evidence may have been tampered with, or even possibly that there may have been another witness that the marshal hasn't spoken to."

"Objection overruled. Continue Miss Foster."

"So, which was it, Marshal? Five-fifteen or five-twenty?"

"Five-twenty, I suppose."

"Thank you. So, what do you think may have happened during that nearly twenty minutes?"

"Objection, Your Honor," interrupted McLaury again. "She is asking the witness to speculate."

"He's right, Miss Foster," said the judge.

"May I approach this a different way, Your Honor?"

"We will see where it goes. If it drifts into speculation I will stop you before Mr. McLaury has an opportunity to object."

"Thank you, Your Honor. Marshal, during your tenure I assume you have investigated a good many shootings, both deadly or not?"

"I have."

"Have you investigated any, where either you or your deputies arrived say fifteen or twenty minutes past the time the event occurred?"

"Yes."

"In these circumstances, did you at any time find that evidence may have disappeared by say, souvenir hunters?"

"It's happened, sure."

"During any of these investigations did you ever find that somebody placed a gun, or a knife or even a rock there, that may not have been there to begin with?"

"Once."

"May I continue, Judge," Imogene asked.

Judge Beckham was beginning to believe that Miss O'Neill had been pretty shrewd in hiring Miss Foster. "You may."

"So, it is not beyond the realm of possibility that such may have occurred in this event?"

"Well, those usually happened at night."

"Day or night, it is still a possibility, is that correct?"

Rea growled, "Yeah, I suppose it is a possibility."

"Just one last thing, Marshal. Just because the witnesses said they didn't see anyone else in the alley, does not make it an impossibility that someone else may have been there?"

"It's not an impossibility," Rea said, begrudgingly.

"I have nothing else, Your Honor," Imogene sat down.

"Mr. McLaury?" asked the judge.

"Yes, Judge," answered McLaury. "Marshal, is there anything in your investigation that would lead you to believe that anybody either took evidence from or planted evidence at the scene?"

"None."

"Did any witness say there was anybody else any place near the alley when the shooting occurred?"

"No, sir."

"In your experience has the coroner ever misdiagnosed a cause of death?"

"Not to my knowledge."

"Do you have any reason to believe that anybody, other than Miss O'Neill shot and killed Ned Blakely?"

"No, I do not," Rea slapped his hand on the arm of the witness chair, for emphasis.

"Thank you. That's all I have, Judge," said McLaury.

"Arguments? You may start, Miss Foster," said Judge Beckham

"Your honor I think there are several important things to mention. First, there is no reason, I have heard, that the coroner could not have been here to testify about his report. Next, I believe, from the testimony that there is nothing conclusive that says Deidre O'Neill was the only person there that may have shot down that alley. And lastly, we have presented doubt that there was no one else in that alley, other than Ned Blakely. I suggest to Your Honor that there is not enough evidence of probable cause to believe that Miss O'Neill committed any crime. One, last thing, if it please the court, even if you believe Miss O'Neill did shoot Ned Blakely, there is no evidence that it was not in self-defense. Thank you, Your Honor." Imogene was pleased with herself as she sat down.

"Mr. McLaury?" said the judge.

"Your Honor," began McLaury. "We have established that Mr. Blakely was shot in the alley and the wounds were caused by bullets from a forty-five caliber pistol. We have established, from several witness statements, that Mister Putney dropped two such guns at the scene. We have those guns in evidence. From those same witnesses, we have established that Miss O'Neill picked up one of those guns and fired it in the direction of the alley five times. That alley is the same one in which Mister Blakely's body was found. There can be little doubt that Miss O'Neill is the person who shot and killed Mister Blakely. We have established all the probable cause necessary to believe that Miss O'Neill is the person responsible and that she should be held over for trial on the charge of murder, in the first degree."

"Is there anything else I should consider?" asked Judge Beckham.

Imogene stood. "Yes, Your Honor. Even if you believe that Miss O'Neill did shoot Ned Blakely, there certainly is not enough evidence to justify a charge of first degree murder. That being the case, we would ask that you set a bond for Miss O'Neill."

Looking at the prosecutor, the judge said, "Well?"

"Judge, I believe we have established probable cause for first degree and that bond is not something you should consider. Miss O'Neill is a woman of some repute, not all good. She is a foreign national and would present a risk of flight. The District Attorney's Office firmly opposes any bond in this case."

Imogene stood again. "Your Honor, Mr. McLaury has not established that Miss O'Neill has any reputation, good or bad. Additionally, Miss O'Neill owns and operates a substantial business here, in Fort Worth, and were she to leave the jurisdiction, not only would she risk forfeiture of any bond you may set, but she would also put that business at risk. I also submit that we would be able to accept any restrictions you may set, to ensure Miss O'Neill's appearance."

77

"Alright," said the judge. "You both have given me a lot to consider." He leaned back in his chair produced his little finger building and put the steeple against his chin. He closed his eyes and contemplated for several moments. "Finally, he opened his eyes and spoke. "Here is my ruling. The prosecution has produced probable cause that Miss O'Neill did shoot and kill Ned Blakely. However, I don't think the evidence presented rises to the level of first degree murder. So, I am ordering the district attorney to present this case, with all their evidence, to the grand jury. What the grand jury decides will provide the direction we will go. In the meantime, until when and if the grand jury returns a true bill of first degree murder, I am going to release Miss O'Neill on a cash bond of two thousand, five hundred dollars. Additionally, I am ordering that Miss O'Neill contain all her activities within the confines of her hotel and restaurant, where I presume, she can obtain lodging." Looking over to the prosecutor's table, he continued, "I further order that Deputy Forsythe visit the business, daily and at random times, to include late night and early morning hours, to ensure Miss O'Neill's compliance with my order and that he provide me a written weekly report on this endeavor."

Chapter Twelve

It had taken Imogene and Mary about an hour to make it back to the jail, where Deidre was waiting in her cell. Deidre was not in a good mood. "Where have you been," she asked. I've been here for at least an hour." She plopped down on the bunk to give emphasis to her question.

"You came back directly through the tunnel from the courthouse, we didn't have that luxury," Imogene grimaced thinking that luxury was probably not a good word to use in this situation.

"Oh, luxury, is it?" Deidre confirmed Imogene's thought.

"You know what I meant. Besides, we had some legal things to deal with and the judge wanted to meet with me. Sometimes things don't operate on Deidre time."

"Easy for you to say. You're not stuck in this miserable dungeon."

"You're right Deidre, but you need to look on the good side. We had significant victories today."

"Yes," Mary spoke up for the first time since entering the cell. "Deidre, don't you see. They can't just charge you. McLaury has to get a grand jury to indict you, and the judge set bail."

"And don't you know McLaury can have a grand jury eating out of his hand. And twenty-five hundred dollars. Where am I going to come up with that kind of money?" Deidre threw up her hands in exasperation.

"Can you borrow against your business?" Imogene asked.

"I doubt it. I owe half that much on my original loan. The rest I made up from my own money, and what we have left we need for operating expenses."

"Mary crossed the room and took Deidre's hand in hers, "Don't worry dear, we will figure something out."

Deidre held the smaller woman's hand tightly as if pulling strength from her. Mary had always been stronger than her size led people to believe. "I know dear, I know," then more cheerfully, "Here I am going on about my own woes when I should be asking about Nahum. How is he doing?" The concern in her voice was genuine.

"Betsy says he is improving daily. Asking for steak and potatoes. And yesterday he had her bring him some pants and a shirt. He said he couldn't tolerate that hospital night shirt anymore."

This brought laughter to Deidre, "I'll just bet he can't." then standing she twirled around in her striped shift. "Wouldn't we just make a fine picture together?" All three women laughed. Mary was glad to see Deidre's spirits lifted.

Halting her dance Deidre looked at Imogene, "So what do we do now?"

"Let's sit down at the table so we can speak more quietly," Imogene said softly. The three women sat at the plain table on the stools the sheriff had provided. They all leaned in to keep their voices low. "Nahum has Henry Morgan running all sorts of errands. Tomorrow Henry is hiring a photographer to take pictures of the alley. I don't exactly know what Nahum has in mind, but you can be sure he's on top of everything. Henry gives him reports, daily."

"Oh, that's good," said Deidre.

"The twins told me he also has something else going on. They wouldn't say what it was," Mary was excited to throw in her part of the news. "And Betsy said he had a visitor yesterday. Nahum didn't say who the man was. Betsy figured it was somebody important. She said Nahum was in really good spirits over the visit. But she said it may have also been over getting some britches." The women all laughed in conspiratorial giggles.

Imogene calmed down first. "I will go visit Nahum after lunch and see what he thinks about the bond. If he has any suggestions. Getting you out of here has to be our primary priority."

Deidre asked for some paper and a pencil. "Sure and that's true," she said as she began writing. When she had finished, she folded the paper and handed it to Imogene. "Take him this note, would you?"

"Certainly."

"Now the two of you get out of here. I need my beauty rest." The women laughed again. This time out loud.

Putney was seated in a chair, wearing trousers, shirt, hospital slippers, and pistols sitting crossed on his lap, when the doctor came in with the nurse. "See Doctor, what did I tell you?" The exasperated woman said, folding her arms.

"I see, Miss Carter," said the doctor, then to Putney, "I see you are feeling better today."

"I reckon I have to," Putney told him. "Since I'm leaving here today."

"I'm sorry, Mister Putney, but I don't think that is at all advisable."

"Advisable or not, it's happening. Look, Doctor, I've got nothing against the nurses and nuns, but the fact is I'm not safe here. I had two visitors during the night, neither of which I am sure were approved by anyone."

The doctor turned and frowned at Miss Carter. "This is the first I've heard of it," she said.

"I will see what we can do about stepping up security, Mr. Putney, but I wouldn't be doing my job if I allowed you to leave in your condition."

"What are y'all going to do for me that I can't do for myself, somewhere else, doctor?"

"Well, there's changing the dressings and helping you walk and making sure you get the rest you need…"

Putney cut him off. "None of that is going to be worth a tinker's damn if someone sneaks in here and shoots me in my sleep. I promise I can get all that sort of care at my hotel. Maybe more. And there I will be much better protected. Besides how would it be if some villain snuck in here and ended up killing one of your staff? No, Doctor. I am determined. There will be a carriage arriving soon. Elizabeth will be coming with my breakfast. I will send her back for a full set of clothes. I need to wait for some other visitors. After that, I will be leaving. All I need now is for someone to bring me a bill and a blank check I can write it on my bank in Galveston. And I promise if I get worse, I will come back here to see you."

"If that's the way it's going to be, I can't stop you, but remember what happens to you when you leave here is your problem. Not mine. Not the hospital's."

"We find ourselves in agreement, Doctor."

When Elizabeth came with his breakfast, Putney sent her back to retrieve some more clothes so he wouldn't feel half-naked leaving the hospital. He ate his breakfast sitting up, facing the open door. He wasn't having anyone else sneaking in on him. He waited for Marshal Cabell and Judge McCormick to arrive. Elizabeth returned before the marshal and judge. She brought his road clothes since the new ones Deidre had bought had been discarded at the hospital. Elizabeth helped Putney walk to the veranda where they both awaited the officials. They hadn't waited long until a fine Studebaker Landau arrived. The driver hopped off the front bench and opened the door to the carriage. The first out was Marshal Cabell who was followed by a thick-set man of average height. The second man was dressed in a black vested suit, wearing a top hat, and carrying a large leather-bound book. When they arrived at the steps to the porch Cabell said, "You look better today than yesterday." Directing his comment at Putney. "And who do we have here?"

Putney introduced Elizabeth and the marshal greeted her warmly, holding her hand with both of his. Cabell then said, "I would like to introduce Judge Andrew Phelps McCormick." Putney started to rise but McCormick motioned for him to stay seated.

The judge ascended the stairs and pulled a wicker chair over to sit across from Putney. He removed his silk top hat and handed it to Cabell. He placed the large book, face down, in his lap, leaned back into the chair, and looked Putney up and down for several seconds. Finally, after making his assessment the judge cleared his throat and said, "I've heard a great deal about you, Mr. Putney." Putney thanked him. McCormick's face turned dour. "Not all of it good. When the marshal first told me he was thinking of appointing you as a deputy, I did some research of my own. I sent a wire to Judge Duvall in Austin." Putney grimaced. "Judge Duvall is of two minds about you. To your credit, he says you are a capable officer and you have had great success in bringing criminals to justice." Putney waited for what he knew was coming next. "But it seems you mete out your own justice through the barrels of those pistols you wear." Putney wanted to tell the judge that the guns he was wearing were new and hadn't meted out any justice. Yet. But he held his tongue until the judge asked, "What have you to say to that?"

Putney thought about how to frame his answer, tampered down his tendency toward impudence, decided, and looked directly into the judge's eyes. "Every man I have ever sought has always had the option as to how he will face justice. A few have decided they would rather kill me than to face that justice. Fortunately for me, it has always turned out to be poor decision making on their part." Putney and the judge stared at one another, each trying to look into the other's soul.

McCormick had a half smile on his face when he spoke, "That's as good an answer as I have heard. Since Marshal Cabell has the authority to hire and fire as he sees necessary, my approval is a formality." The judge paused for effect. "But when I issue a warrant, I expect for them to arrive in my court, mostly alive, at least."

Putney was still fixed on the judge's eyes. "I will do my best."

The judge nodded. "Well, let's get to the business at hand then. You will need to stand now."

Putney stood and Cabell stood on his right side, taking the book from the Judge, and turning it so Putney could see it was a Bible. Elizabeth stood on Putney's left, holding his hand as the judge cited the oath of office. Elizabeth was proud to be with Putney and was proud to be in the company of the two prestigious officials. With the ceremony over, McCormick said, "I understand you served in the Confederacy."

"I did sir," There was not a hint of pride in Putney's tone.

"That's fine, son. So did I. Now it is incumbent on us to hold the law to the highest standard, lest our service be called into question." McCormick shook Putney's hand and started walking back to his carriage.

Marshal Cabell pulled a box from his jacket pocket and opened it to show a shiny, new badge. The one he had worn in Austin had been plain steel in the shape of a shield with a star in the center. This badge was a large circle with a five-pointed star in the middle. The words UNITED STATES had been hand carved on the top and MARSHAL on the bottom. On the sides, fine filigree swirls had been etched. Marshal Cabell pinned the badge on the lapel of Putney's vaquero jacket. "I'm glad to have you on board, Nahum. Now, get yourself well. I will check on you when I return from Graham."

"Thank you, sir," Putney told Carell, "But I will be at O'Neill's Hotel, not here."

Cabell at first looked surprised, "Of course you will."

Imogene and Mary had decided to return to the restaurant for a late lunch before going to the hospital to see Putney. When they walked in, they were surprised to see Putney sitting at one of the tables. Elizabeth sat to his right and in front of him was a plate with a half-eaten steak and a pile of fried potatoes. Both women smiled then Imogene frowned. "Why aren't you in the hospital?"

Putney winked at the Shakespeare brothers behind the two women, He smiled at Mary, then Imogene "Figured this was the only way I was going to get a steak."

Mary stepped quickly to the table and hugged Putney around his neck. Putney winced slightly from the pain in his chest. Imogene sat across from Putney and stared at the badge on his jacket. "Where did you get that?"

"He was just sworn in, Miss Imogene. He's a deputy marshal, now," Elizabeth blushed a little because she knew it wasn't her place to say so, but she was so proud it had just blurted out. It didn't occur to Elizabeth that Putney had already been a deputy marshal, just in a different jurisdiction.

"That's enough about me, what about Deidre? How did the hearing go this morning?"

It was Mary's turn to be exuberant. "You should have been there to see Imogene. She danced circles around that McLaury fellow and Marshal Rea.

Imogene was more reserved in her optimism. She laid out everything that had happened in court. She was dispassionate in the telling but ended with, "At least we got a bond set, although twenty-five hundred is a lot of money. Deidre doesn't know how she will raise it."

"I'll pay it," Putney said it like he was picking up the bill for lunch. "I'll go to the bank this afternoon and make arrangements to have money sent here for deposit. It might take a couple of days. Afterwards, I'll go see Deidre. Put her mind at ease."

Nobody said anything, but their thoughts were all the same. *How does he have that much money?* Putney never spoke about his wealth. Most people had no idea that after his parents had been killed T. J. McKinney, a friend of the family, had bought out his father's ranch and combined both herds. Because the war had caused beef prices to soar, Putney had become better off than most, especially since McKinney had always required to be paid in U. S. dollars and not Confederate script. When Putney returned to Texas after five years in the Wyoming territory he began investing more and more in cattle, mining, and railroads. He had amassed a small fortune. Enough to live on, comfortably. His work as a deputy marshal was to repent for things he had done from the end of the Civil War and his return to Texas. It would be his lifelong vocation. He had worked the last fifteen years, atoning for the sins he had incurred as Jack Callahan.

"So, why did you leave the hospital so soon? I thought you were going to need to be there at least another week?" Imogene wasn't willing to let that subject drop.

"I already told you. A good steak, and ..." Putney added, "a comfortable bed." There was no way he was going to tell them about his nocturnal visitors. There was no need to worry anybody. "Speaking of which, I'm a bit tired, I'm going to lie down for about an hour before heading over to the bank." Putney finished his steak and potatoes and washed it down with luke warm coffee. He rose from the table. Before he left, Imogene handed him Deidre's note. He politely dismissed himself. As he walked to Deidre's apartment, he tapped Caesar on the shoulder, "Come with me. Leave Brutus to watch over the ladies."

After Caesar had closed the door to Deidre's office, Putney leaned on the desk. "Shit. I'm sore," he told Caesar. Help me to the bedroom. And not a word to anyone else." Caesar half carried Putney to the back room, helped Putney off with his jacket, and when Putney was laid down Caesar pulled off the lawman's boots.

After he had made himself comfortable on Deidre's bed, Putney opened his shirt and looked at the bandage around his chest. *No blood*, he thought, *that's a good thing.* Well, has there been any word from that shine boy, what's his name again?

"Tommie," said Caesar. "Yeah, a couple of things. One of us was going to come see you tonight. The most important is about Bull Dawson. He's out of jail and wound up here in Fort Worth."

"I know about that."

"How?"

"Never mind. What else?" Putney's eyelids were heavy.

"Tommie says there's a younger man, named Clint Doby, used to hang around quite a bit with Blakely. Tommie ain't seen him since the shooting. That got Tommie to thinking and he talked to old man Ben. Ben's a negro hostler down at one of the liveries. The one where Clint kept his horse. Ben don't talk to white folk, lessen he has to. Old Ben told Tommie that the day of the shooting, he saw this Clint saddle his pony and head out in a big hurry. He also said Clint was hurt in some kind of way. Ben didn't know how Clint was hurt, but he said it looked bad and there was blood on the hay in the stall where Clint keeps his horse."

"Doby was the last name?"

Caesar nodded, "Yep. I know of him. He does 'hard' work for Courtwright."

Doby, Putney thought to himself. *I wonder....* And he let his thoughts trail off. "You don't know what kind of gun this Clint Doby carries, do you?"

"Nope. Marshal Rea keeps a tight lid on people carrying guns outside their clothes."

"Reckon where Doby would run to? If he's hurt, he'll need some kind of help."

"I'll get Tommie to snoop around. See if he can find out."

"That's a good idea. Look I need you and Brutus to know why I really left the hospital. Henry Morgan, too. But you have to keep it to yourselves." Putney explained about his visitors of the prior night. "I'm going to have to rest more than I had hoped. I'll need somebody to watch at the office door when I am. Especially with Dawson in town."

"We will take care of it, Nahum," the giant assured him.

"Don't let me sleep more than an hour, I need to get over to the bank." After Caesar left Putney pulled Deidre's note from his pocket. He read the note, smiled, then drifted off to sleep.

Chapter Thirteen

It was a quarter to three when Putney arrived at the First National Bank of Fort Worth. Although it was close to closing time, when the bank manager was told that Putney wanted to transfer five thousand dollars to his bank, the manager was more than happy to take the time. The manager said he would wire Putney's bank in Galveston as he left for home when the bank closed. He was sure the Galveston bank would have the wire first thing in the morning. If everything worked out right, the money would be transported to Fort Worth by train and be in the bank no later than Friday. Putney thanked the manager and left for the county jail.

The clerk behind the window at the jail almost fainted when Putney told him who he was and that he wanted to visit Deidre O'Neill. Putney was told to wait while the clerk got the sheriff. Sheriff Maddox came to a side door. He was surprised to see Putney standing there. "Mr. Putney. I thought you were in the hospital," he said.

"Turns out the hospital was becoming hazardous for my health."

Maddox directed Putney to his private office. The sheriff sat behind his desk, adjusted his glasses, and picked up the burning cigar from the ashtray, "What can I do for you, Mr. Putney?"

"I told your clerk that I wanted to see Miss O'Neill."

"So, he said, but we don't let just anybody in to visit prisoners when they want. There are established rules."

"I thought maybe you could bend the rules. Just a little. For a fellow law officer," a growl was beginning to grow in Putney's throat.

"Well, that is often true, but the last I heard you were a deputy marshal out of Austin. You don't have any jurisdiction here in Fort Worth."

Putney pulled his long wallet from an inside pocket of his jacket. He took out the hard pasteboard card with the seal of the United States embossed on it, tapped it on the silver badge, and handed it to the sheriff. The card named him as a Deputy U. S. Marshal for the Northern District of Texas and was signed by the marshal. Sheriff Maddox hemmed and hawed then finally said, "Now that's a horse of a different color, but what business does a federal marshal have with one of my prisoners?" Maddox was stalling, trying to think of a good reason to deny Putney's request.

"I'm investigating the attempted murder of a federal officer and I believe Miss O'Neill may have information, pertinent to that investigation."

"Well, this is sort of irregular, deputy," Maddox was now recognizing Putney's position. "I think I may have to clear this with the prosecutor, Mr. McLaury. You come back tomorrow. I'm sure we can have an answer by then."

Any other time, Putney would have been on his feet with his knuckles on the sheriff's desk, hovering over him and demanding to be let in to visit Deidre. But right now, he wasn't feeling up to those sorts of theatrics. Instead, Putney leaned back in the wooden chair, folded his arms across his chest, and hoped the sheriff hadn't noticed the wince he made from the pain. "Sheriff, if I have to come back tomorrow, I'm coming back with a writ of habeas corpus from Judge McCormick. He's going to order you to place Miss O'Neill in my custody, according to the supremacy clause of the U. S. Constitution. Then I am going to escort her to Dallas, where she will be held there until her bond is paid here and I no longer need her for my investigation." This same sort of bluff had worked many times on recalcitrant sheriffs and town marshals.

Sweat popped out on Maddox's forehead and his glasses fogged up. He removed the spectacles and wiped them with a handkerchief from his pocket. "I don't think there's any need to bring a federal judge into this."

"Your choice."

"Well, you will have to leave your guns here in my office."

Putney had no reason to believe that Maddox was corrupt. It just seemed like McLaury was giving all the orders on this case, "I've no problem with that. As long as you give me a receipt."

"Nahum!" Deidre shouted when she saw the tall deputy marshal being escorted to her cell. "Oh, God I am so glad to see you. But why aren't you in the hospital? Are you all right? I have so many questions."

The matron stopped Putney at the cell door. "Sheriff said no contact with men so I ain't opening the door." Putney stared down at the short, squat woman in the gray shift. His look shook the woman who then said, "But you being a lawman and all, I guess it will be alright." She unlocked the cell door, letting it swing open.

Putney stepped inside and Deidre nearly flew to him. The hug she gave Putney almost caused him to collapse and Deidre felt it. She held him at arm's length and said, "My God, you're still ill. What are you doing here?"

"Let's sit," he said. "I will tell you everything."

Deidre barely breathed as Putney relayed the story of the last forty-eight hours of his hospital stay. When he finished, she exhaled slowly, "Lord," she said "What are you going to do now?"

"I have arranged for a sum of money to be transferred to the bank here," Putney told her. "As soon as it arrives, I will post your bond. That's the first step. Then I'm going to start looking into the shooting. I'm going to find that second man in the alley and make sure he's here to testify about his involvement. That should have you in the clear easily enough. There will be plenty of time to discuss what we will do, after that."

"Do you think Courtwright put those men up to shooting you?" asked Deidre.

"I don't think so. He's too crafty to take that kind of risk. If Blakley had missed and I managed to capture him or the other man, alive, they would have flipped on him in a heartbeat. Courtright wouldn't chance that sort of exposure. But I do think he is trying to take advantage of the situation. For what reason, I haven't quite figured."

"So how are you going to find out who the other man is?'

"I'm going to take a few days to rest up at the hotel. In the meantime, I have the twins and Henry Morgan working on some things. By the time I bond you out, there's a good chance we will know who the other man was, or at least who we can pressure into telling us."

"Promise me you will stay at the hotel and not go out until you're well."

" I promise I will be careful, but Marshal Cabell is looking for a place to set up an office. When he finds something, he will want me to come take a look. Probably he will want me to start organizing some things. Maybe hire a couple of part-time deputies and possemen. But until then I will work out of the hotel."

Deidre rose and stepped toward Putney. He stood to meet her. Their bodies met and they held each other so close they almost became one. No words were spoken between the two lovers. Words were not necessary. They kissed lightly then released their embrace. Putney turned and exited the cell.

The matron who had been standing a respectable distance walked forward to close the cell door. Putney stopped and turned to see Deidre had one hand on the steel bars of the door. He reached and covered her slender fingers with his large hand. "I love you," he said. The first time he had said such a thing since Mandy had died.

"I know," said Deidre.

Chapter Fourteen

Clint Doby massaged the meaty part of his shoulder Where the bullet had passed through. It was still sore, but all things considered, it wasn't bad. He had trouble lifting his left arm and was glad he hadn't been hit in the right side. Sitting at the desk where he used to do his school work Doby was thinking about what he should do next. His mother's care and cooking had helped him heal up quickly but he knew he couldn't stay there much longer. It was certain that someone would come looking for him at his mother's house and he didn't want to bring that sort of trouble to her doorstep. He was considering his options when a light rap on the door told him his mother had brought up his dinner. Emma Lou walked in and placed the plate of fried ham, mashed potatoes, and succotash on the desk. She sat on the bed and asked how her son was feeling.

"Pretty good, Ma. Everything is healing up fine. Thanks to you and Barney," he told her.

"We need to talk about what you're going to do now," his mother said.

"I was just thinking about that. I was thinking maybe I would head down south to Mexico, or maybe out west to New Mexico. A man could get lost out there,"

"I don't know, son both of those are far away and you don't know anybody in either place."

"You have a better idea?" There was sharpness in Doby's tone.

"I think so. Barney and I have been talking about it. Barney has a cousin that married a Creek woman and they have a farm outside of Checotah in the Indian Nations. The Katy railroad runs through Checotah. You could ride over to Denton and you could catch the Katy. You would be in Checotah by tomorrow night."

"What would I do in Indian country?"

"Barney's sure his cousin would put you to work or maybe help you find a job."

"Well….," Doby was hesitant about this idea.

"Look at it this way, son, nobody's going to be looking for you in Checotah and you will have a roof over your head. If it doesn't work out there, the Katy runs as far north as Saint Louis and as far south as Galveston. You can go anywhere from Checotah."

Doby chewed on a bite of ham, thinking, then said, "You know Ma the more I think about it the better I like the idea. But what if Barney's Cousin won't take me in?"

Emma Lou took an envelope from the pocket of her apron. "I been saving up egg and milk money. There's fifty dollars in there along with a letter to Roscoe Stegall, Barney's cousin. Barney said Roscoe's had a few scrapes with the law so he will understand your situation. But Barney didn't say what kind of trouble you are in. We thought it best not to put that into words."

Clint felt his throat tightening and tears started to well up in his eyes. Fifty dollars was not easy to come by, much less save. His hand trembled a little as he took the envelope. "Ma," his voice trembled, "I don't know what to say."

"Just take it, son, with our blessing. And stay out of trouble," tears rolled down Emma Lou's cheeks. She wiped them away and said. "Now you get some rest. It would be best if you leave tonight, after dark so as nobody sees you. Barney will ride over with you so he can bring Molly home. Keep to the Denton Road. It won't have many travelers on it at night." Emma Lou stood in a hurry and left the room before she began bawling out loud.

The only reason for the office in the back of the Emerald Saloon to be darker or mustier than usual was Courtwright's mood, at least that was the way it seemed to Montague Russell. Jim Courtwright was seated at the table along with James McIntire. "Who's this then?" Courtwright snarled at Russell.

"This is the man I told you about, Jim, William Dawson," said Russell.

"Oh, yeah," said Courtwright. "You're the one they call Bull, right?"

"That's me," pride showing in Dawson's voice.

"And you have some sort of grievance against Putney, am I right?"

"I did fifteen years in prison because of him, so yeah I guess you could say I have a hard-on over him."

93

Courtwright's chair flew against the wall, behind him, he stood so quickly. And just as quickly a thirty-two pocket pistol was pointed at Dawson's head. Courtwright's words were slow and dangerous as they oozed through his clenched teeth. "That's the sort of attitude that has us in this fix now. Maybe I should shoot you right now and save me the trouble your attitude will bring me later."

Everyone in the room was silent. Even James McIntire, who usually wasn't troubled by Courtwright's explosive temper. Dawson felt his bowels loosen slightly. Courtwright stared into Dawson's eyes, thinking, *If you say one God damned word, I'll drop you right here.* McIntire finally found his wits and spoke quietly, "Now, Jim, let's just cool down a little. I'm sure Dawson fully understands the situation."

"Do you, Bull? Do you fully understand how pissed off I am at this very moment?" Dawson could not find his voice. He could only move his head up and down, signaling he did not doubt how things stood. Courtwright slowly lowered the hammer of the pistol with his thumb, then let the barrel drop down to the side of his leg. "And you Russell? Do you understand?"

"You have made things brilliantly clear, Jim," Russell's southern drawl was more pronounced than usual.

"Fine, everyone sit," McIntire retrieved Courtwright's chair while Russell and Dawson took a seat. Max Poe and Martin Caine were already seated. "Marty," started Courtwright. "I'm concerned about Clint. Nobody has heard from him since the shooting. I need to know if he had anything to do with it. You and Max ride up to Decatur. See if you can find him up there."

Caine would gladly be out of town and away from Jim Courtwright for a while. "Sure, Jim. I'll be happy to do that."

"And Max," said Courtwright. "You do what Marty tells you. Don't try thinking on your own."

"Sure thing, Boss," the slow-witted boxer replied.

Courtwright appraised the room and then said, "And Marty, take Bull with you, it will put me a little more at ease. Him being out of town."

Well, crap, thought Caine, but with his cheerful manner said, "Sure, Jim, it will be a nice little jaunt." Caine knew full well it wouldn't be nice or jaunty.

Chapter Fifteen

Nahum Putney sat behind the desk in Deidre O'Neill's office with a series of photographs spread out in front of him. Henry Morgan sat in front of the desk while Gustav Rhine, a German photographer, stood over the desk explaining the photographs. Rhine explained about lighting, flash powder, exposure time, aperture, and dozens of things that neither Putney nor Morgan understood. The main thing that concerned Putney was that the photographs were clear and excellent. Morgan had also done good work. Making sure he had gotten a ruler in every photograph. The most interesting series of pictures were those of Morgan removing a bullet from a wooden wall. It had taken Morgan and Rhine half the morning to build a scaffold that would support the two men and keep the camera steady. Morgan had used his initiative by having Rhine take a picture of several bullets. Rhine had perfectly centered the bullets ranging from thirty-two to forty-five caliber. To the left of the bullets was a ruler and to the right was the bullet Morgan had retrieved. From the photograph, it was obvious the bullet from the wall was a thirty-eight caliber. It was also clear to Putney the bullet marks on the brick walls were of a larger caliber, probably from his forty-five Schofield.

"This is amazing," Putney was enthusiastic about the work the two men had done. "Gustav, can you come back Wednesday? Imogene Foster, Deidre's lawyer, will be back from Dallas by then and you may need to go over all this with her again."

"I would be most pleased to meet with Miss Foster," Rhine brushed his thick side whiskers back and there was a gleam in his eye. Putney looked askance at the photographer, then let it pass.

"You and Henry here are going to have to testify to the work ya'll did. Are you okay with that?"

"Okay?" asked Rhine.

"It means all right. Will you be all right with testifying?"

"Oh, certainly I will be O-Kay with testifying," Rhine was pleased to have learned a new English word.

The week had been a busy one for everyone. Imogene had returned from Dallas late Tuesday and was very excited about the photographs. She was anxious to meet with Rhine and Morgan and question them in depth about their findings and their work. Mary's days were spent worrying about the drop in business since Deidre's arrest. The editorial by Buckley Paddock had been harmful to the reputation of the hotel. She started taking out advertising in the Evening Mail a newspaper recently created by J. W. Burson. The Evening Mail's circulation was still small, but Burson was a well-respected businessman and the ads would help the hotel business.

Putney, Imogene, and Mary divided up the times they would visit Deidre. Imogene had returned from Dallas Tuesday evening and decided that mornings were the best time to visit with Deidre. They would discuss developments and plan strategies. They decided that they would proffer two defenses. The first would be self defense and the other would be the second shooter. Mary would visit at lunchtime and tell Deidre about the business and get any suggestions Deidre had, but mostly Mary saw her mission was to keep Deidre's spirits up. In the evenings, Putney would go to the jail. The evenings felt right to Putney but it also gave him time to work on setting up his new office and carrying out other tasks that were important on his list.

After meeting with Gustav Rhine, Putney went to the offices of the Daily Gazette and asked to speak with Buckley Paddock. A female clerk asked Putney if he had an appointment. "Just tell him Nahum Putney is here. I'm sure he will see me." The woman turned and went down a hallway that appeared to have offices on either side. She returned a moment later and told Putney to follow her. She led him down the passage which ended at a door. She opened the door and motioned for Putney to enter.

Paddock was sitting behind a massive desk marking a pile of papers with a blue pencil. He had the look of a man Putney could dislike easily. He looked more like a snake oil salesman than Soapy Smith did, with his hair parted in the middle and stuck down with pomade, each side ending with a little flip. He had a small mustache that was curled at both ends and looked heavy with mustache wax. He wore a vested suit and a rosebud was pinned on the left lapel. "Well, if it isn't the famous Marshal

Putney," Paddock nearly leapt from his chair and walked quickly to greet Putney with his hand held out. "Or should I say infamous?"

Putney left the smaller man's hand suspended between them. After a couple of heartbeats, Paddock understood that Putney was not in the hand-shaking mood. "You could just not say anything. Especially nothing about Miss O'Neill."

"Why, Marshal you sound as if you are miffed about something," Paddock turned his back on Putney and walked to his desk. "I assume it is about the editorial I wrote." Paddock touched a button on a teak box that sat on his desk and a cigarette exited a hole in the box. Paddock took the cigarette and lit it before pushing the button a second time. "Would you like a smoke, Marshal? It's a Kinney. The same brand you smoke, I believe."

"I'm off cigarettes for a while," Putney felt his ears turning red. This dandy was toying with him and it intensified his anger.

"That's right," said Paddock. "You were wounded in the chest. Pierced your lung if I'm not mistaken. Is it very painful?"

"I didn't come here to talk about my wound."

"Oh, I know. You're here to talk about my editorial. I suppose you want me to print a retraction of some sort."

"That's the idea."

"And if I don't, what then? Arrest me? Beat me to a pulp? I do not doubt that even in your condition you could easily do that. What a marvelous story that would make."

This was not going the way Putney had expected. In his indignation, he hadn't thought this plan through. He could see that Paddock wasn't intimidated, so it was time to adjust his approach. "Why would you write an article that you know are insinuations and half-truths?"

"Why, Marshal? That's easily answered. Innuendos and half-truths sell newspapers. Much like the violent stories about you sell dime novels. It would be incredible to believe the tales written about you. You would have to be some sort of demigod to accomplish some of those feats. So, you see Marshal, it's only business."

"Those stories aren't authorized by me and I make no money off them."

"That's a shame. Still, they probably do give you an edge when confronting gullible outlaws. The same applies with newspapers. I print a scathing editorial and the truth does not matter, because it is merely opinion. But the real benefit to the Gazette is that no matter if Miss O'Neill is found guilty or innocent, I already have an edge over my competitors. If she is found guilty, I can say 'I told you so.' If she is found innocent I can print a grand story about my error. Show some humility. That sells newspapers, also." Paddock took a last drag from his cigarette and stubbed it out in an ashtray on the desk. "It simply isn't personal."

"So when she is found not guilty you will print a retraction?"

"Of a sort. If she is found not guilty, of course."

"She will be."

"You know what Marshal? I'm going to add in a bonus. Just for you," Paddock grinned like a monkey eating shit. "I'm not going to print anything about this meeting."

"Why wouldn't you?"

"Because, it wouldn't do for me to sully your name. I have a feeling you will move heaven and earth to set Miss O'Neill free. And that, Marshal, sells newspapers."

Putney had been defeated. He knew it and Paddock knew it. Putney turned on his heel and exited the office and the building in a pout. *Rat bastard*, he thought.

Putney walked to Main Street and Fourth. He saw Marshal Cabell standing outside a building in the middle of the block near Fifth Street and he walked to meet his boss. "Here it is Nahum," Cabell turned the key in the door. Inside was a spacious room. There was a roll-top desk against one wall and shelving on an adjacent one. There were four straight-back chairs around a table in the middle of the room and one rolling low-backed chair at the desk. On the wall opposite the bookshelves was a pot-bellied stove in the front corner. "Not bad, huh?" said Cabell. "And look here." Cabell opened a door on the back wall to show another room just as large. Opposite the door they entered was another that exited to an alley. To one side was a sink with a single spigot. On the same wall was another pot belly stove. "I have already opened an account here in Fort Worth so you can draw money for more furnishings, like maybe a steel cabinet you can lock up guns in.

You might want to put a cot in here, too." Putney nodded his head. As they left Cabell handed his deputy keys to the doors and a bank passbook. I'll send some pre-printed forms over when I get back to Dallas. The judge will have his clerk send over any writs and warrants starting Monday. Here is the key to the Post Office box."

The two parted company with Marshal Cable going south toward the train station and Putney, north to the county jail. Putney stopped at Dunn's Mercantile. The store had some single, steel frame beds and mattresses, and Putney bought a set along with some sheets, blankets, towels, free-standing shelving, a coffee pot, four porcelain coated cups, some hand soap, and various other sundries. He gave the clerk, a sturdy looking woman the address and told her to have the goods delivered the next day. They didn't have any locking cabinets, so he ordered a steel one from a Montgomery Ward catalog that Dunn's kept for just such purchases. Putney left Dunn's still fuming over his meeting with Paddock. He hated losing to such a man and chastised himself for going in angry instead of with a good plan.

Putney had learned that the matron usually on duty when he came, had a sweet tooth, so he stopped at a candy store on his way to the jail and bought a bag of assorted hard candy. At the jail, Putney told Deidre about his day, leaving out the meeting with Paddock. If she had known of the meeting she would have teased him about it and he wasn't in a teasing mood.

The rest of the week moved along in the same manner. Each person going about their business and duties. On some days, Putney would let Elizabeth join him. He enjoyed her company and she kept his spirits up. By Thursday, Putney was feeling the strain of his duties and the healing wound in his chest. Even though the wound had been sewn closed he was still sore and found he got short on breath quicker than he could ever remember. His tiredness caused him to oversleep on Friday morning and he wasn't up and dressed and eating breakfast until eleven o'clock. Elizabeth had just brought his food when a messenger from the bank arrived with a note saying that his cash had been deposited in the bank. Putney ate in a hurry and gulped down his coffee so he could get to the bank before the noon lunch break. He told Elizabeth to tell Mary and Imogene to meet him at the jail.

It was two o'clock by the time the bond had been paid and Deidre was released from custody. Putney, the ladies, and the Shakespeare twins were halfway down the block when Deputy Sheriff Hubert Forsythe caught up with the group. "Whew," he puffed. "I'm glad I caught up with ya'll. Sheriff Maddox told me to make sure Miss O'Neill got to her hotel. You remember the judge told me to keep tabs."

"So, then," Deidre was feeling snarky. "I suppose you should tag along. We wouldn't want the sheriff to think I hopped a train to Galveston, now would we?"

"No, ma'am," Deidre had a way of making men nervous and it affected Forsythe doubly.

Nobody in the entire gaggle spoke on the walk back. Nobody wanted to say anything in the presence of the young deputy sheriff. At the entrance, Deidre gave Forsythe a stern look. "Run on back to the sheriff, young man," she said. "You can tell him your work is done. I suppose I will have to see you, again, tomorrow, sometime."

"Yes ma'am," Forsythe's timidity in front of the Irish woman showed for all to see. "But Mister Putney, I need to talk to you about something. In private, if I could."

"Whatever you have to say to Nahum can be said in front of all of us," snapped Deidre.

"Leave the poor boy alone," Putney scolded. "He's just doing his duty. Sure, Hubert. Come on in. When we get everything settled, you and I will go over to the White Elephant for a drink. That be okay with you?"

"Sure, Marshal. Whatever you say." Forsythe beamed knowing Putney had stood up for him.

Inside the foyer of the hotel and restaurant, the whole staff was waiting. Henry Morgan shouted, "Hip, hip, hooray!" and everyone followed his lead. Elizabeth hurried over to Deidre and gave her a big hug.

"We are all so glad to see you, Miss," She gushed.

"And I'm glad to see you all," said Deidre, and then addressing everyone, "I am very happy to see you all and I want you all to know that everything will be all right. Now back to work," she laughed. "Betsy, this is Deputy Sheriff Hubert Forsythe. I want you to keep him company for a few minutes.

Don't you be letting him snoop around. You hold him right here. Henry, bring a bottle of Bushmills to my office," Then she led her cadre to her office.

As the group left the foyer Elizabeth looked sternly at Forsythe who was standing with his hat in his hand, moving it round and round by the brim. A smile came to Elizabeth's face as she looked at him and thought what a handsome young man he was. "I hope you haven't caused Miss Deidre too much trouble, Deputy Forsythe."

"Oh, no ma'am," Forsythe stammered. " I didn't have nought to do with her at all until today. But I'm told she was treated very well."

"Well, Deputy, I hope so, for your sake."

"Yes ma'am. And please call me Hub. Everyone else does."

"Then, Hub, let's go into the restaurant. We can have a glass of lemonade. Everyone calls me Betsy, but you may call me Elizabeth."

Inside Deidre's office Morgan had arrived and cracked the seal on the bottle of Bushmills and poured everyone a drink. "I toast you all," said Deidre, "for standing by me and keeping the faith. Slainthe'." Everyone toasted her back. Nahum gave Deidre a big kiss and everyone cheered.

"I need to go see what Forsythe wants," Nahum told the group. "I won't be long." He gave Deidre another big kiss and was walking toward the door.

"You better not you big galoot. I have plans for you tonight," Deidre called after him. Putney blushed as everyone else laughed.

Forsythe and Elizabeth were sitting at the first table inside the restaurant. They seemed transfixed on each other with Elizabeth batting her eyelashes and Forsythe looking cow-eyed at her. Putney cleared his throat loudly. Forsythe looking around saw the big red-haired man and leaped up, hitting the table with his knees and nearly knocking the glasses of lemonade over. "Y-y-yes, sir," he stammered.

Speaking as a father might, Putney said, "You better come with me before you get in trouble."

It being mid-afternoon, there were few patrons at the White Elephant. Still, Putney guided the young deputy sheriff to a booth as far from the others as possible. A waiter came and Putney ordered two beers. Forsythe started to speak but Putney motioned for him until the waiter had come and gone. Once alone Putney asked, "What is it you wanted to tell me, Forsythe."

"Well sir, there's two things. First Mr. McLaury had us deputies serving subpoenas for grand jurors all this week. They are all to report on Monday morning. He's been bragging that he will have a true bill by Monday afternoon."

"That's pretty quick, but nothing surprising and nothing we wouldn't know by Monday morning. So why the secrecy?"

"No, sir. I knew you would find out about it soon enough, but that's not the important thing."

"Then out with it son, I have plans."

"Yes sir. It's about the coroner's report. You see, I picked that report up for the sheriff. At the hearing last week I saw the report on Mr. Mclaury's table. It said that Ned Blakely was shot twice with forty-five caliber bullets."

"No surprise there. What's got you worried?"

"I read the report I picked up from the coroner. It said that Blakely was hit once by a forty-five caliber bullet, but the wound wouldn't have been fatal. The bullet that lodged in Blakely's heart was a thirty-eight."

"You sure about that?" quizzed Putney.

"As sure as I am that the Trinity River runs through the middle of town."

"Who else knows about this?

"Nobody. I swear."

"Not even Maddox?"

"No sir. I don't know how that report got changed. And I don't think the sheriff is rotten, but I just didn't know who to trust, except maybe you and this is the first time I could tell you."

"All right, Hubert. You keep this between you and me. When the time is right, you may need to testify about this, but right now it's best to keep your head down. Don't bring it up to anyone. Just keep your eyes and ears open. If anything else comes up, you bring it to me."

"I hope I've done the right thing here. I don't like going behind the sheriff's back but I don't want to see Miss O'Neill hang for something she didn't do."

"Miss O'Neill's not going to hang. You can trust me on that."

"Oh, I will sir."

"One other thing you can trust me on."

What's that, sir?"

"Don't let Miss O'Neill see you going all sweet over Elizabeth. At least not until this is all over."

That evening Mary had closed down the private dining room to throw a welcome home party for Deidre. There wasn't much business to be lost. Ever since Paddock's editorial, the ladies of the line had taken to having their assignations with their gentlemen friends elsewhere. She had the staff set up a buffet with all sorts of vegetables, fruits, sliced beef, ham, and desserts. All the staff were invited. Those who were working would be spelled by those who weren't on duty, so everyone could participate. There was champagne iced down at every table and Mary had hired some Irish musicians to come play on a makeshift bandstand.

Everybody was having a grand time and Mary was sure the hoopla could be heard on the street. Dancing and gaiety were going strong when Mary went to the front to make sure everything was running well. She returned a few minutes later and tapped Putney on the shoulder. "There's a woman here that says she needs to see you. She said it was very important. I tried to put her off, but she wouldn't have it. She said she has to see you, urgently. I had her wait in Deidre's office." Deidre was dancing a country dance with some of the other women, so Putney slipped out quietly.

The woman stood when Putney entered the room. She was older than Putney remembered but he recognized her right away. *Emma Lou Doby*, he thought. *Clint Doby. It makes sense now.* "Mrs. Doby," said Putney.

"This is quite the surprise. What's it been? Fifteen years?"

"Thirteen, Mr. Putney. Tragedy befell us then and it has befallen us now." Putney could see her knees start to buckle and he crossed the room with one giant step and caught her before she collapsed. He lowered her into one of the plush chairs, poured a glass of water from the pitcher on the drinks bar, and knelt beside her, helping her sip it.

"What in the world are you doing here?" he asked.

Emma Lou took a few more sips, fanned herself with her palm, and let out a deep sigh. "It's about my son, Clint. Do you remember him?"

When he had first heard the name earlier in the week he hadn't made the connection. But it was clear as spring water now. He remembered the adobe house south of Fort McKavett. He remembered the dusty landscape. And he remembered the young boy cradling his father's head and blood seeping into the dry West Texas sand. He remembered the boy looking up at him. Tears making mud rivers on the boy's dusty face. He remembered the boy yelling, "I hate you! I hate you!"

Putney had tried to take Claude Doby alive, but Claude had snuck out the back of his ranch house and around the side. He had let loose with a short-barreled shotgun but somehow managed to get all the pellets from the scattergun into the ground. Putney had pivoted and fired twice before Claude could break open the shotgun to reload. Putney had been deadly.

"What can I do for you, Mrs. Doby?"

"It's Stegall now. I moved Back to my parents' house near Decatur after Claude died. I met the man that owns a general store there and after two years we married."

"What happened to Clint?"

"That's what I came to tell you," said Emma Lou. She went on to explain about Clint arriving wounded at her house and how they thought he had killed Putney. "I sent him off until things could blow over," she said. "Then Tuesday these three men came to town asking around about Clint. Someone told them about me and Barney. They came to our house. There was this one young man. At first, he was real polite. Made out like he was Clint's friend. We told him we hadn't seen or heard from Clint. That was when this big guy started yelling at us that we better tell him where Clint was or he was going to hurt someone."

"Who was the big guy?"

"I don't know. There were two big guys, but one of them acted like he didn't have much sense. The younger man tried to calm the big man down. He called the big man Bull. But the big guy, Bull, he had dark hair, he grabbed Barney and started hurting him. I couldn't take it, Mr. Putney. I finally told them he had left the day

104

before for the Nations. When they saw that hurting Barney got me to talking they threatened to hurt him some more. So I told them he was headed to Checotah."

"How far ahead of them do you think Clint is?" asked Putney.

"That's what I didn't tell them. I made out like he went on horseback, but the truth is he rode over to Denton to catch the train. I'm sure he was in Checotah by Monday night. I figure it will take them a few days to get there. Then this morning I read in the newspaper where you weren't dead at all. I figured you were the only one that could help me, so I caught the Denver down here to Fort Worth. I had read about you and this place, so I come here in hopes to find you."

"Where is Clint staying in Checotah?"

"He's at a farm a few miles out of town. It's owned by Barney's cousin, Roscoe, Roscoe Stegall. Please Mr. Putney, can you help us."

"I will. Let me get you set up with a room here. I'll catch the first train I can to Checotah. I think you came soon enough that I can beat them there. I'll bring Clint back here safely. You just wait a minute."

Putney left the office and found Mary waiting at the reception desk. "Get Mrs. Stegall a room, please and show her there. She's pretty upset. Have Elizabeth take her some food. Then tell Deidre I need to see her in her apartment."

The two went back into the office. "Mrs. Stegall, you go with Mary here she will fix you up. Tomorrow send a telegram to your husband. Tell him you're all right and you will be staying here." Emma Lou started to protest, but Putney stopped her. "Don't you worry about a thing. I'll pay for anything you need. I will be back in a few days with your son."

Deidre came into her bedroom and found Putney packing. "And where on this green earth do you think you're going, Mr. Man?"

"I'm going to the Indian nations. I'll be back in a few days."

"The hell you are. You're in no fit condition to go traipsing off to wherever for whatever."

"Calm down. Pour yourself a drink and listen to what I have to say," Putney told her. Deidre filled a glass with Bushmills as Putney packed and told her about Clint Doby and about what

Forsythe had told him. "Look, Clint Doby could be the person that holds this whole thing together. If I can get him back down here, you're off with no trouble. Beside's I feel like I owe him."

"Owe him, hell," Deidre yelled. "He tried to kill you."

"But he didn't kill me. The boy needs help and I'm going to help him. Besides, I think one of the men after him is Bull Dawson. I can't let that stand."

"If you get killed, I'll never forgive you."

"If I get killed I won't expect for you to forgive me."

Chapter Sixteen

The train pulled out of the Fort Worth station at nine in the morning. Putney had gotten no sleep the night before. He smiled as he thought back on the night he had spent with Deidre. It had been like no other in his life. Near exhaustion, Putney had risen at five so he could get to the livery to get his horse and mule. He had decided to take his own animals in a stock car instead of taking a chance on renting from a livery in Checotah. Besides he could pack the mule with all he might need. It was always better to be prepared than caught with your drawers down.

Putney took a seat in the first class dining car and ordered breakfast and coffee from the porter there. He caught the other passengers in the car looking at him. Putney's outfit was more suitable for the trail than the clothes worn by the fashionable men in women in first class. They certainly weren't used to seeing a man wearing two pistols and carrying a Winchester in a posh rail car. To put the spectators at ease, he took the badge that was hidden by his vaquero jacket and pinned it on the lapel. The other passengers' change in demeanor was obvious. Putney smiled again.

By the time the train had pulled into the station at Denton, Putney had finished his breakfast and was seated in the main first class car. There he eased himself into one of the elegant bench seats and pulled a Kinney out of the silver case and lit it. He looked at the case with the sailing ship engraved on it. Through years of use, the engraving had worn down but was still visible. Putney felt a quickening of his heart as he thought of the Christmas day, nearly twenty years earlier, when Mandy had given the case to him. He loved Deidre, deeply, but his love for Mandy would never die. Smoke billowed around his head which itself was lost in its own fog of memories. Memories of the women and girls he had lost in his life. His mother and sisters were killed by Comanche renegades when he was fifteen. Erin, his first love was violated and killed by vicious outlaws. And his young bride, Mandy, who had died at the hands of a one-time friend, seeking revenge. He had loved each one. And he had lost each one, violently. It was the reason it had taken him so long to admit his love for Deidre. He had nearly lost her once at Crying Rock and he feared that professing his love was inviting disaster.

The train clattered noisily into the Denton Station where it would take on more passengers and freight before traveling on to the main line in Denison. The train would have scheduled stops at Denison, McAlester, and Muskogee, but there were nearly a dozen whistle stops in between, of which Checotah was one. The train only stopped at these stations when there were passengers or freight to load. Not even counting on the whistle stops the trip was going to take several hours, so Putney stretched out his legs, lowered his sombrero over his eyes, and quickly fell asleep. He woke briefly when the train pulled out of Denton but the rhythmic clacking of wheels on the tracks soon lulled him back to sleep. At Denison, Putney had to change trains which meant he had to supervise the stockmen who were responsible for getting his animals out of the stock car and onto the next train. The two-hour nap between stops had not been enough, but he knew he would have plenty of time to catch up before he arrived in Checotah.

The station in Denison was a long building made of red brick. Putney detrained to catch the mainline train. While there, a man walked onto the platform and was yelling something that Putney could not make out over the noise of the trains. As the man walked closer, Putney heard the man call his name. Putney signaled the man over. "You Nahum Putney?" the man asked.

"That's me," Putney told him.

"I have a telegraph for you," the man produced a clipboard with a yellow telegram envelope attached. He handed Putney the envelope, then gave him the board with a receipt clipped down and a pencil. "Sign here." Putney signed the receipt and watched the man walk away. He tore open the envelope and removed the telegram. It was from Marshal Cabbel it read:

"Message received STOP Witness subpoena issued for Doby STOP Return with witness"

Putney was glad the marshal had acted quickly to give Putney the legal authority to be in the Indian Nations and to return with Clint Doby. He folded the telegram and stored it in the long wallet. He boarded the train and settled down in the first class car for another nap. After three hours the brakes of the train ground it to a stop in McAlester. There was a scheduled half hour stop there so Putney stepped onto the platform to stretch and wake himself up. He would be in Checotah in another hour and a half and he wanted to shake the sleepiness from his head. He asked a station employee if there was a privy with running water. He walked to the privy and soaked his neckerchief and used the cool cloth to wash his face. He was back in the car before the train chugged it's way toward Checotah. He was probably the only reason the train would stop in the small town.

As the train pulled up to the small station, Putney removed his badge from the lapel of his coat and pinned it on his vest where it would be covered. He saw no advantage to advertising who he was until it was necessary. It was dusk by the time he retrieved his horse and mule from the stock car. Checking his watch he noted it was half past seven. He put on gloves to lead his animals to a nearby livery. Putney didn't want to try to find Roscoe Stegall's farm in the dark so he decided to get a room in a hotel and leave early the next morning. He got directions to a hotel from the liveryman where he boarded his animals for the night.

Piano and fiddle music rang out into the street from the Checotah Hotel. Putney stepped up on the boardwalk and entered through the double doors with stained glass windows. Stepping inside it became obvious that the hotel was a combined saloon, gaming house, and bordello. He took two steps through the doors and stood to survey the surroundings. To his right was a poker table with a variety of players, none of whom had the look of stalwart citizens. On his left was another poker table, a dice table, a roulette wheel, and in the back corner a faro game was getting the most action. In the center of the large room was a circular couch covered in tufted purple upholstery. Beyond that were several tables of men drinking and ogling the whores who stood on a raised platform on the far side from Putney. There was a wide staircase and a music stand between the prostitutes' perch and the faro table. Just past the poker table on his right was a long, polished bar with customers sitting on stools. The room was filled with men from nearly every stage of society. There were what looked like bankers and merchants, cowboys, trappers, gamblers, and the dregs of the world. They were black, white, Indians, and Mexicans. The prostitutes reflected their customers and were garishly and scantily clad. When Putney stepped through the door the entire room, except the musicians stopped and eyed the tall red-haired man carrying a satchel and a Winchester. The scrutiny lasted two heart beats then everyone returned to their activities. Everyone except one. A large black man sat on a stool at the end of the bar nearest Putney. He was wearing a plainsman's hat with a round belly, a black coat pulled back exposing a Colt in a cross-draw holster, and striped pants tucked in mule skinner boots. A huge bushy mustache hid the center portion of the man's face and narrow eyes showed only the pupils staring at Putney under thick eyebrows. It had taken Putney less time than a blink of his eyes to recognize this was the only real dangerous man in the saloon.

Putney pushed his way through the crowd to the end of the bar opposite the dangerous man, where a bartender stood. The barman was a tall thin Indian with a sparse, wispy mustache and chin whiskers. He wore a dingy white shirt with red sleeve garters and a red string tie. The skinny man leaned over the bar and speaking over the noise said, "What will it be mister?"

"I heard I could get a room here," Putney said.

"Depends," Skinny said with a chuckle. "By the hour or for the night?"

"You have one that's away from the noise where a man can get a night's sleep?"

"Sure, on the third floor at the back, overlooking the alley. Quietest room in the joint."

"I'll take it," Putney said.

"Seven dollars."

"Seven? Isn't that a bit steep?"

"Quiet comes at a price," a half sneer, half-smile appeared on the bartender's lips, exposing yellow teeth.

Putney removed one glove and pulled out his coin purse, dug out a silver eagle, and placed it on the bar, "Will that cover a meal, too?"

"Only if you want beef steak, boiled potatoes, and frijoles." The bartender turned his body and ran his finger along a row of keys hanging from pegs. He plucked one. "Number twenty."

"Two other keys are hanging from that peg."

"Yep. Spares," Said Skinny.

Putney fished in his coin purse and fished out a Trade dollar, "I'll take those keys."

The barman hesitated, looking at Putney whose blue eyes seemed to pierce his own. He reached and grabbed the other two. Laying them gingerly on the bar. "If you want to go on up, the steak and a beer will be ready by the time you get back. The waiter won't have no problem finding you, Red."

Picking up the keys, Putney turned, purposefully to his right, seeing the large black man looking over a broad shoulder, trying to appear as if he weren't. Putney crossed the room and walked up the five steps to the landing where three ladies of the line ogled him. As he turned to his right to go up the first flight he looked and saw an Indian wearing a high-crowned bowler with an eagle feather and a beaded vest enter the doors. He climbed the stairs, walking past several more spoiled doves until he got to the second floor landing. There were no people on the stairway to the third floor.

Room twenty was sparse. There was a bed with a wood headboard but no footboard. The gas light from the hallway allowed him to see a short table with a lamp. He put his satchel and rifle on the bed along with his gloves and covered everything with his frock coat. He lit the lamp and looked around the room. To the left of the door was a straight-back chair that stood by a small table with a basin and pitcher of water. On the wall over the table was an unframed oval-shaped mirror and under the table was a steel chamber pot. He poured a little water in the basin and washed his face and hands with a shrunken bar of soap, then dried his hands on a towel hanging on a peg next to the mirror. Putney had the feeling that something wasn't right, and it had to do with the man sitting at the bar. He crossed the room and trimmed the lamp then before leaving the room he pinned his badge on the inside of his vest.

Putney walked down the stairs and onto the landing overlooking the saloon. The room was quieter and the people more still than when he had ascended the stairs. Hackles raised on the back of his neck. The tables that had been crowded were now vacant, except for one where the Indian with the bowler sat, his head down as if he were dozing. Putney noticed there was no pistol in the holster that hung on the man's right side. Now he knew something was wrong, but he hadn't figured out what. A waiter with a plate of food and a beer caught Putney's eyes and with his head motioned to an empty table. Putney stood on the landing as if he had been nailed there. Putney looked to the bar and saw the large black man standing with his hand behind his back. The cross-draw holster was empty. The men who had been close to him before, were now huddled together at the other end.

Putney spoke slowly and clearly to the man staring at him, "The first thing you need to do is tell the mope with the bowler to slowly place that hog leg back into his holster. I would hate to ruin that spiffy hat with a forty-five caliber hole."

The Indian's head raised, and he looked at the man at the bar who nodded. Sliding his right hand from his lap he replaced a Colt in his holster.

"Now," said Putney, "I expect you're about to swing up that Colt behind your back. Before you do that, I would like to know the name of the man that's about to die."

"Only dyin round here is going to be you if you decide to jerk one of those Schofields," The man's voice was a low growl, but the words were as clear as Putney's had been. "I'm Deputy U. S. Marshal Bass Reeves and I mean to take you to Fort Smith to face Judge Parker, Red. Whether it's riding straight up or laying over a saddle is up to you."

Chapter Seventeen

Instead of easing the tension in the room, when Putney smiled everyone fell silent. The roulette wheel stopped and the gamblers at all the tables were watching to see who was about to die. None of them knew Putney but all of them knew who Bass Reeves was and the most preferred that Reeves would lose this match. Reeves was known to Putney as well, though the two had never met.

Bass Reeves had started life as a slave in Arkansas. The story was that during the Civil War, Bass' owner, a state senator named William Reeves had taken Bass along to the battlefields of the war. Sometime during the war Bass Reeves had escaped and fled to the Indian Nations where he lived among the various tribes. The legend was that Reeves had learned to scout and hunt among the Indians and even learned several languages. After the war, Reeves reunited with his wife and they settled in Fort Smith, Arkansas. Because of his tracking abilities Bass was first hired as a Marshals' posseman and shared in bounties collected by Deputy Marshals. He was recognized for his work and in 1875, Marshal James Fagan appointed Reeves as a full deputy. Every marshal since had kept Reeves on, due to his impressive arrest record.

"You may be Bass Reeves," the strange cheerfulness in Putney's voice was unnerving. "But I'm not who you think I am, and we need to slow our horses before this gets out of hand."

"Iffin you ain't Benjamin "Red" Dewberry, who the hell are you and why should I believe you?"

Putney slowly raised his right hand, palm out and open, but his left hand was still ready to strike if needed. Moving cautiously, he pulled the round star badge from inside his vest. "You, Bowler Hat," he ordered, "take this to your boss." The scrawny Indian gingerly stepped toward Putney and plucked the badge from Putney's hand as though Putney might snatch him. Cautiously, the Indian backed away from Putney, never taking his eyes off the tall redhead.

When he felt safe, the Indian looked at the badge, "Damn it, Bass, it's a Marshal's badge."

"Let me see that, Joey," barked Reeves. Joey did as he was told, and Reeves examined the badge. It wasn't like his, which was a simple five-pointed star, but Reeves knew different Marshals designed their own badges, so it could be possible. "How do I know you didn't take this off someone you killed?" Bass asked Putney.

"Same as I don't know you a really Bass Reeves out of Arkansas," Putney answered. "I reckon we're just going to have to trust each other."

"And I reckon your steak is getting cold. We better have a seat and talk about this." Reeves slowly replaced his Colt in the cross-draw holster and started walking to the table the waiter had indicated. Joey followed behind. Putney walked down the five steps from the landing and to the table. All three men sat at the same time, Reeves and Joey watching Putney and he watched them. Disappointed that they hadn't gotten to watch a killing, the rest of the people in the room went back t their noisy activities.

The waiter set Putney's plate and beer on the table, shaking with fear that something could still go wrong, and he would be in the middle of it. Reeves placed the badge next to the plate. Putney let it rest there. Mind if I take a look at your left hand?" asked Reeves. Putney gave him a quizzical look. "Red Dewberry's supposed to have a large star tattooed on the back of his left hand." Putney picked up his badge with his left hand. "Well, at least you ain't Dewberry," said Reeves. "This is Joey Barton, my posseman, so, who are you and what are you doing in the nations?"

Putney gave a quick rundown of what had led him to Checotah, then asked, "What made you think I was this, Benjamin Dewberry?"

"Well, you fit his description and the barman called you Red, so I just naturally figured," Reeves cut the sentence short.

"I guess you didn't stop to think that someone that looks like me might be called Red by a stranger?" asked Putney.

"Nope. I didn't know how much time I had, so I needed to get things set up a might quick. But it wasn't quick enough for you. You must be part Injun to read a trap that quick."

"None at all. When you've been at it as long as I have you know to be cautious. When I sized up the room, I knew that if I were to have trouble, it would come from you."

Reeves rubbed his chin and stroked his massive mustache. "I need to keep that in mind," then looking to Barton, "Ain't the Stegall place up near Honey Springs off the Texas Road?"

"That's right, Bass," said Barton. "Roscoe Stegall married a cousin of mine, Fannie."

"You're in luck Putney," Reeves said, "We got business up in Muskogee and are headed up that way tomorrow. Honey Springs is on the way. We can guide you up there."

"Bass," said Barton, "Stegall is known to cook up bootleg whiskey. It might be best you give me an hour's head start, so's I can prepare him for the idea of two Deputies showing up. He could get a might sketchy."

"Good idea, Joey," said Reeves, then he called over the waiter. "It looks like Deputy Marshal Putney's food has gone cold, bring him a fresh plate and one for me and Joey to boot."

Putney and Reeves met in the saloon for breakfast at seven the next morning. The patronage in the saloon had dropped off but there were still quite a few hangers-on at the gaming tables. Most of the prostitutes had retired for the day, sleeping until the evening would bring in more business. The two men ate ham and eggs with biscuits and red-eye gravy. A pot of coffee was on the table from which they helped themselves. By eight the two men had retrieved their animals from the livery and were riding towards Honey Springs. It had been a short ride along what the people in the Nations called the Texas Road, which ran from Fort Leavenworth, Kansas to Denison, Texas. About ten the two deputies cut off the road to a wagon trail that led to the Stegall farm.

Joey and Roscoe Stegall were sitting in rough hewn chairs outside a split log cabin, smoking pipes. Joey waved at the two as they rode in. Reeves and Putney were tying their animals to a corral rail and Joey came over to them. "We missed 'em, Bass," he said. "They left yesterday afternoon. You better come over and get it straight from Roscoe."

An average sized man with a big belly, bald head, and scruffy beard remained in his chair, smoking his pipe and occasionally taking a swig from a crockery jug. "Yep, that boy showed up here out of the blue on Tuesday morning," he said when questioned by Reeves. "I didn't know him from Adam, but he had a letter from my cousin Barney. I didn't have no work for him, but he had some money for his keep, so's I let him stay. Figured I could get him a job down in Checotah, sooner or later."

"Why did he leave?" asked Putney.

"Didn't have no choice, now did he?" Stegall took a swig from the jug. "These three fellas showed up day before last about supper time. Clint said he knowed 'em, so's I didn't think nothing of it. All kinds of folk pass through here. There was one about Clint's age. Really friendly young feller. They got along pretty good. He told Clint some feller named Jim wanted him to come back to Fort Worth."

"How did Doby act about that?" Reeves asked.

"Am I telling this story or what?" said Stegall. "Hold your horses and I'll get to it." Stegall took another swig. "Anyways, like I was saying, Clint said he didn't think it would be a good notion for him to go back to Texas. He never told me what the trouble was, but I figured the law was after him down there. Looks like I weren't far from wrong. Well, them boys didn't have much to say, just asked if they could pay for a couple of meals and camp out for the night. Said they'd be leaving the next morning. Next day they didn't act like they was in no hurry to leave and they hung around till noon time. We was havin a couple of swigs when one of the big guys, they called Bull, said it was time for them to leave and told Clint he was going back with 'em. Clint said hows he weren't going with him and this Bull figure grabbed him up and said Clint was going with 'em, like or not. Then he slapped Clint around a bit. That was when Fannie came out with my old Henry and said they was to leave and take Clint with 'em. Since Clint didn't have no horse, I let him have one of my mules and rigging. I figured Barney had sent fifty dollars and that more than covered the cost of the animal. They left about an hour later. That's all I know, cept I knowed they weren't no law dogs."

116

Reeves thanked Stegall for the information and signed for Putney and Joey to come away where they could talk without Stegall overhearing them. "What do you think, Nahum?"

"I don't know who the other two are but I'm pretty sure the one called Bull is a man named William Dawson."

"Have you dealt with him before?"

"Nearly killed him twice and arrested him once."

"So, you're saying you're not the best of friends," Reeves laughed.

"I'm sure Bull wouldn't think so. He spent the last fifteen years in prison down in Huntsville. He's sworn he would kill me one day."

"It don't sound like his time behind bars simmered him down much."

"No, Bass, I doubt it did. Men come out of Huntsville either meaner than before or broken. I don't think Bull has been broken."

"I don't reckon we can let that stand," Turning the conversation to Joey, Reeves said, "Joey you take the wagon on up to Muskogee and meet Deputy Lucas. Tell him I have business to tend to helping out a fellow Deputy from Texas. Ya'll go on ahead without me. I'll meet you back in Fort Smith in a week or so."

"Sure thing, Bass. Be careful," said Joey.

"Shouldn't be much problem, just looking for a witness," said Bass.

Putney and Reeves agreed that the most likely route for the four men to take was the Texas Road to Denison. Dawson's band had one day on them which meant it was likely they were between Canadian and McAlester. At the earliest, they would make Denison in two more days. The Katy railroad and the Texas Road ran parallel a few miles apart. If they were lucky there would be a southbound train to Denison leaving that afternoon. That would put them ahead of their quarry by more than a day. The two deputies pushed their animals to get back to Checotah as soon as they could and arrived a few minutes before two o'clock. They were just in time since a southbound was due through Checotah at four that afternoon. The Station would put up a red flag, signaling the train that there were passengers or freight to be loaded. Putney purchased two first class tickets to Denison and paid the stock fee while Reeves took the animals to the stock manager so they would be ready to load when the train arrived. With everything set, the two deputies went to a nearby café for a quick meal.

Putney and Reeves were sitting facing each other on the comfortable benches of first class. The other passengers stared at the two men who must have looked like bandits had it not been for the badges on the lapels of their coats. Before the train pulled out of the station a conductor stopped where the two men were sitting and addressed Putney. "Excuse me, sir," the conductor said, then when Putney produced the tickets, "I'm sorry sir, but there is a mistake. Negroes aren't permitted in first-class."

Reeves started to rise. He was used to the treatment, but Putney signaled him to stay seated. "You're right," Putney glared at the conductor. "There has been a mistake because there are no negroes sitting here."

"B-b-ut," the train man stuttered and gestured at Reeves.

"Two Deputy U. S. Marshals are sitting here. No negro, no white. Just Marshals. See the badges." Putney was brooking no disagreement.

"S-s-sir, it's just not permitted. Think of the other passengers."

Putney stood, towering over the small conductor. "I don't care about the other passengers. Punch the tickets and move on."

The conductor hesitated but seeing the fire in Putney's eyes decided the argument wasn't worth the trouble. He took the tickets and using a hand punch, perforated each ticket. Putney pocketed the tickets and sat down.

"You didn't need to do that for me," said Reeves.

"I didn't. I did it for me," Reeves gave Putney a quizzical look and Putney smiled. "It was either the both of us ride here or back in third class and I'm not suited to third class."

"Marty, that's I think that's McAlester up yonder," Max Poe pointed to the lights in the distance. "You think we could go into town and maybe get a room for the night and a hot meal?

Marty liked Max, even though he sometimes didn't have the sense to pour water out of a boot, even with the instructions written on the heel. "Max, how much money do you have on you?"

"I dunno. Maybe a dollar and six bits." Poe said.

"Okay, I think I have about three dollars, myself," Martin Caine knew he was going to have to explain things so the slow-witted Max Poe could understand. "Bull how much you got?"

"Enough for a bottle of cheap whiskey and a can of beans, maybe," Dawson's temperament had been bad the last two nights, and the conversation did nothing to improve it.

"So, Max, between the three of us we barely have enough money for one room and one meal," said Caine. "That's the reason we can't go to town for a room and meals. We got to save some money to get something to eat until we get back to Fort Worth." The three men hadn't kitted out well before going to Decatur because they figured they would just go up and back and probably spend one night camping before returning to Fort Worth. They had only brought a coffee pot, a small bag of coffee, a frying pan, some bacon, and a few cans of beans. Caine had wanted to go back to Fort Worth and tell Courtwright what they had found out and let him decide on what to do next. But Dawson had been insistent that they ride on to Checotah. 'I don't want to test that man's temper,' Dawson had said about Courtwright. At the time Caine had seen the sense in Dawson's reasoning, but now they were down to nothing to eat, and Caine knew he needed to make a decision.

"Not only that, dimwit," Dawson was speaking to Poe. "What if this tadpole saw a sheriff or town marshal and started running his mouth. I don't feel like spending any time in a back water jail house."

Wanting to diffuse the building hostility, Caine interrupted, "Clint, I don't reckon you have any money."

"I sure as hell don't, and I wouldn't give it to you if I did," Doby was still angry at being dragged away from Roscoe's. "If y'all hadn't pissed off Roscoe's wife the way you did, I might have come along nice and easy and maybe got a small poke from Roscoe. So no, I ain't got a dime." He didn't say anything about the five dollars he had squirreled away in his boot.

"I bet if I held you by the heels I could shake it out of you," threatened Dawson.

119

Doby didn't reply for fear the big man would do just that or worse. He didn't know Dawson and didn't know what he would or wouldn't do. Dawson had already taken his pistol and that was the only defense a man Doby's size had against a man like Dawson. When it came to it his only hope was that Max Poe would stop him.

"Clint's right Bull," said Caine. "There was no need for all that and now we are in a fix. We'll be lucky to make it back to Fort Worth without nearly starving."

"I might just take you off your horse and shake you," Dawson wasn't in the mood to be talked down to by the likes of Martin Caine.

Max Poe kicked his horse in the ribs and swung it around in front of Dawson's. "Ain't nobody gonna be shakin nobody, lessen I take you from your horse and shake you. And If I start that I might just beat you while I'm at it," the former boxer snarled.

As usual, Dawson wasn't willing to take on anybody his equal. "I was just fooling, Max. I didn't mean nothing. I guess I'm a little short on account of the long trip and being hungry. You ain't got to worry about me."

"Y'all tamp it down," snapped Caine. "We're all on a short string. Max, give me what money you have."

"Sure, Marty," Poe said. "But he just better watch how he talks, that's all." Poe pulled a small pouch from his vest pocket and handed it to Caine.

Caine emptied the pouch into his gloved hand and counted a dollar and eighty-five cents then put the coins back in the pouch. He removed a glove so he could fish in his pants pockets and pulled out three dollars and a quarter. He combined the money with Max's and started to hand the pouch to Dawson but paused for a moment. "Bull, I want you to put this money with what you got and go into town. Buy some beans, bacon, and coffee. Maybe some canned stew or something like that. This is a good road and the old Butterfield Road to Fort Worth is also. If we move as fast as we did to Checotah, we can be home in three days, so that's how much food we need." Caine passed the pouch to Dawson. "We will make camp here and wait on you, so don't dally."

Dawson took the pouch and stuffed it inside his shirt. "Sure thing, I ought to be back in an hour or so."

"And Bull," said Caine. "Don't be wandering into a saloon and squandering our money."

Dawson just nodded and rode toward town, waving his hand over his head as he did.

"You think we beat 'em?" Reeves asked Putney as they were recovering their animals from the stock manager at the Denison station.

"We had to," replied Putney. "But they made good time getting up to Honey Springs. A lot better than I would have thought, maybe they won't push so hard on the way back."

"Do you want to take them here or on the other side of the Red?"

"I think you have more leeway in the Nations than either of us would have here in Texas."

"Most likely you're right. Don't nobody much question me in the Nations. What are the chances of gunplay?"

"I can't say," Putney climbed into the saddle. "I don't know those other two, but I can tell you about Bull Dawson. If he could bushwhack you, he wouldn't hesitate, but in a straight-up fight, he will tuck tail and run, if he can."

"Typical," Reeves pulled his horse up next to Putney's. "Outlaws got no gumption unless they got the upper hand. Come on, the ferry's this way."

Leading the way to Colbert's Ferry, Reeves said, "Old man Colbert began operating this ferry before the war. Made himself a pile of money over the years. At one time he built a bridge over the Red River, but that got washed away in a flood back in seventy-two sos he started up the ferry again. He's hauled everything from Butterfield stages to cattle. Used to ferry Rebs back during the war. It's Chickasaw land on the other side and he worked a deal with the Chickasaw sos even if you ford the river in this area, you still have to pay a toll. I see no reason to get wet and still have to pay."

After crossing the Red River, the two deputies rode north through Colbert's Station on the Texas Road. Outside of town, Putney asked Reeves if he knew the country. "Well, enough,"

Reeves told him. "I've tracked down a bootlegger or two from Texas a couple of times. Bringing rot gut up to sell to the Indians."

"Where do you think will be the best place to intercept them," asked Putney.

"North of Caddo a piece, at Clear Boggy Creek. This time of year it's usually up a little. There's a good ford there, but wagons and riders have to take it slow or get bogged down. That will be as good a place as any."

Putney relaxed in his saddle as he took a Kinney from its case and lit it. "Sounds like a plan."

Chapter Eighteen

Deidre O'Neill was sitting in her office going over the business finances and they weren't good. Mary had done the best job she could but since the editorial in the Gazette customers had been staying away in droves. The clock on the wall struck once and she looked up to see the time was two-thirty, then she sighed. Putney had been gone four days and she missed him. Over the years she and Putney had been apart for months at a time, but she had never missed him like the last few days. She supposed it was the circumstances that created her anxiety. She knew he lived a dangerous life and had always been able to accept it because he had always seemed invulnerable. Of course, she knew he wasn't. Over time she had memorized the many scars on his body. But he had gotten them before she knew him, and when asked about them he would play them off as if they were some mere scratches, he received from a long time ago. Now, she had seen his mortality. She knew he wasn't invincible. She longed for him to be back in her arms, under her protective shield.

A knock on the door shook her from her thoughts. Mary opened the door and announced that Deputy Forsythe was there. "Show our little tattletale in so he can see I haven't fled the country."

Hubert Forsythe entered the office, hat in hand. He wouldn't have admitted it to anyone, but he was a little afraid of Deidre. Not that she would do him bodily harm, but that she could give him a tongue lashing that would cut as deep as any knife. "Miss O'Neill," he said quietly. "I hope you are having a good day."

Deidre almost felt sorry for the young deputy sheriff. After all, he was just doing his job, and he was doing his utmost to be pleasant, even helpful. But she couldn't help herself and she wasn't letting him off the hook. "You've seen me," she said in her most derisive tone. "Now run along and tell your masters that I haven't left for Galveston.....yet."

"Thank you, ma'am, but I need to tell you something."

"Well out with it then, boyo. You don't think I have all day to chat over tea with you, do you?

123

"No ma'am. I just wanted to tell you that the grand jury has made its decision."

Deidre knew this information would be coming, but now that Forsythe was about to deliver it her heart began pounding in her breast. She found herself helpless to utter any response.

Forsythe seemed to sense her trepidation. "Well, Miss O'Neill, they came back with a true bill for manslaughter."

Deidre propped her elbows on the desk and let her head drop into her hands. She wasn't surprised but she had hoped for a verdict of no bill.

"I know that wasn't what you wanted to hear, Miss Deidre, but you ought to look on the bright side," Forsythe tried to give an optimistic smile.

This last statement caused Deidre to snap her head up. "Oh, and just what may that be, that I'll spend the next ten years or more in a state penitentiary in some God forsaken out of the way place in the deepest bowels of Texas. Is that the bright side?" Her voice was raised enough that Mary rushed into the room to see what was wrong. "Well, is it Mr. Forsythe? Tell me how pleasant you think that will be."

"I'm sorry, miss, I just meant that at least they didn't charge you with first-degree murder. That's a hanging offense."

"Well, thank the saints for that information, Mr. Forsythe. Now if that is all you may leave. And don't let me catch you gawping around Betsy."

"I'm afraid there's more."

"Well for the sake of Saint Jude tell me."

"The judge has ordered that the trial will start on Monday."

"Is there more?"

"No ma'am."

"Then you may leave. And mind what I said about Betsy. You think I haven't seen you, but I have."

"Yes, ma'am," Forsythe hesitated before saying, "I have to leave this summons with you." He stepped to the desk and laid the paper warily on the desk, then quietly left the room, nodding to Mary as he left.

"Well, I guess that's for it," said Mary as she closed the door behind the deputy.

"I guess it is," said Deidre. "Go tell Imogene. She'll need to know, and we will need to be making plans." Mary nodded and left to get Deidre's attorney.

In fifteen minutes the three women were sitting around Deidre's desk. "What do we do now, Imogene?" The flame was gone from the usually fiery Irish woman.

"I think the first thing is that I should go to McLaury's office and ask for discovery and a witness list. Ordinarily, he would have more time, but since the judge seems to be putting a rush to the trial, we need to get that as soon as possible," said Imogene.

"When do you think Nahum will be back?" Mary asked of either of the other women.

"I've no idea," said Deidre. "We don't even know if he's located Doby yet and we don't know what sort of trouble he may have run into. I'm worried about him. I wish he would have taken one of the twins or Henry with him."

"You know he wanted to make sure we had them around for protection," said Mary.

"We could have spared one of them," returned Deidre.

"That's true but you know how hard-headed he can be," Imogene was blunt in her assessment.

"Don't I ever," said Deidre. Just then the clock struck three. "Mary, would you be a dear and turn the chimes off that damn thing. It sounds like a death peel.

It had taken Imogene some time to collect some papers and law books but by four that afternoon, Imogene was in William McLaury's office, Henry Morgan at her side. McLaury came out of his office into the general waiting room and invited Imogene and Henry into his office. McLaury wasn't the elected district attorney, but he was the chief assistant prosecutor, and his office reflected his status. It was a compact room with a nice desk, but not a grand one. A padded banker's chair sat behind the desk and there were three curved wooden back chairs in front of it. The only other furniture was a bookshelf crammed with law books and a filing cabinet. Stacks of books topped the shelves and the cabinet while more were piled on the floor. McLaury made a show of straightening papers on his desk before sitting down and asking,

"What may I do for you, Miss Foster?" as if he were ignorant of the recent developments.

"It's about the indictment," Imogene said in an icy voice.

"Oh, I think it's a little late to be offering a plea deal, Miss Foster," McLaury smirked and chuckled at what he perceived to be a sense of humor.

Miffed, Imogene returned with, "I couldn't agree more, Mr. McLaury so I thought I would come here to accept your offer to drop all charges."

Taken aback by the young attorney's audacity, McLaury sputtered a little before saying, "That is completely out of the question. Miss O'Neill should count herself lucky the grand jury only returned with manslaughter."

"Whatever," Imogene dismissed his comment which raised his ire another degree.

McLaury was through playing nice, "What is it you want, Miss Foster? I'm a busy man and, as you know doubt know, I have a trial to prepare for."

Imogene was thinking how easy it was to goad McLaury to anger and how she would use it against him in the courtroom. "Really? Why you're so smart I figured you had your case all tied up with a blue ribbon. I'm surprised that you any planning to do at all."

"Don't you worry, Missy. This case will be a walk in the park."

"I couldn't agree more," Imogene was enjoying needling the arrogant prosecutor. She then put on her best Southern Belle accent. "But I thought you might give little ole me a chance. Yore so smart an all," then back to her regular tone. "I want your witness list and discovery of evidence you mean to present."

"And if I say I'm not prepared to provide that yet?"

Imogene stood and signaled Morgan to do the same. "Henry," she said. "Do you know the way to Judge Beckham's office? We will go there, and I will apply for a continuance. I think Mr. McLaury's reluctance gives me plenty of justification. My bet is the judge will grant my request, or he will order Mr. McLaury to do exactly what he knows he should have done in the first place. Either way, it will be a win for us."

Morgan took his hat out of his lap and standing said, "Have a good day, Mr. McLaury."

"Now, wait a damn minute," McLaury was angry because he knew he had been out maneuvered.

"Language, Mr. McLaury," said Morgan, reminding him a lady was present.

"Yeah, sorry," grumbled the prosecutor. "Just a minute." He stepped over to the filing cabinet, thumbed through some files, and pulled out some papers. "Here," he thrust the papers towards Imogene.

Morgan reached and took the papers. "Thanks, Mr. McLaury," chuckling in the same manner as McLaury had, before.

Deidre had assembled her war council in her office. Mary and the Shakespeare twins were present as well as Imogene and Morgan. This time though it was Imogene sitting behind the desk. On Deidre's request, Brutus had moved the coffee table in front of the desk and Elizabeth had brought in cold cuts, bread, condiments, and two bottles of bourbon. Everyone, except Imogene, sat in a semi-circle around the low table, with Deidre at the apex. Elizabeth had been allowed to stay, but only if she sat in a corner and kept quiet.

Henry Morgan poured three fingers of whiskey and laughing said. "Whew boy, I wished you could have seen McLaury," He laughed again. "Miss Imogene had him trussed up like a yearling at branding time." He took a drink of the bourbon and continued, "If he had a tail, she would have tied knots in it. Then when she said we were going to see the judge I thought he was going to shit his pants. Excuse me, ladies, Betsy."

Imogene blushed, "I don't know it was all that, Henry, but I must admit it was easy to get his goat."

"Don't sell yourself short Miss Imogene," said Henry. "His feathers were ruffled and of that, there is no doubt."

Everyone in the room was laughing at Morgan's telling of the encounter with McLaury. As the gaiety slowed Deidre asked everyone to calm down so they could get down to business. "So, Imogene, what have we got?"

Imogene shuffled some papers. "There are no surprises here," she said. "The only direct evidence he has is the coroner's report, so of course the coroner is on the witness list. Other than that, there is Marshal Rea and one deputy city marshal who conducted the investigation. Then there are four eyewitnesses, I have their statements here. Three of the statements are suspect because they are almost identical. All three say they didn't see who shot Nahum, but they insist that they all saw Deidre pick up a gun and start shooting at Ned Blakely. I think I can shake their testimony, but they may stick to their stories. It depends on how well they have been coached."

"What about the fourth?" asked Mary.

"He may be a problem," Imogene furrowed her brow. "He doesn't have anything to add to the other three. Except, he says that he saw Deidre shooting, and from where he was it looked like she might have hit Blakely."

"How could he be a problem?" Deidre wanted to know.

"Not because of what he has to say, but who he is," Imogene admitted.

"Well, who is he and what can he say that is more important than the others?" The question came from Caesar.

"He's a prominent man, therefore his testimony may hold more weight," the worry in Imogene's voice was evident.

"You mean Quanah Parker," Deidre's remark was more a statement than a question.

"That's exactly who I mean."

"If he saw no more than what you say, how can he hurt us?" again it was Deidre.

"There is no reason for McLaury to bring him down here from the reservation, except one."

"Jesus, Mary and Joseph, Imogene," exclaimed Deidre. "What would that one reason be."

Imogene cleared her throat. "To get at me," she said. "It's obvious to me that McLaury has done his homework. I do not doubt that he's checked into my background and knows I was taken captive by the Comanche and that Parker was one of them. He thinks that confronting Quanah Parker will scare me and that I will fumble my cross-examination. He thinks if that happens, it will strengthen his other witnesses."

Still sitting in the corner, Elizabeth jumped up from her chair, breaking her promise to remain quiet. "Well, that just won't work," she was adamant. "That can't scare you."

Imogene's head dropped a fraction and she cast her eyes down. "No. If that is his gambit, he will be right. Facing that man scares the hell out of me. Just the thought has me trembling."

Elizabeth ran to Imogene's side and hugged her. "I have faith in you, Miss Imogene, I know you can do it."

Any gaiety was gone like a wind it had blown out of the room. Nobody spoke for several moments until Deidre finally said, "Well, you will have to cross that bridge when you come to it, and we will all cross it with you dear."

Imogene looked at the woman she sometimes viewed as her rival. Her eyes were red from the tears that had welled up in her eyes. "Thank you, Deidre. I will depend on your confidence."

Silence again fell on the room, for a moment, then Mary asked, "Is there anything else?"

Wiping the tears from her eyes and sitting up straight as a rod Imogene said, "There is one last thing. He has Nahum on his witness list."

"What," The room shook from Deidre's outburst. "How can he do that? Why would he do that?"

Imogene let the lawyer in her take over. "He can do it, because Nahum is a witness, although from what Nahum has told me, he doesn't remember anything past getting shot. So, the how isn't important. It's the why that matters."

"Please explain to us mere laymen," said Deidre.

"It's very simple. He knows that once Nahum is served with a summons to testify, he can't discuss the case with me. The only thing I can talk to Nahum about is what he witnessed, which we all know is nothing. But Nahum will be out of the picture with helping me, or more importantly, you," Imogene looked directly at Deidre. "He will have to move out of the hotel. None of you can talk to him, otherwise, it will prejudice our case."

"What about before he is served with a summons?" asked Morgan.

"As long as he hasn't received the summons, it's all fair game. After that, and I mean this, nobody in this room can have anything to do with him. It will ruin everything we have worked for."

"Well," said Morgan, "That leaves us no choice but to get to Putney before he can be served. We can explain what's happening. Maybe he can think of something to work around this problem."

"We have no idea where he is, how can we get to him?" asked Deidre.

Morgan shook his head. "I don't know but we have to figure it out."

Everybody, except Elizabeth, poured a stiff drink, even Mary who usually did not touch whiskey. The room was so quiet that one could almost hear the thoughts whirring in each person's brain. After a few minutes, Elizabeth finally asked, "Where did Mr. Putney go, anyway?"

Mary had advised everyone, before, not to tell Elizabeth, for fear that she might blurt it out to Hubert Forsythe. Mary looked at Deidre and Deidre looked at everyone else in the room. "Well, we may as well tell her," Deidre said.

After Deidre had explained Putney's plan to Elizabeth and why they hadn't told her, Elizabeth asked, "How was he going to get to this town called Checotah?"

"He took the train," explained Deidre.

"Well, how does the train go there?"

Deidre was getting exasperated, "It goes from here to Denton then up to Denison, and on into the Indian Nations."

"Isn't Denison on the Red River?" Elizabeth asked. Deidre said it was and figured that was the end of the conversation. Deidre went back to thinking how they could get word to Putney. If anybody had been looking at the teenager, they would have seen she was thinking hard as well. Finally, Elizabeth said, "Why it's simple."

Every head turned to her, and everyone smiled their amusement at the girl for thinking the problem was just that easy.

Almost mockingly, Deidre said, "Well, why don't you tell us, dear? How simple is it?"

"Well," Elizabeth's confidence was sinking a little, but she kept on. "When me and my family came down from Saint Jo, we traveled on what everyone called the Texas Road, in the Indian Nations."

"And," Morgan urged her on.

"I remember there's a ferry that crosses the river at Denison."

"Go on, Betsy," said Mary.

"What if Henry took the train up to Denison and then waited at the ferry? If Mr. Putney comes across the river on the ferry, Henry will see him and tell him what's all has happened."

"But what if he comes back on the train?" This came from Imogene.

"Easy. I've been at the train station when a train comes through and sometimes there is a telegram for somebody on the train. The telegram boy walks up and down the platform calling out the name of the person the telegram is for. We send a telegram to every station between here and Checotah, telling Mr. Putney to go see Henry at the ferry in Denison. And since you're all worried, I might spill the beans to Hubert, I could go with Henry up to Denton. I could wait there and look for Mr. Putney on every train that comes through. If I find him, I could give him the message."

Every person in the room looked at Elizabeth in awe.

"Out of the mouths of babes," said Deidre.

Chapter Nineteen

Henry Morgan and Elizabeth Sikes arrived in Denton by eight-fifteen the following morning. There had been quite a heated discussion over Elizabeth staying in Denton on her own. It was Mary Johnson's argument that finally won out. "She's nearly seventeen," Mary had argued. "Lots of girls are married and expecting their first child by her age. Besides, Deidre, you can't go anywhere. Imogene must stay to work on your defense. I must stay and run the business. Henry's going to Denison which means we are down a bodyguard, and I don't think Nahum would want us to bring anybody else in. Betsy's all we have."

After everything was settled, Mary took Elizabeth to her room. "You need some proper clothes to travel in and we are about the same size," Reaching into her wardrobe, Mary pulled out a respectable tweed suit and a beige blouse. It had a high collar with ruffles at the top and on the sleeves. "Here try this on." There was no screen or other divider in the room, and Elizabeth was a little embarrassed. Seeing her reluctance, Mary told her, "Don't worry dear, we are both women here. If this is the worst humiliation, you have to endure in your life you can count yourself fortunate. Mary turned her back to give Elizabeth some privacy and thought back to her first encounter with Charlie Johnson, who had saved her from Comanche warriors. *Yes dear*, she thought, *it could be much, much worse.*

Elizabeth told Mary to turn around. The outfit fit perfectly. Mary opened a drawer in her chifforobe, retrieved a bag that matched the suit, and handed that to Elizabeth. Then she pulled out a wooden box. "If you reach between these pleats, "Mary directed the teenager's hands, "You will find pockets." Then opening the box, she showed Elizabeth a pair of matching parlor pistols. Mary showed Elizabeth how to operate the small caliber, single-shot pistols, then loaded each with a short twenty-two bullet. "Keep one in each pocket. If you have trouble with anyone, use one. That is usually good enough to stop the trouble. If it doesn't stop the trouble use the other, that will surely stop it." To finish off the look, Mary placed a brown, velvet hat on Elizabeth's mouse-colored hair. "There you look perfect." Mary directed her to a full-length mirror that hung behind the door.

Looking in the mirror Elizabeth gasped, "Gosh, I look like a fully grown woman. I wish Hubert could see me in this. Thank you, Miss Mary."

"You're welcome, dear," said Mary. "Now change back, go home, and tell your parents we have an important job for you and that you won't be home for a few days. Don't tell them what, just say it's really important and you will be getting extra pay. Come right back. You can sleep in here tonight. I expect I will be up half the night keeping Deidre calmed down. Her Irish doesn't do well with things she can't control."

Morgan had gotten Elizabeth off the train and gave a few words of fatherly advice before he had to reboard for the trip to Denison. Deidre had given Elizabeth plenty of money for meals and to get a room at a boarding house for the times the trains weren't arriving. Before she and Morgan had left for the Fort Worth Depot, Deidre had pulled her aside. "Here," Deidre said, "Put this in your handbag, in case you have trouble." It was a double-barreled, thirty-six caliber derringer.

Morgan hopped on the train as it started chugging out of Denton. He waved at Elizabeth and watched as she grew smaller and smaller. *I hope she will be all right* he thought and walked to sit in the second-class car." By eleven that morning he was in Denison. He went to the stock car and gave the manager a receipt for his horse, cinched up the saddle, and rode off to find the ferry.

Martin Caine was still angry with Dawson who had returned to the campsite with several tins of food. "I got these for a nickel a can," Dawson had gloated. "I got 'em cheap because they didn't have labels." With the money he had saved on the tins, Dawson had bought a bottle of whiskey. When they started opening the cans they found nothing but stewed tomatoes and spinach. Caine couldn't think of two foods he disliked more, but, like the others, he was hungry. He hoped the next cans they opened would bear something more edible. At least Dawson had had sense enough to buy a bag of coffee. That night they passed the bottle around. Everyone but Doby was offered a drink. Doby was happy to have the coffee, though he wished there had been some sugar. Most of the liquor was downed by Dawson and Poe. Both being big men, the alcohol had a lesser effect than it would on Caine, who only had a couple of swigs so he could wash out the taste of Tomato and spinach and maybe wash down the ball of anger he felt toward Dawson.

Caine had hoped to make it to the Red River before nightfall, but the food and the whiskey had a bad effect on Poe who had to stop several times to run to the bushes. This was the main reason Caine was still fuming over the food. At the rate they were going, they would be lucky to make Fort Worth in a week. "You know," Caine told the others, "If we push a little harder we just might make it to Caddo, at least. The road is sloping downhill, so there may be a creek or something where we could water the horses. But we can't be dallying."

⊠

Bass Reeves had climbed a tree, on the south side of Clear Boggy Creek, to get a better vantage point for watching the Texas Road. It was late afternoon when, using his twin telescope binoculars, he saw four men riding south and one of them was on a mule. He whistled a signal to Putney, who was in the bushes on the other side of the road. Reeves shinnied down the tree and set up on the south bank of the creek. Normally, during the dry season, the south bank was hard-packed dry clay, a foot or so thick. But with the creek up that clay became a sticky glob that could weigh a horse's hooves down. Reeves waited until the four men were well bogged in the sticky clay when he stepped onto a dry portion of the bank, with a shotgun, and called out, "Halt! U. S. Marshals!"

Bull Dawson didn't see the badge and thought it was a joke and a bad attempt at a robbery. Dawson was reaching for his pistol when Putney stepped out of the brush and in a loud voice said, "I wouldn't do that Bull. You've never been very good at a straight-up shoot-out."

Dawson looked to his left and saw his tall red-haired nemesis. Staring down the barrel of a Winchester, Bull thought better of his actions and his hands up, away from his sidearm. The other three men followed suit. "Good thinkin, boys," said Reeves. "Now, you boys slip down from them saddles, real smooth and nobody will get killed today."

When the men were standing up to their shins in the creek, Reeves signaled with his shotgun for them to cross over out of the creek. "Keep them hands up where I can see 'em boys," ordered Reeves, "You don't want to cause this scatter gun to go off, now do you?" As Reeves kept the four at gunpoint, Putney stepped forward and searched them for guns. Caine, Poe and Dawson all had forty-fours and Dawson had an extra thirty-eight stuck in his cartridge belt.

Having retrieved all four guns, Putney stepped over to where Reeves was standing and said, "That's all the pistols. Have them tie up to that picket line we set up and I'll get their saddle guns." Once they had tied their animals, Putney searched for rifles and found two, which he confiscated. "I think we are pretty safe from one of them doing something stupid now."

"I think you may be right Nahum," laughed Reeves, then pointing to all but Clint Doby. "Why don't you boys go across the road and have a seat, while Marshal Putney here has a talk with this boy?" The three men did as they were told and Reeves crossed the road with them.

"Marshal Putney," said Doby. "I thought you were dead."

"Don't say anymore in front of these men," Putney told him. "Your mother came to see me when she read in the newspaper that I was alive. She's told me everything she knows. You and I are going to have plenty of time to talk in a bit, but I don't want anybody else to hear us." Doby nodded that he understood. Then to Reeves, he said, "I think we're ready. I'll get our animals and we can be on our way."

Putney walked down the road and into the brush where the animals were hidden and came back. "You ready, Bass?"

I'm ready, Nahum," Reeves told him. "You boys have been detained for interfering with a federal witness," he said to the three men on the ground. "But since I ain't got no warrant on any of you, I'm going to let you go." There was a sigh of relief from each of the three, but then he continued. "But I don't want to be dogged by any of you, so I'm just going to take your mounts on down to Caddo and I'll leave them at the livery for you. I'll tell the liveryman you'll be around after a few hours. They'll be paid up

135

for you, so there won't be any problem. Oh, and I'll leave your guns with him, too." Reeves untied the picket rope from the trees and tied one end with the leather strings attached to his saddle. "You boys need to go on back to Texas. Iffin I see you here in the nations again, I might not be so nice."

He took to his saddle and Putney told Doby to do the same. "Before we go, y'all shuck your boots. And toss them over to this side of the road." He said to the three men. Grumbling, they did as they were told. Putney picked up the boots and tied each pair to the saddle thongs. "You can pick these up in Caddo, too. And Bull, maybe you should try some other place besides Fort Worth to live." Putney climbed into his saddle and he, Reeves, and Doby rode south.

Putney checked at the rail Depot in Caddo, with Doby, while Reeves took the outlaws' horses to the livery. He found that there was one more local train due through at seven. Putney checked his watch. It was six thirty. He asked if there was time to signal the train to stop and the station man told him there was. He bought two second class tickets to Fort Worth. Both he and Doby had been on the trail several days and he didn't want their stink assaulting the noses of the first class passengers. He also paid for his horse and the two mules to be boarded on the stock car. They sat on a bench outside the small depot house and waited on Reeves who came along in five minutes. Putney told Reeves that the train would be along shortly.

"Well, Nahum Putney," said Reeves. "It's real good working with you." He held out his hand and the two deputy marshals shook."

"And with you, Bass, especially since we didn't kill each other." Both men laughed at the jest. "If you're ever down in Fort Worth, look me up. I'll buy you a steak at O'Neill's."

"I'll do that for sure, Nahum," said Bass. "Good Luck with this boy here." Reeves got on his horse and headed toward the center of town.

By a quarter after seven, the train was headed toward Denison, Texas with Nahum Putney, and Clint Doby on board. Putney directed Doby to two facing seats away from the other people in the car. "We will have about an hour stopover in Denison," Putney told Doby. "I'll buy us a hot meal there, it looks like you could use one."

"I could, Marshal." Doby was showing signs of embarrassment.

Putney lit a cigarette and offered one to Doby who politely refused. "Okay Clint, I think it's time for you to tell me how you got mixed up in this business. I want you to tell me in your words. If I have a question, I'll ask."

"Well, it started the day Jim, Jim Courtwright that is, got a message you wanted to see him. Me and Ned Blakely was working for Jim at the Emerald Saloon. There were quite a few folk in there that day and they needed the extra help. Jim was sitting at a table with Jim McIntire and Soapy Smith and another guy I had seen around but didn't know. Ned had taken a bottle to the table when this other man came in and said Luke Short had sent him with a message that you wanted to see him. Ned and me had talked about you before and we both knew each other had grudges against you." Hurriedly Doby added, "But I don't know more, Marshal. Not after Mama explained everything to me."

"That's all right, son," said Putney. "Go ahead."

It didn't seem to set too well with Soapy Smith either because he left pretty quick after the man had told Jim. Courtwright and McIntire also got up and went tot the back room, leaving this other guy sitting at the table by himself with a nearly fresh bottle. That guy had a few drinks, corked the bottle, and left. Took the bottle with him too. About half an hour later, Ned left but wasn't gone long. Neither was the other guy, but he went straight to the back room and knocked. He must have been okay with the bosses, because they let him in.

Putney stopped him. "And you didn't know who the man was?"

"Not then. I learned later that night he was a guy everyone called Captain, but in a joking way, kind of. Like they was making fun of him. They said he was a shill for Soapy Smith. So, there were three night bartenders came in and the drinks girls, so Ned and I got some time off. We went down to Frank's Saloon for some drinks. Jim Doesn't like us drinking at the Emerald. While we was drinking Ned asks me how I would like a chance at getting even with you having killed my father. Like I said, I was young when that happened, and I never knew my Pa had tried to backshoot you."

"I told you, Clint, don't worry about it. We've all made mistakes in our lives. Believe me, I know. Go on."

"I guess I had a few to drink and said I sure would. And Ned says it would even be better if we got paid to do it. And I said it sure would. That was all he said that night. We finished our drinks and went to the Nance Hotel to check out the ladies of the line." Doby stopped to think for a minute. "Don't tell Mama about that, would you?"

"Don't worry, Clint, your secret's safe with me."

"Well, the next day, Ned comes to me and says that there was this guy willing to pay us fifty dollars each if we was to kill you. He asked if I was up for it. At the time I told him hell, yeah. But I thought we were going to challenge you in the street, like the ones I read about Billy the Kid, Jesse James, and the Earps. I didn't know he was planning to bushwhack you. So anyway, that day, we went to this alley where he said we was going to wait on you. We waited about an hour when we saw you coming down the street. He told me to get behind some boxes and that's when I knew what he had planned, but it was too late. And I was afraid if I backed out, he'd kill me. Ned was real mean when he wanted to be. When you was even with him he came from behind those boxes and shot you. Then that lady she picked up your gun. I thought she was going to shoot Ned, but he was already face down and she began shooting at me. Well, I just started shooting wildly and that was when I saw you fall. Before I could run a bullet hit me right here." Doby pointed to the fleshy part of his chest. "I was scared to death. I ran quick as I could to where I keep my horse and I skinned out of there like a bat out of hell. That's about all Marshal, I swear."

"Is this the gun you had that day?" Putney wanted to know.

"Yes, sir, that's the only gun I ever had."

Putney had already smoked two cigarettes while Doby was telling his story. He propped his feet on the bench beside Doby and lit another one. "I believe you. I need to think a bit now. We will be in Denison soon.

As Putney had predicted they had an hour before they caught the train from Denison to Denton. After making sure the animals would get transferred, the two walked to a close by café and ate. Putney had fried pork chops with mashed potatoes and greens while Doby had a steak, fried potatoes, and black-eyed peas. Putney checked his watch and saw they had a little time. He asked a waitress if they had peach cobbler. She said they did, so he ordered two. They had just enough time to make it back to the station and board the train. The clacking of the wheels on the rail soon had Doby to sleep. Putney kicked back again and smoked and thought.

The jerking of the train jolted Doby awake and he was looking out the window at the depot platform. He saw a young woman walking up and down the platform. She seemed to be yelling something, but over the noise of the train, he couldn't make it out. She was a pretty girl and Doby found himself wondering about her. As he was staring at the young woman, he finally made out what she had been yelling. He nudged Putney. "That girl yonder is calling your name."

Putney looked out the window and saw Elizabeth. He grabbed Doby by the arm and said, "Come on."

They rushed out to see an exasperated Elizabeth Sikes, when she saw Putney, she yelled out, "Thank God." And ran to him and gave him a big hug.

"What in the world are you doing here?" Putney asked her.

I've been here since yesterday, looking for you. It's important," she said. Then seeing the young man with him she said, "Who's this?"

"In a minute, tell me what you are doing here."

"We had to get a message to you before you got back to Fort Worth," Elizabeth said. "it's important and I don't think Miss Imogene wants you to come back just yet."

Just then a conductor walked passed and said to Putney, "Train's moving out in twenty minutes, mister."

"Is there another train to Fort Worth tonight?" Putney asked.

"Nope, not until eight-thirty tomorrow morning," said the conductor and he walked on.

"Elizabeth, this is Clint Doby," Putney told her in a hurry. "Y'all go sit on that bench until I get back."

Putney rushed back to the stock car to get the horse and mules off before the train could take off with them. When he had accomplished that task, he tied them up at a hitching rail and went to where Elizabeth and Clint were sitting. Neither was talking to the other. "Where have you been staying?" Putney asked Elizabeth. She told him the name of the boarding house where she had been checked in. "I hope they have two more rooms. Come on, show me. Then you're going to tell me what's going on."

Chapter Twenty

Putney was glad that Mrs. Avery, the woman who owned the boarding house, was an early riser. She had breakfast on the table by six-thirty. "Lots of folks want to catch that eight-thirty to Fort Worth, or the nine o'clock going to Dallas. This gives them plenty of time to eat a decent meal before they do." Putney had been smoking on the front porch when she had come and told him the food was ready. He hurried up the stairs and knocked on Elizabeth's and Doby's doors, telling them to shake a leg.

Putney was already seated with a plate of eggs, bacon, and potatoes in front of him when the other two made it to the table. He had placed three sealed envelopes next to his plate and when Elizabeth had filled her plate he passed them over to her. One was addressed to Imogene, one to just 'The Twins', and the other to Luke Short. "I did a lot of thinking last night," he said. "When I finish, I'm going to go send a telegram to Henry at the Colbert's Ferry on the Texas side, telling him you found me, and he is to get on back to Fort Worth as quick as he can. Clint, I want you to get Elizabeth over to the depot. If I don't make it over there in time, make sure she gets on the Fort Worth train." Doby took a mouthful of potatoes and nodded his head.

"I can take care of myself," Elizabeth was put out thinking Putney had placed her in the charge of this ne'er do well. "I've done all right by myself, so far."

To calm her, Putney said, "I know that, but Clint may need some help finding the place." Elizabeth smiled at the little joke.

"Anyway," said Putney. "When you get to Fort Worth, it is very important Imogene reads the letter. It tells her what I am going to do and then there is a very important instruction that only she is to read. But you need to tell her I said it is of the utmost importance that she follows it to the letter."

"I'll make sure she knows what you said and how important it is."

"Give the others to one of the twins," Putney told her. "Whoever takes the one for Luke Short is not to read it, just to make sure it gets to Short." Putney finished the last bite on his plate. "Short will know what to do, one way or the other." Putney fished in his vest pocket and handed a key to Elizabeth. "Once he's read it, if Short is agreeable he will need this key. The third letter tells Brutus and Caesar what I need for them to do."

Putney rose from the table, thanked Mrs. Avery, and paid her a little extra for the rooms and the kind service. "I'm going now to get our animals and send the telegram to Henry. You two don't dawdle." Before he left the dining room he stopped, bent over Elizabeth, and kissed her on top of her head. "Thank you, Elizabeth. It was a genius plan." Doby looked and saw Elizabeth blush at the compliment and thought how pretty she was with the red on her cheeks.

Putney had made it back to the station in time to get the animals on the stock car for Dallas and to see Elizabeth off. He and Doby caught the nine o'clock to Dallas, but this time in first class since they had an opportunity to clean up at Mrs. Avery's. Putney took a cigarette from its case and lit it thinking he would need to find a tobacco shop in Dallas. The train was fifteen minutes out from Denton before Putney spoke. "I sent a telegram to Marshal Cabell in Dallas. He should meet us at the station there. I didn't want Elizabeth to know, because it's important that things be kept as quiet as possible. You understand?"

"Yes, sir, I do,"

"I have some instructions for you, also. We will be in Fort Worth tonight. If we're lucky Luke Short will meet us at the station. We're going to take you to my office. Once you are there you cannot leave, for any reason. If Short doesn't meet us, I will have to come up with another plan, but I think he will."

"I'll do whatever you say, Marshal," Doby agreed.

"Good, because your life may well depend on it."

Doby shuddered at that remark.

Putney signed for Doby to lean in closer and spoke softly as a father might to his son. "Clint, I'm doing what I can to keep you out of jail. I want you to understand that."

"Yes, sir."

"You are going to have to testify in Deidre O'Neill's case. Once you are on the stand her lawyer, Imogene Foster, is going to ask you a few questions, just to make you comfortable. But you are going to have to listen very carefully to everything she asks. When she's ready she will ask you a very important question. I can't tell you what it is."

Doby looked confused. "Why not? I don't understand."

"Because if I told you, you would know what I want you to say, and that could get us both in trouble. I'm walking on the edge, already. You just need to trust me. Anyway, she is going to ask you this question. You need to listen very carefully. Unless he isn't as smart as I think he is, McLaury will object. Then Imogene will ask the question again, but this time a little differently. You are the only person alive who knows the answer. Whether you stay out of jail or not will depend on what that answer is." Putney leaned back in his seat hoping he had gotten through to the young man.

Doby leaned back in his seat, more confused than ever.

"Well, Nahum," Marshal Cabell said as Putney and Doby stepped off the train. "Seems you've been busier than a one-legged man in a butt-kicking contest."

"Yes, sir. A little," Putney responded. "This is Clint Doby." The marshal shook the young man's hand. "Clint is an important witness in the conspiracy to have me assassinated."

"Oh, he is?" Cabell patted Doby on the back. "Then it is indeed very good to meet you, young Doby." Cabell turned to Putney. "I have a carriage to take us to my office."

"I need to get my horse and two mules first," Putney told his boss. "I'll meet you out front."

Putney got the animals from the stock manager and tied them up behind the marshal's carriage. It was a brougham-landau, so Putney told Doby to ride his horse because he needed to speak to the marshal in the carriage. "Marshal," he started. "I'm severely pressed for time. I need to get an order for the exhumation of Ned Blakely's body."

"I trust you, Nahum, but whatever for?"

"I have an informant who told me the original coroner's report said Blakely was shot once by me, with a forty-five. Then he was shot with another bullet, this one a thirty-eight. That was the fatal

143

wound. But the report the sheriff has says both bullets were forty-fives. Doby can testify that he was the one who shot the thirty-eight. I have it here in my satchel. But without evidence to back him up, its just a story."

"Should I ask who this informant is, or do I not want to know?"

"It's going to come out at Deidre's trial, so there is no reason you shouldn't know, but I want to keep it as quiet as possible until then. It is a deputy for Sheriff Maddox."

"All right, I think we can take care of that," said the marshal.

"I need to get my affidavit as soon as I can to Judge McCormick."

"When is the trial?"

"It starts up Monday."

"That won't do. There is no way you can get to Graham, get back, get the body dug up, and get a second report." Putney looked confused. "The only way you could do that is to take a train to Graham. Which there is none."

Putney's head dropped. *Damn it.* He thought, *what am I going to do now?*

"Don't worry though," said Cabell. "We'll get it done. Let's get to my office. You can write up the affidavit. I'll take care of getting the order you need."

"At the office in downtown Dallas, Putney was given a desk where he could write his affidavit and the application for the order. Doby was told to have a seat in the anteroom and given a couple of copies of The Boston Illustrated Police News to read. When Putney had finished, Cabell told a clerk to get Doby some lunch as he and Putney needed to make a visit. As they were walking Cabell told Putney, "When McCormick decided to start holding court in Graham he appointed two Commissioners here in Dallas. They work on a fee basis, but they can authorize arrest warrants and search warrants. I don't see why they can't authorize an order for exhumation."

The two men walked to the office of Judge George Aldredge. "Aldredge is a county judge, but McCormick also appointed him as a federal Commissioner. I'm sure we can get what we need from him." A receptionist greeted Marshal Cabell when he entered. "This is my deputy, Nahum Putney," said Cabell. "We

144

were hoping to see Judge Aldredge for a few minutes." The receptionist said she was certain that the judge would see the two men then turned and went through an office door. She reappeared in a few minutes.

"The judge will see you now," she said.

"Marshal," Judge Aldredge greeted Cabell. "How are you?"

"Fine, Judge, just fine," then Cabell introduced Putney.

"Didn't I read where you were badly wounded in Fort Worth, young man?" inquired the judge.

"I suppose you did," said Putney. "It seems to have been big news."

"It was indeed," said the judge then to Cabell, "I'm guessing this is not a social call."

"No, it isn't judge," said Cabell. "Putney has been investigating a conspiracy in Fort Worth and he has uncovered some irregularities." Cabell went on to explain about the discrepancies with the coroner's report and presented him with Putney's affidavit and application for an exhumation.

Aldredge read the two documents and then said, "I see you haven't named who provided this information, Deputy."

"No, sir, I didn't. It's going to come out sooner or later, but right now I wanted to protect him from reprisals."

"Is this person reliable?"

"Yes, sir," said Putney. "In my experience, he is as reliable as any man who has provided me information over the past fifteen years."

"That's good enough for me," said the judge. "Now raise your hand. Do you swear that the information in the affidavit you have provided is the truth?"

"I do, your honor," swore Putney.

Sitting, the judge signed the application then walked to the door and spoke to the receptionist. "Have Taylor type an order of exhumation, according to this affidavit, and add that the body will be brought to the Dallas County Corner for examination." The judge then asked the two lawmen if they would like a drink while they waited.

After a few minutes and some polite conversation between the judge and Cabell, a man entered the office. "Here's the order, Judge."

"Thank you, Taylor," Judge Aldredge read over the order. "It looks like everything is in order." He handed the document to Putney. Good luck Deputy. I look forward to learning the results."

Putney and Cabell thanked the judge and left the office. "What are your plans now?" Cabell asked Putney.

"I'm going to take Doby on the last train over to Fort Worth. I don't want to get there until after dark. I have someone meeting me there. By the way, I'm going to need to deputize this man so there will be a little expense."

"As long as there are results, Nahum, that's what I'm looking for."

Chapter Twenty-One

Elizabeth hurried from the train station to the hotel. She was anxious to tell everyone that she had seen Putney and that he was all right. Mary saw Elizabeth first and motioned for her to go to Deidre's office. Mary followed her through the door. When Deidre saw the girl, she ran to hug her. "How are you, dear? Did you have any problems? Did you see Nahum? Is he all right?"

"Slow down, Deidre," Mary said. "She hasn't even had time to catch her breath."

"It's fine," said Elizabeth. "I'm fine, I didn't have any problems, and yes I saw Mister Putney and he is doing fine, too."

"Well, where is he, then?" Deidre asked.

"He's gone to Dallas. He said he has a plan and he wanted me to tell you all not to worry."

The word of Elizabeth's return had spread quickly and by the time she finished her last sentence, the Shakespeare twins were in the office asking the same questions. While she was repeating what she had told Deidre, Imogene entered the office, so she started her answer over.

"Well, then, dear," said Deidre come over here and sit. Tell us everything."

She told them about arriving in Denton and getting a room at Mrs. Avery's. She had gotten a train schedule and was at the station every time a southbound came through. She would walk back and forth on the platform calling out Putney's name, but it wasn't until the night before that she had seen him.

"Did he find the man he was looking for?" Imogene asked.

"Yes. He had Clint with him. He was polite and seemed nice."

"Well, if he is the same one that was in the alley, he's not," said Deidre.

There was a knock on the door and Mary answered it. Mrs. Stegall stood in the opening. "I'm sorry to bother you all. I see you must be having a meeting. I just wondered if you had heard from Mr. Putney and if he had been able to reach Clint."

"As a matter of fact, Mrs. Stegall, yes on both questions," Mary told her. "We have just gotten word that Nahum and your

147

son are both well," Mary didn't want to say more than that, just then.

"Thank God for that," Emma Lou said. "Where is he?"

"We don't know just yet. When we know I will be sure to tell you," Mary assured the older woman. "But as you said, we are having a meeting now and I must get back to it."

"Thank you, Mrs. Johnson. You have been so kind," Mary closed the door softly and went back to the group gathered around Elizabeth.

Everyone was looking at Elizabeth who was enjoying the attention. "Well, Mr. Putney and Clint have gone to Dallas. I don't know why, but I'm sure it is important. I wrote some things down. I have them here," Elizabeth produced the envelopes. "Brutus, Caesar," she said. "This one is for you two." She handed over the envelope marked 'The Twins'. "And this is for you, too, only you're not to open it but take it to Mr. Short, along with this." She took the key from her purse. "But you're only to give it to him if he is agreeable." Then she gave an envelope to Imogene. "This is for you, Miss Foster. He said it was very important and that there is something in it only for you and you're not to tell anyone."

"And me?" asked Deidre. "Is there nothing for me?"

"No, Miss Deidre, that's all he gave me."

"Harumph. Big galoot," Deidre said in disappointment.

The Shakespeare's had gone to a corner of the office and read their letter. Imogene sat and opened her envelope. Deidre and Mary stood over her. "Excuse me," she said.

"Come on, Mary," Deidre walked over to the drinks table, even though it was still morning. "Let's have a drink while the others read their important letters."

After reading their letter, Brutus said, "I'll go find Luke Short and give him this, you go take care of the other, Caesar." Caesar nodded his agreement. "We're headed out," he said to the rest. "We shouldn't be long, so y'all don't go nowhere until we get back." Their obligation as bodyguards was still intact.

They got another harumph from Deidre and a weak smile from Mary. Imogene hadn't seemed to hear. The wait finally got the best of Deidre. "Well, Imogene, what does he say?" Imogene waved for her to be quiet. "Harumph," said Deidre as she poured another glass of Bushmills.

148

After a minute, Imogene folded all but the last page of the letter. She put the rest back in the envelope and folded the page and placed it in her lap. "He says he has gone to Dallas to see Marshal Cabell. He said he will be back soon. We will know about it, but he won't be seeing any of us. He said he will be busy, and we will know all about it by noon tomorrow. He said he is with Clint Doby, but that Doby is in danger, so we won't be seeing him until the trial. I am to put him and Doby on our witness list, as well as Hubert Forsythe. It's a good thing he let me know because I have to have that list to McLaury by this afternoon. There was something else, but I have to keep it a secret for now."

"Why does he want to be on your witness list?" asked Mary. "He's already on McLaury's."

"He said he has seen the prosecutor do the same thing in Austin. He said that if he's on McLaury's list, I won't put him on mine, because I can just question him on cross-examination. The trick is McLaury won't call him to the stand and because he's not on my list, I can't. So, any evidence he has won't be entered. This way we block McLaury's play."

"Well, that shifty little bastard," said Deidre. "McLaury, I mean. Anything else?"

"Not much except this," Imogene handed the paper to Deidre. "He said he only had three envelopes in his folder, so he had to put this in mine."

Deidre snatched the folded paper from Imogene as a petulant child might snatch a piece of candy from a teasing adult's hand. She read it quickly and smiled broadly. She folded it back, went to her desk, and slipped it into a drawer.

Brutus had tracked Luke Short down at the Planter's Restaurant. He had to wait at the maître d desk since black people could only enter through the back, unless they were with a white man. A message was sent to Short who came out and greeted the ebony giant. "My lunch just arrived," said Short. "Come on with me." Brutus looked to the maître d. "Don't worry about him. Come on." Brutus went with Short to his table. "You want a beer?" asked Short.

"Sure, but," started Brutus.

"I said don't worry, you're with me," Short called a waiter over and ordered another beer. "Now what can I do for you, er."

"Brutus."

"I just couldn't tell which one you were."

"Yeah, we get that a lot. Anyway, I have this here letter from Marshal Putney," Brutus handed the envelope and Short opened it. After reading it, Short placed it face down on the table. "You have something else for me?"

"Then you're agreeable?"

"Of course. I wouldn't miss being a part of this for love or money." A discontented waiter placed a beer in front of Brutus. "Drink up, Brutus. I think we have a few exciting days ahead of us."

Brutus smiled and chugged his beer.

While Brutus had been searching for Luke Short, Caesar was scouring Hell's Half Acre for Tommie Fogg. He finally found him behind Maddox Flat eating a sandwich. "Hey, Mr. Shakespeare," Fogg hailed Caesar. "I don't know which one you are."

Caesar laughed. "It's me, Caesar."

"Sure, I knowed it all along." Fogg laughed with him. "What can I do for you, boss."

"I got a job for you. You interested?"

"Who do I have to kill?" Fogg was a jovial young man and was always cracking jokes.

"Nobody, today. You know the trial of Miss O'Neill is coming up next week?"

"I read about it in the Gazette. Reckon she'll get off?"

"We're doing everything we can to make sure she does."

"What can I do to help?"

"There's two things. First, I need you to keep track of Jim Courtwright for a few days. Note where he goes and who he sees. Think you can handle that?"

"No trouble at all. I shine his boots all the time. He won't suspect nothin."

"Good," Caesar liked Tommie Fogg, partly because he was witty and partly because he was a bright boy who knew how to keep his mouth shut, especially around white people. "Do you know where the new U. S. Marshal's office is?"

"Yeah, I saw them painting the door the other day, but I ain't seen nobody in there."

150

"That's about to change. I need you to go to the back door twice a day. Knock and say 'It's Tommie Fogg.' Someone will answer and give you instructions. You got it?"

"Sure. Easy as falling off a log."

"I'm going to get serious now Tommie, so pay attention. If anybody sees you or tries to make you get someone to answer the door then you say, 'It's Tommie Fogg the shine boy.' Then duck."

"Why duck?"

"Believe me, if you say what I told you, you don't want to be standing in front of that door when it gets answered."

"Whoo wee. I hope this job pays well."

"Better than you've ever been paid before."

"Then I'm your man."

"There's just one more thing. You may have to take care of a chamber pot every day. You okay with that?"

"If the pay is good, I only have one thing to say. Well, shit." Tommie Fogg laughed at his joke and Caesar laughed with him."

Brutus returned to O'Neill's first and Imogene asked him to escort her over to McLaury's office to take her witness list. McLaury was in the outer office when they arrived. "My, my, Miss Foster, your escort seems to have grown," McLaury grinned. "And darkened, too."

"Have you ever thought about taking your act to vaudeville?" Imogene's snarkiness was not lost on McLaury.

Annoyed, McLaury said, "Come in my office." When he had closed the door he asked, "What can I do for you, Miss Foster?"

"Nothing, actually. I just came to bring you my witness list," she handed a document to McLaury who perused the paper.

"Who's this Clint Doby?" McLaury asked.

"A witness," Imogene clipped her answer.

"And when can I expect to interview him?"

"I couldn't say. I don't know where he is right now."

"When do you think you will know?"

"Couldn't say. But I will let you know just as soon as I do."

McLaury was tiring of the young attorney's arrogance. "I see you have Nahum Putney on here. Why? I already have him on my list."

"Oh, I don't know. Just in case you forget, I guess."

"I don't suppose you know where Putney is either."

"As a matter of fact, I do. He's in Dallas. But I understand he will be in Fort Worth soon."

"How soon?'

Imogene shrugged, "Oh I don't really know, but I understand it won't be a secret. In fact, it will probably be most public."

"What about this Henry Morgan and Gustav Rhine?"

"Gustave is a photographer. I'm sure you can speak with him anytime. Henry Morgan is out of town, but I expect him back tonight. I will make sure he's available to you."

"And how about this last one, Deputy Sheriff Hubert Forsythe?"

"Why, Mr McLaury I would think even you can find one of Sheriff Maddox's deputies."

"Well, sure, but what's he going to testify to?"

"I'm not obligated to tell you. You may interview him yourself. "If there's nothing else, Mr. McLaury, we shall take our leave."

"Wait," said McLaury. "What's your defense going to be?"

"Come now, Mr. McLaury, what fun would there be in telling you now?"

It was nine-thirty that night when the train from Dallas pulled into the Fort Worth Depot. Putney had been very happy that Luke Short had telegraphed him saying he was willing to help, he just hoped Short had been able to make all the arrangements Putney had asked for. Putney and Doby had taken the one-hour ride to Fort Worth in the stock car. The stock manager had said it was highly irregular, but Putney gave him five dollars and saw the irregularity fly away. It wasn't the most comfortable Putney had ever been, but by no means was it the least. Putney had wanted to ride in the stock car because the depot would be well-lit, and he didn't want to expose Doby any more than he had to. The stock car was behind the luggage car and just in front of the caboose so there wouldn't be as much light. When the train stopped Putney told Doby to wait as he looked for Short. Putney was not disappointed. Short was standing there with a short-barreled shotgun, in front of a small wagon with a canvas bonnet of three bows. Short wasn't dressed as his usual dapper self, more like a cowboy in a pair of denim trousers, a cotton work shirt and a

152

canvas jacket, which covered a Colt Peacemaker. Putney walked over to Short. "Good to see you, Short."

"My pleasure, Putney. Let's get your cargo on board and over to your office."

Putney nodded and went to the stock car. First, he took the animals out of the car and then got Doby, using the two mules for cover. When they reached the rear of the wagon, Doby climbed over the tailgate and settled in for the short ride. Putney and Short climbed into the front seat.

"Were you able to get everything?" Putney asked.

"Two bunks and mattresses, extra bedding and towels, extra coffee and sugar. A couple of pots and frying pans, bacon, salt, and so forth. I got some iron fittings to put up two door braces and some tools to install it. I only got one shotgun since I already had one of my own. Did I miss anything?"

"I don't reckon. I think I've arranged for delivery of extra food, as needed. We will know soon after we get to the office. I brought something for you, too," Putney produced a badge similar to his, but smaller and made of tin. He handed the badge to Short who read the words 'Special Deputy U. S. Marshal."

"It's been a while since I wore one of these. Does it mean I have to go straight?"

Putney smiled. "Only until the job is done."

Chapter Twenty-Two

Waiting for Sheriff Walter Maddox, William McLaury paced outside of the sheriff's office, and he was spitting mad. Maddox came through the main entrance and seeing McLaury said, "William, what's so damned important I had to leave my home just as I was about to turn in?"

"We best talk in your private office," said the lawyer.

After closing the office door behind them, Maddox asked, "Well?"

"I just finished speaking with your deputy, Hubert Forsythe."

"And that's what has you so riled up?"

"Damn right, it is," McLaury pulled a leather cigar case from his coat pocket, took out a cigar, bit the end off, with purpose, and spat it on the floor. "He's being called as a witness for the O'Neill woman and do you know what he's going to say?"

Maddox was lighting one of his own cigars and almost burned his fingers. "What? No. What are you talking about?"

Blowing a big cloud of smoke McLaury said, "He told me that the coroner's report, I'm entering in evidence has been falsified. He says when he picked it up from the coroner it said Blakely had been shot with a forty-five and a thirty-eight. Not two forty-fives."

All Maddox could say is, "What?"

"That is what he's going to say," McLaury, who hadn't sat, was puffing at a furious pace.

"I'll fire that boy," said Maddox.

"No, don't do that. Not yet anyway. We don't want to do anything like that before the trial. That wouldn't look good. But you sure as hell can fire him after that."

"Then what are we going to do?"

McLaury paced and smoked. "Let me think." After a bit, he said, "You know what else?" he didn't wait for a reply. "She has a photographer and some other guy going to testify that they dug a thirty-eight bullet out of the wood wall over the tobacco shop." Maddox remained silent while McLaury paced and thought. Finally, he said, "I got it. "I'm not going to call Forsythe. I'll call you."

"What?" Maddox's cigar nearly fell out of his mouth.

"Sure. You're the custodian of record. All you have to testify to is that the report and the two bullets have remained in your custody since Forsythe picked them up."

"But she's still going to call him. And those other two."

"Yeah, yeah," agreed McLaury. "I have an idea how to discredit them. Don't say anything to anyone about this. Certainly not Forsythe." Then changing the subject, "Has Putney been served yet?"

"No," said Maddox. "Nobody has seen him for nearly a week."

"I think he and Foster are cooking up something. If they've been colluding I'll have the judge cook their goose, I'll tell you that."

Luke Short had set the room up perfectly. There was one bunk set against the wall farthest from the door and another on the wall that faced the door. The third was on the wall between the back door and the office door. He had set up the table in the center of the room. Leaning against one wall was an iron bar and two steel brackets with a bag of tools and parts in a canvas bag between them. The shelves were lined with various tin goods, among them five cans of peaches, two dozen eggs, and a bag of coffee. Two pots and two frying pans were hung on the wall, next to the stove. A slab of bacon was hanging from the ceiling. There were small tables near each bed with lanterns and a lantern was suspended above the table. One small table was next to the sink stacked with towels. Short had added some touches of his own. The first was a dressing screen, behind which he put the chamber pot and a carton of medicated papers. Putney raised one eyebrow. "For the sake of decorum, Putney. We don't know how long we will be here, and we can't leave for an outhouse. The other addition was three decks of cards and a box of poker chips, to which Short said, "Have to practice. I don't want to get rusty. Maybe I can teach this boy a few things about gambling."

Putney nodded his approval, "I reckon we ought to get started putting these bars up." Short emptied the contents of the canvas bag on the table. In half an hour they had long lag bolts securing the brackets to the two doors and dropped the iron bars into place.

"That may not keep somebody out forever, but it will slow them down."

"I'll put us on some coffee while you run down your plans," Short told Putney.

"First, as I said in my letter, you and Clint may be holed up in here for several days. It depends on how long the trial lasts. I wouldn't think more than a week though. Clint should always sleep in the bunk farthest from the door. You take the one next to it and I'll take the other when I'm here. First thing in the morning I'm going to the Oakwood Cemetery and serving an order of exhumation for Ned Blakely on the caretaker."

"What?" Short was surprised. "Why would you do that?"

"That's right, you don't know. Hubert Forsythe told me the coroner's report had been altered. It shows Blakely was shot with forty-five caliber bullets. Forsythe says the report he took to the Sheriff's office showed there was one forty-five and one thirty-eight. I'll be taking the body over to Dallas for another examination."

"That ought to throw a kink in McLaury's case," said Short.

"It will," agreed Putney. "But I'm afraid Hubert's career with the sheriff is going to be short."

"Yeah, integrity can have its drawbacks."

"I'm going to try to take care of him as best I can. Maybe put him on as a posseman. Anyway, that will take all day, so on Friday I will need to make myself available to McLaury. Wouldn't want him telling the judge I was dodging him."

Short placed three cups on the table and filled them with coffee.

"What about me, Mr. Putney?" asked Doby, "Am I going to have to talk with Mr. McLaury?"

"Probably at some point, but we will have to do it away from here. I would like to keep this a secret if I can." As Putney finished, there was a knock on the back door. Clint Jumped to his feet. Short calmly picked up the shotgun and Putney, just as calmly pulled a Schofield. Putney waved Doby to get behind the screen and stood to one side of the door. "Who is it?" he asked.

"It's Tommie Fogg," came the answer.

Putney removed the bar, unlocked the door, and allowed Fogg to enter. Short stepped into the alley, looking both ways to ensure

Fogg hadn't been followed. "Lord, Almighty," exclaimed Tommie Fogg. "Caesar should have warned me I'd be facing famous pistoleers."

"Tommie, I'm Nahum Putney and this is Luke Short."

"You didn't have to tell me that, you two are famous." Clint came from behind the curtain. "This ain't Billy Bonny's ghost, is it?" Fogg laughed at his joke.

"No," Putney smiled broadly, then getting serious. "You don't need to know his name. It's safer for everyone."

"If you say so. Caesar told me to come here after eleven, so here I am. What can I do for you?"

"Nothing, tonight. I just wanted to put a face to the name and let Luke know who you are. Did Caesar give you the code?"

"Yes, sir. If I'm alone, I do just like I did tonight. If someone is with me, I say I'm the shine boy."

"That's good, Tommie," Putney said. "I want you to come by as early as possible every morning. Luke will tell you if he needs anything. Then go keep tabs on Courtwright. Later come back here, but only after dark. I probably won't be here so report everything you see to Luke."

"And empty the shit can, I guess."

"If needed, I'm sure Luke will appreciate it."

"Man, the things I'll do for money," said Fogg.

Putney was sitting in a wagon outside the entrance to Oakwood Cemetery. With him were two workers he had picked up near the train yard. They were all smoking cigarettes that Putney had provided. They had been there half an hour when a wagon carrying two black men in coveralls and work shirts and a white man drove up. The white man was short wearing denim trousers, an open collared shirt and vest, a beat-up straw hat, and had a corn cob pipe stuck in his mouth. "What are you doing here at this time of day?" the white man asked Putney.

"Are you the caretaker," Putney asked as his answer.

"That's me. Billy Bob Tyler. What can I do for you?"

Putney introduced himself and his title. "I have a federal court order here for an exhumation."

"A what?"

"An exhumation. You know dig a body up."

"I know what exhumation means. I ain't no dumb cracker. I mean what kind of order you have." Putney explained what a federal court order was. "I don't know about all that. I think I need to see what Sheriff Maddox has to say about this."

"I will make that easy for you. If you don't show me to Ned Blakely's grave and start digging, I will arrest you and you can talk to Sheriff Maddox from inside one of his jail cells."

"You can't do that," complained the caretaker.

"Watch me," Putney told him.

Tyler gave it some thought then said, "Well, the grave's still pretty fresh, it ought not be too hard. Follow me."

The two wagons drove down a path until Tyler pulled his to a spot that was about twenty feet from a grave where the grass hadn't started reclaiming the earth. "Boy's," he said. "I know it's early, but you better get started while it's still cool. I'm going to go into town and see the sheriff or Marshal Rea about all this. I'll bring back a couple of buckets of beer." Turning to Putney Tyler asked, "Are them boys going to help?"

"That's what they're here for. And to load," said Putney.

"Then two buckets it will be," Tyler was suddenly agreeable.

"Make it three. Stop at the icehouse for a couple of blocks to keep it cold. I'm paying," said Putney.

×

It hadn't taken Tyler long to spread the word. Within an hour people started arriving on horseback and in carriages and wagons to gawk at the event. Some people pushed in too close, and Putney warned them to stay back. He enlisted the two workers to keep the crowd from closing in. About a half hour later Sheriff Maddox and Marshal Rea showed up in a buck board. "What in hell is going on here?" Maddox demanded to know.

Putney only replied, "An exhumation."

"I can see, that. By whose authority are you digging this body up."

"By the authority of the federal court," said Putney who showed the sheriff his copy of the order.

Maddox read it over with Rea looking over his shoulder, doing the same. "What's this pertaining to?" asked Rea.

"Who are you?" asked Putney.

"City Marshal Bill Rea."

"I thought it would have been obvious, Marshal Rea. It is pertaining to an investigation by the federal court."

"Don't get smart with me," Rea was angry "What do you expect to find by doing this?"

"I don't know," said Putney. "I expect that's up to the Dallas County Coroner."

Rea almost choked. "Dallas County? You'll take this body to Dallas County over my dead body."

"Do you mean to try and prevent me from carrying out my sworn duties, Marshal?" Putney backed up two steps. "Because if you are, Ned Blakely's body may not be the only one making the trip to Dallas."

Sheriff Maddox jumped between the two lawmen. "Whoa, here, now," he ordered. "Let's not let this get out of hand." Gesturing for Putney to back off a little, Maddox continued, "Let me just talk to Marshal Rea for a minute." The sheriff stepped closely to Rea, "Bill, this man is a real shootist. You push him and he'll kill you and there won't be shit I can do about it. He has a legal court order. Now just cool down before something bad happens."

"You think I'm afraid of him because he has that fancy silver star?" asked Rea.

"Not because of that silver star, but if you're not afraid of him you're a hell of a lot stupider than I gave you credit for. Now just go back to the buck board. I'll smooth this over."

Rea gave one more hateful glare at Putney, turned, and walked away, glad the sheriff had intervened because he knew Maddox had been right about Putney's ability to kill him.

Maddox walked over to Putney. "That's taken care of, Putney. You know you trod awfully heavily around here. That star doesn't mean you can go around threatening local law officers."

Putney knew that in the end, Rea would have backed down, but he needed to show him, the sheriff, and all the spectators that he wasn't going to be pushed around. "Sheriff, I think you recalled it wrong. Rea threatened me first. But I tell you what, you can tell him I forgive him because I know the ignorant can't always help themselves."

159

"Damn it, Putney, I don't have to put up with your smart ass. You keep it up and I'll find something to put you in jail for. You just keep this crowd from getting out of control."

"You could always send a couple of deputy sheriff's to help me out," Putney told him.

"Oh, yeah? Like Hubert Forsythe, I suppose," under his breath, Maddox cursed himself because that was a slip he shouldn't have made.

"If you think he will work, I reckon that will be all right," Putney didn't know what Maddox knew or whether he was trying to draw something out of Putney.

"You handle it," said Maddox.

The crowd at the cemetery had continued to grow each hour. By noon people were bringing picnic lunches. Children were playing around the gravestones like it was a park. A couple of men that Putney had never seen, showed up with cameras. Even Buckley Paddock showed up in a fringe-topped surrey. Paddock walked to where Putney was standing under a tree watching the men working. They were digging around the coffin so they could get a purchase on the box to lift it. "Deputy," said Paddock, "I never knew you were such a showman."

"Not my idea," Putney replied. "But people are always going to gawk at the macabre. Why do you think so many people turn out for hangings? It's something that can't be helped."

"I usually would have sent a reporter out, but I just had to see for myself, as well," said Paddock. "I don't guess you have a statement you would like to give for the readers of the Gazette?"

"Sure, I do," said Putney.

"Wait, let me get out a notebook, so I get it all down," Paddock reached in the pocket of his linen jacket. When he had it open and pencil in hand he said, "Go ahead."

Putney stared at the newspaperman in his linen suit and boater hat. He couldn't believe Paddock had taken him seriously, so he said, "Buckley Paddock is an ass."

"You're not making friends, here, Putney," an aggravated Paddock said.

Putney couldn't resist one more remark. "And here I thought we were becoming such great pals."

As Paddock left, Putney saw Hubert Forsyth riding up, he dismounted and walked over to Putney. "I have a subpoena for you, Marshal," the deputy sheriff told him.

"I was expecting it. Thanks."

"Can we talk?" asked Forsythe.

"It wouldn't be wise now that you've served me. We don't want anyone to think we are getting our stories together."

"Yeah, I guess so. Thanks anyway," Forsythe was dejected but he knew Putney was right.

Putney walked over to the grave. "Almost there, Marshal," one of the black laborers told him.

"When you're ready, let me know. My men will help you," Putney told them.

Martin Caine, Bull Dawson, and Max Poe stomped into The Emerald Saloon and walked up to the bar. Caine and Poe ordered a beer and Dawson ordered a whiskey. The three looked around the bar to see that other than the bartender and two drovers, the only other person in the room was Montague Russell. They walked over to where Russell was sitting and sat down. "Where is everybody?" asked Caine.

Russell looked at him like he had two heads. "Haven't you heard? That son of a bitch, Putney is out at Oakwood digging up Blakely's body. Everybody's out there watching it."

"We just got into town," said Caine. "We had to sell Max's horse and saddle in Denison to buy train tickets here."

"Did you find Doby?" asked Russell.

"Yeah," said Dawson. "But that damn Putney and some darky named Reeves surprised us and took Doby with them. We had to walk three hours barefoot to get our horses."

"Bass Reeves?" said Russell. "I've read about him. I bet he's killed more men than Putney. You were lucky walking was all that happened to you."

"Where's Courtwright?" Caine asked.

"He's out at the cemetery with McIntire. I guess they wanted to take in the show as well. I think one of you should get out there and tell Courtwright about your failure."

Everyone was surprised when Poe spoke up. "I'll go. He owes me money for a horse and saddle."

"Well, you're the man to tell him," said Russell.

"I'll take your horse, Marty," Poe didn't seem like he was asking.

"Sure, Max," said Caine as he finished his beer. "I'm going to my room and get some rest. See you later."

"What about you, Bull?" asked Russell.

"I'm gonna sit here and get drunk."

Russell smiled. "Good man," he said.

Putney had seen Courtwright and another man, sitting their horses, talking back and forth. They didn't bother trying to talk to Putney. Putney recognized a third man who rode up as one of the men who had taken Doby. He and Courtwright seemed to be arguing about something, then the big man rode off.

"We're ready, Marshal," Tyler called from the graveside. Putney thought it was humorous since the little fat man hadn't turned a shovel. Putney signaled for his two men and told them to go help get the coffin out of the hole. The gravediggers had thought ahead and hadn't piled any dirt on one side so the coffin could be lifted up and pushed over until they could climb out. The four men struggled but the box was finally on ground level. One of Putney's workers drove the wagon over so the coffin could be placed in it. The two gravediggers helped Putney's men, even though they hadn't been asked.

"Thanks, men," said Putney handing each of the black laborers a five-dollar coin. "I hope that's enough."

They looked at the silver coin in their hands and one said, "Yes, sir, Marshal, thank you. That's more than we woulda made in two weeks."

Putney Climbed onto the wagon a began driving out of the cemetery. Now Putney was leading a parade. At first, he thought it was strange, but then realized it made sense because everybody had to travel the same road to get back to town. He hoped the crowd would thin as they got nearer the train depot. He was disheartened when the crowd only seemed to grow.

They reached the freight area of the depot and Putney arranged Payment for the coffin and himself. His two laborers loaded the box into a freight car that would be hooked up to the next train going to Dallas. Putney told the men to wait with the wagon and mules and he would wire them from Dallas when he was returning. He paid them each a couple of dollars to eat on and said he would pay them the ten dollars he had agreed to, after Blakely's body was reburied.

With the coffin loaded the crowd finally began to disperse, but Courtwright and the other man stood around, glad-handing folks as they left. Putney leaned one shoulder against the box car and was getting ready to light a cigarette when he heard someone holler, "Putney, behind you!"

Putney was spinning around, pistol in hand, when two bullets slammed into the side of the box car. Three hooded men were coming at Putney, firing at him. Before Putney could get off a shot, the sound of another gun from a different direction broke the air and one hooded man fell to the ground. One of the others was aiming when Putney fired, and his bullet hit the center of the hood. The man's head snapped back, and the body followed as if jerked by a rope. The third hooded man turned and ran with the man who had been with Courtwright chasing after him. Putney looked behind him and saw Jim Courtwright holstering his pistol. Putney started to run after the third man, but Courtwright called out, "McIntire's after him. You need to stay with your cargo."

Of course, Courtwright was correct. Putney had been acting reflexively. Putney stopped and for no reason looked at his left hand. The cigarette was still between his fingers which Putney found funny and laughed. Courtwright stood next to Putney. "You always laugh when you almost get killed?" he asked.

Putney held up the cigarette and both men found it funny. Courtwright struck a match. Putney took the light off the match and blew it out. "Who yelled out the warning to me?" he asked.

"That was Tommie Fogg, a shoeshine boy around town," Said Courtwright as the two men walked over to survey the men on the ground. Each pulled a hood off a different man. "Do you know them?" Putney asked.

"Never seen them before. Looks like saddle tramps," answered Courtwright as he searched one man's pockets. "Look what I found." Courtwright held out two double eagles and a ten-dollar coin.

Putney searched the other man and found the same. "Where do you think they got this kind of money? Cowboys never have this much at one time."

"It's a mystery to me," Courtwright admitted. "But it looks like somebody has put a price on your head. Maybe McIntire will catch the other one and we can get some answers.

Putney blew smoke rings and said, "Whoever did isn't getting their money's worth. By the way, thanks for taking this one down."

Courtwright smiled and said, "Think nothing of it. I may be a lot of things, but I can't tolerate a back shooter. I mean it's just downright rude."

Chapter Twenty-Three

"Were fixin to hook up the baggage car," A depot attendant told Putney.

"Hold on a minute," said Putney. "I guess I'm going to have to get this coffin off the train," he said to Courtwright.

"I don't know what you're up to, Putney," said Courtwright, "but you might as well see it through."

"I don't think Marshal Rea will take it too kindly. We had a standoff earlier today."

"Don't worry about Bill, I'll get him settled down."

Putney nodded and then told the attendant to hook it up and that he would be riding with the baggage. Putney hopped into the box car, "Tell Rea, I hope to be back before nightfall." He called to Courtwright.

The train pulled into the Dallas Depot where Marshal Cabell was waiting. "I already got a telegram from Sheriff Maddox," he told Putney. "You can tell me about it while we get this body to the coroner."

Waiting outside the coroner's examining room, Putney finished telling Cabell everything that had happened that day. He told him about his run-in with Rea, his discussion with Paddock, and went into detail about the attempt on his life. "And you say Courtwright and McIntire jumped in to the fray?" asked the marshal.

"If it hadn't been for them and Tommie Fog shouting a warning, I probably wouldn't be here now. but I have to say those boys were about the worst shots I ever ran into."

"What does that tell you about Courtwright?"

Putney thought before answering. "I don't think he was behind this or when Blakely ambushed me. He's up to something, I just haven't figured it out."

"Then who do you think is behind these attacks?"

"It's a puzzle to me. I had thought maybe Montague Russell but from what I've seen and been told, he doesn't have the means. By my figure, there has been nearly two hundred dollars in bounty money spent on me with no results. I've seen Russell. He was shilling for Soapy Smith but Smith has gone back to Denver. There were some other people I sent to prison over the Knights of the Rising Sun, back in seventy-one, but I haven't seen any of them or heard anything about them. If it's one of them, they are keeping low."

"Who do you think the third man was?" Marshal Cabell's concern was real.

"Could have been Bull Dawson, but he would have had to catch a train in Durant or Denison. It's possible, but he certainly wouldn't have the money to pay out a hundred dollars and he was still in prison when Blakely shot me."

Just then the corner came out of the examining room, pulling off his thick rubber gloves. "Well, gentlemen," he said. "Here's what I can tell you. This man was shot twice. Once with a forty-four or forty-five caliber bullet. One can't determine the actual size without the bullet available. That wound would not have been mortal. At least not immediately. Without attention, he may have bled to death. The other wound, as far as I can tell, was from a smaller bullet. Probably a thirty-eight, but it may have been a thirty-two or even a thirty-six. Not many people use thirty-six anymore. There again, without the bullet, it is difficult to tell."

"Could the second bullet have been a forty-four," asked Cabell.

"Where the bullet enters it appears it was a thirty-eight. Where the bullet stopped in the heart, there was more damage so it would be difficult to say for certain, if that were the only place to examine, except it definitely killed him. So, from my experience, it was a thirty-eight caliber bullet that inflicted the wound."

"And that is what you would testify to, if necessary," asked Putney.

"It is," the coroner said. "If you give me a few moments I will have my report typed up for you."

"Thank you, doctor," said Cabell.

"There you have it, Nahum. I guess you better get that body back over to Fort Worth. It's an hour before the next train leaves. You get the body to the station. And talk to Rea as soon as you can. In the meantime, I'm going to find a fellow that has worked for me a few times. I'm going to send him with you. He's a good hand, by the name of Ed Hoy."

166

"Don't you think that's overkill, Marshal?"

"That's exactly what I'm trying to prevent."

"What do you mean you told Putney to go on to Dallas?" Marshal Bill Rea was livid with Courtwright. "I could have him sitting in my jail right now for killing these two men."

"You going to have me sharing that jail cell with him, Bill?" Courtwright was not about to be upbraided by Rea. "This was an attempt to waylay Putney by back shooting scum. If it hadn't been for that shine boy yelling a warning Putney would be dead. Even for that and me getting one, Putney still should have been killed. It was his good luck that they were bad shots, drunk, or both. No, Bill, we're already losing one legal fight. No sense in losing another."

"That's what I mean Jim. He's going to get that body over to Dallas and the coroner over there is sure to be able to tell that two different types of bullets shot Blakely. If you hadn't let him go, we could have kept that quiet until after the trial."

"I don't think it would make any difference. Max Poe filled me in on what happened up in the Nations. Putney went up there to track down Clint Doby and he enlisted the help of Bass Reeves. You've heard of him, right? Why would Putney go to all that trouble if Clint didn't have something to say? No, that battle is almost lost to us," Courtwright was being practical about the situation. "Putney has that boy squirreled away somewhere. If we can figure that out and if we could get Doby away from him, we might be back in business."

Rea shook his head, "What are you going to tell McLaury? If this trial takes a bad turn, he won't be happy."

"I don't know why I would tell McLaury anything. We set this up for him to hit a home run. If he strikes out, I don't want us connected to this in any shape, form, or fashion. Right now, we need to make Putney think we are on his side, or at least not against him."

"Then, what do you want to do?"

"Putney said he would try to be back before nightfall. There's a train comes in around seven. We'll meet it. You're going to tell

Putney that you and I talked and you are just going to file it as self-defense. That ought to take a little tension out of the rope."

Putney was waiting by the baggage car when a man, who looked like he had just walked out of Buffalo Bill's Wild West Show approached him. He wore a fringed buckskin jacket highly decorated with colorful beading over a turquoise, double-breasted shirt, fringed buckskin pants tucked into knee-high mule skinner boots. On his head, he wore a grey John Bull hat with three crow feathers. His hair was long and black and sleek. Over his left breast was pinned a badge like the one Putney had given to Luke Short. He was carrying a rifle in a buckskin sleeve, decorated with similar beading to the jacket. "I think you must be Nahum Putney," he said.

"I am, and I'm guessing you're Ed Hoy."

"That's me. Marshal Cabell sent me. Looks like I got here just in time." Hoy reached out his hand and Putney shook it.

"Kind of stand out, don't you?"

"Asks the man with long red hair and a red beard, wearing a Mexican jacket and two Schofields."

"Point taken," said Putney. "You have side arms?"

"Two short-barreled Batt forty-fours under my jacket. They frown on carrying pistols openly, here in Dallas."

"Yeah, in Fort Worth, too, but They've gotten used to me. Don't know if they will be able to get used to you."

"What? They don't like Indians over there?" Both men laughed.

On the platform, a conductor was yelling "All aboard."

"I guess we better hop in," said Putney

Putney had wired ahead for his two workers to meet him at the seven o'clock train. The train was slowing as it was approaching the Fort Worth station. Putney leaned out of the box car door and saw his men waiting on the wagon. He also saw Marshal Bill Rea and ex-Marshal Jim Courtwright. Leaning back in the car he spoke to Ed Hoy. "Looks like Rea and Courtwright have formed a welcoming committee. If Rea chooses to arrest me, don't kill him.

Just see this body gets planted," He pulled out his coin purse and gave Hoy two silver coins. "See that those workers get this."

The train lurched to a stop and Putney climbed down to meet Rea and Courtwright. As he was walking to meet them Rea said, "What the hell are you doing here?" Putney was surprised at the greeting until he realized that Rea was talking past him and at Ed Hoy.

"Bill Rea is that any way to speak to an old friend?" asked Hoy.

"You've never been a friend, old or new. And I've told you Fort Worth is a place you should give a wide birth to," Rea told him.

Great, thought Putney, *Cabell set me up with a bodyguard that has history with Rea.*

"You might say I'm on a protection assignment, Bill," Hoy flashed his badge. "It seems you folk in Fort Worth have taken a dislike to Marshal Cabell's favorite deputy and I'm here to make sure that dislike doesn't get out of control."

"Simmer down, men," Courtwright stepped in to cool things down. He didn't like Hoy any more than Rea, but another gun battle in Fort Worth just wouldn't do. Especially with his name connected to it. "We've all had our moments," Courtwright explained to Putney. "But I think we can put that all aside for the time being. Why don't we walk over to the White Elephant, have a drink, and be friends."

"Ed & I have business in the cemetery," said Putney. "And it's been a long day, so I would like to get our business settled here and now. How about it Bill?

Bill Rea didn't like Putney to begin with and seeing him with Ed Hoy, a man he despised was adding fuel to the fire, but thinking of his conversation with Courtwright, he let it go. "Yeah, I agree," he said. "I just came down here to tell you that Jim explained everything. I've got deputies looking for the third shooter, but we haven't come up with anything yet. But as far as you're concerned, you're in the clear. I'm going to file it as self-defense. I think the District Attorney will accept it."

"Well, that's just fine, Bill," Putney told him. "I'm glad Jim, here could get things worked out so congenially." His sarcasm was not lost on anybody in earshot.

"I don't guess y'all want to help us hoist ole Ned on the wagon?" Asked Hoy.

In obvious anger, Rea spun on his heel and walked away. Jim Courtwright looked at Putney, shrugged, and then also turned to walk away.

"Was it something I said?" asked Hoy.

"You could have told me that there was animosity between you and Rea," Putney told him.

"I know," said Hoy. "And truthfully, I thought about it, but I thought it would be more fun this way."

Putney shook his head and thought of Jimmy Two Feathers who had the same sense of humor. "Christ," he said. "Let's get this body in a hole and call it a night."

Putney was dressing when Luke Short woke. "Where you headed this early," asked Short.

"Going to McLaury's office. Wouldn't want him to say I was dodging him." Putney looked in the mirror and ran a brush through his hair before putting his hat on. "I'm going to go out through the main door," he said. "I don't want anyone to see me going out through the alley and start getting ideas."

Short rose and unbolted the office door, "Bring some newspapers when you come back. I'm bored stiff." Putney nodded and went through the office and listened for Short to replace the iron bar. Sitting in the chair at the desk was Ed Hoy. Putney had given Hoy a key to the office the night before, so he could come and go as he needed. They figured using the front door would make it look like business as usual. Putney had also given Hoy the Dallas coroner's report to give to Imogene and told him to check into the hotel. They agreed that Hoy would meet Putney every morning and would return to the office every evening.

Outside the courthouse, Hoy produced a meerschaum pipe carved with fancy scrolls and turtles on each side. He stuffed the pipe and lit up. Putney thought that was a lot of trouble to go through, produced a Kinney, and lit it.

Looking down the block, Putney saw a man of average height with a long beard and a mustache so thick it was as if the man had no face below his nose. He was dressed in a three-piece suit with a day coat and a silk top hat. For his part, William McLaury saw the two men smoking in front of the courthouse and wondered if Buffalo Bill was in town, but he knew it wasn't so. He didn't know who the Indian was, but he was certain the red-haired man was the infamous Nahum Putney.

McLaury walked directly to the two men. "I assume you're Nahum Putney," he said.

"That's right," said Putney. "And this is Ed Hoy, a fellow deputy marshal.

Having heard of what happened at the train station, McLaury said, "I hope this isn't a prelude to another shooting. Something I am determined to stamp out in Fort Worth."

"We're both fine with that, is it Mr. McLaury?" said Putney.

"It is. I guess you better come on in my office," the attorney walked past Putney and Hoy and into the court building to his office. The two deputies followed. Once inside the office, McLaury hung up his coat and placed his hat on the books that topped his filing cabinet. He motioned for his visitors to sit. "Now, what can I do for you?"

"I'm just answering my subpoena," said Putney.

"And you needed this man to do that?"

"No, he just likes me, so he came along," Putney was already disliking McLaury.

"Do you think all this is funny, Mr. Putney?" McLaury already knew he didn't like Putney.

"Not at all. Why do you ask?"

"It seems like you make a show of everything. Nothing seems serious to you and now you bring this Apache with you."

"Whoa, Chief," said Hoy. "I ain't done or said nothing for you to start insulting me. I ain't Apache or Kiowa or none of those heathens. I'm full-blooded Creek."

"I do apologize, Mr. Hoy, I never realized there was a difference. Thank you for correcting me."

"Look," Putney was angry, "I don't know what bug crawled up your ass, but I came here out of respect for the law. But neither my friend, nor I have to put up with your crap. So, if you have any questions for me, before the trial starts, let me know, otherwise we are leaving."

171

"All right, when was the last time you spoke with Imogene Foster or Deidre O'Neill?"

"Last Friday, before I left for the territories."

"And what took you to the Indian Nations?"

"Federal business."

"Then that's all I have for you."

Putney rose to leave, followed by Hoy. Before opening the door he turned to McLaury, "You never had any intention of calling me to the witness stand, did you?"

"You might think that Mr. Putney, but if you don't mind, I will keep my strategies to myself."

Chapter Twenty-Four

For Deidre the last week was more tedious than life aboard ship, sailing from Ireland. She had managed, then, to scrape enough money together to purchase a second-class ticket which gave her the privilege of having meals served and being able to amble about on the quarter deck. Other than that, there wasn't much to do except listen to some boring scholar or his even more boring wife. But it was preferable to what she was now enduring.

She had not seen Nahum in over a week, although she had a great deal of news about his activities. There had been his letter of course, which she cherished, and which was her only consolation. But then she had also been told of his actions at the cemetery, where he had the body of Ned Blakely dug up, which in her twisted way she found a little humorous. But there was also the attempt on his life at the train station. When she first learned of that endeavor she panicked, because she first had been told he was killed, and later someone said he was only wounded. The rumors nearly drove her mad, so she dispatched the twins to find out what happened. They returned that evening to tell her that Putney was safe and had not been harmed at all. She was bewildered when they told her Courtwright had most probably saved Putney's life. She couldn't imagine Courtwright risking himself for anyone, much less Nahum Putney. But she was relieved at the news.

Then on Thursday night, a colorfully dressed Indian had checked into the hotel, using Putney's name as a reference. Mary had brought Ed Hoy to Deidre when he first arrived, and he told them that Marshal Cabell had hired him as a sort of bodyguard to Putney. Deidre was quite comforted by that news. On Friday, she learned from Imogene that Putney had been to see McLaury, but that was the last news she had of him.

Now, on a Saturday night, which was usually filled with gaiety as she played hostess to the customers in the private dining room, she sat with her elbows propped on her large desk and her head in her hands. Mary was taking care of the few customers in the private dining room, while Deidre moped in her office. Mary had reported that the private diners were disappointed because Deidre was not attending them personally, since they all knew she was out of jail. "To hell with them," she told Mary. "Where were the likes of them when I was sitting in jail? Not one letter or note did I get from any of my so-called admirers. I didn't see any of them stepping up to help with my bond. You just tell them that when I'm found not guilty, I'm going to throw a big party and none of them are invited." Mary didn't tell them of course. Business was already bad enough without antagonizing good customers.

When the clock chimed twelve Deidre sighed, deciding she might as well go to bed. Feeling sleep would elude her, she rose from her desk walked to the drinks cabinet, and poured herself a large glass of Bushmills, mixed with honey, hoping it would relax her enough that she could at least rest. She drank her elixir as she undressed and donned a white sleeping gown. It was senseless to wear one of her more elaborate gowns, as Nahum wasn't there to see her in it. Having finished the drink, she lay on the bed worrying about the upcoming trial, worrying about the business but mostly worrying about Nahum. The whiskey and honey had done its work and without even knowing it she slipped into a deep sleep.

She had no idea of the time when she thought she heard something in the outer office, but her mind was overwhelmed with sleep, and she decided it was one of those things people sense in their dreams. She couldn't even tell if she was dreaming or not, but she quickly drifted off to a dream about her childhood home on a hill overlooking Lochfingrean. Suddenly she felt as though she couldn't breathe. Her dream was becoming a nightmare. She struggled to wake, and it was only then that she realized there was a hand clamped over her mouth. She began to struggle under the grip when a voice whispered, "Shhh. It's me, Nahum." Deidre's eyes sprang open to see her lover's face mere inches from hers. One hand was over her mouth while the other had a finger to his lips making the gesture for her to be quiet.

Nahum Putney slowly lifted his hand and Deidre breathed, "Am I dreaming?"

"No," whispered Nahum. "I could stay away no longer. I had to see you."

Still dazed from being woken, Deidre, asked, "What time is it?"

174

"Near three, does it really matter?" returned Nahum.

Finally, fully aware, Deidre said, "No it does not. Now kiss me."

Deidre laid silently on Nahum's shoulder, smoking a cheroot as he just as silently smoked a Kinney. Putney had read of a fight between Arthur Chambers and Johnny Clark in Canada. The fight lasted one hundred thirty-six rounds and took two hours and twenty-three minutes. Putney would have bet neither man was as tired as he was after one hour with Deidre. Finally breaking the silence, Deidre asked, "When do you have to leave?"

"Shortly," he said.

"I worry about you."

"You don't need to. I'll be all right."

"All right?" she said. "You were nearly killed just two days ago."

"But I wasn't"

"How can you be so indifferent about it?" Deidre was getting wound up.

"I'm not indifferent about it. I'm just not worried about it," said Putney as he rolled over and stubbed out his cigarette in an ashtray. "It's just part of the job."

Deidre sat up in bed, "Yes. And it's a job you should quit."

Putney rose from the bed and stumbled in the dark, looking for the gas light. He found the light and put a match to the gas but kept the light low. "Which I will. When it is time."

"And when will that time be?"

Putney didn't want to argue, so he just shrugged his shoulders.

"When you're dead, that's when."

Putney hunted for his long johns, picked them up off the floor, and sat on the bed. "I don't think so, but that's not up to me."

"Well, who is it up to then?"

Nahum gently took Deidre's hands in his. "I'm going to tell you something I never told anyone before," he said. "Remember when I told you about the time I went on a rampage of revenge, using the name Jack Callahan?" She nodded her head. "I told you about how my wife, Mandy was killed." Deidre nodded again.

Then I told you how Imogene found me in McKinney and the shape I was in."

"Yes, you told me all that. And my heart breaks for you. But that does not explain what we are talking about."

"There were four years between the time Mandy died and Imogene found me. For four years I wandered around Wyoming, Montana, the Dakotas, and Idaho working for despicable men and doing despicable things. Things I will keep to myself until the day they put me in the ground. This work I do, is me repaying those wasted years."

Tears ran down Deidre's cheeks, "But that was fifteen years ago. When will you have paid for those years?"

"The only way I know how to tell you is when God lets me know."

"That's too ambiguous."

"I know and I wish I could explain it differently," Putney had finished tucking his shirt in his trousers and was pulling his galluses over his shoulders. He sat on the bed to put his boots on.

Deidre stood on her knees and put her hands on his shoulders and gently kissed his neck. "I wish I could take all that pain away," she whispered to him.

"One day you will and then you and God will let me know it's time to quit."

"Do you have to leave now?"

Nahum pulled on his jacket and looked at his watch, "It's nearly four thirty and I need to get out of here before your kitchen staff starts showing up."

"Well at least you didn't come calling in that awful Mexican jacket and sombrero," Deidre forced a laugh.

"I only wore this because I love you," said Nahum. He kissed her passionately, turned, and walked toward the door.

"And I love you, too," said Deidre as he turned the door knob.

[x]

Putney went through the kitchen and opened the door he had jimmied to gain entry. He walked nearly to the corner of the building where he would look down the narrow passage between the hotel and the next building to make sure he wasn't seen when a

176

figure came out from the passage. "You're not near as sneaky as you think."

Putney had a pistol out and was squeezing the trigger when he recognized Ed Hoy. "Shit," said Putney. "Do you know how close you came to dying?"

"Yeah, that was probably a mistake on my part," said Hoy.

"Don't you ever sleep?"

"Marshal Cabell ain't paying me to sleep. Come on, we'll follow the alley a couple more blocks. There's a place down aways we can get breakfast. It will just look like we're early risers for church."

Thinking about his conversation with Deidre, Putney said, "It wouldn't hurt me to go to church."

Chapter Twenty-Five

By the time the sun had been up for ten minutes on Monday morning, a line had already begun to form outside the courthouse. Sheriff Maddox had expected that interest in the trial of Deidre O'Neill would be high, so he had brought in deputies to ensure orderliness. The courthouse was a stone octagonal building with wings off every other side of the octagon, giving it a cross shape, with offices and courtrooms in each wing. It had originally been built with a dome in the center but in 1882 the dome was replaced with a third floor, topped with a clock tower, to make room for more offices and courtrooms. The front entrance faced Weatherford Street, and, with stantions and ropes, the deputies had created four paths to the entrance. The first line was for trial spectators the second was for people conducting business, other than the O'Neill trial, the third was for the trial attorneys and witnesses, leaving the last for potential jurors.

Since court was to start at nine o'clock, participants began arriving at eight. Jurors were shuffled to the Clerk's office to be registered and left waiting in a large room with straight-back wooden chairs. Witnesses were escorted to one of two witness rooms, depending on whether they were McLaury's witnesses or O'Neill's. Ed Hoy had met the early train from Dallas and brought the Dallas County coroner to the courthouse. Putney arrived early to avoid a chance meeting with either Deidre or Imogene, who at Deidre's insistence arrived in a grand open-air carriage. Reporters and photographers from both Fort Worth papers and a reporter and photographer from Dallas were present. She obliged the newsmen by posing for photographs. Buckley Paddock from the Fort Worth Gazette was the first man in the spectator's line. McLaury, Marshal Rea, and Sheriff Maddox were seated at the prosecutor's table by a quarter to nine, and Deidre, Imogene, and Mary were seated at the defense table. At that time deputies allowed spectators to enter. The first row, behind McLaury, was reserved for the reporters and Paddock, while the row behind Deidre had been reserved for her supporters. This is where Ceasar, Brutus, and Elizabeth now sat. Promptly, at nine o'clock, Judge Beckham's clerk entered the courtroom and called, "All rise."

With the formalities of the court opening, the pledge of allegiance, and a prayer, Judge Beckham took his seat behind the bench and addressed the crowd. "I am only going to say this once," he said. "This is a court of law and all of you seated in the gallery will act with proper decorum. Should any of you act otherwise, sheriff's deputies will remove you and you will be barred from the remainder of the trial."

The judge then turned his attention to Imogene. "Miss Foster, I see you delivered a motion to my office early Friday morning, requesting to amend your witness list. I will now hear your oral argument on why I should permit this amendment."

Imogene stood and said, "Thank you, your honor. If it pleases the court my motion requests the addition of Doctor Thomas McLeod, the coroner for the County of Dallas."

"For what purpose?" asked the judge.

"To testify to the findings of an autopsy he performed on the body of Ned Blakely."

"And why was this brought to my attention at so late a date?"

"Your honor, I was not aware of the autopsy until I was informed by U. S. Marshal William Cabell through Deputy U. S. Marshal Ed Hoy, on Thursday evening, when Deputy Hoy delivered the message to me, along with a copy of Doctor McLeod's report."

"I read about the exhumation of Mr. Blakely. Do you have any knowledge of why the exhumation and autopsy were performed?"

"Your honor, the only information I have is from a note by Marshal Cabell stating that the exhumation and autopsy were performed pursuant to an investigation by the U. S. Marshal's office, for the federal district court, regarding a possible conspiracy to assassinate a Deputy U. S. Marshal."

"Mr. McLaury already has a coroner's report from Doctor Cramer," said Judge Beckham. "What would be the purpose of submitting another report and testimony from Doctor McLeod?"

"We believe that Doctor McLeod's report and testimony will show a different result than that of Doctor Cramer's and thus is important to our case, your honor."

"I see and what say you Mister McLaury?" the judge asked the prosecutor.

McLaury stood. "Judge, I see no purpose in this testimony, and I strongly object. Doctor Cramer is a well-respected citizen of Tarrant County. To have his judgment called into question by an official of any county, but especially Dallas County is disrespectful to Doctor Cramer, Tarrant County, and honestly, your honor, this court itself."

"Very good, you may both be seated," the judge cleared his throat and began again. "I have heard your arguments and I have read both of your commentaries on this matter. I will be honest with you, Miss Foster, I am not fond of having the findings of our own county officials questioned. And to be blunt, I do not appreciate the federal government sticking its nose into what is obviously a local matter and falls under the jurisdiction of this city and county." Clearing his throat again, Judge Beckham continued, "However, this is a serious charge facing Miss O'Neill and it falls to this court to afford her every opportunity to defend herself. Therefore, I am going to allow this testimony and the introduction of the second autopsy report."

McLaury stood. "Your honor, for the purposes of the record, I wish to reiterate my objection."

"Objection overruled, Mister McLaury," said the judge. "We will now take a fifteen-minute break, while deputies clear all but the first two rows so we can bring in the jury pool."

"Your honor," said Imogene, standing, "Before we take a break, I have an objection of my own, I would like to file."

"Yes, Miss Foster, you may continue," the judge allowed.

"Your honor, I see seated at the prosecution table are two law officers, both of whom are on the prosecution's witness list. I understand the prosecutor may need an investigating officer to assist in his case, but I believe two presents an unfair obstacle for the defense to overcome. I ask, therefore, that one of these officers be required to wait in the witness room during testimony."

"Mister McLaury," said the judge. "Do wish to be heard on this objection?"

"Your honor, Marshal Rea is here as the investigating officer in this case and Sheriff Maddox is an officer of this court, responsible for the safety and security of the court. I see no reason why both cannot be present during the trial."

"I agree with Miss Foster," said the judge. "She is not allowed to have any witness other than Miss O'Neill to be present in the courtroom. Sheriff Maddox has deputies he can depend on to ensure the safety of the court. However, the decision is yours. You may of course bring in another person from your office who is not on your witness list to assist you. Objection sustained. Now without further objection, we will take a fifteen-minute recess."

The potential jurors were all seated in the courtroom when Judge Beckham reentered. The judge began, "Gentlemen, you have all been selected as prospective jurors to sit in this case. We will soon begin the process of *voir dire*, or in plain English the process by which the attorneys in this case, and I, will select who will serve on the jury and who will be excused. The attorneys will have an opportunity to ask you questions. They will also have the chance to what we call strike certain of you from serving on the jury. This should not be construed that they or this court find you are not good and honest citizens, it simply means they have the right to try and select the men, they deem most likely to assist this court in finding justice in this case. Is there anyone who does not understand this concept?"

Nobody answered the judge's question.

"Good," he said. "Before we begin with the attorneys there are some questions I need to pose." With that statement, he had each person seated at the attorneys' tables stand. He introduced each person and asked if the jurors knew that person or knew of that person and if that knowledge would prevent them from deciding the case fairly. Several raised their hands, and the judge questioned them further after which he excused two men.

"Next, as you no doubt, recognize, counsel for the defense is a woman. I myself have had any reservations as to her qualifications or her ability to ably defend her client. But after due diligence, I am satisfied with her abilities and find she is more than qualified. Gentlemen, this is a sign of the times. However, are there any among you who could not render a fair verdict based upon the sex of defense counsel?"

181

Five men raised their hands and the judge excused them all.

"Now," said the judge. "Are there any of you who have read news articles or editorials about this case?"

Most of the men raised their hands.

"Finally, of those of you who raised your hands, did these articles or editorials influence you so much that you could not render a fair verdict in this case?"

Five men raised their hands, and these were also excused. The judge thanked those who remained and began the voir dire process.

Questioning of the jurors lasted until one o'clock that afternoon. Upon completion, a jury of twelve men were seated in the jury box and were sworn in. The judge cautioned the jurors that they were not to discuss the case with anyone or amongst themselves until the evidence had been presented and the judge handed the case over to them to decide. The judge directed that the court would recess for one hour at which time they would reconvene and opening statements would be made.

Before voir dire was completed, Mary signaled for Elizabeth to leave to go get the lunch Mary had directed the kitchen to prepare for their lunch. Elizabeth was waiting on the courthouse steps when Deidre and the rest exited. Deidre saw Elizabeth with the basket. "My, Mary," she said. "How efficient of you. Let's sit under that big oak over there and eat." They were all seated around a blanket Elizabeth had spread on the ground. She placed paper-wrapped sandwiches in front of everyone and got out a one-gallon crockery jug filled with chilled lemonade then dealt out tin cups to everyone.

"So, tell me, Imogene," said Deidre, "What do you think?"

Imogene was chewing part of her sandwich and waggled her head, showing she didn't want to commit.

"Well," Deidre continued. "You know I first had my doubts, but you clobbered McLaury with the coroner and your objection."

Imogene swallowed, "Let's not get overconfident," she said. "Yes, we had a good morning, but I have to tell you there are one or two of the jurors I think could be a little shaky."

"I'm not worried, Miss Imogene," Elizabeth spoke up. "I think you were brilliant."

Imogene reddened at the girl's compliment. Then Mary spoke up. "No, Imogene is right. We don't want to put the cart before the horse. I think Imogene did very well, but McLaury is no slug, but he is a snake in the grass. He hasn't really started yet."

"What about me," Deidre pretended to pout. "Didn't I do an excellent job keeping my mouth shut?" Everyone laughed. "Lord, none of you understand how difficult that is." They all laughed some more until a man walked up. The laughing immediately stopped.

"It's very good to see such frivolity in the face of such dire circumstances," said the man who was wearing a straw hat and a beige linen suit. "Permit me to introduce myself. My name is Buckley Paddock. May I ask the cause of your gaiety?"

"Oh, so it's yourself, then is it Mister Paddock," as usual when she was aggravated, Deidre's Irish brogue was becoming more pronounced. "Aye. I'll tell you the cause of our gaiety. We were laughing about something Betsy here had said."

"And that was?"

"Well, when she saw you walking this way, she said you walked like a banty rooster that had his goolies cut off."

"Goolies?" questioned Paddock, which caused them all to burst out in a fit of laughter. He didn't know what had been meant, but Paddock knew he was being ridiculed, and he didn't like being humiliated. "Let's see how much you laugh when you read tomorrow's paper."

Mary couldn't stop snickering but said, "Deidre, you shouldn't have said that. He's going to write something nasty about you again."

"I know. I just couldn't help myself," said Deidre.

Elizabeth broke in with, "What's goolies?" which set them all to laughing again.

Chapter Twenty-Six

"Gentlemen," William McLaury began. "I'm not going to make a long opening statement because this is a very simple case and to bore you with a drawn out opening is just not necessary. What I intend to do is show you, through evidence and witnesses, that the defendant killed Ned Blakely out of malice. Now, she did not murder Mister Blakely through premeditation and that is the only reason that today, she is here charged with manslaughter and not homicide in the first degree. But the fact remains that she shot and killed him for revenge. Evidence will show that Mister Blakely had already been disabled from a wound given him by Deputy U. S. Marshal Nahum Putney."

"Before I go any further, I'm going to let you in on a secret. One that the defense will certainly bring out. Ned Blakely was not a good man. The fact is he was a very bad man. But that does not mean he deserved his life to be taken from him. If he himself acted with malice and criminality, he should be sitting here in this courtroom, not lying in a pine box in Oakwood Cemetery. He deserved his day of justice, just as we are affording Miss O'Neill hers. But why is he not here instead of her? Why indeed? Because Miss O'Neill decided to take justice into her own hands and deprive Mister Blakely of the justice he so rightly deserved."

"But, as I was saying, Mister Blakely was on the ground having received a wound that may have well killed him if not attended to."

"Objection, your honor," Imogene had hopped up from her seat.

"On what grounds, Miss Foster?" the judge inquired.

"Mister McLaury has made a statement of fact that has not yet been entered into evidence. This is supposed to be an opening statement, not testimony."

Judge Beckham made a tent with his hands and thought for a minute. Mister McLaury has a right to lay out what he thinks evidence will show. Objection overruled."

"Thank you, your honor," said McLaury. "As I was saying, Mister Blakely was suffering from a wound that made it

184

impossible to continue his attack on the marshal, so, shooting him was an unnecessary act by Miss O'Neill. But why did she shoot him? She did it out of vengeance for the attack on the marshal. I will show you evidence that not only did she shoot Mister Blakely for that, but also because Mister Blakley was trying to extort her into paying protection money to keep her infamous establishment safe."

"Objection," Imogene was on her feet again.

"What for this time, Miss Foster?"

"The characterization of O'Neill's Hotel and Restaurant. Using the word infamous denotes that there is illegal or immoral activity at the business owned by Miss O'Neill, which is sanctioned by Miss O'Neill. This characterization prejudices the jury against my client."

"Attorneys approach the bench," said Judge Beckham. McLaury and Imogene came to the judge's dais. Judge Beckham leaned over and whispered, "Miss Foster, this is Mister McLaury's turn. He may say what he wants within certain parameters, which I will set. Not you. Do you understand?" Imogene nodded. "Mister McLaury you know better than to use inflammatory statements which may incorrectly influence the jury. I do not find your characterization one of those, but you came mighty close. I advise you to tread lightly. Do you understand?"

"Yes, judge," McLaury whispered.

"Good, you may both return," then in a voice, the whole court could hear, the judge said. "Objection Overruled."

McLaury returned to the podium in front of the jury and continued speaking. Deidre leaned into Imogene at the defense table and asked, "What did he say?"

"It wasn't good," whispered Imogene. "I will tell you later."

".... And not only that, but I will present a witness that this deputy marshal, one Nahum Putney had history with Ned Blakely and there will be further evidence that Mister Blakely feared Nahum Putney. Now it would stretch the bounds of reason that Miss O'Neill did not know of this history, given the close relationship of Miss O'Neill and Deputy Putney."

"Lastly gentlemen, I will present physical and scientific evidence that the bullet that killed Mister Blakely, did in fact come from the gun that Miss O'Neill used to kill Mister Blakely."

"Gentlemen, when I began, I told you I would be brief because I don't need to convince you with what I say, but because the evidence will be so overwhelming that you will only be able to return a verdict of guilt. Thank you."

Judge Beckham told Imogene it was time for her opening statement and as she was approaching the podium Deidre whispered, "Imogene, you forgot your notes."

Imogene held up a finger to Deidre and turned to the judge, "Your honor, may I have a moment with my client?"

"Quickly, Miss Foster," the judge advised.

Imogene returned to the table and leaned over to Deidre and Mary. "I'm not going to need them, I'm going a bit of a different direction," she said. "Trust me." She approached the podium and started.

"Gentlemen, I want to thank Mister McLaury for his brevity. I too shall be brief because I barely know what to say in rebuttal. You see the story that Mister McLaury wove is a total fantasy. It was a yarn worthy of being included as part of the Grimm Brothers' Fairy Tales for it was a grim scenario, indeed. But the problem is that Mister McLaury couldn't make up his mind as to the purpose of his story. First, he wants you to believe that Miss O'Neill shot Mister Blakely out of revenge for his shooting Nahum Putney. But wait, that may not have been the reason. No, it may have been in retribution for Ned Blakely's attempt to extort Miss O'Neill. But then he makes another turn and wants you to believe that it had to do with some history between Blakely and Nahum Putney. The only thing Mister McLaury was consistent about was giving the role of the wicked witch to Deidre O'Neill. My, my, my what a tale."

"But you gentlemen are not children given to believe in fantasies. No. You are intelligent men to whom the responsibility of sussing out the truth has been given. So, I am going to tell you the truth, and it is simple. Miss O'Neill is not guilty of the crime she has been charged with. But more than that she is in fact innocent."

"Now, as his honor, Judge Beckham told you previously, there is no burden on either Miss O'Neill or me to prove her innocence. The burden falls to Mister McLaury to prove guilt and that proof must be beyond a reasonable doubt. But the truth is Mister

186

McLaury will not provide you with anything to doubt what he will try to prove. So, that task lies with me and Miss O'Neill. And I tell you, good sirs, we are up to the task."

"We will present evidence that will show that Miss O'Neill never even shot Ned Blakely. I will present to you our own scientific evidence that the fatal wound couldn't have come from the pistol used by Miss O'Neill. We will have fact witnesses to the evidence and, gentlemen, in the end, you will have no alternative but to bring a verdict of not guilty. I want to thank you for your time, and I want to thank you, in advance, for your diligence."

Judge Beckham pulled a pocket watch from under his robe and after looking at it said. "Mr. McLaury, how long do you think it will take to present your witnesses and evidence?"

"Your honor I estimate no longer than a day," McLaury answered.

"It is three o'clock. I don't like to start testimony, only to get less than a quarter of the way through. We will recess until tomorrow at nine in the morning," the judge rapped his gavel on the bench. Everyone stood and the judge exited the court.

McLaury stepped over to the defense table. "Fairy tale, Miss Foster?" he said, "That was very good, but I wonder if the fairy tale isn't really yours or are you going to produce a magic bullet?" he smirked and walked toward the exit.

The team had gathered in Deidre's office. The gaiety at lunchtime was gone. Deidre poured whiskey and passed the glasses out for everyone, except Elizabeth. She finally smiled, "Grimm's Fairy Tales," she said. "I admit I never expected that. Very well done, Imogene."

Everyone agreed that Imogene had perfectly encapsulated their case. For Imogene's part, she blushed at the compliments. "I think, all and all, it was a good day," she told the group. "I know my objections were overruled, but it doesn't matter, the jury can't unhear what I said. I think I may have even won over one of the shaky jurors. I guess we'll see."

"I think everyone should get a good night's rest," said Deidre. "Tomorrow is going to be a long day of lies and innuendos and it will take all of our spirit to suffer through it." All agreed and began leaving the office. "Brutus, you and Ceasar wait a moment," Deidre said. "I worry over Nahum. Can you get a message to him to find out how he is doing?"

"I'm sure we can, Boss," said Brutus. "We'll let you know if we hear anything."

"Thank you."

⊠

In the back of Putney's office things had become animated. "I tell you, Marshal," said Clint Doby. "I'm going crazy in here. Mister Short is good company and all but I'm tired of looking at the walls every day. Why, if nobody told me I wouldn't know if it was night or day."

"Calm down, Clint," Putney told him. "I'll think of something to get you some relief. Have a seat, I sent Tommie to get some steaks for dinner, that should help. First, I want to talk to Luke."

Putney and Luke Short stepped into the office. "What do you think, Luke?"

"I can tell you I am in sympathy with the boy, Nahum. It's like being locked up in jail. I could use some air myself," Short told him.

"Fine," said Putney. "You go take some air. Find Ed Hoy and y'all come back here. I think I may have something that will help. Bring a bucket of beer when you return. That may take the edge off, at least for a bit."

188

Chapter Twenty-Seven

City Marshal William Rea was the first witness for the prosecution. McLaury asked him several questions about Reas's experience as a police officer in Fort Worth and how many years he had been city marshal. Rea had said he started with the city marshal's office in 1879 and was one of the first five deputy city marshals and that he had been elected in 1883 and held the office for a little over a year. When asked about the number of murder investigations he had participated in or led, he said dozens. He said he learned of the shootout between Putney and Blakely when a citizen ran to his office and told him. He also said he had arrived at the scene of the shooting within twenty minutes. "Marshal Rea," said McLaury, "I would like you to take a look at the blackboard." And he walked to a swiveling blackboard that had been moved into the courtroom the previous day. He spun the blackboard over to reveal a map showing the parallel streets of Main and Houston, an alley between the two off of Second Street which intersected the other two. "Marshal Rea," he asked does this drawing accurately depict the scene where Mister Blakely's body was found?"

"It does."

"Would you walk to the blackboard and place an X where the body was found?"

Rea did as he was asked and was about to return to the witness stand when McLaury stopped him. "Before you sit down, would you place a small circle near the X that would indicate where the head of the body was, so that we know how the body was laying?"

Rea did this and returned to the stand. "Marshal, I see that you placed the X inside the alley and that the circle is above the X indicating that the head was away from the alley entrance."

"That is correct."

And this accurately depicts the scene when you arrived?"

"It does."

"Was there anyone else there?"

"Several bystanders and gawkers. My deputy and I had to move them back."

"Then neither Nahum Putney nor Deidre O'Neill were at the scene."

"They were not."

"Did you find anything other than Mister Blakely's body?"

"Yes, I found two Schofield forty-five pistols in the street, along with a great deal of blood."

"Did you speak to any witnesses at the scene?"

"I did."

"And what did they have to say?"

Imogene stood, "Objection, your honor. Hearsay. If Mister McLaury wants to know what witnesses said, he should call them to the stand. In fact, several are on the witness list."

"Sustained."

"All right," continued McLaury, "Did you call for the coroner?"

"Yes."

"And how long was it before he arrived?"

"About half an hour."

"And he examined the body?"

"He did."

"Did he say anything about the position of the body?"

"Objection, your honor," said Imogene. "Doctor Cramer is on the witness list also. He can testify to what he saw."

"Your honor," said the prosecutor. "I believe the witness can testify to a conversation he had with a fellow official assisting in the investigation."

"Doctor Cramer can tell us what he said. Objection sustained," said Judge Beckham.

"All right let's try this. Marshal, how many murder investigations have you been involved with in your career as a law officer?"

"I'm not certain. Probably a few dozen."

"Then it would be fair to say that you are experienced and well-qualified to make certain judgments in such a case."

"I believe I am."

"Did you examine the body?"

"I looked at it."

"Was the body face up or face down?"

"Face down."

"What did you notice, if anything?

"I saw there was one bullet wound in the back."

"Did you see any wounds elsewhere on the body?"

"No. I didn't touch the body because I was waiting on the coroner?"

"And when the coroner arrived, did he touch or move the body?"

"He did. After his initial examination, he turned the body over."

"What did you observe then?"

"There was another bullet wound in Mister Blakely's lower abdomen."

"In your experience, what did that indicate to you?"

"What I think it showed was that Mister Blakely had been shot in the lower abdomen first. The force of the bullet spun him around and the second bullet struck him in the back."

"Now, without saying who told you what, during your investigation, did you come to any conclusions?"

"Yes. I concluded that Mister Blakely fired one shot at Deputy United States Marshal Nahum Putney, striking him in the chest and that Mister Putney had fired at Mister Blakely once, hitting him just below the stomach area."

"Then what happened after that?"

"Miss O'Neill picked up a Schofield that Mister Putney dropped and fired it five times in the direction of Mister Blakely."

"I just want to make sure I have the sequence of events right, according to your investigation," Said McLaury. "What I understand is that Mister Blakely fired at Nahum Putney, hitting him once. Then Mister Putney returned fire hitting Mister Blakely once, which, in your opinion, spun Mister Blakely around. Then Miss O'Neill picked up a pistol and fired five times in Mister Blakely's direction after his back was turned. Is that right?"

"If I could make one correction?"

"Go ahead, Marshal."

"I don't know how many times Blakely fired. Witnesses said there were several shots fired from his direction."

"Does it make a difference in what we are trying to get at today?"

"Not really except it tells me Ned Blakely was a terrible shot."

This comment brought giggles and snickers from the gallery and the judge banged his gavel once and the laughing stopped.

"Be that as it may, if Mister Blakely's back was turned, is it possible Miss O'Neill was acting in self-defense?"

"I don't see how. He wasn't shooting anymore, and he couldn't have been shooting at her if he had?"

"Thank you, Marshal, that's all I have for the present."

Judge Beckham indicated it was Imogene's turn.

"Marshal," Imogene began. "The scenario you and the prosecutor just laid out is actually conjecture, I mean you didn't personally see this happen the way you said, correct?"

"No, but..."

Imogene cut him off. "You said you spoke with several witnesses. Did any of these witnesses say they saw Miss O'Neil strike Ned Blakely when she was firing in his direction?"

"No, but..."

Again, Imogene stopped his response. "As the officer investigating this event, did you look to see if you could find any of the bullets Miss O'Neill allegedly fired?"

"I didn't see the need. There were only two bullets that mattered, and they were in Blakely's body."

"I see. So, by the same token, you didn't see any sense in looking for bullets that Mister Blakely or anybody else may have fired."

"No, I did not."

"Where, if you know, were Mister Putney and Miss O'Neill when you arrived?"

"When I got there, I didn't know where they were."

"But you did find out later, didn't you?"

"Yes."

"Well?"

"They were at the Railway Hospital."

"Did you ever ask the doctor at the hospital for the bullet that struck Mister Putney?"

"No."

"So, all in all, a very thorough investigation, I see."

This had McLaury standing, "Objection your honor. Miss Foster Can't be making off-handed, sarcastic remarks toward a witness."

192

"Judge Beckham looked at Imogene over his glasses. "You know better Miss Foster. Or at least you should. Objection sustained. Miss Foster's remark will be stricken from the record and the jury will disregard her statement."

"I apologize to the court, your honor. I have no further questions for the Marshal."

"Marshal, you may step down," said the judge. "Mister McLaury, call your next witness."

"I call Doctor Reginald Cramer." The coroner took the stand, was sworn in, and gave his name and his occupation before McLaury began his questioning.

"Doctor Cramer," said McLaury. "How long have you been coroner for Tarrant County?"

"Fifteen years," said Cramer.

"And before that, did you practice what I will call regular medicine?"

"I did."

"Can you tell us where and when?"

"After the war, I moved here to Fort Worth, in 1866 and I began practicing medicine."

"During that time did you have occasion to treat gunshot wounds?"

"Oh, yes. In the early days after the war, this was a mighty rough place. Mighty rough. There were plenty of gunshot and stabbing wounds that needed mending. Or people that needed burying."

"I see. And once you became coroner you have examined numerous gunshot wounds of deceased people."

"Oh, Lord yes. When all those drovers started coming through with the cow herds, shootings were a common event. Then once the railroad came in, it got even busier."

"Thank you, doctor. I would now like to ask you about your time during the war. Were you active during the war?"

"Oh yes. I was a surgeon under General Lee's command."

"That is a battlefield surgeon?"

"Yes, sir."

"And as such I suppose you saw many gunshot wounds?"

"More than I could count."

McLaury turned to the judge. "Your honor, in light of Doctor Cramer's extensive experience with gunshot wounds, I request he be recognized as an expert."

"What say you, Miss Foster," asked the judge.

"No objection, your honor." She said.

"Doctor," said McLaury, "Did you have the opportunity to conduct an investigation at a shooting on Second Street, between Houston and Main?"

"Yes, I did." The doctor replied.

"When you arrived at that location, what did you see?"

"I saw a man lying face down in an alley."

"And did you examine this man?"

"Yes, I did."

"Let me direct your attention to the blackboard. Is this an accurate depiction of the scene?"

"As far as I can tell. It appears there is an X marked in the approximate location of the body."

"I see. If X is the body where would the head be?"

"Again, there is a small circle over the X and that would be where the head was."

"So, the head was toward the alley and the feet would then be pointing toward Second Street?"

"That is correct."

"We will come back to that in a moment. Now, upon examining the body what did you see?"

"I noticed there was what appeared to be a large caliber bullet hole in the back."

"Could you tell what caliber bullet hole it was?"

"No, not until later examination."

"Then what did you do?"

"I rolled the body over and saw there was another large caliber bullet hole in the lower abdomen."

"And could you tell what caliber that hole was?"

"Not at that time."

"Did you form an opinion of what may have happened at the scene?"

"Yes, it appeared that the man had been shot first in the lower abdomen and then in the back?"

"How did you come to that conclusion?"

"Well, if the man had been shot in the back first, he would have fallen face down with his head facing the street, not the alley."

"Then what about the wound in the front?"

"In my opinion, it would have been very difficult for a man to be shot in the back first and then in the front unless there were two assailants."

"So, what, then, was your final conclusion?"

"I concluded that the man had most probably been shot in the front. Where the wound was, it probably would have caused the man's hip and knee to collapse, sort of turning him around, then he was shot in the back, causing him to fall face down with his head facing the alley."

"Now, doctor, I would like to show you a document I have marked as Prosecution Exhibit 1. May I approach your honor?"

"You may," said the judge.

McLaury walked to the witness stand and handed the doctor the paper. "Doctor, do you recognize this document?"

"Yes, I do."

"And is that your signature at the bottom?"

"It is."

"Doctor, would you tell the jury what this document is?"

Facing the jury Doctor Cramer said, "This is a report of the autopsy I performed on the body in the alley. A man I later learned had been identified as Ned Blakely."

"Thank you. In that report did you come to a conclusion about the wound received in the front and about its lethality?"

"Yes, That wound entered the abdomen in a downward path and lodged against the hip. The only way that wound would have been lethal would have been if Mister Blakely had not received treatment. Then he may have eventually bled to death."

"Were you able to determine the caliber of the bullet?"

"Yes. Let me look at the report. Yes, it was a forty-four or forty-five caliber bullet."

"Again, look at the report and tell us about the second wound."

"That wound was different."

"How so?"

"It was lethal. The bullet passed in an almost straight line directly hitting the heart where it lodged. It is definitely the bullet that killed Mister Blakely."

"What caliber bullet does your report say that bullet was?"

Looking down at the report, the doctor replied, "That bullet was also either a forty-four or forty-five caliber bullet."

"Doctor, do you happen to know what caliber bullet is fired from a Smith and Wesson Schofield pistol?"

"I do. That particular weapon uses a forty-five caliber bullet."

"Thank you. Doctor I would now like to show you what I have marked as Prosecution Exhibit 2. May I approach, your honor?"

Judge Beckham signaled that McLaury could approach the witness.

"Would you describe this to the jury?"

"It is a manilla envelope."

"Do you recognize the envelope?"

"Yes, it is the sort I use to place bullets in when I have retrieved them from a body."

"Do you recognize this envelope specifically?"

"I do."

"How?"

"I have written the name Ned Blakely on it and placed the date."

"Anything else?"

"Yes, on the flap of the envelope are my initials."

"Are there other markings on the envelope?"

"Yes. The initials of Deputy Sheriff Hubert Forsythe."

"Why are Deputy Forsythe's initials on the envelope?"

"It is my practice to place the evidence in the envelope in front of a witness. I then write my initials, and have the witness write theirs."

"And why do you do that?"

"To ensure the integrity of the evidence."

"Thank you. Would you please open the envelope and tell the jury what is inside?"

The doctor opened the envelope. He poured the contents into his hand and said, "There are two forty-four or forty-five caliber bullets."

"Can you tell us which?"

"I think the second bullet would have to be a smaller caliber than the first. If they were the same caliber the power of the first bullet would already begin slowing and the power of the second bullet would overcome the first causing him to fall forward, instead of the direction he did fall."

"So," Imogene could hardly control her enthusiasm, "If I understand you correctly if the first bullet was say a forty-five and if the second bullet hit a fraction of a second later, but was a thirty-eight, the second bullet wouldn't overpower the first and the body could have possibly fallen the way it did, as you indicated?"

"Yes, you understood me correctly."

"Thank you, doctor. Your honor, I have no further questions for this witness."

McLaury leapt to his feet again, "Redirect your honor."

"Go ahead," allowed the judge.

"Doctor, everything that Miss Foster asked you is merely conjecture, am I right?"

"Yes."

"And you stand by the testimony that you gave under direct, that being both bullets were forty-four or forty-five calibers?"

"I do."

"Thank you. That is all your honor."

"Doctor Cramer, you may step down," Judge Beckham said. I see it is just past eleven. Mister McLaury, how many more witnesses do you have?"

McLaury consulted his witness list. "Six, your honor."

"Is there a witness that would be brief enough that we wouldn't go past noon?"

"Yes, your honor, I believe Sheriff Maddox's testimony will be brief."

"Very good then, call Sheriff Maddox."

Maddox entered the courtroom and approached the witness stand. He found it eerie to be in the position of not knowing what had transpired before him. He thought that Doctor Cramer had been on the stand longer than expected and it worried him. After being sworn Maddox took the stand, stated his name and occupation, then McLaury began.

"Sheriff, I told the judge that we will be brief, and I certainly expect it to be so."

"Okay."

"Sheriff, am I correct that the sheriff's office is the custodian of all evidence in criminal trials?"

"That is right."

"If I may approach, your honor?"

"You may," said the judge.

Handing the envelope to Maddox, McLaury said, "Sheriff, I am handing you an envelope marked as Prosecution Exhibit 2. Do you recognize it?"

"Yes, it is the envelope that was picked up by Deputy Hubert Forsythe from the coroner and brought to my office for safekeeping until the trial."

"Thank you. Be careful not to spill the contents but look at the writing on the envelope and describe it, please."

"It says Ned Blakely and has a date."

"How about on the flap of the envelope?"

"Well, there are to be two sets of initials."

"Do you recognize those initials?"

"The first one I recognize as Doctor Cramer's The second are those of Deputy Forsythe."

"Do you trust Deputy Forsythe? Is he an honest man?"

"Yes, I believe so."

"Evidence of this nature, do you just leave it lying around the office where anybody could touch it, move it, tamper with it?"

"Certainly not. We keep it in a locked cabinet inside our walk-in safe."

"Who has access to that cabinet?"

"Well during the day, we leave the safe open so we can get stuff we may need. But there are only three people who have a key to the cabinet. That would be me, my chief deputy, and the chief clerk."

"And that is all."

"Yes, sir," Maddox was emphatic.

"Thank you, Sheriff, that's all I have."

"Miss Foster," said the judge.

"Sheriff, even though the cabinet is locked, it sounds like anybody could have access to it. I mean they could touch it, lean up against it, stump a toe on it."

"Well, that may be, but they don't have a key to it."

"Do you keep a log of when the cabinet is accessed, by whom, and when?"

"Yes."

"Why do suppose the prosecution did enter that log into evidence?"

"I don't know you would have to ask him."

"Is there a possibility that the log hasn't been kept up to date and that's the reason he didn't want the court to see it?"

"No, I don't think so?"

"You don't think so what, that it is not possible the log isn't up to date or that the prosecutor had his doubts it would be up to date?"

"The log is up to date. I'm certain of it."

"Your honor," Imogene addressed the judge. "I find it odd that Mister McLaury would call the sheriff to testify as to the security of the evidence cabinet, but not provide it in court to be examined. I request that you order Sheriff Maddox to produce the log and I request that I have an opportunity to review it before I question Sheriff Maddox further."

The judge rubbed his chin, "Mister McLaury, do you have any thoughts on Miss Foster's request?"

"I do, your honor, but I request a sidebar so it can be discussed."

"Very well, the attorneys may approach." Both Imogene and McLaury came to the side of the judge's bench that was farthest from the jury, so the discussion couldn't be overheard. "Go ahead, Mister McLaury."

"Judge this is another of Miss Foster's tactics to confuse the jury. The sheriff has already testified to the security of the cabinet and there is no reason to disbelieve him."

"Miss Foster?" said the judge.

"Your honor, I don't see what all the huff is about. If the log is accurate and up to date, there should be no problem and I would gladly give up my lunch time so I can review the log. That way it won't take any of the court's precious time."

"This is outlandish judge," McLaury was livid. "There is no way I'm going to let her review that log without me present, especially over lunch."

"Your honor, Elizabeth who works at O'Neill's Restaurant has brought a basket with very good sandwiches and I believe iced tea. She always prepares too much, and I am certain there is plenty for Mister McLaury and he is welcome to join me at my table, have a bite, and review the log with me."

"It is settled then. Y'all may step back." The two lawyers returned to their respective tables. Imogene gave Deidre and Mary a wink. McLaury was beating his fist into the side of his leg. Judge Beckham addressed Sheriff Maddox. "Sheriff, I am going to recess in a moment and when I do, I want you to go to your office, retrieve the log in question, and return here as quickly as possible. You are to give the log to Mister McLaury, but only in the presence of Miss Foster. We will address the log when we return from lunch."

Before the judge could lower his gavel Sheriff Maddox asked, "Judge can I stay with them while they review the log?"

"No, you may not. We stand at recess. Court will reconvene at one o'clock.

Chapter Twenty-Eight

A clerk answered the knocking at the door of Judge Beckham's chambers to find Imogene and McLaury standing together. "The judge is eating. May I help you?

"Yes," McLaury said. "Miss Foster and I have reached an agreement, but we need to discuss it with the judge before we can go further."

"Let them in, Harry," the judge called to his assistant. "If these two have agreed to anything it will be a pleasure to hear them out."

Harry was peeved, but he waved them to a long conference table where the judge was eating. It was obvious what upset Harry. His meal sat on the table uneaten. Judge Beckham gestured for Imogene and McLaury to sit. "What do you have?"

"Miss Foster, would you like to begin," asked McLaury.

"Thank you," Imogene said. "Judge the log is full of discrepancies which, if nothing else shows sloppy record keeping."

"She is correct, Judge, but the entries for the evidence in this case appear to be accurate and untampered with," said McLaury.

Imogene broke in, "The problem is that the way the log was kept, in my opinion, is a sign that evidence could have been handled and simply not logged. Honestly, it borders on criminality."

"Do you agree Mister McLaury?" asked Judge Beckham.

"Unfortunately, I do Judge."

"Then what is the remedy?" the judge asked.

"We have agreed that an instruction to the jury, from you, could be stated so that neither case is prejudiced, and the jury can give it the weight they see fit," "said McLaury.

"I see," said the judge. "I will give it some thought and will make an announcement in court. I want to thank you each for your diligence."

It was fifteen minutes until court resumed when Imogene found Deidre and told her to come to the courtroom because they had something to discuss. At the table, Imogene explained what she and McLaury had found and the agreement they had taken to the judge. She told Deidre, "I have to know whether or not you agree. If you don't, I will have to let the judge know, before we proceed."

"If the log isn't correct, why wouldn't you push the point?" asked Deidre.

"Because there is no sign that the log isn't correct as far as the evidence in this case is concerned," Imogene insisted. "If I push it McLaury will ask the judge to instruct the jury that, as far as our case goes, the log is correct and that will be the end to it. If we let the log be entered without commentary, the jury can see the whole log and they can make up their own mind. It is a risk, but it is better than the alternative."

"You've done well up to now, so I think I will trust your judgment. But next time let me know, before you make a deal."

"You're right," Imogene agreed. "I just didn't know if we would have time enough to talk to the judge. I'm sorry."

"If it works, you won't have to be sorry."

After court opened in the afternoon, the judge called the attorneys to the bench. "Miss Foster," he said, "Have you discussed with your client what you, Mister McLaury and I spoke about?"

"I have, your honor and she is in agreement."

The judge continued, "It seems to me that since you brought up the issue of the evidence log, it should be you that enters the logbook into evidence. However, you should know that I will be instructing the jury that they can only consider the entries that are pertinent to this case. Do you understand?"

"I do your honor," the disappointment showing on her face.

"Knowing that, are you willing to proceed on this course?"

Imogene gave it some thought and then said, "I am."

Speaking to the prosecutor, the judge said, "Are you in agreement, Mister McLaury?"

McLaury gave a broad grin and said, "Certainly, your honor."

"Don't gloat, Mister McLaury, or I may change my mind."

"Of course not, your honor," McLaury's expression became sober.

"Very well, Miss Foster, The sheriff is still your witness. You may both step back."

Both of the attorneys returned to their tables and Maddox was called to return to the stand. Imogene held the logbook in her hand and asked the judge for permission to approach the witness, which was granted.

"Sheriff," she said, "I have a ledger here that I would like for you to examine." Maddox gave a cursory look at the logbook, then Imogene asked, "Sheriff, is this the ledger that your office uses to log in all evidence and transactions concerning evidence?"

"It is," he answered.

"And as far as you know it is accurate in every respect?"

"Objection your honor," said McLaury. "That question is outside the bound you just instructed Miss Foster."

"Objection sustained. Nice try, Miss Foster, but stick to my instructions."

"Certainly, your honor, I apologize."

The judge asked, "Do you have more questions for the sheriff?"

"No, your honor, I only want to offer this logbook as Defense Exhibit 1."

"Without objection, so entered," said the judge. He then addressed the jury. "Gentlemen, I am allowing entry of this evidence, but I must instruct you that you may only consider such entries as concern this case. Entries from other cases are not the concern of this court and you should not consider them. I will reiterate this instruction before you receive the case for your deliberations. Mister McLaury call your next witness."

McLaury called two men to testify to what they had seen and heard at the time of the shooting. Their testimonies were similar and straightforward. They were on Second Street when they heard gunshots. They turned to see Putney fall in the street and Deidre O'Neill pick up the gun Putney dropped and shot several times in the direction of a man who was falling face down in the alley. When they were cross-examined by Imogene, they both admitted that things happened quickly and neither saw Deidre's shots hit the man in the alley.

The third witness McLaury called was Quanah Parker. Parker said he had been on Second Street when he recognized Putney. He was walking toward Putney to greet him when a man stepped from the shadows of the alley and shot Putney, Parker said Putney had pulled a pistol and shot the man, then fell to his knees. He said at that time Deidre picked up the gun Putney had dropped and started shooting at the man in the alley. He said from his point of view it looked like Deidre may have hit Blakely, but he couldn't be absolute. Parker then told how he had commandeered a wagon and drove Putney to the Railway Hospital. McLaury then passed the witness to Imogene.

Imogene stood at the podium looking down, trying to bring up the courage to face her one-time captor. After a long pause, Judge Beckham said, "Miss Foster, do you have any questions for this witness?"

Pulled out of her trance Imogene managed to say, "Yes, judge I do, but may I have a moment?"

"Be quick," the judge said.

Imogene returned to the table and huddled with Deidre and Mary. "I don't know if I can do this," she said. "My knees are literally trembling."

Deidre reached out and touched Imogene's hand. "We talked about this, dear," Deidre consoled her lawyer. "It is important. Just as you said, because he is famous, his testimony is going to mean more than the other eyewitnesses."

Mary went a different route. "I've been with you daily for three weeks, Imogene. I know you have the strength for it."

"Miss Foster," said the judge. "May we continue?

Imogene gave herself a shake, straightened, and said, "Yes, your honor." She walked to the podium and began. "I don't know whether to call you Mister Parker or Quanah."

"Whichever you think is right. It will be fine with me," said the tall Comanche.

"Mister Parker will do," Judge Beckham instructed her.

"Yes, Judge," obeyed Imogene. "Mister Parker, we have met before, have we not?"

"We knew each other many years ago."

"Objection, your honor," McLaury said, standing. "I don't see what Mister Parker and Miss Foster's relationship has to do with this case."

"Miss Foster?" said the judge.

"If the court will allow, my line of questioning should bring out the motive behind Mister Parker's testimony."

"I will allow it, but if you don't make your point, I will strike it from the record."

"Thank you, your honor. Mister Parker, how was it we met those many years ago?"

"You were a guest in the camp of Chief Big Looking Glass."

"By guest, don't you mean captive?"

"Those were different times Miss Foster."

"While I was detained in your camp, did there come a time when you met a man named Nahum Putney?"

"These are strange questions for me. You know that I knew Nahum Putney."

"I know, Mister Parker, but the jury does not. Would you please answer the question?"

"Yes, I knew Nahum Putney."

"How did you meet him?"

"He was a warrior against the Comanche, and I captured him."

"What was your intent should happen to Mister Putney?"

"I took him to Big Looking Glass and the council to decide."

"And what did they decide?"

"They decided to free him and you."

"But that wasn't your desired outcome, was it?"

"I obeyed my elders," Parker was trying to hedge his answer.

"That wasn't what I asked. Let me ask it differently. If it had been your decision, what would have happened to Mister Putney?"

Parker stirred in his seat. He knew the answer she was looking for, but he knew it wouldn't set well with the white men on the jury. His hesitation gave McLaury another chance.

"Your honor, I just don't see how this can get us to the matter at hand and I renew my objection."

Parker's lack of responsiveness and McLaury's objection strengthened Imogene. "Your honor, I am trying to get the witness to be specific with his answers so I can bring this to an end. If you allow me a few more questions and direct the witness to answer

207

directly instead of trying to obfuscate we will get to the crux of it quickly, I promise."

"Very well," said the judge. "But I'm not going to let this drag on forever. Mister McLaury your objection is overruled for the moment. Mister Parker, please answer Miss Foster's questions as directly as possible."

Imogene restarted. "Let me ask this so you can give just a yes or no answer. Wasn't it your desire to see Nahum Putney put to death?"

Any chance of delaying a direct answer gone, Parker straightened himself and looked at the jury with all the pride of a war chief. "Yes, that was my desire."

"But Big Looking Glass did not allow that?"

"He did not."

"What did he decide?"

"He decided to free Putney in trade for information against the Gray Army."

"And that was not all, was it?"

"No. Big Looking Glass allowed Putney to take you with him."

"And what were your intentions toward me?"

"Putney was the best warrior the Gray's had. Capturing him was a triumph. I had hoped Big Looking Glass would give you to me as a bride."

"You wanted me as a bride? Do you know how old I was at the time?"

"I doubt you had yet bled."

This time McLaury jumped from his seat. "Your honor," he pled, "Surely this is beyond the pale?"

"I'm not sure I disagree, Miss Foster," Judge Beckham was shocked at the witness's answer.

"I fully understand your honor, but I beg just a few more questions and all will be clear."

"It better or I will be striking all this testimony."

"So, Mister Parker, you failed in having Nahum Putney executed and you failed in receiving me, a twelve-year-old girl as your wife, and that made you angry."

"Yes."

"And you swore revenge, did you not."

"Not exactly."

"Well then, what, exactly."

"I said we would meet again, and I would hold Nahum Putney's life in my hand."

"And by that, you meant you would kill him?"

"It was more of a prophecy."

"But you failed in killing him because he is still alive today."

"I could have let him die."

Imogene felt she was on fire. "That's not the question. You had failed in your revenge. And what better way to avenge your long-time enemy than giving testimony in a trial against a person he loves, with hopes of sending that person to prison for a long time, maybe the rest of her life? Sending Deidre O'Neill to prison?" Imogene snapped her arm out and pointed at Deidre to make her point.

"That was never my desire."

"Oh, wasn't it, Quanah Parker, Great War Chief?"

"Your honor," McLaury shouted.

"Miss Foster that was out of line," said Judge Beckham. "You had already made your point. Miss Foster's last remark will be stricken from the record, and it will be disregarded by the jury."

"I have no further questions," said Imogene and returned to the defense table exhausted.

McLaury tried to rehabilitate his witness, but the damage was done, and he knew it. What the jury would remember was that a hostile Comanche was seeking revenge on Putney, not to mention what would amount to rape of a child in the minds of the jury. It was a fruitless effort.

☒

Putney knew that McLaury would be calling Russell and Parker that day. He figured that the testimony of a well known figure such as Quanah Parker create a great deal of interest, so he had made a plan with Luke Short and Ed Hoy. Hoy would wait outside the courthouse and when Russell was called, Putney would go outside for a smoke. That would be Hoy's signal. Hoy would go back to the office and he and Short would sneak Doby to the O'Neill for a short visit with his mother. Putney had also arranged for Tommie Fogg to help. Fogg's job was to go ahead of the two deputies, checking out the way. As much as possible they would stick to the alleys and narrow passages between buildings and avoid the main streets.

By two o'clock they had gotten Doby to the back door of the hotel. The lunch rush being over, most of the staff was eating in the private dining room and it was a simple task to get Doby through the kitchen and to the back stairs with little notice. When Mrs. Stegall opened the door and saw her son she nearly fainted and Doby had to catch her. With Short and Hoy's help he managed to get his mother to a chair and sit her down. Emma Lou opened her eyes and seeing her son, again, began to cry.

"It's alright, Ma," Doby told her. "I'm here and I'm safe."

"Thank the mercies," cried Emma Lou. "I was worried sick about you. Where have you been? Where are you staying? And who are these men?"

"This is Mister Short and Mister Hoy. They're deputy marshals working for Mister Putney. They're helping me. I can't tell you where I'm staying, Ma. It's safer if you don't know. You just need to rest easy that I'm safe and everything is going to be alright."

"Lord have mercy, son, are these men going to take you to jail?"

"No, Ma. At least that's nothing you have to be troubled about right now. Mister Putney has helped me. I don't know how everything will shake out, but I ain't worried."

By now Emma Lou had gained her composure, she stood and thanked Hoy and Short for their help.

"We can't stay long, Missus Stegall," Short said. "Nahum wanted to make sure you knew your son was safe and being taken care of. Ed and me are going to wait just outside your door and give you and Clint some time alone, but we will need to leave in about ten minutes." Short wanted this to be over and get Doby back to Putney's office before the streets got busy. After giving the two some time, Short knocked on the door and said, "Clint. It's time to go."

Clint opened the door and he and Emma Lou stepped into the hall. Emma Lou hugged both Short and Hoy and kissed each on the cheek, thanking them again for looking after her son.

The three snuck out through the kitchen again and into the alley where Fogg was waiting. Fogg stayed ahead about a block's length and would signal when he thought it was safe. As they crossed through the alleys connecting Fourth Street, Hoy noticed a large man looking at them. He stopped the other two and whispered something in Short's ear.

"Let's see what he does. We will quit following Tommie. If it looks like the guy is following us, I have an idea."

Chapter Twenty-Nine

The next witness McLaury called was Montague Russell. Since
Russell had refused to be interviewed by Imogene, she had no idea
as to what he would testify, but she had no grounds to object.
Russell was wearing a new suit, and his boots were buffed, but he
still did not have the polish of the once-proud Confederate Army
captain. Russell was sworn in and asked to give his name and
employment.

"Captain Montague Russell. I am employed by the TIC
Commercial Detective Agency," said Russell.

"Objection your honor," said Imogene.

"Yes, Miss Foster?" asked the judge.

"I object to his use of the title of captain. Mister Russell is not
a captain of anything and to my knowledge hasn't been in nearly
twenty years. His use of that title denotes some sort of authority
not given to other men."

McLaury started to speak but the judge motioned for him to
stay silent. "Miss Foster it is a well-established tradition,
especially here in Texas that a title once earned by a man stays
with him unless he is stripped of the title beforehand. Objection
overruled."

McLaury began by emphasizing the title. "Captain Russell, do
you know a man named Nahum Putney?"

"I do," replied Russell.

McLaury wanted to make a point, "And when I say know him,
I mean personally, not just by reputation."

"I know Mister Putney."

"Good, then would you tell the court how you know Mister
Putney?"

"Objection your honor," Imogene stood again.

"What, now, Miss Foster?" asked the judge.

"Since we are using Captain Russell's former title, I think it is
only appropriate to refer to Nahum Putney by his current title.
Deputy Marshal."

"Approach," said the judge. The attorneys huddled at the judge's bench. "Miss Foster, are you deliberately trying to aggravate this court?"

"No, your honor."

"Then I suggest you keep your objections to matters of law, not social niceties."

"But your honor, titles infer authority and I think it only fair…."

Judge Beckham cut her off, "Did you not understand what I just said?"

"I understand your honor."

"Then return to your table. Mister McLaury, you may continue."

McLaury thanked the judge. "Now Captain," again McLaury emphasized the title and Imogene knew it was only to twist the knife. "How do you know Mister Putney."

"I first knew him as a soldier under my command."

"Was Mister Putney a good soldier?"

"To a point."

"What do you mean by that?"

"Putney was a good Indian fighter and probably the best scout the Mounted Mountain Rangers ever had. But he often had problems with authority."

"How is that?"

"He would sometimes question my orders and he had a particular dislike of two soldiers I recruited, late in the war."

"Let's skip to the end of the war. Did you have an issue with Mister Putney at that time?"

"Yes, I did."

"Please tell the court what that problem was."

"He deserted."

"Deserted?" McLaury feigned credulity. "That is a serious charge. Was there a witness to this desertion?

"Ned Blakely."

"The same Ned Blakely left dead in the streets of Fort Worth?"

"The same."

"I see. And when was the next time you met Nahum Putney?"

"About five years later, in Llano, Texas."

"What were you doing in Llano, at the time?"

"Land speculation."

"Did Mister Putney do anything of note in Llano that you are aware of?"

"Yes, he murdered two men employed by me and murdered two members of a posse sent to capture him."

This time Imogene could not contain herself. She leapt from the table and nearly hollered, "Objection your honor."

"Yes, Miss Foster?" the judge asked.

"Captain," she spat the word as if she had been eating scorpions. "Captain Russell knows full well that grand juries in both Llano and Gillespie counties failed to indict Deputy Marshal Putney of those claims and that he was fully exonerated."

This time Judge Beckham addressed Russell, "Captain Russell, are you aware of this?"

"Well, yes judge."

"Then what possessed you to slander Deputy Putney in this manner," the judge waved off Russell before he could answer, then addressed McLaury, "Mister McLaury, I hope for your sake that you did not know this witness would knowingly say a thing of this nature."

McLaury stammered, "I did not, your honor."

"It is obvious to me that your witness made this statement in hopes of negatively influencing the jury and I suggest you take a moment to speak with your witness and make clear to him that if he says anything like it again, I will strike his entire testimony and I will instruct the jury to disregard anything this witness has to say. As it is I will have his comment stricken and the jury may not give any consideration to it. We will recess for five minutes while you instruct your witness," the sound of Judge Beckham's gavel was like the crack of a rifle shot.

McLaury began questioning Rusell again with, "Captain Russell you understand the judge's ruling about your testimony, don't you?"

"I do."

"And we shan't have any such repetition, will we?"

"We shall not."

"Thank you."

"Now, during the war, it was your responsibility to protect people from marauding Indians, wasn't it?"

"It was."

"And in the course of your duties did you encounter hostiles?"

"We did."

"I guess the resulted in battles."

"It did."

"Did Mister Putney participate in these battles?"

"He did."

"Was Mister Putney proficient in these battles?"

"He was, without a doubt, the best combatant in my company."

"He was, in fact, feared by the enemy."

"He was."

"How do you know this?"

"I later learned that the Comanche and the Kiowas had given him a nickname."

"And that was?"

"I don't know how to say it in their language, but I know it translated to Red Panther."

"And why do you suppose they dubbed him so?"

"He often fought alone and often from ambush."

"Would you say Mister Putney was proficient at killing the enemy?"

"Yes."

"Did Mister Putney ever express a particular enmity toward the enemy?"

"Yes, he hated the Comanche, in particular."

"Do you know the reason for this?"

"Yes, the Comanche killed his parents and sisters when he was young."

"Would you say he was vengeful toward the Comanche?"

"Objection, your honor, the question calls for the witness to come to a conclusion," said Imogene.

"Lay a foundation, Mister McLaury," the judge instructed.

"Captain, was part of your duties to counsel with those under your command?"

"It was."

"Did you counsel with all the men under your command?"

215

"At one time or another, yes."

"That means you counseled with Mister Putney?"

"Several times."

"Did he ever tell you he desired retribution against Indians?"

"From the very start, he told me he joined the Rangers in revenge for the deaths of his family."

"Did he ever repeat this desire for vengeance?"

"On many occasions."

"Was Mister Blakely aware of Mister Putney's vengeful attitude?"

Imogene was about to say something again but decided that her continued objections could put the jury off.

"He was."

"Did it worry Mister Blakely?"

"He was afraid of Mister Putney."

"How do you know he was afraid of Mister Putney?"

Imogene couldn't stop herself. Objection your honor. Dead man's rule."

"You should be aware that the dead man's rule only applies in civil cases, Miss Foster," the judge admonished her, then addressing the jury, "Gentlemen, the dead man's rule is a portion of the law that says a person cannot testify as to what a deceased person said, but it only applies in a civil trial. This is a criminal trial, and the rule does not apply. Continue Mister McLaury."

"You may answer, Captain."

"The night before the shooting, Mister Blakely told me he had seen Mister Putney in town, and he was worried that Mister Putney was here to find him."

"Why would he have thought that?"

"He told me he had tried to get Miss O'Neill to pay for a service where he would provide security for her business. Mister Blakely feared that Miss O'Neill had told Mister Putney that he, Mister Blakely, was trying to extort Miss O'Neill."

"And that caused him concern?"

"It did. He told me he thought Mister Putney was here to gun him down."

"Did he say he was going to address this fear with Mister Putney?"

"He did. He told me he had seen Mister Putney and Miss O'Neill walking around town and he decided he wanted to talk with Mister Putney."

"Why would he do such a thing if he was afraid of Mister Putney?"

"He told me he was going to approach Mister Putney in the daylight, while he was with Miss O'Neill and there were plenty of witnesses around. He didn't think Mister Putney would shoot him down under those circumstances."

"So, in your opinion, it was never Mister Blakely's intention to confront Mister Putney by using deadly force?"

"I don't believe so."

"So, what do you think happened when Mister Blakely approached Mister Putney?"

"Objection, your honor," Imogene couldn't let this pass. "Mister Russell has no idea what happened on the street that day."

"You are correct, Miss Foster," Judge Beckham finally agreed with her. "Objection sustained. Captain Russell, you will not answer that question. Mister McLaury?"

"I have no further questions for this witness."

"Miss Foster, it is your turn," said the judge.

During the direct examination, both Deidre and Mary had been furiously writing notes and passing them to Imogene. But Imogene had been too focused on Russell's testimony to pay the necessary attention to the notes. "Judge," she said. "May I have a couple of minutes to confer with my client and assistant?"

"Please keep it short, Miss Foster," he said.

Deidre and Mary started whispering to Imogene at once and Imogene told them one at a time and started with Deidre. "Nahum didn't desert," she said. "Lee had already surrendered and Russell, the bastard, knew that. He was intending to rob a Union gold shipment."

"Yes, I know all that," said Imogene.

"Well, it wasn't Blakely that was trying to extort me, it was Courtwright. Blakely would just stand around outside, trying to intimidate me. A couple of times he roughed up some waiters, but I never spoke with him."

"Alright. Mary?" asked Imogene.

"Two things, Putney put Russell in prison over the Ku Klux Klan Act and Russell had been working for Soapy Smith."

"Alright. I think I know what you both are saying, and I think we can tear down his testimony. If I run into trouble I will come back here for suggestions."

Both of the other women agreed. "I'm ready now your honor."

"Proceed," said the judge.

It was now Imogene's turn to make a point about Russell's title. "Mister Russell," she purposefully stressed the word mister. "Let's start with Mister Putney's service while in the Mounted Mountain Rangers." She deliberately didn't say anything about being under Russell's command. "You said Mister Putney was proficient in his duties, didn't you?"

"To a point."

"He was proficient enough that he was promoted to Corporal, is that not true?"

"It is true."

"And it is true that he was so proficient at scouting that he scouted for the Rangers, almost to the exclusion of anyone else."

"He was good at that job."

"You also said he was a good combatant?"

"I did."

"In combat, did Corporal Putney ever wound or kill anyone that wasn't already trying to kill him or another one of the soldiers?"

"It was combat, so yes."

"But in your testimony, didn't you infer that Corporal Putney was just a killing machine?"

"I didn't say that."

"But you did say he was vengeful?"

"I did."

"Were the Rangers mostly successful in their engagements with hostile tribes?"

"I'm proud to say we were."

"After a battle, did any of the troops ever take scalps or otherwise disfigure dead Indians?"

"Some did."

"Did Corporal Putney ever scalp or disfigure anyone?"

"Not that I ever saw."

218

"Wouldn't a vengeful man make the most of the opportunity to scalp these enemies?"

"I can't say."

"Fine, now let's talk about Mister Blakely. He wasn't a regular soldier, was he?"

"I don't know what you mean by regular soldier."

"I mean Mister Blakely was a Missouri Bushwhacker that fought with the likes of Bloody Bill Anderson and William Quantrill."

"If that is your definition, then yes Blakely was an irregular soldier."

"Did Mister Blakely participate in the raid on Lawrence, Kansas where civilians were massacred by bushwhackers?

"I don't know if he did or not."

"But he could have?"

"Objection," said McLaury. "The witness already testified that he didn't know."

"Sustained," said the judge.

"What was the name of Mister Blakely's commander?"

"Captain Tidwell."

"Did Captain Tidwell trust Mister Blakely and expect him to follow orders."

"Captain Tidwell was a demanding but good officer."

"I'll take that as a yes."

"Let's talk now about the supposed desertion of Corporal Putney. Before that, did you give Corporal Putney and Mister Blakely a specific mission?

"What was that mission?"

"They were to scout out a for a troop of Union soldiers."

Was it your plan, and Captain Tidwell to attack those soldiers?"

"It was."

"For what purpose?"

"They were supposed to be transporting a shipment of gold to New Mexico."

"But these soldiers weren't traveling alone, were they?"

"No, the cowards had imbedded themselves with a civilian wagon train."

"Was it possible that the Union troops were not only transporting gold, but they may have been providing protection to the convoy of settlers?"

"It's possible."

"Why would you order an attack on Union soldiers and civilians?"

"We weren't attacking the civilians, just the gold shipment which, by the way, is a legitimate military target."

"We will get to that in a minute."

"Did Mister Blakely have orders to murder Corporal Putney, if he didn't go along with the plan?"

"I gave no such order."

"Did Captain Tidwell?"

"I couldn't say."

"Whatever the case, Corporal Putney, at some point, made it evident that he was not going to follow orders to attack the wagon train, is that correct?"

"Yes, he got the drop on Blakey while Blakely was asleep. Took his clothes and weapons and left him to fend for himself."

"This was the moment which you say Corporal Putney deserted?"

"Yes."

"In your opinion is it desertion when a military unit is no longer functional?"

"I know what you're getting at and yes it was desertion."

"Isn't it true that you were aware that General Lee had surrendered some weeks before and that the war was over?"

"We were still under orders."

"Yes, let's talk about that. Weren't your orders only to continue patrolling against hostile Indians and that you were to cease any operations against Union forces?"

"Did Putney tell you that?"

"It doesn't matter who told me that. Is it a fact or not?"

Grudgingly Russell said, "Yes. The war was technically over."

"So, a raid on a gold shipment was not a legitimate military target and your real objective was to rob the gold shipment and keep the gold for yourself and Captain Tidwell?"

"We were acting as soldiers and doing what soldiers are supposed to do."

"But you were no longer soldiers, only place keepers until relieved by Union forces, at which time you were supposed to surrender."

"I guess it is a matter of opinion."

"Oh, come on Captain," Imogene was now ridiculing Russell. "You knew that General Lee had surrendered, and you were under orders not to engage Union troops? That is a yes or no question."

"Alright, then, yes," admitted Russell.

"And Putney knew this."

"Yes."

"So, any attack by troops led by you would have been illegal."

"If you say so," Russell didn't want to openly admit that Imogene had him over a barrel.

"No, Mister Russell, the law says so. But let's continue. You were trained in a prestigious military academy, correct?"

"Yes."

"Did they teach you that a soldier has no obligation to obey an illegal order?"

"They did."

"So, Corporal Putney was simply following his right to not obey an illegal order."

"You've made your point."

"Let's move on to something else," said Imogene. "You said that Mister Blakely was trying to get Miss O'Neill to pay him to provide security at her hotel and restaurant, is that correct?"

"That's what I said."

"But that's not true, is it? Mister Blakely worked for someone else who was trying to extort miss O'Neill?"

"Maybe."

"Mister Blakely never had any discussions with Miss O'Neill."

"I don't know if he did or didn't"

"Mister Blakely was just the bully boy to create security problems for Miss O'Neill?"

"I can't say."

"Can't or won't?"

"Your honor," said McLaury, "The witness already said he couldn't say."

"That's what he said, yes, Mister McLaury," Judge Beckham said. "Objection sustained. Continue Miss Foster."

"Mister Russell would it be fair to say you hold another grudge against Nahum Putney?"

"I'm not certain what you mean."

"Let me start another way, have you ever been in prison?"

"Objection your honor," said McLaury. "I don't see why it should make a difference whether or not Captain Russell has been in prison."

"Your honor, it makes every difference in the world," retorted Imogene. "It goes to his character and I expect to show he has a motive for testifying."

"You may continue Miss Foster," said the judge.

"Please answer the question," Imogene said to Russell.

Russell didn't like the question, but he answered anyway, "Yes, I have been in prison,"

"For what offense and for how long?"

"I was convicted of violating the Ku Klux Klan Act and conspiracy. I was sentenced to ten years."

"Who was the arresting officer in this case?"

Russell mumbled, "Putney."

"Would you please speak up?" said Imogene. "I'm not sure the jury heard you."

"Nahum Putney," Russell showed his contempt for Imogene.

"I would imagine that would give you a good reason to hold a grudge against Mister Putney, wouldn't it?"

"I haven't thought of it one way or another."

"You haven't?"

Russell spat out an emphatic, "No."

"I see, well let me ask you something else, have you ever heard the term shill?"

"I have."

"What is your understanding that word means?"

"It is somebody who helps a con man."

"Would you say a shill would be a dishonest man?"

"Probably."

"Have you ever heard of a man called Soapy Smith?"

"Yes."

"Would you call Soapy Smith a con man?"

"Some might?"

"But would you?"

"Probably."

"Did you ever shill for Soapy Smith?"

"No."

"Did you ever buy soap from Soapy Smith?"

"Yes."

"Did you ever win money in a packet of soap you bought from Soapy Smith?"

"Some."

"How much?"

"A little, I don't remember exactly."

"Did you ever see anyone else win money in a packet of soap?"

"I don't keep up with other people's doings."

"Do you consider yourself an honest man?"

"I do."

"So, you plan to rob a gold shipment. You go to prison for violating federal laws and you may have been a shill for Soapy Smith and you say you're an honest man?"

"I never said I was a shill for Soapy Smith and all I can say is, people change."

"Some people change, Mister Russell, but I don't think that applies to you. From the beginning, your testimony tried to paint Mister Putney as a hardened killer. You wrongly accused him of murder. You insinuated that Mister Putney's only purpose was revenge and by inference, Miss O'Neill was part of a plan to murder Blakely. You came here only to try to persuade the jury that Blakely was the victim. You should be ashamed of yourself."

"Your honor," shouted McLaury.

"Settle down, Mister McLaury. "Miss Foster, you have overstepped. It is up to the jury to decide the validity of a witness's testimony. You can save all your conjecture for your closing argument. Objection sustained. That last diatribe by Miss Foster will be stricken and the jury will disregard it. Miss Foster, you are on thin ice, and I suggest you control yourself, lest there be consequences."

Imogene knew it was time to show some contrition. "Yes, sir, your honor. I humbly apologize to the court."

"Do you have anything else?" the judge asked.

"No, your honor, I am finished with this witness," she was really thinking, *I finished this witness.*

"Mister McLaury, do you have anything further for this witness?"

McLaury was realizing how much he had underestimated Imogene Foster. He was going to have to start making some points or this trial was all but over and to question Russell further would be fatal. "No, your honor. The prosecution rests."

"You still have one more witness on your list. You don't wish to call Deputy Putney?"

McLaury still had an ace in the hole. If he released Putney the deputy would be able to resume contact with Foster. He couldn't afford that. "Your honor, I would like to reserve Mister Putney as a rebuttal witness."

"Fine," said the judge. "Miss Foster you may present your case tomorrow, for now, court is in recess."

Chapter Thirty

There was another small celebration in the private dining room at O'Neill's. When Deidre got back to the hotel after that day's court, she told the chef to cook a roast with all the trimmings. There was wine and beer, iced tea, and lemonade. Mary, Elizabeth, the twins, and Harry Morgan were there. Deidre had gone to get Imogene as she wanted it to be a surprise. When Deidre and Imogen walked in, Imogene was shocked. "What's all this?" she asked.

"We are celebrating how you kicked Russell's teeth in. It was great," Deidre told her.

"Well, I guess we did have a pretty good day," Imogene was a little embarrassed. "But you know there is more to come and McLaury may be doing the same to us tomorrow."

"That's not possible, Miss Imogene," said Elizabeth.

Brutus broke in, "I thought I was going to have to leave, being afraid I was going to bust out laughing."

"That's right," said Ceasar. "I think it was about the funniest thing since we locked the Gant brothers in a pantry." Then both he and Brutus broke out in uproarious laughter.

"You all calm down," said Mary, giggling a little herself. "Imogene is right, McLaury isn't stupid. There's no telling what he has up his sleeve."

They all sat down around a large circular table and began passing the food around. "Are we still going to follow the order we discussed?" asked Deidre.

"I see no reason to change. I just wish I knew what Clint Doby was going to say," said Imogene. "That has me worried."

"What about Putney," asked Harry.

"I don't think we should be too worried about him," said Deidre. "This isn't his first rodeo."

☒

Jim Courtwright and Bill Rea were having drinks in the office of The Commercial Detective Agency when Martin Caine entered.

"Have a drink, Martin," Courtwright told him. "I guess you heard about what happened in court today."

"Yep," said Caine. "Russell's been down at the Emerald spitting venom for the past hour. I got tired of hearing it, so I went and had dinner. I ran into Max, and he had some interesting news I thought you two might like to hear. I didn't know where you would be, so I tried here first."

"He's not still grousing about that horse and tack, is he?" asked Courtwright. "I paid him a fair price."

"No, I think he was pretty happy about that. He bought a big sorrel. I bet that horse is close to eighteen hands."

"Well, Max is a big man," said Rea. "He needs a big horse."

"Then what did he have to say?" asked Courtwright.

Caine smiled. "He said he knows where Putney is hiding Clint Doby."

Courtwright jumped up from the comfy chair he was sitting on, nearly spilling his drink. "What? How? Where?"

"He wouldn't tell me where," said Caine. "He said that anybody that wants to know that information is going to have to pay for it."

"Shit," said Rea. "I guess he ain't the dumb ox we all took him for."

"No," growled Courtwright. "What did he say?"

"He said he was just wandering around uptown while everyone was up at the courthouse, and he saw Jimmie Fogg slipping around. Didn't have his shoeshine gear or nothing." Caine told him. "So, he stepped back around a building corner, and watched a little and it looked like Jimmie was waving someone forward. Sure enough, it wasn't a minute when Luke Short and that fancy Indian stepped out of an alley and skittered across the street, with Clint between the two of them. Said Short and the Indian were armed to the tooth."

"Please tell me he followed them," said Courtwright.

"He said he did."

"And?"

"And he wouldn't say anything else, except he was thinking about asking Putney for money to keep quiet about what he saw."

Courtwright had walked over to the bar. He slammed his glass down on it and said, "You get back out there and get Max before he gets to Putney. Bring him here as soon as you find him."

When Putney left the courthouse, Ed Hoy was smoking his pipe, waiting for him. "How did things go?" Putney asked.

"Fine, just fine," said Hoy and he smiled.

"You look like you have something to say."

"Sort of," Hoy laughed.

Putney lit a cigarette and said, "Am I going to have to beat it out of you?"

"Reckon not," Hoy smiled. "We was taking Clint back to the office when Luke spotted a big man named Max Poe. You know him?"

"We've met."

"Luke said this Poe fella was looking shady so instead of following Jimmie, we took a detour. We kept an eye out for Poe and sure enough, he was tailing us."

"Please tell me you didn't go to the office."

"Nah. We ain't stupid. No, we ambled around a bit then headed toward the Acre."

"What?"

"That's what we did. Luke took us down an alley and we ended up in back of a saloon. Turns out it was the Trinity pool hall. Luke said he knew the owner, so I stayed in the back room while Luke went to talk to him. Luke came back and we sat around for about an hour. I guess curiosity finally got the best of Poe. He came in and asked the owner if he had seen Luke. The owner said he hadn't seen Luke in two weeks. Poe called him a liar and stomped out. We figured Poe would have come back around to watch the alley, so we slid out the front and went straight to the back of the White Elephant. Luke got a couple of the boys there to scout around for Poe. When they reported back nobody had seen him, we went to the office. Got back safe and sound."

It was Putney's turn to laugh. "Where do you think he is now?"

"Probably still in the alley behind the Trinity," They both laughed.

"Just in case someone is watching us, let's go to the Planter's House for dinner, then you can head on back to O'Neill's."

"Soon as I see you safe home."

Chapter Thirty-One

The first witness Imogene called was Doctor Thomas McLeod, the Dallas County Coroner. "Doctor," said Imogene, "Would you tell us where you received your medical training?"

In a slight Scottish accent, Doctor McLeod answered, "I received my degree from the University of Edinburgh in Scotland. From there I went to Saint Bartholomew's Hospital in London for my residency. I left there in 1865."

"Did you go into private practice after that?" asked Imogene.

"No, I was hired by the British East India Company."

"You practiced medicine in India, then?"

"No, I was in Malaysia."

"And after that?"

"My contract with The Company was up in sixty-nine so I went to Australia for a time, where I worked at the Sydney Infirmary and Dispensary. I worked there until 1871."

"Is that when you immigrated to Texas?"

"Yes, I met a man in Sydney who said Texas had a rapidly growing population and needed good doctors. Working for The Company and at an indigent hospital had taken its toll on my own health and I thought private practice in Texas would be a welcome respite."

"And you settled in Dallas."

"Yes, I considered settling in Galveston, but after a month there I saw a doctor just beginning wouldn't have much of an opportunity. So, I took a packet boat up the Trinity River to Porter's Bluff and then a coach to Dallas."

"So, you've been practicing medicine in Dallas for thirteen years?"

"Aye, give or take a month."

"When did you become the coroner for Dallas, County?"

"County Judge Burke appointed me in 1881."

"Since you left school in Edinburgh until today, have you had much experience with gunshot wounds?"

"I think so. At Saint Bart's I saw a few, mostly from shotguns or cap and ball pistols. While serving with The Company it was not unusual for the troops to engage in battles with Chinese gangs and smugglers, so I tended a goodly number of rifle wounds. The hospital in Sydney was an indigent hospital. It was also the hospital where people brought emergency victims. Most of those were gunshot or stabbing victims. In my practice, I haven't seen many in Dallas, as it is a private practice, but I have seen quite a few as coroner."

Imogene turned to the judge and said, "Your honor I would like to submit Doctor McLeod as an expert in gunshot wounds."

Judge Beckham asked McLaury if he had any objections. McLaury asked if he could ask Doctor McLeod a few questions, which the judge granted.

"Doctor McLeod," McLaury began politely. "I took some notes as Miss Foster was asking you questions. I noticed that you said when you were at Saint Bartholomew's you said you tended to a few people with gunshot wounds, mostly shotgun. Is that correct?"

"Aye, that would be correct."

"Could you define a few?"

"Ach, I don't rightly know, maybe two or three dozen."

"Of those two or three dozen, how many would you say were bullet wounds, not from shotguns?"

"Maybe half."

"So, twelve to eighteen," McLaury made a note.

"I would say so, yes."

Of those twelve to eighteen, how many were wounds from cartridge-type bullets?"

"There weren't many of those guns around then, so it would be hard to say. Less than three, I would think."

"Now about your work with the East India Company, when discussing your encounters with bullet wounds there you used the term goodly number. How many is a goodly number?"

"Probably around one hundred."

"But you said those were mostly rifle wounds, did you not?

"I did."

"Correct me if I'm mistaken, but those would have also been cap and ball rifles, or maybe even muskets?"

"Well, aye, the Chinese usually had muskets."

"Then your short time in Sydney, you said it was an indigent hospital and you treated emergency victims there."

"Yes."

"Most of those were gunshot or stabbing victims?"

"Yes."

"But you were only there about one year?"

"That would be about right."

"Can you give us an estimate of how many gunshot victims you treated?"

"Again, probably two or three dozen."

"Then in Dallas, you treated very few, if any gunshot wounds, and most of your experience with that type of wound has been as coroner for the last three years."

"Yes."

"Do you have any knowledge as to the number of shootings that have occurred in Fort Worth or Tarrant County since you arrived in Texas?"

"Only what I read in the newspapers."

"How many do you think that would be?"

"I have no idea. I don't keep a scorecard, you know."

"I'm sure you don't, but if you would help me out for just a moment, do you think in the last ten years that Fort Worth has had more or less shootings than Dallas?"

"Ach, more, much more."

"My last question to you is this; Who do you think has more experience with bullet wounds, a man who was a surgeon during the American Civil War, then worked as a doctor in Fort Worth since 1865, or a man with your experience?"

"Obviously, the first man would have more experience."

"Thank you, Doctor," said McLaury, then speaking to the judge. "Your honor, may we approach?"

The judge waved the two attorneys forward. "Judge," said McLaury, "Given Doctor McLeod's testimony, I don't see how it is possible to equate his experience with Doctor Cramer's."

"Well," Miss Foster," said Judge Beckham.

"I'm not asking the court to equate the two, only to acknowledge that Doctor McLeod has enough experience to be considered an expert in gunshot wounds," Imogene argued.

McLaury interjected, "Judge, if you do that, then I request an instruction to the jury that they can consider the experience level of the two doctors and the jury can decide which of the two is most believable."

Imogene was worried that if she didn't compromise, she would lose the entire argument, so she told the judge that she had no objection to McLaury's suggestion. The judge told them to step back, he accepted Doctor McLeod as an expert witness but instructed the jury that when two expert witnesses disagreed, they could balance the experiences and reach their own conclusion.

Imogene returned to questioning Doctor McLeod. She asked about the autopsy report he had written. Over several questions, Doctor McLeod confirmed that the wounds received by Blakely were caused by two different caliber bullets. It was then McLaury's turn to cross-examine the doctor. "Doctor Mcleod, how long after Mister Blakely was buried did you conduct this examination?" he asked.

"My report shows it was four weeks and a day."

"Do bodies change when they decompose?" asked McLaury.

"Depending on the circumstances, they can," agreed the doctor.

"How long would that take?"

"Generally speaking, human remains begin decomposing immediately but there is no noticeable decomposition for forty-eight hours after death."

"So, a body could be significantly changed, especially after four weeks."

"That is true."

"Is it possible that the decomposition of Mister Blakely's body was such that the wounds could have deformed, making identifying the types of bullets nearly impossible?"

"It would be possible, except for one thing."

"That being?"

"Mister Blakely had been embalmed. Something that is common in urban areas and less common in rural areas. Embalming slows down the decomposition such that it would take several months, if not years, to cause the kind of effect you are talking about. Even then it would not be impossible to deduce the caliber of bullets used."

232

"Are you saying it is entirely impossible for a body to deform, even if embalmed?"

"Nothing is impossible, I suppose."

"Thank you. I have nothing else for this witness," McLaury returned to his table and the judge excused the doctor.

The next witness Imogene called was Harry Morgan. She asked him about investigating the scene of the shooting. How he went about it and what he had found. She then turned the witness over to McLaury.

"Mister Morgan, what is your usual occupation?" he asked.

"I'm a bartender at the O'Neill."

"How long have you been investigating crime scenes?"

"Only this once."

"So, you wouldn't compare your experience to that of a seasoned law officer like Marshal William Rea, would you?"

"I don't reckon."

"How did you know what to look for."

"Deputy U. S. Marshal Putney told me what to do."

"Do you know what sort of experience Deputy Putney has investigating crime scenes?"

"No, sir."

"Now, these markings you say looked like ricochet markings, how do you know that's what they were?"

"It's what they looked like to me."

"But they could have been caused by anything, say a hammer, for example?"

"I guess."

"Or a rock from a boy's sling shot?"

"I guess."

"The truth is you don't know, for certain, what caused those marks, isn't that right?"

"I guess so."

"Could you tell how long it had been since whatever made those markings did so?"

"No."

"Those marks could have been made weeks, or months or even years ago, as far as you know."

"I guess so."

"How about this supposed thirty-eight caliber bullet you found in the wood? When did that bullet get there?"

"I don't rightly know."

"Was it weeks, months, years?"

"I can't say."

"So, your testimony is that you saw some markings on brick walls, and you don't know what made the marks or when they were made. Then you found a thirty-eight caliber bullet in a wooden wall, yet you don't know when that got there or who may have fired the gun at that wall. Is that right?"

"Yes."

"No further questions your honor."

The next witness for the defense was the photographer, Gustav Rhine. Imogene went over with Rhine the methods he had used in getting the photographs. She asked who had assisted him and why they had taken the photos of the various comparison bullets. Rhine was very methodical in his explanations and his testimony had gone well. Imogene entered all the photographs into evidence and said she had no further questions of Mister Rhine.

"Mister Rhine," said McLaury, "You are a professional photographer, is that right?"

"Yes, I am."

"From your testimony, I understand you take a great deal of pride in your work."

"I do."

"What kind of photographs are you best known for?"

"Portraits and landscapes."

"You came from New York, is that correct?"

"Yes, and Bavaria before that."

"Thank you. How many scenes of crimes did you photograph in Bavaria?"

"None, I was just a boy when my parents brought me to America."

"Well, then, how many scenes of crimes did you photograph in New York?"

"I never took a photograph of a crime in New York."

"Isn't it true, that you don't even know that the photographs you took here in Fort Worth were even that of a crime scene?"

"It is what Mister Morgan told me."

"And we all know how much Mister Morgan knows about crime scenes."

"Objection your honor," said Imogene.

"Sustained," said the judge.

"I retract that statement, judge," said McLaury. From there McLaury asked Rhine the same questions about the markings and the thirty-eight bullet he had asked of Morgan. And he got the same answers.

By the time they had gotten through the first three witnesses, the judge broke for lunch. Imogene told the others to go ahead and set up their picnic at their usual spot, but she wanted to talk to Deidre and Mary for a minute. When no one else was around to hear, Deidre said, "It's not good is it?"

"I'm afraid not," said Imogene. "McLaury beat us up pretty good this morning. I about half expected what he did to Harry and Gustav, but I didn't plan on the judge agreeing with him about Doctor McLeod."

"So, what's the plan now?" asked Deidre.

"That's why I wanted to talk to you," said Imogene. "I plan to call Hubert Forsythe next. But I don't know."

"What is it don't you know?" asked Deidre.

I don't know if he will stand up. I mean what if he gets weak in the knees? I mean after this you can bet he won't have a job. Can we depend on him?"

"I think we can," said Mary. Deidre asked what made Mary think so. "I think Hubert has a good heart and he just wants to do the right thing. And..." Mary stopped what she was about to say.

"And, what?" asked Imogene.

"Now, Deidre, don't get upset," said Mary.

"Why?" asked Deidre. "What would I get upset about?"

"Well, Hubert's been at the hotel several times."

"I know that," said Deidre. "The little twerp comes around every day to make sure I'm still in town, even though I've been in court all day."

"I don't mean that, sometimes he comes to the kitchen door to walk Betsy home."

Deidre's eyes were beginning to blaze. "What do you mean sometimes," she asked.

"I mean every night. He comes to the kitchen door to walk Betsy home."

"Why that little," Deidre was fighting to contain herself.

"But Deidre," said Mary. "Don't you understand? He wouldn't back out now. If he did, he would disappoint Betsy. The young man's sick in love with her."

"He's got to be six or seven years older than Betsy," said Deidre. "He'll for certain be sick when I get through with him."

"No, Deidre," said Imogene. "Mary is right. If he thinks he's in love with Betsy, then we know he is going to stay on our side. So, don't do anything until after the trial. Let's not waste this opportunity."

The flame was receding in Deidre's eyes. "Alright then, but he'll get a tongue-lashing from me when this is over."

"Then, he's set," said Imogene. "Now who do we call next? Nahum or Clint Doby? I think Nahum, but I want to hear from you two. Especially you Deidre."

Deidre thought for a moment then said, "I'm thinking Nahum, but I want to hear your reason before I make a final decision."

"Mary?" asked Imogene.

"I want to hear what you have to say, also," said Mary

"My reason is that I have no clue what Doby is going to say. I know Nahum gave us his gun and it is a thirty-eight, but I don't know, and I hate to have a witness that I don't know what they are going to say. I'm hoping we can get a clue from Nahum if he testifies first. If he doesn't provide us with a clue, we are no worse off. If we have Doby on the stand first, I'm afraid McLaury will devastate us again."

"I hadn't thought of Doby," said Deidre. "I was just hoping Nahum could make all this make a little more sense. But what you say has its merits."

"I guess I'll make it unanimous," said Mary.

"Good," said Imogene. "I think we can wrap up today. Mary, go find Ed Hoy. Tell him we are going to need Doby this afternoon. I hope he's close enough by."

Mary went off to find Hoy while Deidre and Imogene went to their picnic tree. Imogene thought about the question Nahum had told her to ask Doby and thought, *I hope Nahum isn't suborning perjury.*

Chapter Thirty-Two

Hubert Forsythe was nervous as he took the witness stand. He knew that, after his testimony, he would most likely be out of a job. The Chief Deputy Sheriff stood at the back of the courtroom, with his arms folded across his chest, glowering at Forsythe. But he had already told Putney what he knew and besides he cared what Elizabeth would think of him if he backed down now. "*No, sir*, he thought, *I ain't gonna crawfish.*

"Deputy Forsythe, how long have you worked for Sheriff Maddox?" asked Imogene.

"A little over a year," said Forsythe.

"During that time the sheriff has assigned you several types of duties, is that correct?"

"Yes, ma'am."

"In fact, weren't you the person that arrested Miss O'Neill?"

Forsythe stuttered a little, "Y, y, yes, Ma'am."

"You took that duty seriously, didn't you?"

"Yes, ma'am."

"As you do all your duties?"

"Yes, ma'am."

"Did there come a time when the sheriff assigned you to pick up a coroner's report and evidence from Doctor Cramer?"

"Yes ma'am."

"And you took that duty seriously, too?"

"Yes, Ma'am."

"When you retrieved the coroner's report, did you read it?"

"Yes, ma'am."

"Did you see the evidence the doctor gave you?"

"Yes ma'am."

"What did the report say?"

"It said that Mister Blakey had been shot twice. Once with a forty-four caliber bullet and once with a thirty-eight."

"You are certain that is what it said?"

"Oh, yes ma'am."

"And the evidence, what was that?"

"It looked like one forty-four bullet and one thirty-eight bullet."

"How did Doctor Cramer give you the evidence?"

"He put both bullets in an envelope."

"Did he seal the envelope?"

"No, ma'am."

"What did you do with the report and the evidence?"

"I brought it to Mister Handy, the chief clerk."

"Did he look at either the report or the bullets?"

"I don't think so."

"Did he log the evidence in a ledger?"

"I didn't see him do that, but I don't know he didn't."

"As far as you know, did anyone else handle either the report or the evidence?"

"Not as far as I know."

"Thank you, Deputy," said Imogene, then to the judge, I have nothing further, at this time.

McLaury stood up, shuffled some papers then asked. "Deputy, when did you first notice this discrepancy?"

"The day Miss O'Neill first appeared in court."

"About four weeks ago, then?"

"Yes, sir."

"When did you first tell anyone about this discrepancy?"

"About two weeks ago."

"Was that the sheriff you reported it to?"

"No, sir."

"The chief deputy, then?"

"No, sir."

"Anybody in the sheriff's office?"

"No, sir."

"Well in heaven's name who did you report it to?"

"Deputy Marshal Nahum Putney?"

"Nahum Putney?"

"Yes, sir."

"Why didn't you report it to one of your superiors?"

"I don't know."

"Oh, I think you know. You didn't trust Sheriff Maddox or anyone else in the sheriff's office, isn't that right?"

"That's not exactly right, no, sir."

"Wasn't it your duty to report it to the sheriff?"

"I guess."

"But you didn't?"

"No, sir."

"Do you have a copy of this phantom report?"

"No, sir."

"Do you see Miss O'Neill, often?"

"Yes, sir, every day. Just like Judge Beckham told me to do."

"Do you see anyone else when you go to check on Miss O'Neill?"

"Yes, sir."

"Who?"

"Different people, like Miss Johnson over there."

"I see. The other day at lunch break did I see you speaking with a young lady outside of the courthouse?"

"I don't know, sir. I don't have any idea who or what you see."

"How about that young lady seated behind Miss Johnson? The one with the picnic basket beside her? Do you ever see her when you check on Miss O'Neill?"

"Yes, sir, sometimes."

"Do you know her name?"

"Objection your honor. This has nothing to do with Deputy Forsythe's testimony."

"I think you may be wrong, Miss Foster. I will allow Mister McLaury the same leeway I allowed you with Captain Russell. You may continue, Mister McLaury."

"Well, Deputy, do you know her name?"

"Elizabeth, sir."

"She's a pretty young thing isn't she, Deputy?"

Imogene jumped up, "Your honor."

"The court will take judicial notice that the young lady, Elizabeth, by name, is attractive. Go ahead, Mister McLaury."

"It wouldn't take much for a young man like you to be sweet on a pretty girl like that, would it?"

"Please your honor," said Imogene. "This line of questioning is doing nothing but causing embarrassment to the witness and the young lady in question."

"I agree, Miss Foster. Mister McLaury, do you have a purpose in this line of questioning?"

"Yes, sir, judge. I am trying to determine if the witness has some feelings for this girl, who I believe to be an employee of Miss O'Neill, and whether those feelings could influence the witness's testimony."

"Very well," said the judge. "You may continue."

"Would you like for me to ask the question again, Deputy?"

"No, I understood it."

"Well?"

"I don't see any harm in a guy liking a pretty girl."

"It happens to us all, but my question is does your feelings for this young lady have anything to do with you deciding to concoct this testimony?"

"Objection to the word concoct."

"Sustained," said the judge. "I think you have made your point Mister McLaury. Do you have anything further for this witness?"

"No, your honor."

"Redirect," said Imogene.

"Go ahead," allowed the judge.

"When did you first meet Miss Elizabeth Sikes, the girl in question?"

"The day Miss O'Neill was released on bond."

"How did that come about?"

"The sheriff told me to make sure Miss O'Neill got to her hotel and stayed there."

"When did you tell Deputy Marshal Putney about the coroner's report?"

"The same day."

"So, you had only a passing acquaintance with Miss Sikes at the time."

"Yes, ma'am."

"I have no further questions, judge."

"You may step down, Deputy," said the judge. "Miss Foster, call your next witness."

"The defense calls Deputy U. S. Marshal Nahum Putney," Imogene said a little louder than necessary.

The entire courtroom became alive with whispers. "Order," commanded Judge Beckham and slammed his gavel down. The courtroom fell quiet.

Imogene had already discussed, with Deidre, her first round of questions for Putney, so she jumped right in. "Deputy Putney, do you know the defendant, Deidre O'Neill?"

"I do," said Putney.

"How long have you known her?"

"Fourteen years."

"What is your relationship with Miss O'Neill?"

Putney knew the questions needed to be asked and that it was better to be asked by Imogene than McLaury. "Miss O'Neill and I are lovers."

This started the courtroom buzzing again. This time Judge Beckham stood behind the bench and banged his gavel three times. "If I hear one more peep I will clear everyone out of the gallery and that is my last word." The sudden quiet in the courtroom was almost painful.

Imogene began again, "That is a bold admission, Deputy. Wouldn't it have been better to hedge your answer?"

"Why, Mister McLaury would have insisted I admit it and it is nothing for which I am ashamed."

"Why haven't you married her?"

"My occupation keeps me out on the road nearly constantly and honestly the nature of my job means the next day I may not return. I found no reason to try and make her a widow."

"But you love her?"

"Naturally."

Imogene exhaled deeply, glad that part was over. "Now, Deputy, did you know Ned Blakely?"

"I did."

"Tell us about when you first met him."

"I was a soldier in the Confederate Army, a scout for the Mounted Mountain Rangers. I had come in from a scouting mission and I was summoned by the commanding officer."

"That would be Montague Russell?"

"The same. At his tent, I was introduced to a man named Thomas Tidwell and to Ned Blakely."

"Did they have ranks?"

"They were bushwhackers, so as far as I was concerned, no."

"Was anyone else present, besides these two and Russell?"

"Yes, Sergent Andrews and a blackheart named Brandon Starnes."

"A blackheart?"

"Yes, a criminal Russell had recruited from the state prison in turn for clemency from the Confederacy."

"I apologize for interrupting, please tell us about the conversation."

"Russell and Tidwell told me that the war was over and had been for weeks. Then they told me about a plan to rob a shipment of Union gold. They wanted me to scout out where the Union troops were and report back."

"Was anyone to be sent with you?"

"Yes, Blakely."

"Did you agree with the plan?"

"I told them I did because I figured Starnes's purpose there was to kill me if I didn't."

"What happened next?"

"I went to get some sleep. I was awakened after about two hours by Sergent Andrew. He told me I was to leave right away."

"Did anything else happen?"

"Yes, when I went to get my horse Tidwell and Blakely were at the picket line, talking. Tidwell told Blakely that as soon as we had the Union troops spotted, we were to return but if I gave any sign of hesitancy Blakely was to kill me."

"But you went on the mission anyway?"

"I did. I figured I had a better chance in the wilderness with one thug than a whole camp full."

"Did you find the troops?"

"We did."

"What happened then?"

"We were supposed to watch until we figured which pass they would be taking, so I told Blakely to get some sleep. We had been up nearly twenty-four hours. I told him I would take the first watch."

"What did you do next?"

"I had decided to see which direction the Union troops were going to go, so I could go the other. As soon as I had it figured out, I woke Blakely."

"Gently, I suppose?"

242

Putney laughed, "Hardly. I chucked a rock at him as I held a rifle on him. I made him give me his pistol and shuck off all his clothes except his long johns. Then I took all the horses and left."

"You left him defenseless, in the middle of Indian country?" Imogene feigned shock.

"No, I left his pistol and a canteen of water and pointed him to the Union troops and told him good luck."

"If he was going to kill you, and you knew it, why didn't you just kill him instead?"

"I achieved my goal, there was no need to kill him. I don't kill unarmed men."

"When was the next time you saw Ned Blakely?"

"I didn't."

"But isn't he the man that shot you?"

"That is what I have been told, but at the time I didn't recognize him, or at least I don't remember recognizing him."

"But didn't you shoot him?"

"I did, but not because I recognized him, but because he was shooting at me. I would have shot at anybody trying to kill me or Miss O'Neill."

"Did you see Miss O'Neill shoot anyone?"

"Not that I remember. I guess I went out soon after I was hit."

"Were you seeking out Mister Blakely for some sort of vengeance?"

"I didn't even know Blakely was in Fort Worth."

"Judge," said Imogene, I have a piece of evidence in my satchel. It is an unloaded revolver, but I would like one of the sheriff's deputies or the bailiff to first inspect it."

The judge told the bailiff to check the gun. "It's empty, judge."

"Fine Miss Foster," said the judge. "Continue."

"May I approach the witness?" the judge nodded. "Deputy, do you recognize this weapon?"

Putney inspected the weapon and finally said, "I do. It is the gun I took off Clint Doby near Clear Boggy Creek in the Indian Nations."

"How do you know it is the same weapon?"

"Here on the side plate next to the letters S and W on the grip handle are where I scratched my initials."

"Could you describe the type of revolver it is and what sort of ammunition it uses?"

"It is a Smith and Wesson thirty-eight caliber model two revolver, top break."

"Why did you take this revolver from Mister Doby?"

"As part of an investigation directed me by Marshal William Cabell."

"What led you to believe Mister Doby might have information regarding your investigation?"

"His mother came to me and told me she was afraid that her son had been involved in the shooting on Second Street. She also told me where I could find him."

"Did you have to take the gun from Mister Doby by force or use of arms?"

"No. He gave it to me willingly."

"As part of your investigation, did you have the body of Ned Blakely exhumed?"

"I did."

"For what purpose?"

"For an independent examination by the Dallas County Coroner."

"Why not use Doctor Cramer, the county coroner here in Tarrant County."

"I had information that the coroner's report from here had been tampered with or forged. So, the Federal Commissioner in Dallas ordered the examination to be conducted independent of the Tarrant County examination."

"Was that information about a discrepancy in the Tarrant County report provided to you by Deputy Sheriff Hubert Forsythe?"

"Yes."

"Why did you believe his information was truthful."

"Because he had nothing to gain and everything to lose. In my experience that usually stands the test."

"Your honor, I would like this revolver entered into evidence as Defense Exhibit ."

"Without objection?"

"No objection," said McLaury.

"About Mister Doby. Have you or Marshal Cabell had him sequestered?"

"I have."

"Why."

"I feared his life would be in danger if he were walking around Fort Worth."

"Why would you believe that?"

"Deputy U. S. Marshal Bass Reeves and I had to track him down after we discovered he had been abducted near Honey Springs?"

"Abducted?"

"Yes, by three men."

"Do you know these men?"

"I know one of them, William Dawson."

"How do you know William Dawson?"

"He tried to kill me twice near Llano. I arrested him on warrants in a place called The Flat near Fort Griffin."

"What were the warrants for?"

"There was one each for the murders four family members near Llano. One for the rape of the wife and mother of that family. One each for the murders of two Army soldiers and one for the attempted murder of a Deputy U. S. Marshal."

"It sounds as if Mister Dawson is an extremely violent man."

"He is that."

"So, did Mister Doby come with you willingly?"

"He did. Although I did have a subpoena for him as a material witness."

"I want to show you what has been entered as Defense Exhibit 1. "May I approach, judge?"

The judge allowed it.

"Do you recognize this document?"

"I do. It is the coroner's report from Doctor Mcleod in Dallas County."

"Does this report say how Mister Blakely was killed?"

"It says he was killed with a thirty-eight caliber bullet."

"The same caliber bullet that might be fired from a gun like Mister Doby's"

"Objection," said McLaury. "Mister Putney has no way of knowing what gun was used to kill Mister Blakely."

245

"Your honor, I did not ask that. Only that it was the same caliber that might be fired from such a weapon," argued Imogene.

"That's what she said," the judge told McLaury. "Overruled."

"You may answer, Deputy," Imogene told Putney, emphasizing the word deputy.

"Mister Doby's gun would fire the same type of ammunition."

Imogene took the report from Putney and turned to go back to the lectern when she saw Ed Hoy sitting on the front row signaling to her. "May I have a moment, your honor."

"Make it quick, Miss Foster."

Imogene went to Hoy who leaned over the rail and said, "Doby is outside. Luke Short and me are watching him."

"Thank you," said Imogene. Turning back to the judge, she said. "I have no further questions for this witness.

"Mister McLaury, it's your turn," Judge Beckham said.

"Thank you, your honor. Mister Putney, you are quite famous, are you not?"

"I don't know about that."

McLaury walked back to his table and picked up a box. "May I approach the witness, your honor?" Judge Beckham nodded, yes.

"There is no need to be modest, Mister Putney. Please take a look in this box."

Putney looked to find a dozen dime novels, each one about him."

"Could you tell the court what is in the box?"

"Books."

"What or who is the subject of the books?"

"Me."

"How many books are there?"

"Twelve."

"Your honor I would like to enter these as Prosecution Exhibits 3 through 12."

"So entered," said the judge. "Give them to the clerk so he may mark them."

"A dozen books about you, right Mister Putney."

"I said there were twelve, yes."

"Why it seems to me that you're more famous than Bat Masterson, Billy the Kid, and Wyatt Earp and his brothers, wouldn't you say?"

"I would say I'm almost as famous as the Tombstone Cowboys and your brothers."

By the redness that suddenly took McLaury's face everyone in the courtroom could tell Putney's answer had angered him." "Judge, would you please direct the witness to answer the question?"

"I believe he did, Mister McLaury," said the judge. "But Deputy Putney the question was about certain other persons. Please direct your answer to those persons."

"I reckon in some circles I might be as famous as those men."

"And like those men isn't what makes you most famous is your tendency toward violence."

"Having never read those books or ones about the men you mentioned, I wouldn't know what they say I'm famous for."

"You've never read any of these books?"

"No."

"Why not?"

"From what I've been told about them, they are all a pack of half-truths if not out-and-out lies."

"How do you know, if you haven't read them?"

"I told you, from what I heard."

"But you do have a reputation as a violent man, don't you?"

"Maybe in some circles, I reckon."

"You have killed quite a large number of men, haven't you Mister Putney?"

"Including Comanche, Kiowa, and Wichita, that would probably be true."

"Let's exclude the Indians. That would still leave a large number, correct?"

"Define large."

"More than five?"

"Yes."

"More than ten?"

"Yes."

"More than fifteen?"

"Not as many as that."

"So somewhere between ten and fifteen men?"

"Well, to be correct, two were women."

"Oh, well, that makes it better."

"Objection your honor," said Imogene.

"I withdraw the statement, your honor," McLaury knew the jury wouldn't be able to disregard it, no matter how they tried."

"You also have a reputation as a person with a temper, don't you?"

"I don't pay much attention to what people say."

"Two weeks ago, didn't you storm into the office of Mister Buckley Paddock and threaten him if he didn't print a retraction of an editorial he had written about Miss O'Neill?"

"I didn't storm, and I didn't threaten."

"But you were angry about the editorial."

"I wasn't happy."

"You would like to have beaten him, wouldn't you?"

"I don't beat or otherwise harm defenseless men."

"When you consider your size and reputation wouldn't you say a man like Mister Paddock might be intimidated by your presence?"

"From our conversation, I didn't think much intimidated Mister Paddock."

"Why would you think that?"

"I don't know, by the way he handled himself I thought he might have been a professional boxer."

"Your honor, Mister Putney is trying to make this a joke."

"You asked the question, Mister McLaury," the judge told him. "I don't know what Mister Putney thinks or doesn't think."

"You don't like me, do you, Mister Putney?"

"I don't dislike you any more than I dislike most people I don't know."

"Your honor, half the time I can't get a straight answer out of this man, so I have no further questions."

Imogene stood and said, "Redirect, your honor."

"Go ahead," Miss Foster.

"Deputy Putney, those books Mister McLaury started with, did you write them?"

"No."

"Did you authorize anybody else to write them?"

"No."

"Nothing more, your honor.

Judge Beckham looked at his watch then said, "Miss Foster, it is four o'clock. Do you think we can finish with your next witness in a reasonable amount of time?"

"I do your honor. I expect the testimony to be short."

"Very well, call your next witness."

"I call Clint Doby."

"Is he actually here?" asked Judge Beckham.

"I have been advised he is, yes sir."

"Very well."

Doby walked into the courtroom with Luke Short on one side and Ed Hoy on the other. "Miss Foster," said the judge, "There are three men here. Which one is Clint Doby?"

"The one in the center, Judge," If Imogene hadn't known Short and Hoy she would have had to guess herself.

"Well, who are the other two?"

"This gentleman is Luke Short," Imogene pointed at the gambler. "And the other is Ed Hoy."

"Why arc thcy here?"

"They are both Special Deputy Marshals hired to protect Mister Doby, judge."

"Mister Hoy," said the judge. "Do you understand this is not a circus?"

"I am aware of that, judge."

"Nor is it a Wild West show."

"I am aware of that, also, judge."

"Then why have you come to my court dressed like that?"

"I am a Creek Indian born on the Muskogee reservation after my people were forced to leave their native lands and marched in The Trail of Tears. This is the traditional dress of my people. Fit for the most serious of ceremonies," The part about the dress was a lie but Hoy knew most white people would be ignorant of that and be embarrassed to question it. Ed Hoy liked playing small tricks on white people.

"Then, I suppose it is appropriate," said the judge. "You and Mister Short may sit behind the defense table. Mister Doby come forward and be sworn."

"Your honor, I renew my objection over Mister Doby's testimony, since I have not had an opportunity to interview him."

"From Deputy Putney's testimony and the statement made previously by Miss Foster, it seems nobody has had an opportunity to interview him. Is that correct, Mister Doby?"

"Yes sir, judge," Doby said.

"Let me ask you this, young man. Knowing you didn't have to grant Mister McLaury or Miss Foster an interview; would you have spoken to either of them?"

"I don't think so, judge," Doby was being honest.

"Then I see it makes no difference Mister McLaury, overruled. Take the stand and be sworn, Mister Doby."

Imogene didn't know where to start. The question Putney had written for her to ask Doby still bothered her. But she put on her best face and stepped to the podium. Mister Doby, I know the judge already asked this, but I just want the jury to be clear. Have we ever spoken or met?"

Doby remembered what Putney had told him about listening carefully to every question asked. "No, ma'am, we haven't."

"Have you discussed your testimony with anyone either inside or outside of this court?"

"Not really, no."

"What do you mean by that?"

"Well, Mister Putney told me to listen to every question, carefully."

"Did he tell you anything else?"

"Only that I should answer every question as honestly as I can."

"Sound advice. May I approach your honor?" Judge Beckham nodded. "Mister Doby," said Imogene. "Do you recognize this revolver?"

"Doby inspected the gun carefully then said, "Yes, ma'am. This is my gun."

"How can you tell this is your gun?"

"Right here on the side plate, behind the cylinder, this fancy scrollwork is my initials. I paid for it when I bought the gun."

"Why did you buy this type of gun and not another?" Imogene was still working her way to the question, and this was really a stall for time.

"It's illegal to carry open here in town and this is smaller than a forty-four, so it's easier to keep under my coat."

"Are you proficient with firearms?"

"I'm okay, I mean I shoot pretty well most of the time."

"Do you know a man named Ned Blakely?"

"Well, I did, but he's dead now."

"How did you know him?"

"We worked together for Mister Courtwright."

"As detectives?"

"That's what we called ourselves, but we didn't have no badges or nothing."

"What did you do for Mister Courtwright?"

"We had regular rounds where we went to saloons and well, I don't know if I can say it in public."

"Saloons and what other establishments? It's important."

Doby blushed, "Well, you know where the girls worked."

"You mean bordellos?" asked Imogene.

Doby blushed again, "I've heard called that and other names."

"We will just stick to bordello. When you say you had regular rounds, what do you mean by that?"

"Well, some of the business in the Acre pay Mister Courtwright for security."

"By security, do you mean protection?"

"I guess. We was to make sure nothing happened in the joints."

"Did people pay willingly?"

"Some did, others needed a little convincing."

"Who did the convincing?"

"It was my job to talk them into it if they started crawfishing."

"What if they still didn't want to pay?"

"That's when Ned would go to the back with them and have another talk."

"And after a talk with Ned, they paid?"

"Yeah, Ned had a convincing way about him."

"Was Mister Blakely a violent man?"

"Objection, judge," McLaury said. "The question calls for a conjecture."

"Lay a foundation, Miss Foster," the judge told Imogene.

"Did you ever see Mister Blakely rough anybody up?"

"Sometimes."

"When you were making collections?"

251

"Sometimes."

"Were there other times?"

"Well, ole Ned could get mighty mean, especially if he had a snoot on."

"Was that often?"

"Pretty much every night after we made our rounds."

"Did Mister Blakely ever mention Deputy Putney to you?"

"Oh, yeah. When he was drunk, sometimes he would go into the story about when Mister Putney had gotten the drop on him, out west. He sure didn't like Mister Putney."

"When Deputy Putney first came to Fort Worth, was Mister Blakely aware of it?"

"Yeah, he told me a man told him about Mister Putney down at the White Elephant. He told me this man said he would pay fifty dollars, silver to the man that killed Mister Putney."

"Did Mister Blakely say he intended to collect this bounty?"

"He sure did."

"How did he say he was going to collect the bounty?"

"He said he was going to follow Mister Putney, sneaky like and when the time was right, he was going to call Mister Putney out."

"Do you mean he was going to challenge Deputy Putney to a duel?"

"Yes ma'am."

"So, you had no notion that Mister Blakely meant to ambush Deputy Putney?"

"No, ma'am."

"Were you present when Mister Blakely shot Deputy Putney?"

Doby had thought about each question before it was answered, but this one seemed like it needed extra thought. Finally, he said, "Yes, ma'am."

"Were you in the alley?"

Again, Doby thought hard before answering. "Yes, ma'am, I was."

It's now or never thought Imogene. "Is it true you were there to protect Deputy Putney from Mister Blakely?"

As Imogene expected, McLaury jumped up saying, "Objection your honor. That's a leading question."

Judge Beckham glared at Imogene, "You know better, Miss Foster," he said. "I'm going to sustain the objection and direct the witness not to answer that question."

"I apologize, your honor," said Imogene, thinking she was lucky the judge hadn't held her in contempt.

"Ask another question," the judge directed.

Flustered, Imogene shuffled her notes, shuffled her feet on the floor, and finally came up with another question. "Mister Doby, do you know who shot Mister McLaury after Deputy Putney had shot him?"

Doby now understood why Putney had told him to think carefully before answering each question, "Yes, ma'am, I do.

"Was it the defendant, Miss O'Neill?" asked Imogene pointing at Deidre.

"No, ma'am."

"Can you tell who it was that shot Mister Blakely?"

"To protect Mister Putney, I shot Ned Blakely in the back."

Chapter Thirty-Three

Judge Beckham stopped the testimony, "Young man." he said. "I have to warn you you have just made an admission, and I want you to know that you don't have to say anything more until you have an attorney to advise you. Do you understand?"

"Yes, sir," Doby told him, "I understand."

"Knowing that, do you wish to continue?"

"Yes, sir, I do."

"Miss Foster," said the judge, "Do you have anything further for this witness?"

Imogene was in shock at Doby's statement. "I don't think so, your honor"

"Very well, Mister McLaury?"

If Imogene was shocked, McLaury was flummoxed. "In the light of this admission, I would like to have a short recess to discuss my case with Marshal Rea."

"Good idea," said the judge. "We will recess for ten minutes. The witness will remain on the stand and not discuss anything with anyone."

After the recess, McLaury started with Doby. "Mister Doby, do you know that extortion is a crime?"

Doby looked confused, "I'm not sure what you mean."

"I mean demanding money for protection, that's extortion."

"I never really thought about it, I was just doing my job."

"And when you collected this money, what did you do with it?"

Doby had been following Putney's advice to think carefully

"Judge," said Doby, "You told me I might oughta have an attorney and now he's telling me that money collection is a crime. Do I have to answer that?"

"No, son," the judge told him. "You do not have to answer that question or any question that implicates you in what might be a crime."

"Then I don't think I want to answer that question."

"That is your right," said the judge. "Mister McLaury, move on."

"Your honor, since Mister Doby doesn't want to answer that question, I request a recess until tomorrow morning, to confer in depth with Marshal Rea and Sheriff Maddox."

"What is your thought, Miss Foster?" asked Judge Beckham.

"Your honor, to give him extra time, simply because he doesn't like what a witness says, seems to me to give him an unfair advantage."

Judge Beckham removed his glasses and massaged the bridge of his nose. After several moments of thought, he said, "Gentlemen of the jury, we find ourselves in a position where I must discuss some legalities with the attorneys. What we need to discuss has nothing to do with the case before; therefore us, it is inappropriate to discuss it in front of you. So, I will ask the bailiff to escort you to the jury room during this discussion. When I am ready, I will call you back and advise you of my decision. Bailiff, please escort the jury out."

With the jury gone, Judge Beckham continued. "Mister McLaury?"

"Judge," said the prosecutor, "I think the one with the unfair advantage, here, is Miss Foster. I've never seen a witness make this sort of admission. To not allow us to investigate this statement puts an undue burden on the state. The purpose of the court is to find the truth. I need the opportunity to investigate."

"Miss Foster?"

Imogene thought for a moment, then said, "Judge, Mister McLaury rushed to have this trial when there was no need. Mister McLaury could have taken his time to investigate to determine whether or not a crime was even committed. Had he done his due diligence Marshal Rea or Sheriff Maddox could have discovered the information provided by Mister Doby. But he had a bee in his bonnet and was determined to bring Miss O'Neill to trial. Why he was in such a rush, I can only speculate, which I will not do here. Miss O'Neill is a well-established and successful businesswoman in this community. She was going nowhere. Mister McLaury had ample opportunity to investigate this case and the only person to blame for the position we now find ourselves in is Mister McLaury. Now he wants to investigate. What's next? Will he be

255

asking to bring in a new witness he drags up somewhere to say who knows what? "Will I be given access to all witnesses, like Deputy Putney, to prepare to counter anything the state produces? I sincerely ask your honor not to allow this.

"Thank you, Miss Foster, Mister McLaury, I appreciate your comments," said the judge. "I am going to retire to my chambers for a few minutes to consider your points. I will return momentarily and give you, my decision."

Nobody left the courtroom while the judge was out. At the prosecution table, the atmosphere was panic as McLaury, Rea, and Maddox huddled together, whispering frantically. Anyone could tell McLaury was intensely disturbed. "I'm telling you both this right now," said McLaury, "If the judge rules for us, I want you to find everyone and anyone that knows about Doby and have them in my office by seven o'clock." The conversation continued with Rea and Maddox offering suggestions.

At the defense table, Imogene was trying to tamp down Deidre and Mary's enthusiasm. "You shouldn't get your hopes up," she said, "There is as good a chance he will rule against us as he will for us."

Judge Beckham entered the courtroom after fifteen minutes. He sat behind the bench and cleared his throat. "From time to time, we as judges are called on to have the wisdom of Solomon. I think we most often fail to reach that lofty goal. Here I am given the task of deciding which could easily tip the scales of justice. I pray my decision will not make that happen." The judge rubbed the bridge of his nose, again, "Mister McLaury, I am going to grant your request for a recess, and I will give you until tomorrow morning to investigate Mister Doby's statement." McLaury stood up straight as a rod and was about to speak, but the judge intercepted him by saying, "Don't thank me yet, because I am going to restrict you. You may bring any witness you want to bolster your position, but not any new witness. It must be someone from your published witness list, but they cannot give testimony outside of the topic of Mister Doby's testimony."

"Yes, sir, your honor," McLaury said with a big grin on his face.

Judge Beckham then addressed a crestfallen Imogene Foster. "Miss Foster, all is not lost for your client. While I am granting

256

Mister McLaury's request, I am also granting your request. You may have full access to any witness, including Deputy Putney. With that, Bailiff, bring the jury in and we will dismiss for the evening."

Chapter Thirty-Four

McLaury looked at Bill Rea and Jim Courtwright, "That was the best you could bring me? One man who couldn't find his ass with both hands and I can't call as a witness even if he could and the other an already discredited witness."

"If Max hadn't lost Short and that Indian protecting Doby, we could have had him and found out what his testimony would be," said Courtwright.

"If ifs and ands were pots and pans there would be no more ifs and ands," said McLaury. "The fact is he lost them, and you didn't get your hands on him."

"Will, I don't think it's as bleak as you might think," Rea told McLaury. "I bet you a hundred dollars that Doby was in the alley to help Blakely with the dirty work. He had never been shot at before and when the O'Neill woman began blasting away, he was scared shitless and accidentally hit Blakely. Russell can testify that Doby hated Putney for killing his father. Keep it to that and Foster won't have a chance to beat him up again."

"That doesn't help. Either way, it puts Doby's bullet in Blakely," said Courtwright.

"Let me think," said McLaury. The two other men kept silent as McLaury closed his eyes, leaned back in his chair, and tried to think of a way to salvage his case. They could see his eyes moving behind his lids, as if he were trying to will chess pieces into place with his mere thoughts. After a few minutes he opened his eyes and said, "I have an idea. Have Russell in the courtroom first thing. I may be able to pull this thing off after all."

It was eight in the evening when Putney walked into Deidre O'Neill's office, with him was a slender, bespectacled man wearing a gray tweed suit and a bowler hat. "Where in hell have you been?" Deidre asked. "Court's been out since before five. We looked all over for you."

"Luke came out and gave me the news before the jury returned," Putney told everyone in the room. "Let me introduce

Mister Abernathy Pool. Mister Pool is Clint's new lawyer. From what Luke told me, he's going to need one. I took him to see his client and then we came over here for drinks. "Right, Mister Pool?"

"Well, yes, I...." Imogene cut him off.

"Mister Pool," she said. "I need to speak with Nahum about this case and it might conflict with Mister Doby's problems, so if you don't mind, could you please go somewhere else for your drink?" Imogene was noticeably irritated, so Pool nodded and left the room. When he was gone Imogene turned to Putney. "What in the hell have you done?" she asked.

Putney walked over to Deidre and kissed her on the cheek, then to the drinks cabinet and poured himself a glass of whiskey. With glass in hand, he turned to Imogene and asked, "What has your knickers in a twist?"

"Let's try suborning perjury," said Imogene.

"I have no idea what you mean." Putney took another drink.

"Didn't Luke Short tell you that Clint Doby said he shot Blakely, trying to save you?"

"Sure, he did, but what makes you think he lied and what makes you think I encouraged him to lie?" Putney asked.

"You know good and well he was in that alley trying to kill you. Or Deidre. Or both. And you got him to lie about why he was there."

Putney turned his back on Imogene and poured himself another drink. He was beginning to get angry with her and the action gave him time to tamp down his ire. "First," he said as he turned around, "I don't know what his purpose was in the alley and second, I damn sure didn't tell him to lie about it. Whatever he said, lie or truth is on him, not me."

"Then what about that question you had me ask him, you know the leading question you knew would be objected to?"

"Look," said Putney. "The only thing I told Clint was to listen to every question carefully before answering. If you didn't like his answers, I can't help that."

"I'm a representative of the law," said Imogene. "How can I continue, knowing I am complicit with cheating?"

"It isn't cheating," said Putney. "It's simply putting an edge on the knife. Cheating is what was done with the coroner's report and switching out the bullets in evidence. I may have toed the line, but I didn't step over it. But I will tell you this one thing, I would gladly step over it to save Deidre, or you or anyone else in this room. The people in this room are the only family I have. You, Mary, Brutus, Ceasar, Elizabeth, and most especially Deidre. I would do anything to protect any of you. That's the main law in my life."

Imogene knew she had lost the argument. She had also lost her steam, "So, that's it? You live by Putney's Law?"

Putney stepped over to Imogene and put his long arms around her, giving her a gentle hug, "I'm sorry I've upset you, Sweetie. I reckon my edges are a little harder than they ought to be."

"They are," she said, then whispered in his ear so that only he could hear, "And that's why I love you."

"Mister McLaury," said Judge Beckham, "I hope you resolved your investigation and are ready to proceed."

"I am ready, judge," said McLaury. "However, I would like to take things a little out of order, if I may. Before continuing my cross-examination of Mister Doby, I would like to recall Captain Montague Russell to the stand for a very few questions."

"That is quite out of the ordinary," said the judge. "Miss Foster, what do you have to say about this?"

Imogene thought for a moment. She had already torn up Russell on the stand once and figured she could do it again if it was necessary. She couldn't imagine what he could add to the story, so she told the judge she had no objections.

Abernathy Pool had gone to Judge Beckham's office before court began and told him he had been hired as Clint Doby's attorney, so Judge Beckham asked, "Mister Pool, do you have any objections?"

"None, your honor," said Pool.

"Then take your client and his guardians and sit in the hall until we are ready for him."

"If I may, Judge," Pool said, "I would prefer to remain in the courtroom while this other witness is testifying. It would be well for me to know what he says, as it affects my client."

"Certainly, Mister Pool. Mister McLaury, call Mister Russell."

260

After the judge advised Russell that he was still under oath, McLaury started with, "Captain, do you know a man named Clint Doby?"

"Yes, sir, I do."

"How do you know him?"

"We work together for Mister Courtwright."

"Are you friends?"

"I don't know that I would say we are friends, but we are friendly."

"I suppose from time to time, while working together you may have had friendly discussions?"

"Yes, we have."

"During these friendly discussions, did Mister Doby ever mention Deputy Marshal Nahum Putney?"

"Yes, he did."

"Did he seem fond of Mister Putney?"

"Quite the contrary, it seemed to me he had a great dislike for Putney."

"Oh? And why is that?"

"He told me that Putney killed his father."

"Judge, that's all I have for this witness."

"Judge Beckham scratched his head and said, "Alright. Miss Foster do have anything?"

Imogene thought for a second and decided that anything she asked would just drive this last point home, so she said, "No, sir."

"Very, well. You may step down Mister Russell. Mister Pool, please return your client to the stand," the judge instructed.

Judge Beckham told Doby he was still under oath and that now that he had an attorney in the courtroom should he have a problem with a question he could certainly consult with his lawyer before answering.

McLaury started by asking, "Mister Doby before Nahum Putney came to Fort Worth, had you ever met him?"

Doby answered that he did.

"Tell us, under what circumstances did you meet Nahum Putney, the first time?"

Doby took time to form his answer, then said, "When he came to our ranch near Mason to arrest my father."

"There is more to it than that isn't there?"

261

"I guess."

"Please tell us what more happened."

"Mister Putney shot my father."

"Did your father die because of Mister Putney's action?"

"Yes."

"Did that make you angry?"

Following Pool's instructions about when he was uncertain if he should answer a question, Doby looked at Pool who was sitting on the second row of the gallery next to Luke Short. There was no signal from Pool, so Doby said, "Yes."

McLaury changed his approach and asked, "Do you know if Mister Blakely had ever met Mister Putney before this event?"

"Yes, he did," said Doby.

"Did he tell you about it?"

"Yes."

"What did he tell you?"

"He said Mister Putney had left him in Indian country where he either had to turn himself in to Yankee troops or get captured by Indians."

"And Mister Blakely was angry about that."

"I reckon so."

"Come on Mister Doby, didn't the two of you commiserate about your dislike of Mister Putney?"

"I'm sorry I don't know what that word commis...whatever means."

"Judge Beckham broke in, "It means talking about similar misfortunes."

"Yeah, I guess we did."

"Did Mister Blakely tell you he was going to confront Mister Putney?"

"Yes."

"Did he ask you to come along with him?"

"Yes."

"And you did?"

Pool stood up and said, "If it pleases your honor, I think Mister McLaury is treading awfully close to Mister Doby's Fifth Amendment right." Pool didn't go into what that meant. He didn't want the jury to think about what testifying against one's own interest could mean.

262

"You may be right, Mister Pool," said the judge, "But he hasn't stepped over the line. You may answer, Mister Doby."

"Yeah, but I didn't know Blakey was going to try to ambush Mister Putney," said Doby.

"What did you think was going to happen?"

"I thought Blakely was going to try Mister Putney to a showdown, you know like what you read in dime books."

"You mean like a dual in the middle of the street?"

"Yeah, that's what I mean."

Then why did he need you there?"

"I don't know."

"Weren't you part of Mister Blakely's plan to assassinate Mister Putney?"

Pool stood again. "Your honor, I am advising my client not to answer that question."

"That is his right," said the judge. "Mister Doby, you don't have to answer that question."

Doby sat silent.

McLaury changed directions again. "Mister Doby, were you ever in the Army?"

"No."

"Did you ever serve with an organization like the Texas Rangers, fighting Indians?"

"No."

"Before this event, were you ever in any battle with firearms?"

"No."

"When this particular battle began, who fired the first shot?"

"Blakely."

"Then who?"

"I don't remember."

"You don't remember if it was Mister Putney, Miss O'Neill, or yourself?"

"No."

"Were you scared?"

"Yes."

"So, scared that you shot wildly?"

Standing again, Pool simply said, "Your honor."

"Mister Doby has already admitted that he used his gun during the event," said the judge. "I see no harm in answering this question."

"I reckon," said Doby.

"Did this gun battle happen quickly or did it take a long time?"

"It seemed it only took a few seconds."

"And bullets were flying all around?"

"Yes."

"I guess you tried not to get shot."

"Well, yeah, I ain't crazy."

"Did you get shot?"

"Yes."

"Where did you get shot?"

"Right here," Doby pointed to the fleshy area under his arm.

"Who shot you?"

"I didn't see. I don't know."

"Was it Mister Blakely?"

"No."

"How about Miss O'Neill or Mister Putney?"

Pool stood again, "Judge he already answered he didn't know who shot him."

"That's right, Mister McLaury, move on," the judge instructed the prosecutor.

"Thank you, your honor," said McLaury. "Things were happening fast, weren't they Mister Doby?"

"Yes, sir."

"What were you doing as all this was happening, I mean besides shooting?"

"I was trying to get the hell out of there."

"Is it possible you didn't see who shot Mister Blakely?"

"I already said I shot him."

"You testified that things were happening quickly. Is it possible that you may have thought you shot Mister Blakely, but you didn't really see him fall when you shot in his direction."

"Well, I didn't see him fall.

"So, you don't really know who shot Mister Blakely?"

"I guess not."

"It could have been Miss O'Neill?"

This time it was Imogene who stood. "Objection your honor," she said. "The question calls for speculation."

"Objection sustained," said the judge.

"Now, Mister Doby let's discuss something different. "You've spent quite a few days in the company of Mister Putney, lately, is that right?"

"Yes, sir."

"Spending all that time together, I guess you discussed all sorts of topics? Sports, politics, jobs, that sort of thing?"

"Well, yeah, I guess."

"Did you ever discuss your testimony in court, on this case?"

"A little, yeah."

"Did he tell you to say that you shot Mister Blakely?"

"No, he never."

"Then what did he tell you?"

"He told me to listen to every question carefully and to tell the truth."

"That's good advice. Have you told the truth here today?"

"Yes, sir."

"And yesterday, when you said you shot Mister Blakely to defend Mister Putney, Was that the truth?"

Pool was on his feet again, "Your honor I am again advising my client not to answer the question."

"I don't see the harm," said the judge.

"May I approach the bench, your honor," asked Pool.

"I suppose, Mister McLaury, Miss Foster please approach, also."

With the three attorneys in front of him, Judge Beckham said, "You have the floor, Mister Pool."

"Judge," he said. "If my client answers 'no', then he is admitting to perjury. If he answers 'yes' but in fact didn't, he opens himself up to a possible perjury charge. Either way, it could be a statement against his interest."

"Mmmmm," said the judge. "Miss Foster, Mister Doby is your witness, do you have anything to say about this?"

"I have no objection to him not answering, your honor," said Imogene. The truth was, she did not want Doby to answer.

"How about you, Mister McLaury?" asked Judge Beckham.

"Judge the point here is to get to the truth. Either he has testified truthfully or not. It is important the jury knows."

"Would you agree to not prosecute him if he answers, no?" asked the judge.

After giving it a moment's thought, McLaury said, "If your honor would allow it, I would prefer to reframe the question in a manner so that Mister Doby would not be in jeopardy."

"If you can do that, I will allow it. If the question should give rise to the possibility of perjury, I will sustain Mister Pool's objection and not require Mister Doby to answer. Does this suit everyone?" asked the judge.

All three attorneys agreed and returned to their positions in the court.

"Mister Doby," McLaury started again, "Let me put my question differently. You stated that you were scared, things were happening quickly, you were wounded, you were trying to find cover to prevent further wounding, and everything was confusing, is that correct?"

"Yes, sir," admitted Doby.

"Given all that, even though you may have believed you were answering truthfully, yesterday, upon reflection, with all that was happening and the confusion, is it possible that it was not your bullet that actually struck Mister Blakely?"

Doby looked at Pool who nodded his head that it was alright to answer, then he said, "Yes, sir. That's possible."

"Thank you, Mister Doby," said McLaury. "Your honor I have no further questions for this witness."

"Miss Foster?" asked the judge.

Imogene knew McLaury had done some damage to her case, but she didn't want to risk the chance of Doby saying something that would put Deidre in more danger. "No, your honor, I have no more questions."

The judge allowed Doby to leave the court. He was joined by Pool and followed by Short and Hoy.

"Miss Foster," said the judge, "Do have any more witnesses?"

Imogene and Deidre had discussed the possibility of Deidre testifying. Deidre was concerned that anything she said would get twisted by McLaury and though she wanted to tell her side it was best for her not to take the stand. Deidre truly felt they had already beaten McLaury and there was no sense risking what they had gained. "No, your honor," said Imogene.

"How about you, Mister McLaury, anything in rebuttal?" asked Judge Beckham.

McLaury believed he couldn't get any better testimony from any other witnesses, and he wanted to end with Doby's testimony fresh in the minds of the jury. "No, your honor. The prosecution rests."

The judge looked at Imogene, "Miss Foster?" he asked.

"The defense rests, your honor," said Imogene.

"Fine," said the judge. "It's early in the day yet. We will recess until one o'clock and you can present your closing arguments."

Chapter Thirty-Five

Judge Beckham checked his watch as he stepped behind the bench. After everyone was seated, he spoke to the jury, "Gentlemen, the case in chief is over. The attorneys have presented their evidence and their witnesses. It is now time for them to give their closing arguments. I want to remind you that what the attorneys say is not evidence, but a summation of what they believe the evidence shows. The way this works is that Miss Foster will summarize first and Mister McLaury will go last. This is because the burden of proof is on the prosecution, so Mister McLaury has the last word. When they finish their arguments, you will be taken to the jury room where it is your job to consider the evidence and reach a verdict. The verdict must be unanimous. I will give you further instructions before you retire to the jury room. Miss Foster you may proceed."

Imogene had already arranged the physical evidence on her table so she could refer to it without hesitation. She walked to the podium and began, "Gentlemen, I want to thank you again for the attention you have given this case. When I first addressed you, I told you that Mister McLaury would weave some sort of fairy tale to get you to convict Miss O'Neill. I told you his evidence would not stand up, once we presented our evidence. You may ask yourself, 'How can she make such a statement?' I will remind you of the prosecution's evidence and how we refuted that evidence. I will begin with the investigation of the scene of the evidence. Did either Marshal Rea or Sheriff Maddox do a thorough search of the scene? Their testimony tells you they did not. On the other hand, we presented photographs of the scene, the photos showed how bullets fired from the gun used by Miss O'Neill could not have struck Mister Blakely. The photos also showed the careful collection of a thirty-eight caliber bullet that was fired during the attack. Mister McLaury is sure to tell you that the photographer, Mister Rhine, and the man who collected the evidence, Mister Morgan, were not professionally trained to collect evidence. This may be true, but at least they made an effort, and you can see the care they took."

"Now let's consider the evidence presented by the coroners. Doctor Cramer's report and testimony showed that the fatal wound came from a forty-four or forty-five caliber bullet. However, we presented a second report and testimony from Doctor McLeod, who is totally impartial to this case. He has no reputation to protect. And what did Doctor McLeod tell you? He demonstrated that the fatal wound could not have been made by such a large caliber bullet, rather it had to be from a thirty-eight or smaller. We have twice shown that a thirty-eight was involved."

"Then we have the evidence of two forty-four caliber bullets presented by the prosecution. That looked pretty damning, but we presented testimony from Deputy Sheriff Forsythe that when he received the evidence, one bullet was a forty-four and the other was a thirty-eight. Ask yourselves why Deputy Forsythe would make up such a story. His testimony put his job at risk. He had nothing to gain. Now the prosecutor would have you believe he made up the story due to a mild flirtation. Ask yourself if you would make up such a story, knowing you would be out of a job just to impress a pretty girl. I doubt any of you would."

"How about the witnesses to the event? Every witness said they couldn't be certain who or what Miss O'Neil shot at. Why would they say that? I will tell you why because they are honest citizens."

"Then the prosecution presented witnesses to tell you that Miss O'Neill and Deputy U. S. Marshal Nahum Putney conspired to draw Mister Blakely out and force him into a battle for his life. But as it turns out those very witnesses held grudges of their own against Deputy Putney. Remember the so-called Captain Russell? His plan to commit a robbery was foiled by Nahum Putney. Then later, as a deputy marshal, Nahum Putney was instrumental in sending Russell to prison. How could anyone possibly take his testimony seriously? And can you believe Quanah Parker? A man who at one time swore to kill Nahum Putney. I don't think so."

"Finally, the nail in the coffin of the prosecution case is the testimony of Mister Clint Doby. You remember. Here is his pistol," Imogene reached over to her table and held up the thirty-eight caliber gun. "You heard testimony from Deputy Marshal Putney that he took the gun from Clint Doby, and he marked it so it could not be confused with any similar weapon. And Mister

269

Doby, himself, told you it was his pistol and he identified it by the fancy scrollwork. But what else did Mister Doby say? And this is very important. Clint Doby, knowing he could be prosecuted, told you that the person who shot Mister Blakely was not Deidre O'Neill. No, he told you it was he who shot Blakely. The prosecution tried their best to diminish Mister Doby's testimony, but they failed."

"Gentlemen, Judge Beckham will tell you that the prosecution has the burden of proving Deidre O'Neill committed a crime, beyond reasonable doubt. What is reasonable doubt? 'It is doubt that would make a reasonable man hesitate before acting on a matter of importance.' It means that you, as the fact finders in this case, cannot say with moral certainty that Deidre O'Neill is guilty of the crime for which she is charged. Reasonable doubt, gentlemen. Reasonable doubt. Has the prosecution proved their case beyond reasonable doubt? I say no. Quite to the contrary gentlemen, I tell you we have proved Deidre O'Neill innocent beyond any doubt."

I thank you again for your attentiveness and I know you will return with a verdict of not guilty."

McLaury waited for Imogene to be seated at her table before he rose and stepped to the lectern with a handful of notes. Looking around the courtroom, he took his time before starting. He looked at the gallery, the judge, Deidre O'Neill, and finally the jury. "Good afternoon, gentlemen. Were you amazed at Miss Foster's presentation? I know I was. The truth be told if I were sitting where you are I would be ready to acquit Miss O'Neill. But before you even consider that let me remind you that Miss Foster tried to make a silk purse from a sow's ear. Let me go through her arguments, one by one. First, I will remind you that Marshal Rea did conduct an investigation where the crime took place. Did he take photographs, map out so-called bullet marks, look for bullets in wooden portions of buildings? No, he did not, and for a simple reason, because there is no way of telling whether the marks were made by bullets or some tool. Even her own witness admitted he could not say for certain that the marks were made by bullets or from a rock from a slingshot. And there was no way of telling when the marks were left. And the bullet in the wall? How long had that been there? There is no way of telling. Marshal Rea has years of experience as a lawman, and he knew all this. Had Miss O'Neill's men been more experienced they would have known that. But out of desperation Miss O'Neill's men took direction from a man who was laid up in a hospital and never himself investigated the scene. Join that with the point that Mister Putney also has no real experience investigating murder scenes."

"Let's discuss the battling coroners' reports and their testimony. Who are these men? Well, Doctor Cramer is a longtime resident of Fort Worth. He is a veteran of the War Between the States, a war where he tended to severe bullet wounds, nearly daily. A man who has conducted many autopsies right here in Fort Worth and his judgment has never been questioned. But how about Doctor McLeod? I'm sure he is an honorable man but weigh his experience against that of Doctor Cramer. Who has the greater understanding of bullet wounds? That seems a quite easy one to answer."

"But how about the examination of Mister Blakely's body? Doctor Cramer was able to perform his examination within hours of the shooting. But what about Doctor McLeod? Mister Blakey's body had been buried for weeks. Do you really believe that there were no changes in the body after all that time? That brings us to the accusation that Doctor Cramer's report was altered. There was never any evidence that the allegation was true. It was all innuendo and relies on you taking a leap of faith to believe it. And as far as Deputy Forsythe, would he be the first man to try and impress a woman or girl for his own purpose? It's a story as old as Samson and Delilah.

The people we brought forth to testify to what they witnessed were just a portion of those we could have called. But these were enough. What did they tell you? Each one told you Miss O'Neill was shooting in the direction of Mister Blakely. But Miss Foster wants you to believe Miss O'Neill was shooting at someone else. And we will get to that part of the story in a minute. But what about Quanah Parker? If he wanted to take revenge on Nahum Putney, why not just let him lay there in the middle of the street and bleed to death? That would be easier than rushing him to get medical care, saving his life, and then coming to testify in court so he could exact his revenge against Mister Putney's lover. That just makes no sense. No, Miss Foster wants you to believe that every witness was acting out of some sort of malice.

Let's not forget what Captain Russell told you about Mister Putney. I'll be the first to admit that Captain Russell has an axe to grind against Putney, but you have to ask yourself if his testimony is believable. Put yourself in Mister Blakely's boots. You see a man walking around Fort Worth, wearing two pistols in the open for anyone to see. An act that is illegal for anyone else. This man you see left you in the west Texas desert with little to defend yourself against marauding hostiles. Add to it Mister Putney's reputation. If he weren't wearing a badge, he would be considered a pistoleer, a shootist, no different than the likes of Ben Thompson, or King Fisher. Don't take my word for it. Read the books I put into evidence. What would you do if you thought John Wesley Harding was in town looking for you? By his own admission, he has even killed two women. He is no better than any of the Earps. Men who shoot first and ask questions later. Why, all you have to do is read the Fort Worth Gazette, just last week Putney killed a man at the train station."

"Objection your honor," Imogene almost screamed outraged at McLaury's last statement. "There was nothing offered into evidence about any shooting at the Fort Worth train station."

Judge Beckham sighed, "You are correct, but what do you want me to do?"

"I want you to have that statement stricken from the record and instruct the jury to disregard it," said Imogene.

"Do you really think at this point the jury is going to unhear it?" asked the judge, "But you are right. The clerk will strike Mister McLaury's statement about the train station. Gentlemen of the jury, you are to disregard Mister McLaury's statement," the judge sighed and waved a hand at McLaury as a signal for him to continue.

"Finally," McLaury said to the jury, "That brings us to Mister Clint Doby. What do we know about Mister Doby? Well, we know by his own admission that he is an extortionist. We also learned he is another man with a grudge against Mister Putney. Something that seems quite common. We know that Mister Putney at some point grabbed Mister Doby up in the Indian Nations and brought him here to Fort Worth, or somewhere close by and hid him out until he could be sprung on us to testify. I can't deny that the pistol Miss Foster showed you belongs to Mister Doby, or that it was seized by Mister Putney. But it doesn't make any difference. Nobody could prove that any bullets fired in that alley were shot from that gun. I could have gone to several gun stores in town and bought all sorts of pistols. It wouldn't matter because nobody can say what bullet was fired from what gun if the guns were of the same caliber."

"Now we have Mister Doby, who admits to being in the alley and even admits to shooting Mister Blakely. But don't forget Doby was holed up with Mister Putney for who knows how long. Think about Mister Putney's reputation. Think of the young age of Mister Doby. Do you think a young man like that could be influenced by a man like Putney? And that's not to mention that he was also under guard by a known shootist and gambler like Luke Short and an Indian that comes from who knows where. I would be frightened to death in that circumstance. I would say just about anything to get away from those men. But I have to give Mister Doby credit for finally having the courage to admit that he couldn't say whether he had shot Mister Blakely, or not."

"So here we are gentlemen. Miss Foster has brought more smoke and mirrors into this courtroom than an illusionist at a Vaudeville theater. Her task was to try and confuse you. Make you believe she could suspend a person in midair. But it is all an illusion, a magic trick."

"No, gentlemen, trust the real evidence. Trust Marshal Willaim Rea. Trust Sheriff Maddox. Trust Doctor Cramer, and all the other witnesses who gave undeniable evidence that Deidre O'Neill purposefully shot Ned Blakely in the back. An act of revenge against a man who was already incapacitated. No, gentlemen, your duty is clear, there is no doubt what the truth is. You must retire to the jury room, consider the real evidence, and come back with the only verdict, imaginable. A verdict of Guilty.

Chapter Thirty-Six

The most notable luminaries of Fort Worth turned out at the Freedom Gala held at O'Neill's Restaurant and Hotel a mere week after Deidre O'Neill was acquitted. Deidre was somewhat annoyed by the hypocrisy of the celebrants, most of whom shunned her establishment like the plague had broken out there, during the trial. But Mary, always the person who had a soothing effect on Deidre's temper, had calmed down the Irish woman. "Deidre," she said. "This is vindication for you. It is an opportunity to change our reputation. You will be bigger than ever. Just go out and be your most delightful. You will have all these movers and shakers eating out of your hand. Why, it was in the Gazette that even the most influential women in town are beginning to imitate how you dress. You have won. Be gracious."

Mary was right of course. The Planters House and The Commercial, the other big restaurants in town, had closed for the evening. At The White Elephant, Luke Short was hosting a celebration where the lesser citizens gathered to toast the victorious Deidre O'Neill. Deidre told Mary to go out and make sure everyone was enjoying themselves. "If I'm going to do this, I'll do it with flair," said Deidre, then asked, "Have you seen Nahum or Imogene?"

"Imogene will be down shortly, and Nahum should be here just any minute," said Mary. "He said he had some paperwork to take care of."

"That's fine then. Tell Brutus and Caesar to send him in here the minute he arrives," said Deidre, and Mary said she would. The celebration was getting into full swing with a band playing waltzes and polkas, but the music could barely be heard in Deidre's apartment. Deidre took a moment to enjoy the calm, looking at her image in the three-way mirror. She worried that she might be putting on weight, but it didn't show in her sleek ball gown made from copper silk and trimmed with blue taffeta. It hung just at the top of her ivory shoulders. The bodice was form-fitting to the waist and then billowed out to a perfect bell shape to the floor. It was with pride, not vanity that she admitted to herself, that even at forty-five years of age she could hold her own against any woman in Texas.

A knock on the door was followed by the entrance of Imogene Foster. Her dress was more subdued than Deidre's, yet it had a simple elegance of its own. The dress of gold satin fit her figure perfectly to the waist but then flowed into draped spirals to the floor. The drapes were trimmed in black velvet and a black velvet panel insert, like a vest fit in a V form from her waist to her neck. The long sleeves and collar were trimmed with cream-colored lace and a ruffle of the same lace ran from the neck to the bottom of the V. Her golden blond hair was up with one tight curl hanging over her shoulder and was topped with a small hat adorned with raven's feathers. "Oh, Imogene, you look adorable," gushed Deidre as her lawyer entered her private chambers. "When Nahum gets here, we must sashay into the dining room, one on each arm."

Blushing at the compliment, and at the thought of being on Nahum's arm, Imogene said, "But this is your moment, Deidre."

"Nonsense. If it weren't for you and Nahum there would be no celebration," Deidre swept to Imogene and hugged her, but not so tightly as to wrinkle either woman's outfit.

"Where is Nahum, anyway?" asked Imogene.

Before Deidre could answer, Putney said, "Did I hear someone calling my name?" Both women stood in awe at the man before them. Putney was wearing a black tuxedo over a royal blue satin waistcoat. The tuxedo had tails and satin lapels. His white shirt had a high stiff collar, and, to Deidre's amazement, he was wearing a white, perfectly knotted bow tie. His red hair had been trimmed slightly so that it just brushed his shoulders, and his beard was neatly trimmed. To finish off the look he wore glossy black patent leather shoes. Neither woman had ever seen him wear shoes instead of boots.

"My," said Deidre, you look more resplendent than Prince Edward, himself. And no massive armory hanging off your hips. What shall we do in case of an emergency?" Nahum pulled back one lapel of his tuxedo jacket and showed a small Colt revolver dangling in a shoulder holster. "I should have known," laughed Deidre. "Let's go to the office and have a toast before we face the teeming throng."

The three stood at the drinks table while Deidre poured each a generous portion of Bushmills whiskey. "To my hero and my heroine, without whom I wouldn't be standing here tonight," Deidre lifted her glass. The other two clinked their glasses against Deidre's and they both sipped their whiskey.

"Now," said Nahum, "I would like to make a toast of my own." He raised his glass and said to the two ladies in my life. The women I love."

Both Deidre and Imogene felt slight pangs of jealousy, both wishing they were his only love, but without hesitation, they both clinked their glasses against his. "Slainte," Deidre toasted in Gaelic. The three downed their drinks and went to the main room.

Caesar had been looking for the trio to enter and when he saw them, he signaled the bandmaster who stopped the waltz the band was playing and they struck up <u>For He's a Jolly Good Fellow</u>, except they changed the words to She's a Jolly good Lady. The dancers and other revelers all stopped, joining in the congratulatory song, and at the end broke into applause. From the kitchen, the chef rolled in a four-tiered cake, and everyone applauded again. Deidre was escorted to the bandstand by Nahum and Imogene. Standing a foot higher than her audience, Deidre scanned the room. She saw the mayor and all the city councilmen, doctors, lawyers, businessmen, and all their wives. Even Buckley Paddock was in attendance. Conspicuous by their absence were Sheriff Maddox, Marshal Rea, Jim Courtwright, and William McLaury. Judge Beckham wasn't there either, but he had sent word earlier that it would not be seemly for the judge in her case to attend, though he did congratulate Deidre. He also congratulated Imogene for her brilliant and robust defense of her client. Deidre held up her hands asking everyone for their attention.

As the applause was dying, Mary handed Deidre a glass of champagne, and then Deidre addressed her well-wishers, "Ladies and gentlemen," she began. "I am honored and humbled by everyone's presence here tonight. I want to thank you all for having faith in me," Of course,this wasn't true, but she was following Mary's advice to be gracious. "I want to thank Mister Buckley Paddock for editorial retracting his earlier opinion of my innocence. It takes a big man to admit when he is wrong." She

276

could care less if Paddock dropped dead at that very moment, but she wanted to keep on the good side of the major newspaper in town. She held up her glass of champagne, gesturing toward Paddock, then tried not to choke as she sipped. "But," she restarted, "I want to specifically thank some very special people." She waved to Mary to join her. "For those who don't know her, this is Mary Johnson. Mary has been with me for many years, and she is my rock and has been, especially during this time. Tonight, I would like to announce that starting immediately Miss Johnson will have a quarter interest in my business." There was a round of applause from the crowd, and none clapped louder than Brutus and Caesar. As they were clapping, Deidre signaled for the ebony giants to step up to the bandstand. "For those that don't know, these two lovable bears were born into slavery, before New York abolished the practice. They have been with me for years and have been my protectors in all circumstances." More applause was raised. "Tonight, I am turning over twelve and one-half percent, each, of my business." The Shakespeare twins were blushing from their boss' generosity, though nobody could tell. This time there was polite applause but not nearly as enthusiastic. "The brothers stepped down and guided Imogene to the dais. "Imogene Foster," said Deidre, "I know of no way to appropriately thank you for your representation but know that I will always consider you my sister and will love you forever." This time people called out to Imogene for her to speak. Deidre bowed elegantly to Imogene and let her have the floor.

Imogene was blushing and there wasn't a person in the room that couldn't see it. "Ladies and gentlemen," she said, "I want to thank Deidre for allowing me to represent her and having faith in me the entire time." Though she had been eloquent in court, Imogene wanted to get her speaking over with and get off the stage as quickly as possible.

Deidre stepped back to the forefront and said, "Lastly, I want to recognize the man who started all this trouble." This line got a laugh from everybody. She continued, "But he is, has, and always will be my Sir Galahad. My knight in shining armor," Then raising her voice she announced, "Deputy United States Marshal Edward Nahum Putney."

277

There were shouts for a speech as Putney stepped beside the fiery redhead. She always had a knack for embarrassing him and this was no exception. He held up one hand to quieten the crowd; he stopped the applause immediately. He looked at Deidre, lovingly, then he bowed deeply, rose took one hand and kissed it, then simply said, "Thank you, my lady." His brief address started everyone clapping again. Putney held up his lover's hand, like a champion prize fighter, "Everyone enjoy yourselves." He ushered Deidre off the bandstand and he and she began making the rounds of the crowd, shaking hands and accepting congratulations. Mary and Imogene were doing the same, hoping to leave no hand untouched.

Deidre excused herself from Nahum and made her way over to a corner where Elizabeth Sykes and Hubert Forsythe were standing. Both were shy about mixing with a crowd of such importance. Elizabeth was dressed in a lovely Sunday dress made of white cotton with three lines of blue satin ruffles around the bottom and a matching blue satin sash around her waist. It ended just above her ankles, and she was wearing blue stockings and white pumps. Her hair was combed straight down her back with one long braid tied with a blue ribbon. Hubert was feeling out of place with his simple brown, wool serge suit, cotton shirt and string tie. He had managed to buy a new pair of brown, fancy tooled boots which he wore outside his trousers. Elizabeth gushed over Deidre's attire and her speech. "Thank you, Betsy," said Deidre. "How about the two of you, are you faring well?"

"Oh, yes," said Elizabeth. "We are both so happy for you, and we have a little secret, but only you can know."

"And what might that be?" Deidre asked, as though she couldn't read the expressions on their faces.

Elizabeth leaned over and whispered, "Hubert asked me to marry him."

Deidre had been expecting as much but feigned shock, then said, "Well, that is exciting news." Then looking at Forsythe said, "I guess you will be looking for a new job."

"No ma'am," Forsythe said. "You see, Judge Beckham told Sheriff Maddox that he needed to keep an honest man like me and the sheriff agreed. So, I'm set, at least for now. And Mister Putney said he would take me on as a part-time posseman."

278

"Well, there you have it, but I can't let those two upstage me," Deidre told the couple. "Elizabeth," It was the first time Deidre had called her by her proper name. "With Mary taking over part of the business, I'm going to need someone to help run the front of the house, with Janet and the job is yours. It will come with a rise in pay and your own small room in the hotel."

"Oh my gosh, Miss Deidre. Thank you so much," said Elizabeth.

Deidre then looked at Forsythe with a scowl. "But don't you go thinking you can come and go as you want. At least not until you've tied the knot."

"Oh, no ma'am," an embarrassed Forsythe told her.

Deidre gave them both a hug. "Now I have to go glad hand some more folks. You two get some cake, and no more than one glass of champagne for either of you." Deidre swooshed off to greet more guests.

The celebration had begun to quiet down as people sat at their tables and ordered meals. Mary looked around. Both dining rooms were filled with people standing, waiting to be seated. She thought it was the beginning of a new life for O'Neill's.

Putney and Deidre had managed to make it back to each other when they both saw people's attention being drawn to the entrance. Luke Short and Ed Hoy were standing at the entrance hoping to catch the attention of the couple. They made their way to the gambler and Indian. "Sorry to interrupt, Miss O'Neill," said Short with a tip of his silk top hat. "But there is a clamor across the street for the woman of the day.

Deidre looked at the crowd behind her. "I don't think they will notice my absence," she said and the four stepped quickly out into the street. As the four entered the doors of The White Elephant a loud cheer rose from the whole saloon. This was a much more boisterous crowd and one that truly believed in Deidre.

A voice in the crowd yelled out, "Hip, hip," which was quickly followed by a chorus of "Hurray!" This happened three times then the group started making their way through the crowd. There were no speeches to be made in The White Elephant. Instead, men and women patted the couple on their backs and offered to buy drinks. The couple accepted glasses of bourbon from Luke Short and Putney roared a toast over the din of the crowd. Putney then pulled his long wallet out of his jacket pocket and produced two one-hundred-dollar bills and slapped them on the bar. "Drinks on Miss O'Neill," he shouted. With everyone's attention diverted, Putney and Deidre pushed their way to the door and stepped into the warm night air.

"Nahum," said Deidre, "Let's not go back to either party. Let us go straight to my apartment."

"Sweetheart," said Putney, "I couldn't agree more."

Once in Deidre's bedroom, Nahum couldn't wait to remove his restrictive clothing. The tie was the first to go, followed by the formal jacket and the waistcoat. Deidre ducked behind a dressing screen and began disrobing. Nahum sat on the edge of the bed and shucked the patent leather shoes that had begun to pinch his toes. "A little late for propriety, don't you think," he joked over his shoulder.

"I'm a lady of society now," said Deidre," convention must be obeyed, she jested in return.

"Deidre," said Nahum. "I have something I want to tell you."

"Good," said Deidre, "Because I have something to tell you, too. Get those clothes off and get into bed, when I'm ready you can tell me."

Nahum stripped down to the bottom part of his long johns and lay on the bed, waiting for Deidre. After a few moments, she came from behind the screen wearing a frilly white dressing gown trimmed with yellow bows. She sank into the bed next to Nahum, gave him a light kiss, and then laid her head on his chest. "What did you want to tell me?" Nahum asked.

"Oh, no," said Deidre. "You mentioned it something first, so you go first."

Nahum stared at the ceiling, trying to form his words. "We've known each other a while and you know I have never been one for sentimental talk."

"That, dear, maybe the understatement of the year," she returned.

"I know you've always wanted me to find another line of work. And I've told you why I couldn't."

"Yes," she said. "And it is silly reasoning. You aren't that man anymore."

"Sometimes I wonder, but that isn't what I want to say. I know I've changed, but I must keep on with this line of work. Not because of the reasons I told you before. I see that now as folly. But, Deidre," Nahum propped himself on one elbow, letting her head softly sink into the pillow. "There are just too many wicked men, and someone has to stand for the law."

"So, I guess you'll be telling me you are back to Austin, then."

"No, No," he said. "That's not it at all. No, I'm going to stay here and work for Marshal Cabell, as long as he will have me. Here I'm more or less my own boss. But that's not what I wanted to say either."

"Well, I wish you would get to it, then," Deidre told him.

"If you would let me, I will," he said. "Look, you are going to be here and be successful for a long time. And I'm going to be here," Nahum paused and took a deep breath. "So, I think it's time we get married."

"Well, if that's not the most romantic proposal I ever heard, I don't know what is," said Deidre.

"I'm just being straight. It's the only way I know how."

"I know, dear," she said. "And I love you for it."

"Well, are you going to answer?" Nahum was anxious that she would say no.

"All I have to say is it's a good thing you asked before I started showing."

"Showing what?"

"I'm pregnant, you big galoot. Now shut up and kiss me."

Chapter Thirty-Seven

For a day and a half, neither Nahum Putney nor Deidre O'Neill emerged from Deidre's apartment. Messages had been left on Deidre's desk for Mary, ordering food and coffee. At noon on the second day, Putney exited the hotel wearing pieces of his tuxedo. Absent were the tie and the waistcoat. Putney went directly to his office, put a fresh set of everyday clothes, his Smiths and cartridge belt and boots in a case, then set off to the Buck Head Bath House. After having a fine soak in a private room, Putney dressed and gave his formal clothes and the case to an attendant to take to the laundry. He stopped at a tobacco shop, bought a packet of Kinney ready-rolled cigarettes, and filled his silver case. Standing outside the shop, he lit a cigarette and smoked until it nearly burned his fingers. He stubbed out the cigarette and headed to Hell's Half Acre.

Putney shook his head in disgust at the squaller of the red-light district. Maybe after dark the place didn't look so bad, but Putney couldn't understand how anybody could dismiss the smell of vomit, spilled beer, and open sewage. He walked directly to the Emerald Saloon and passed through the double doors. The bar on the left was typical of saloons on the frontier and seedier parts of cities. There was no polished bar, no grand mirror, no large painting of a round-bottomed temptress. The spittoons appeared to have never been cleaned and the floors were sticky with spilled beer and blood. Putney walked to the bar but resisted leaning his elbows on the greasy top. He was greeted by a burly bartender with two days' growth of beard and a dirty apron. The barman looked at the badge pinned on Putney's vaquero jacket. "Whatcha havin, Marshal?" he asked.

"Information," Putney told him.

"Information comes with two bits and a glass of whiskey," Putney was informed.

"Will half a dollar buy me good whiskey and a clean glass?" asked Putney.

"Sure, but the information will still cost another two bits."

Putney fished in his trouser pocket and flipped a silver dollar onto the bar. "Good whiskey, clean glass, and information," said Putney.

The bartender reached under the bar and produced a bottle of bonded whiskey, broke the paper seal, and filled a glass. "Do you want special information or will just any old information do?"

"I'm looking for Jim Courtwright, have you seen him?"

"Yep," replied the barkeeper and slapped a quarter on the bar.

"Have you always been this surly? Or do you practice at it?"

"The bartender swept away the quarter, "I work at it as hard as you work at wanting information."

Putney reached into his pocket and produced another dollar, gently placing it on the bar this time. The bartender placed his hand on top of the dollar but before he could blink Putney pulled a six-inch knife from its scabbard and punched into the bar a mere quarter of an inch from the bartender's hand. The man's eyes opened wide until they were as large as the dollar under his hand. Glaring into the man's eyes Putney said, "That is a shitload of information under your palm, and if you don't answer me this time you will have to spend it at the sawbones to sew up your hand."

Sweat popped out on the barman's forehead as he said, "Jim's in the backroom." He nodded to his left.

There was no way Putney was going into the backroom of a place like the Emerald Saloon. "Leave the dollar where it is, go back there, and tell Courtwright I want to see him out here. Then you can pick up the dollar."

The bartender slowly slid his hand away from the knife and walked to the closed door in the back. He opened it and said something, came back to the bar, and pointed at the dollar. "As soon as I see Courtwright," said Putney.

It wasn't half a minute when Courtwright entered the barroom. "When Jake said the Marshal wanted to see me, I thought he meant Rea, But I'm alright coming out to talk with you, Putney. Truth is, I wouldn't have gone back to that storeroom either. Jake give us two glasses of whiskey and not the crap I'm sure you tried to pawn off on Marshal Putney." Jake brought out two fresh glasses and a bottle of O. Z. Tyler. "I assure you, Putney this is real whiskey and won't set your gut on fire." Courtwright poured two drinks and lifted his glass, "Cheers," he said and took a drink. "Now, what can I do for you?"

Putney knew he was in enemy territory, so he sipped his whiskey but kept an eye on Courtwright. He knew Courtwright's gun would be under his jacket and if the gunman went for his pistol, Putney would have him dead in a heartbeat. It was the barman that concerned him. "The first thing you can do is have ole Jake hear put his scatter gun on the bar, butt first."

Courtwright glanced at Jake and gave a nod. The barman reached under the bar and gently placed a double barreled shotgun on the bar, following Putney's direction. Satisfied Putney said, "You did me a good turn down at the train station, but that doesn't mean I trust you any farther than I can throw you."

"Why, Nahum, I'm crushed," said Courtwright and taking another drink of whiskey.

"I'm sure you are, Jim," said Putney. "My real business today is what I originally came to Fort Worth for. That is to tell you that O'Neill's is out of bounds. But things have changed. I'm not going back to Austin. I'm going to plant myself here, so I'm telling you, now, you're not welcome at O'Neill's. And you should pass that word to any of the toughs you employ as so-called detectives. As long as you understand that then there is no reason you and I should have any problems."

"That's good with me, Nahum," Courtwright agreed, "As long as you understand one thing."

"And that is?"

"I'm not agreeing because you frighten me. I agree because it just isn't profitable," Courtwright said. "Now, is there anything else?"

"Yes," said Putney. "Where are Montague Russell and Bull Dawson keeping themselves?"

"That's a strange thing," Courtwright answered. "I haven't seen either of them since the trial. The truth is I think you do frighten them."

"If you see either of them, tell them what I told you applies specifically to them."

"I'll pass along the message," Courtwright assured Putney.

284

Putney and Deidre were married two days later. It was a quiet ceremony with only Mary and Imogene in attendance in Judge Beckham's chambers. Mary closed the restaurant that day, so the employees could come to a small party. Putney moved a few clothes into Deidre's apartment but they both agreed most of his belongings would stay at his office until they found a house, at which time Mary would take over the apartment. The day after the wedding, Imogene returned to Dallas. Deidre had tried to get her to set up her practice in Fort Worth, but Imogene declined, saying she had important clients in Dallas who she had to get back to. The truth was that Imogene didn't think she could bear seeing Deidre and Nahum together, day in and day out. She didn't begrudge their happiness, but she knew the only way she would ever be happy was to have distance between the two of them.

In the days that followed, everyone settled into a pattern of normalcy. Mary took over running most of the day-to-day business. One of the first things she did was to close down the private dining room. Certain gentlemen and their paramours would have to find someplace else for their assignations. She combined the two eating areas in order to accommodate more customers. From then on O'Neill's would be a respectable place. Deidre spent most of her days looking for a house to rent. She wanted something nice, but not expensive. Also, at her doctor's insistence, she got plenty of rest daily. The doctor told her childbirth was never easy, but for a woman of her age was especially risky.

For his part, Putney stayed busy, serving writs around the countryside, it was rare for him to begone more than a day. On a couple of occasions, he traveled to Waco to pick up some prisoners and move them to Graham for trial. Because these trips could take a couple of days, he hired Forsythe to accompany him.

Deidre's search for a house had finally ended with a nice two-bedroom house west of the Trinity River just off Seventh Street. The rent was reasonable, and it had a bathroom and kitchen with running water. She and Putney were waiting to move in until they could have all the furnishings. Because she had to rest and Putney was busy, she hired a decorator to purchase the items they would need, all approved by her first, naturally.

Two days after moving into their new home, while at his office, Putney received an urgent telegram from Sheriff Schmick of Eastland County saying the Texas and Pacific train had been robbed outside the town of Ranger. When the gang broke the door of the mail car the postal clerk fired on the bandits, possibly wounding one. The bandits returned fire, wounding the clerk. The take was estimated to be twenty thousand dollars in currency and eight thousand in gold bullion. Sheriff Schmick said that he suspected the robbers were the Nate Reed gang and was asking for immediate assistance. Putney pulled the watch from his vest and checked the time. It was twenty past one. Putney pulled his train schedule for the Texas Pacific Railroad and saw another train was slated to depart west at four that afternoon. Putney knew the time frame would be tight, but he could make it if he didn't dawdle. First, he wrote 'forward to U. S. Marshal Cabell and provided the address on the yellow telegram he had received, then added a request for the postal inspector if he was available. Postal inspectors were city people and rarely ventured into the field and he knew there would be no help from that department, but it was policy always to request one. On his way to the telegraph office, he saw a teenager who he often used as a messenger. He told the boy to go to the stable and have the hostler ready his horse and both mules and bring them to the office. Then he told him to go to the sheriff's office to find Hubert Forsyth and give him a message, then return with the answer to his office and wait for Putney's return. Putney then went to the telegraph office and sent his message.

Putney always kept packs in his office filled with ammunition, canned goods, various tools, cookware, tin plates and cups, and manacles and chains. Usually enough for a ten-day trip. But he had to stop at the grocer's and pick up a slab of bacon, potatoes, carrots, coffee, and sugar. On the way back to his office he stopped at the tobacconist and bought a dozen packs of Kinney's. Back at the office, the teen boy handed him a note and Putney gave the boy four bits. The note said Forsythe had been sent to Samantha Springs to investigate a horse theft and probably wouldn't be back for a day. Putney hadn't had the time to set up any other possemen and was disappointed that Forsythe wasn't around, but he didn't have time to seek out anyone else. He entered the office stowed his purchases in packs and waited for his animals. It was fifteen minutes before the hostler arrived with the stock, Putney checked the animals. They were all in good shape and the pack mule had a bag of grain that should last ten days. He loaded up his supplies, slid a Winchester into its saddle sheath, and strapped a sawed-off ten gauge on top of his packs. He checked his watch. It was two-thirty. He mounted and rode to his house.

Because of the doctor's orders to rest, Deidre had hired a woman to help with housework and cooking. That was her excuse anyway. The truth was that she would have hired someone anyway because she wasn't a very good cook and she abhorred housework. The woman's name was Jeanette, and she was the wife of a rail worker. Except for one thing, she was an excellent cook, but she couldn't cook tamales, a food Putney had grown fond of over the years. But she could cook a ripping good peach pie, one of which was sitting in the kitchen window to cool, and Putney wished he had time to eat some. Jeanette always had dinner prepared by three o'clock and would leave to tend to her own family. Today was no different. At first, Jeanette was startled when Putney entered the kitchen. He was never home at that time of day. "Mister Putney," she said, "This is unexpected."

"I know, Jeanette," Putney replied, "And I hope I didn't frighten you. I'm glad I got here before you left. I have a job I have to go on and I may be gone several days. I was hoping I could impose on you to look in on Deidre at night, just to make sure everything is well. Of course, I'll pay extra for your help."

"Land O'Goshen, Mister Putney. Naturally, I'll look in on the missus. My man, Frank gets off at midnight and I'll have him do a walk by the house before he gets home, too. I just hope your job isn't too dangerous."

Putney was about to lie and say it was just normal business when Deidre walked into the kitchen. "Edward," Deidre had taken to calling him by his first name when she was miffed at him. "What on earth are you doing home at this time of day and what was this word, dangerous I heard?"

Pregnancy had not diminished Deidre's beauty, instead, she grew prettier every day. She was wearing a new day coat made of red and black brocade and trimmed with fur at the collar and cuffs. The colors suited her perfectly. "Let's go into the parlor and I will explain," Nahum told her.

Deidre settled herself into an overstuffed, wingback chair, waiting for Nahum's explanation. He sat on a round ottoman in front of Deidre and was direct with her. He had never sugar-coated his job to her, and he wasn't starting now. "There has been a train robbery about a hundred miles west of here. The mail carriage was hit and I have to go see if I can help track down the bandits."

"Oh, well," said Deidre. "I'm glad it's nothing dangerous." She tried to make light of the situation. "I hope it is someone with a large bounty. We need an icebox." Then she laughed.

Nahum could see the worry written across her face. He took both her hands in his and looked into her deep blue eyes. "It won't be bad. I'm sure the sheriff will have a posse and if I'm lucky maybe a couple of Rangers will show up. With luck, we will run them to ground in no time and I will be back before you know it."

"I know you will be careful," his wife told him. "But be just a little extra careful. You're a family man now." she patted the bulge that was just beginning to show. "When do you have to leave?"

"I just stopped to pick up my thirty-eight. A westbound heads out of here at four. By the time I get to the station and get my animals on board, I can just make it."

"Then you best get started," Deidre said. "No time to dally."

Nahum went to the bedroom wardrobe and took a lock box off the top shelf. He unlocked it and removed the small pistol, his large Bowie, and a pasteboard photograph of Deidre. He placed the box, took the shoulder rig from a hook in the wardrobe, and returned to the parlor. Deidre was walking away from the secretary cabinet that stood in one corner and sat down in her chair. Nahum knelt by her chair, took her hands in his, and kissed them both. "I'll be back soon," He assured her then kissed her deeply on her lips.

"You better be, Mister Man or there will be the devil to pay," said Deidre. She reached into the inside pocket of his vaquero jacket and removed his silver cigarette case. In its place, she inserted a wooden box, the size of a gentleman's cigar case. "For luck," she said and put the silver case in an outside pocket.

Before he walked out the front door, Jeanette caught him. "I fixed you a ham and cheese sandwich and wrapped it in cheesecloth. Mrs. Putney told me you like extra mustard."

288

"That I do, Jeanette," he said and bent to give her a light kiss on her forehead.

Chapter Thirty-Eight

Putney made it to the train station at a quarter past three. Outside the station was a man Putney had met once before. Sam Perkins was a lanky man with skin burned to the color of old leather. The lines in his face testified more to years in the elements than they did his age. He had a thick, gray, bushy mustache and a hat with a larger brim and a misshapened crown. On his vest was pinned the badge of a Texas Ranger. Perkins was rolling a quirly when he saw Putney approaching him. "Ain't seen you since Waco in seventy-eight, what are you doing here?"

"I imagine the same as you," said Putney, shaking the old Ranger's hand.

"Nate Reed?" asked Perkins.

"That's what they say," said Putney. "I reckon we will be riding out to Eastland together."

"If we are it will be tomorrow,"

"What do you mean? There's a train leaving west at four."

"Canceled," Perkins told him, "Sort of."

"What do you mean?" asked Putney.

"Check for yourself," Perkins jerked a thumb to the door of the station.

Putney walked into the depot and immediately realized what Perkins was talking about. Standing just inside the door, on the tracks side, stood three men. Their clothes varied in color, but in every other aspect were uniforms. Each man wore a slicker over cheap vested, wool suits, high-topped lace-up shoes, and bowler hats. Each had a rifle case in their hands. *Damn it,* thought Putney, *Pinkerton's*. Putney had no use for Pinkerton men. Although they had a big reputation for catching outlaws, it was all puffery. Usually, they would join a posse when the bandits were on the verge of being caught, anyway, but they would take the credit. As soon as possible they would telegraph their head office in Chicago about how they had captured the criminals, then that office would send wires to all the major newspapers. In the end, the Wells Fargo reward money would go to the Pinkerton men and the men who did all the real work got squat all.

290

Putney walked to the ticket window and asked for a first class ticket to Eastland.

"Got none," said the clerk.

"There's a four o'clock scheduled," Putney said to the clerk through clenched teeth.

"It's been canceled," the clerk informed him.

"There's a train firing up on the tracks right now and the engine is directed west," Putney was losing his patience.

"Yep, I know, but that's a special train chartered by them gentlemen over there. The station manager canceled all westbound until T and P's main office gives him the go-ahead."

Putney turned from the clerk and walked toward the three Pinkertons. On his way, he bit the inside of his cheek as a reminder to smile.

Tipping his sombrero, Putney greeted the men and introduced himself. The shorter of the men and apparently the honcho said, "What can we do for you, Marshal?"

"It seems you've hired a special train going west. I'm sure y'all are headed to Eastland to investigate the robbery. That is where I am also headed, and there's a Ranger outside that needs to get there, too. So, I reckon I'm asking you to give us and our animals a ride on your special."

"Sorry, Marshal, this train has been paid for by The Pinkerton Detective Agency and only Pinkerton Detectives will be riding," said the short man.

"I'm sorry," Putney gritted his teeth. "I don't think you introduced yourself."

"Ballinger, Josiah Ballinger," said the man and thrust his hand forward for Putney to shake.

Putney ignored the hand. "Mister Ballinger, I am respectfully asking you a second time to let me and Ranger Perkins board that train."

Ballinger rolled his tongue around the wad of tobacco in his cheek, looked around, found a spittoon, walked over to it a sent a stream of spit into the metal bowl. "I already told you, mister, this is a Pinkerton train, for Pinkerton men. You'll have to figure out something else."

"I've already figured something out," said Putney. "Have you ever heard of 28 United States Code, Section 566?"

"Can't say I have," said Ballinger. "And can't say I care."

"You should care. You see it's the law that says as a Deputy Marshal I can command all necessary assistance to carry out my duties. So, I'm going to explain this in terms you and your friends will understand. Either you allow me and Ranger Perkins, and our animals on that train or he and I are going to kick the shit out of your scrawny asses, throw you out of the station and I am going to commandeer that train. And when I return, I will track down the three of you and arrest you for obstructing a Deputy Marshal in the performance of his duties. So, one more time, I'm asking you politely to invite Ranger Perkins and me to join you on your trip west."

One of the Pinkertons started reaching inside his slicker when Putney heard the undeniable sound of a Winchester being cocked. "I wouldn't do that mister," said Perkins. "It wouldn't be healthy."

Ballinger looked over at Perkins then up at Putney. He was still defiant, but he also understood where he and his men stood. "We'll let you come on board, but don't think I'm going to let this pass. I will be reporting it to my superiors in Chicago, as soon as possible."

"You do that," said Putney. He then looked at his watch, turned to Perkins he said, "I reckon we ought to load our animals on the stock car. This train will be leaving in fifteen minutes." Putney then walked back to the ticket window. "Did you follow all that?" He asked. The clerk nodded. "Then you go tell the engineer that if that train moves one inch before I'm ready, what I said would be done to them I will visit on you both. I hope you understand."

"You'll get no trouble from either of us, Marshal. I guarantee it."

⊠

Putney and Perkins sat in the back of the second class car while Ballinger and his men sat in the front mumbling and grumbling about the two lawmen. Putney and Perkins had agreed that they didn't think the robbery had been pulled off by Nate Reed. "Last bulletin I read on Nate Reed was that he was up in Colorado and Wyoming," said Perkins.

"Yeah, I saw that, too," said Putney. "It doesn't make any sense he would be back down here."

"Nope," said Perkins. "But I know one thing. We ain't gonna solve it on this train and I once had a friend tell me to never underestimate the power of a good nap and might be sleep may be a rare thing the next few days." With that Perkins stretched his legs out into the aisle and pulled his battered hat down over his eyes.

Putney went to retrieve his cigarette case, felt the wooden box, and remembered the cigarettes were in a different pocket. After getting the right case he leaned back, smoking the Kinney, watching the landscape fly by. Perkins is right he thought and after a few more pulls on the cigarette stubbed it out and imitated the Ranger.

It was seven in the evening when the train chugged to a stop between Ranger and Eastland. Putney and Perkins waited until the Pinkertons were off the train before discussing what their first steps should be. Putney said he thought they should let the Pinkertons do their preening while he and Perkins would snoop around for information the detectives would more than likely miss. The robbed train had been pulled over to a side rail and the mail clerk had been taken for medical treatment in Eastland. The passengers were waiting, impatiently for the lawmen to get through with their tasks so the train could move on. A sheriff's deputy greeted the detectives and the Pinkertons all but snubbed him. They asked where the engineer, fireman, and conductor were because that was who they needed to interview. The deputy said they were all in the caboose and the detectives stomped off in that direction. The deputy spied Putney and Perkins walked over to them and said, "Mighty uppity, ain't they?"

"They can't help it, they're probably Yankees," said Perkins. "What's your name?"

"Arnold Beamer," the deputy said and stuck out his hand. Perkins introduced Putney and himself. "Tell me Arnold, where's Sheriff Schmick?"

"He took off with the posse as soon as he could gather enough men," said Beamer.

"Which way did they go?" Putney was letting Perkins ask the questions, biding his time.

293

"They headed out south. That's the way the mail clerk said the bandits went."

"How is the clerk, anyway?" asked Perkins.

"Bullet busted his kneecap. The doc says he'll be gimping around in a brace the rest of his life."

"That's too bad. Did the sheriff pick up any tracks?"

"I don't know. By the time I got here, he had already formed up the posse. He told me to wait here for y'all. I didn't know you were bringing Pinkertons."

"We didn't, they kind of brought us."

Putney looked around. "It's going to be dark, soon, Sam. Deputy Beamer, can you take me to the spot where the train was stopped? I'd like to look around for tracks."

"Sure, let me get my horse," said Beamer.

"I have to get mine from the stock car. Meet me down by the caboose," Putney told the deputy. "You coming, Sam?"

"Nah," said Perkins. "I think I'll nose around with the passengers a bit. See what I can garner."

On the way, Putney had his own questions for Beamer. "They didn't pull up any rails or put up a roadblock?" asked Putney.

"Nope. You must have noticed how much the train slows down climbing Ranger Hill. They rode out of the brush and the train was easy to catch. The trainmen told me it was a precision piece of work. Three boarded the engine, some boarded the first class car, some the caboose, and the rest hit the mail car."

"How many did they say there were?"

"At first, they said about ten, but after the sheriff left, we got to talking and I figured it must have been more like fifteen. The conductor is an old coot. Said he worked on trains during the war, and it looked more like a military raid than just a bunch of loose-knit robbers."

"Is that so?"

"Yep, Like on the passenger car. They didn't bother with second class or steerage, just first class. And there they only took cash. They knew right where to look, too. "Money belts, inside hat bands, women's purses, and men's wallets of course," Perkins lowered his voice as if there were people around that could hear. "They even frisked women's corsets. But they left jewelry and watches and such alone."

"How about the mail car?"

"Kind of the same thing, from what I'm told," said Beamer. "After they shot the mail clerk, he gave up the key and combination right away. He said it wasn't his money and he wasn't going to take any more risk. Funny thing he told me, Marshal."

"What's that?"

"There was a lot more gold than they took. He said the leader told them to take forty-five bars, three each, so as not to weigh down the horses. That's how I came up with fifteen bandits. He said they split the gold up right then and there and they did the money, too, except he gave one man half, and he kept the other half. Ain't that strange?"

"It would be if they were all going in the same direction to make their escape. Not so strange if they were planning to split up."

"Here we are, Marshal," said Beamer.

Putney looked to the west and figured he had maybe half an hour of light left to find any tracks. He looked around and saw where the posse had trampled any marks that he could have deciphered but it was plain to see the posse's tracks went south, so that's the way Putney went. After about three miles the light was almost too dim to do any good, but Putney suddenly pulled his horse up and dismounted. Beamer started to ride forward, but Putney held him up. Putney cursed himself for not bringing a lantern, but he was sure the sign was clear. He walked a few yards, bent low, and rechecked the ground. The red soil was loose and mixed with tiny shards of gravel. If the posse had been paying attention, they would also have seen the sign, but he could easily see the posse's trail continued south. He gathered three large stones and stacked them as a marker.

"I don't think we'll find anything else tonight," Putney told Beamer. "Is there a decent restaurant in town?"

"Yeah, but they ain't got nothing left, by now. Anybody that had any spare food has been out selling to the passengers. I had to get on a couple of people trying to cheat those poor folk for something to eat and drink. Why do you think people would do something like that, Marshal?"

"Because, deep down everyone has the potential to be a thief," Putney replied.

By the time Putney and Beamer returned to the train, the passengers were boarding. "What's going on?" Putney asked Perkins.

"Seems the Pinkertons have all the information they need," Perkins said. "They cleared the train to go on. I got your mules and my animals off the train. They are sending the charter back to Fort Worth."

"Did you get anything from the passengers?"

"Yeah," said Perkins, "But it's kind of odd. They all said the robbers kept calling one guy Nate. Kind of like he was boss."

"Why would they do that? I think they would want to keep their identity secret," said Putney.

"That's my thinking, too, but it gets odder," Perkins told Putney. "The Pinkertons said the trainmen told them the same thing." Putney twisted up his face in a quizzical manner. "Yeah, and according to the conductor, the mail clerk said the same thing."

"It sounds like someone was trying to make a point," said Putney.

"I reckon Sheriff Schmick only got the story from the mail clerk and that's why he thought it was Nate Reed. But I don't think Texas Jack is that stupid," The Ranger used Reed's moniker.

"I would bet he isn't," Putney agreed.

"What did you find," Perkins asked Putney.

"I don't want the Pinkertons to overhear. Let's go back to where the train was hit and make camp. I'll tell you on the way."

"That's alright by me."

Ballinger walked over to the two lawmen and said, "We're going into town and get a good meal and rooms. Are you boys coming?"

"Nah," said Perkins. "A soft bed might make my bones hurt. We'll just camp out down the tracks a bit. Y'all try to catch up in the morning. From what Putney says, the tracks won't be hard to follow."

"Fine, then," smirking at the westerners. "Try not to get lost in the dark."

"If we do, I'm sure we can depend on you finding us," said Perkins.

On their way to stake out a camp site, Putney told Perkins what he had found. "About three miles south of the rail tracks, I saw sign where it looked like somebody had used some brush to obliterate tracks heading back east. In the morning, we'll get back there and we ought to be able to tell more then, but I'm willing to bet that at least part of the gang doubled back. I can't see them going back to Fort Worth."

"What do you think the plan is?"

"Why wouldn't they head south?" Putney asked of himself as much as Perkins. "It has got to be three hundred miles to the Mexican border. By the time they make fifty miles, every sheriff between here and there will be on alert. Not to mention Rangers. And they have to go past Fort Concho. That's a risk there."

"What about cutting west?"

"Same thing, too much distance and there's Fort Stockton and Fort Davis."

"So, you're thinking north."

"That's what I would do. It can't be more than a hundred miles to the Red River. They could cross into the Nations, and it wouldn't take much to pay off the Indians to hide them out until things cool down. Then they could scatter out and be free as birds."

"Unless we catch them first."

"That's a big if. How do you feel about crossing the Red?"

"I reckon you could deputize me."

"I reckon I will if it comes to it," said Putney.

Chapter Thirty-Nine

By dawn, Putney and Perkins had eaten breakfast of bacon, beans, and coffee, and were riding south. When they got to the spot Putney had marked, they both dismounted and began their search for tracks. "it's just like you say, Nahum," said Perkins. "If you know what you're looking at, it's plain to see there's been a drag here."

"The posse must have been in too big a hurry to miss it. If they had a good tracker, he couldn't have missed it."

"Well, you didn't and it's a good thing. Now let's see if we can find where they dropped the drag and pick up their tracks," said Perkins.

"What about the Pinkerton's?"

"What about them," Perkins wanted to know.

"If there's fifteen bandits, even the Pinkertons could be some help," Putney said.

"I reckon you're right. Leave a marker with a note. Like as not they'll miss it, but they may get lucky," Perkins laughed.

After half an hour they found where the outlaws had dropped the drag, and a clear trail could be seen by both lawmen. The trail bent gradually north and about half an hour later crossed back over the tracks. It was at the bottom of Ranger Hill which was about two miles from where the train had stopped. The trail skirted west of a farming community called Strawn and continued north. It had been more than a decade since Putney had been in the area, but nothing had changed much. There were wide valleys between hills that grew higher as they rode north. The main difference was that the area had been surveyed and mapped, better than when he had been there previously. One thing that Putney always kept with his packs was a map case. Unfortunately, most of the maps he had were of southwest Texas and not this area. Perkins told him not to be concerned over maps as he knew the area pretty well. "Once these hills grow into the Palo Pinto Mountains it may get a little rough, but no more for us than them. And they've left a pretty good trail." *Maybe too good of a trail*, thought Putney.

The two kept north all day long, rarely losing sight of the tracks they were following. It was close to six in the evening when they came across a campsite. There was a good-sized campfire, but it was cold by the time they had gotten there, and there was a pile of discarded bean cans. They dismounted and scouted around the camp. "I think you were right, Nahum. It looks like they have a day on us," said Perkins. "But there's something I don't understand."

"What's that, Sam?"

"The Brazos can't be more than a couple of miles. Why didn't they go on and cross and make camp on the other side?"

"Maybe it had gotten dark, and they didn't want to ford at night."

"Yeah, that would make sense, I reckon, but it sure doesn't look like men who are on the run."

"Let's take a look around and see what else we can find," Putney suggested.

Each man took a different side of the campfire and began walking in ever-widening circles, looking for anything that might give them some information. Putney's search led him over to a stand of live oaks. He searched around on the ground, then when he was sure of his findings, he called Perkins over. "What do you see?" he asked.

Right away Perkins answered, "Well, from the horse shit, it's plain they picketed their animals here."

"What else?"

Perkins bent over taking a good look at the ground. After a few minutes, he said, "There weren't but ten horses here, at the most."

"Yeah, that's what I saw, too. What do you think it means?"

"Well, the best possible circumstance for us is that we've only been tracking ten horses anyway. It's not like we were counting on the trail. Could be five of them liked their odds of going south better. Or they could have split off somewhere that we didn't see."

"And what would be the worst circumstance you can think of?"

"Probably the same as you," the Ranger said. "Five of them dropped off and waited for us to pass and are scheming to come up behind us."

"And if we were to try and ford the Brazos before dark, the others could be waiting on the other side. Catch us in the middle of the river and it would be a duck shoot."

"Damn it, Putney," said Perkins. "I wish you hadn't said what I was thinking out loud. It kinda gives me the shivers. How about you?"

"I hate to think we've been duped, and the idea doesn't give me a great deal of comfort."

"Look, I ain't saying I'm scared, but let's just say I would prefer us to be wrong at that them yayhoos lit out south like I said. What do you think we should do?"

Putney kicked at a pile of horse droppings, thought for a minute, and finally said, "I think, if this is real, our best hope is that the Pinkertons followed our trail. If five of them dropped behind us, they would probably wait for us to move on. Chances are they won't come at us without the aid of the others. Unless the others come back across the river, I think we could be safe and the Pinkertons may well catch up to us before dark."

"Well," said Perkins. "it's a plan. Not a good one, mind, but I don't have anything better."

Perkins built a small fire and put on a pot of coffee while Putney staked out the animals and fed them grain. Using his hat as a bowl, he poured water into his hat and watered each animal, emptying both canteens. It wasn't much but if their hunch was right, they couldn't risk going to the river for water. Perkins had enough water for them to make it through the night. Putney loosened the cinches on the animals so they could blow but left them saddled and packed. He unstrapped the shotgun from his pack and dug around for a box of shells for the ten gauge and a box of cartridges for the Winchester. He had enough bullets in his shell belt to reload his Smiths twice each. The thirty-eight Colt was for the final round. He also dug out a frying pan, bacon, three cans of beans plates, cups, and forks.

The two men ate while it was still light. They didn't want to be occupied in the dark if an attack came. They had decided to keep the fire burning after dark, so the Pinkertons could see it. When it grew dark, they would crawl away from the fire about ten feet on each side and wait. The last rays of the sun were stretched out over the top of a hill, and it would be pitch dark in seconds. They both slithered on their bellies, away from the fire, as they had planned and waited. After about ten minutes there was a call in the darkness. "Hello, the camp," It was Ballinger's voice.

"Keep to your left, Ballinger," Putney called back. He had called out Pinkerton man's name so he would know the camp was friendly. "Hold your horses there. I will come to you."

Ballinger was confused but figured Putney must have a reason so he led his men to his left and in the flickering light of the fire could just make out where the lawmen's animals were picketed. Putney slithered away from the floor another five feet then rose and walked crouching to the horses.

Ballinger and his men had dismounted and were waiting. With the cover of the horses, Putney stood erect and walked over to the Pinkerton's. "What the hell is going on here," Ballinger asked. Putney filled him in on what Perkins and he thought could be happening. "Well, that's something," said Ballinger. "A Marshal and a Ranger getting caught in a squeeze. You should have waited for us."

"I don't know for sure that we are in a squeeze, but it wouldn't have made any difference if we waited for you. If we had, we wouldn't have found this camp before dark and we wouldn't have figured out that an ambush might be set up."

"Still," said Ballinger, "You have to appreciate the irony of it."

Ballinger was getting under Putney's skin, and he knew it. "Have it your way," said Putney. "Have it any way you want. I don't care. But I'm big enough to tell you that we are glad to see you, in case we are right. "If we're not right then the bandits still have a day on us, and we will need to get after it tomorrow to try and make up time before they get to the Red River."

"Alright, Putney," said Ballinger, "We are on the same side, after all. Let's let by gones be by gones."

"That's good by me," Putney said. "There's coffee in the pot by the fire and a couple of cans of warm beans, if you want them."

"Any meat," asked one of the other detectives.

"Be polite, Stan, and accept what is offered. Besides there's a good ham on the pack horse. You and Paul get these animals staked out and fed, then bring the ham over. We can eat it cold with the beans and coffee." said Ballinger.

"Sure, Josh," said Stan.

"I'll get the rifles," said Ballinger. "Do you think it will be safe by the fire, Putney?"

"Can't say, but I wouldn't make myself too good of a target," Putney advised him.

"Point taken. We will have to take care," Ballinger stopped. "What about the Ranger? Where is he?"

"Sam is on the other side of the fire, somewhere. I'm not certain where."

"Just make sure he doesn't shoot us," said Ballinger.

"He won't," Putney told the detective.

While the Pinkertons ate the five men set a watch. Each man would take two hours while the others bedded down. Given the situation, none of them really slept, they just dozed until it was time for their watch.

Chapter Forty

"What the hell, Bill? I almost shot you. What are you doing here?" a deep-voiced bandit asked.

"The boss sent me," said Bill. "He wants to know what's going on."

"Nothing is going on, that's what's happening," said deep voice. "We weren't expecting those other three. What's the plan now?"

"The boss is bringing everyone across the river, one by one, Dave. By daylight, everyone should be in place. When those law dogs start stirring, we're going to bust in on them. Light the whole camp up," Bill gave a sly giggle. "It will be like shooting fish in a barrel."

"I'm glad you're so sure about it," said Dave. "I've heard about that Putney guy. Some say he don't die. Like a cat with nine lives. And there's a Ranger, too. He won't go down easy. Don't know about them others."

"They're probably just town folk," said Bill. "They'll probably just shit themselves, then die. Easy doings."

"Alright," said Dave. "I'll spread the word over here. You tell the captain we'll be ready when he starts it."

"Adios, Dave," said Bill, and he slinked away into the woods.

Putney had drawn the next to last watch. He felt something burning inside. It was a feeling he knew and he didn't like it. When his time was up, he shook Ballinger. "Your turn," he said.

Ballinger rubbed his eyes. "Guess I did doze off. Didn't think I would," said Ballinger. "Alright. I got it." He rolled over to his knees and then stood, half crouched. "Do you suppose there's any coffee?"

"I cooked some at the beginning of my watch," said Putney. "There's plenty in the pot." Putney walked off to pee, where the horses were tied. The horses stirred a bit but didn't get excited. He set his ten gauge down and walked into the brush about two feet. After he relieved himself, he started back to where his bedroll was, but that familiar feeling told him not to go there. Walking to the other side of the camp, he picked up his Winchester and spare shells. He pushed himself back in the brush, making a small bower for himself, sat, and laid his head on his knees.

Light was peaking over the hills on the east and Ballinger decided to pour himself another cup of coffee before he started waking the others. A rifle crack broke the peace of the morning and Ballinger fell face down, his head just missing the glowing coals of the fire. The morning became alive with gunfire. "They're on us, boys," hollered Sam Perkins. "Defend yourselves."

Stan and Paul jumped up, pistols in hand, suddenly alert. Perkins rolled away from the center of the camp, hugging his Winchester, then got to his knees. Bullets were ripping the air and hitting the earth with thud after thud. Putney stood in his bower, the Winchester to his shoulder. He scanned the landscape and waited. It was still half dark, and each shot the bandits fired showed tongues of flame from their barrels. Putney waited. A rifle cracked from the direction he was looking, He aimed where the flash had come from. It was impossible to tell if he hit anything.

Stan and Paul began firing their Colts as quickly as they could. They were shooting wild into the brush around them. It was doubtful they were hitting anyone. "Get to the trees," Putney yelled at the two detectives who came to their senses and tried to find cover. Another volley of bullets flew into the camp from two directions and Putney feared they weren't going to make it out alive.

Perkins made it to the horses and using them as cover, started trying to pick his targets. One man, in the direction of the river, stood to fire and Perkins dropped him before he could pull the trigger. Paul and Stan managed to reach a stand of live oaks and took time in the cover to reload their pistols. Only Stan had retrieved his rifle. Not being able to strike their targets, the bandits started creeping forward, on both sides. Their mistake was met with deadly fire from Putney and Perkins. Each lawman hit a target which caused the other bandits to duck back into their hiding places.

Putney decided his position was no longer safe, so he picked up the shotgun and ran, along the edge of the brush, for about twenty feet then jumped into the bushes for concealment. The old feeling was growing on him. He came up in a kneeling position, steadied himself, and waited for another man to show. He was rewarded when a tall man stuck his head from behind an elm tree. Putney fired and the man's head exploded like a melon. Putney continued to work his way around in the brush. He was trying to get behind the five he figured had dropped off the trail and come up behind them. He had already shot two. If he could get the others, he could end the crossfire.

By the fire, Ballinger grunted. *Damn that hurts*, he thought. He put one hand up to the muscle next to his neck and felt the sticky blood oozing from his wound. Ballinger was no stranger to battles. He had served with the Union during the war and had been wounded twice. One thing he knew. He was in the open and needed to get somewhere to avoid being shot again. He decided his best option was with the animals. With his good hand, he pulled his pistol from its holster, started running toward the horses, and fired as quickly as he could. He was nearly at the horses when a bullet skittered across the earth and hit him in the ankle. He fell and became an easy target for anyone who wanted to pick him off. Perkins saw the detective fall. He jumped from behind a mule and grabbed the man to pull him to safety. Just as he got Ballinger between two horses, a bullet burned its way through one shoulder blade and out his chest. Perkins fell to his knees and Ballinger grabbed a hand and pulled the Ranger to safety, settling him behind a tree.

Paul and Stan had finally gathered their wits and from their fort stopped firing wildly and started trying to pick their targets. The rising sun started filling the little opening with light and burned away the shadows where the bandits had hidden. Stan had his rifle to his shoulder, and seeing one man laying on the ground, aimed in and fired. The body jumped when the bullet struck the man in the head.

Putney was still trying to get behind his targets when a man jumped up from the brush with a pistol in his hand. Putney had his shotgun in his left hand, with the hammers pulled back. When he saw the outlaw, he brought the shotgun up to his waist and pulled both triggers. His foe flew backward and fell into the bushes where he had been hiding. *That's three*, thought Putney. *Two more to go.* He had left the box of shotgun shells where he had been when the battle had started, so he dropped the shotgun and moved forward with the Winchester pointing the way. Putney was surprised when he looked to his left and saw a man in the brush. He was kneeling on all fours, his body was shaking like a man with the tremors, and a stain was growing on the back of his trousers. "Pitch that rifle out," Putney ordered.

"Please, please," cried the man. "Please don't shoot me."

Putney struggled against the thug pushing its way up from his gut. *Shoot him*, he thought, but he threw the urge aside. "Chunk that rifle and your pistol and you might live today," Putney growled at the cowering man. The outlaw followed Putney's orders and then collapsed on his face sobbing like a baby. "You stay right there," Putney commanded. "If you're not here when I come back, I will hunt you down like a dog and kill you where you lay."

Putney continued making his way around the camp, trying to find the fifth killer. He heard a crashing noise, turned, and saw a man on a horse whipping it for all he was worth. Putney aimed his rifle and fired. The outlaw slumped to one side and slid off the horse. Putney waited to see if the man would stand. He didn't.

Standing on one good leg, behind a horse, Ballinger managed to reload his pistol. He wished he had a rifle, but he knew he had to make do with what he had. Somehow, he realized that there no longer was anyone firing from behind him. He hoped that was a good sign. With his pistol, he aimed in at a tree where he earlier had seen a man popping his head out. Thinking he might have just one opportunity, Ballinger pulled the hammer back so the trigger wouldn't have far to move when he was ready. He waited until his man peeked from around the tree. Ballinger squeezed the trigger, lightly. The bullet struck the tree. *Damn it*, he thought and aimed again. His target again stuck his head from behind the tree. This time Ballinger's shot was true.

Putney was ready to end the battle and with abandon started walking through the center of the camp. The thing inside him was growing out of his control. Bullets whizzed past him and hit dirt and trees behind him. Putney raised his rifle. In his mind's eye he could see his old life in Wyoming and Montana. Now, Jack Callahan totally dominated him and like so many of the times before, he walked toward trouble not regarding his life. He saw one man ahead of him and pulled the trigger on the rifle. The hammer hit an empty chamber. He dropped the rifle pulled a Smith and shot the man in the head. Seeing Putney coming at him another man jumped up and fired. The bullet flew through Putney's long hair. Putney pulled the trigger on his pistol, twice, hitting the man both times. From the bushes, two pistols and two rifles flew out and hit the ground in front of Putney. Two men were yelling, in unison, "I surrender, I surrender."

In a voice as calm as angels' breath, or maybe a demon's, Putney said, "Get up. If you try to shoot, I will kill you where you stand." Both men stood with their hands high above their heads.

"Walk to the fire and sit," Putney ordered.

Paul and Stan slowly crept from their protective trees; guns pointed at the defeated bandits. "There's one more back behind us," Putney said still aiming his pistol forward. By Putney's count, there were only two, maybe three outlaws left. He waited. There was no more movement. No more assault.

Putney walked to the center of the camp, feeling he was returning to himself. Paul and Stan were dragging a man from the brush who was crying, "No, no. He'll kill me if I'm not there."

"Shut up," said Stan, "or I may kill you, myself. They dragged the man to the other two and dropped him.

"Over here, Stan," called Ballinger. "I'm going to need some help."

Stan and Paul went over to their comrade and seeing he was wounded, carried him back to the fire. Putney looked around, "Where's Sam?" he asked.

"Over by the horses," Ballinger said. "I think he's wounded pretty bad.

Putney went to where Perkins was lying behind a tree. He knelt by the Ranger and asked, "How you doing, Sam?"

"I've been better," Perkins tried to laugh.

Putney bent down and picked up his friend, carried him over, and gently set him down by Ballinger. "You rest here, pard, I'll get some bandages," Putney told the two Pinkertons that he had manacles and leg irons in his pack, and they should come get them so they could lock up the prisoners. When the three returned the Pinkertons began locking up the captives while Putney tended to the wounded.

"Take care of Ballinger first," said Perkins. "I just need to rest a minute."

Putney inspected Ballinger's wounds. "Good news is, you'll survive," Putney said. "Bad news, I think you're going to walk with a limp for a while."

Ballinger laughed. "At least I'll walk," he said.

Putney always kept rolls of clean cotton strips and a bottle of carbonic acid. He tore a foot-long strip of bandage, folded it in a square, and soaked it with the acid. He tore away Ballinger's shirt from around the wound on Ballinger's neck, "This is going to burn," he said and placed the square on the wound. Ballinger winced as the antiseptic went to work. The wound was in an awkward place, but Putney wrapped a bandage as well as he could to hold the pad in place. The other wound had broken Ballinger's ankle. Luckily, Ballinger wore high-top laced shoes which, though not practical in the wilds, made it easy to remove. Putney found some sticks, then following the same procedure, placed carbolic-soaked pads on both sides of the ankle then wrapped it. He put the sticks on each side of the ankle, splinting it, and using more bandage to keep them in place.

Putney then turned to Perkins. "How are you holding up?" he asked.

"As well as can be expected," Perkins said, wheezing.

Using his Bowie, Putney cut away the upper portion of Perkin's shirt. The wound in the Ranger's chest was the size of a silver dollar and Putney could hear the wheezing each time Perkins breathed. "It ain't good, is it?" said Perkins.

The wound was similar to the one Putney had received at the hands of Ned Blakely, except worse. "I'm not going to lie to you, Sam. You're right. It's bad. But let me get you cleaned up. I'm going to need to bend you over to get to the wound in your back and it's going to be painful."

"Just get to it and quit telling me about it. It ain't the first time I've been shot."

Putney did as he said he would and saw the bullet hole. Much smaller than the one in Perkins' chest. It looked like the bullet had gone through the right shoulder blade and come out near where Perkins' heart would be. Putney cleaned the dirt off and placed a carbolic-soaked square on it. "Come hold this," Putney said to the

Pinkertons, he didn't care which. Stan knelt by Perkins and held the patch in place while Putney cleaned and treated the front wound. Then between the two of them, they coiled cotton strips around the chest and finally tied it off.

Stan and Paul brought over bedrolls for the two wounded to lay on, then they went to survey the damage that the lawmen had done to the outlaws. While they were doing that Putney unsaddled the horses and mules, tied them in a string, and riding his horse bareback went to the river to water the animals. He was certain they had missed at least two, if not more, of the bandits, so he kept his senses on alert. The Brazos was flowing swiftly, so he found a low bank that formed a sort of beach and took the animals there. When they had their fill, he returned to the camp. Paul and Stan had brought over saddles for the two wounded to prop their heads on and were interrogating the prisoners.

"We know there were fifteen of you," Stan was saying. "Ten of your friends are dead. You make thirteen. Where are the other two?"

"How the hell should we know? We had all we could do to keep our wits about us with y'all murdering us the way you did." said one outlaw.

"Murdering you? That's a laugh," said Paul. "It was all we could do from getting killed by y'all."

"Yeah, well it was a stupid plan," said another bandit. "We should have stuck to the original and waited for y'all to get to the middle of the river."

"What about you?" Stan asked the one man who was still whimpering. "Who were the other two?"

"Between his short sobs, the man said, "Didn't know their real names. Called one Nate and the other Captain."

"You're not going to get much out of these men right now," said Putney. "They're still scared. Let them calm down a bit then they will start getting hungry. That's when you can expect to get some answers. In the meantime, why don't y'all see if you can round up their horses? I know there's one loose on the trail we came in on and there ought to be four others tied up back there someplace. My bet is you will find gold and cash with the horses."

"What should we do with the bodies?"

"I have a rule I learned from my father. Let them lay. They knew the task they set for themselves, and this is the consequence."

"You don't want to bury them?" asked Paul.

"Why? That would be a hell of a lot of work. And you won't get them buried deep enough to keep the coyotes, wolves, and cougars from digging them up. Nah, in two days the crows will have a hard time finding a meal."

Ballinger spoke up for the first time in a while. "He's right boys. It would be a lot of work for nothing. You two go find the horses like Putney said. We need to recover as much loot as we can. And then we need to get to civilization. Chicago will be wanting a report. Putney, where do you suppose the nearest town is from here?"

"It's been years since I've been out this way, but to my recollection, I don't think we're far from Palo Pinto," Putney told him.

"That's right," wheezed Perkins, who could barely be heard.

Putney knelt beside his friend, "Which direction, Sam?"

It was hard for Perkins to talk, but he managed to get out, "About ten miles southeast, I think," he said.

"Thanks," Putney told him then asked Ballinger, "Did you get that?"

"Yeah, thanks. I'll have the boys look around for about another hour for horses. If you wouldn't mind cooking up some ham and beans, and some coffee, maybe we could get out of here by noon."

"I can take care of that. Tell your boys to be careful crossing the Brazos, looking for those horses. It's a tricky river."

Putney got some more beans, plates, another pan, and coffee from his packs, blazed up the fire, and started the cook.

While waiting for the coffee Perkins said, "Nahum come here, I need to talk to you, but I can't speak too loud." Putney knelt by the Ranger, who said, "Nahum, I reckon I ain't going to ride out of here."

Putney wouldn't lie to any man in this condition. "No, I'm sure you won't."

"You know," said Perkins, "I wouldn't mind a panther chewing up my body. A man could say he was something if he was eaten by a lion. But damn it, with my luck, it will be wolves or worse, coyotes. I'm going to ask you a favor."

"You name it," said Putney.

"I would appreciate it and will sing your praises to the angels if you would wait here with me until I pass. I'll try not to keep you too long."

"It would be my honor, Sam."

"I keep an old canvas on my pack mule. If you wouldn't mind wrapping me up in it. I have a nice little house north of Fort Worth in a place called Saginaw. A wife and a fifteen-year-old boy, too. If you'll carry my body there, I'll do my damnedest not to stink overly much."

"Again, Sam, I'm glad you told me. I promise you'll get a decent burial."

"There's just one more thing, Nahum."

"Tell me, Sam."

"There's a bottle of whiskey in my pack. I hope I go to heaven, but if I go to hell, I don't think I could bear to face ole slew foot sober."

Chapter Forty-One

The Pinkertons found eight horses across the river still picketed. They searched the saddle bags but found none of the stolen bullion or cash. They figured the ones that had gotten away had grabbed the loot and high-tailed it north. There was nothing they could do about it now, they had to get Ballinger and prisoners to Palo Pinto. Returning to the camp, they reported to Ballinger, and he agreed. "I suppose you two will have to go up into the Indian Nations and try to track them down after you dump these guys with the sheriff in Palo Pinto. We'll catch a train to Fort Worth. You can telegraph Chicago with a report, and I'll get good medical attention. Putney patched me up pretty good, so I think I'll be fine."

The men ate a lunch of beans, bacon, and coffee, fed the prisoners, and started packing up. "What are we going to do with all these extra horses?" asked Paul.

"They will be a drag on you," Putney advised. "I'd let them go. They'll be alright. There's plenty of grass around here. The Sheriff will probably send someone out to round them and the tack up."

It was just past one o'clock when everything was ready. Paul and Stan hoisted the prisoners aboard horses, then helped Ballinger mount. "Putney," said Ballinger. "I know we got off to a rough start, but I have to tell you I'm glad you were here."

"You boys held your own," said Putney. "Sam and I would probably be buzzard bait if it hadn't been for y'all."

"What do you want me to do with these prisoner irons?"

"Find Deputy Sheriff Hubert Forsythe. He'll take care of them. By the way, don't try to follow the Brazos. That river snakes around so much you wouldn't find your way to Palo Pinto for days. Just cut southeast as straight as you can. I'm sure you'll be alright."

Ballinger bent over to shake Putney's hand. "If you ever want to work as a detective, I'll put in a good word for you."

Putney said thanks, although both men knew that would never happen.

When the Pinkertons rode away Putney settled himself down by Sam Perkins. "Weren't such bad boys in the end," said Perkins.

"Reckon not," replied Putney. "How are you holding out?"

"The whiskey don't hurt," said Perkins.

Putney reached over to the coffee pot and poured himself a cup. Hearing a great wheeze, he looked and saw Sam Perkins had passed. Putney drank his coffee and smoked a cigarette. He thought about Deidre and hoped if was ever killed out in the field there would be someone to take him home to her. He finished the coffee, threw the cigarette butt in the fire, and went to get the canvas out of Perkins' pack.

After he had the Ranger secured in his wrappings, he started packing up all the gear. He would load Sam's body last. He just finished securing the gear on both mules and was throwing the saddle on Perkins' horse when he heard a rustling behind him. The hairs on the back of his neck bristled. He dropped the saddle and started to reach for a pistol when he heard a Winchester being cocked. "I wouldn't do that Corporal," it was Montague Russell's voice. Putney turned slowly and standing before him was his old captain. No longer in the ragged clothes he had worn in Fort Worth, Russell was wearing the trappings of a successful Texas rancher.

There was rustling of brush from a different direction and Bull Dawson stepped into the open. "I wish he hadda gone for that gun, I'da dropped him where he stood."

"That's William for you, Putney," said Russell. "Never one to savor the moment. Just charge ahead, damned the consequences." Putney stayed silent. "William, why don't you go over there and relieve the corporal of the burden of trying to figure out how he's going to draw one of those guns and kill us?"

Dawson came around behind Putney, reached around him, and withdrew both Smiths from their holsters. "Check under that Mexican jacket, William," instructed Russell. "I wouldn't put it past the corporal to have a hideout gun under there." Dawson felt around and found the Colt in the shoulder holster and took it.

"Didn't I see a bottle of whiskey by that dead man?" asked Russell. "William dig that coffee pot out of the corporal's things. Let's have a cup of coffee spiced with some whiskey. Sort of a celebration." Russell motioned for Putney to walk over to the

313

campfire. "Stoke that fire up Corporal but take care not to do something stupid. I would hate to end this early." Russell was enjoying trying to degrade Putney by continually referring to him as Corporal. It didn't bother Putney.

Dawson brought the bag of coffee and the pot to the fire, filled the pot with water, and started the coffee boiling. Russell invited Putney to sit while the coffee was cooking. Putney sat in the dirt with one leg out and one with his knee bent. Russell sat opposite Putney on a log one of the Pinkertons had drug over earlier. "Corporal, you have no idea how long I have waited for this moment. I'm glad now Blakely screwed up killing you in Fort Worth. I couldn't believe it when I saw you in town. I thought of killing you myself, but that may have risked my other plans, so I paid Blakely a hundred dollars to kill you. I guess he must have hired that dunce Doby to help. A bad decision that.

Putney spoke for the first time. "I guess that was you who hired those two cowboys to gun me down at the train station."

"Yes, that was unfortunate, too. I gave William another hundred to do that, but he took it upon himself to hire those two dimwits. Evidently, they didn't have sharpshooter skills. And William, well William does what he does best when he sees the odds are against him. That is to skedaddle." The pot was shaking from the boiling coffee. "William, why don't you pour us all a cup of coffee and put some whiskey in each cup? We will drink to Corporal Putney's success and imminent demise."

Dawson had been standing behind Putney but now came around in between him and Russell. He poured three cups of coffee then a generous portion of whiskey in his and Russell's cup, but just a splash in Putney's. "No sense wasting, huh, Putney."

Putney picked up his cup of coffee and blew in it to cool the hot liquid. He watched as Russell laid the rifle across his lap and reached for his cup. Dawson stood beside Russell.

"I have a question, Russell," said Putney. "Where did you get all this money to pay for my assassination?"

"Oh, I'm sure you will like that story," Russell told him, "Remember back in Llano when you interrupted us? Well, we had managed several stage robberies. Of course, we never had to worry about capture since Oberman was getting paid off. It was a very sweet operation until you came along. Anyway, I had saved all the money from those actions. Then I moved up to Waco, made a few investments, and was doing well. As Fort Worth was growing, I moved up there and as you know, I saw an opportunity to start putting to right what the war had robbed me of. But then you came along. Again. You are kind of like my own private pestilence, did you know that."

"I am happy to serve," Putney said and took a drink from his cup.

"Please, don't interrupt, I have more to tell you before you die," Russell said. "As I was saying, I had a few investments you never discovered and quite a bit in the bank. After I got out of prison, I returned to Fort Worth, but I wanted everyone to believe I was a broken man. I started planning this action. It wasn't until after the trial that I had everything in place. Except for that poor mail clerk. He wasn't supposed to be on that train. There should have been another, whom I had bribed. Anyway, I put together this troop of men. I had waited for William to get out of prison because I had promised him a cut in the proceeds. Then I realized this opportunity."

"What opportunity?" Putney asked.

"Don't be coy, Corporal. This opportunity. This one right here. Of course, it didn't come off exactly as I had planned. Parts did. You see, I knew you would be dispatched to hunt us down. I also knew I could lay a false trail that would draw away the less astute lawmen, but I knew you wouldn't fall for it. I figured that you would have one other helping you, but I must admit I failed to consider the possibility of Pinkertons. It would have been much more accommodating had you and the Ranger had gone ahead and tried to cross the river. We could have avoided all this messy bloodshed."

"I know losing to me must destroy your ego," said Putney. "In the future, I will see what I can do to be less of a disappointment."

"Make your snide remarks now, Corporal, because when I finish this coffee, you too will be finished."

"Since I'm doomed would it be too much for me to ask if I can have a smoke?"

315

"Not at all, Corporal. After all, we are all civilized here. I would never refuse a condemned man a last request. By all means smoke one of your fancy ready-rolled cigarettes."

"If it's all the same to you, my wife gave me some fancy Cuban forty-ones as a wedding gift. I've been waiting for the right occasion to savor one and it doesn't look like I'll get another chance."

"Please do," Russell allowed.

Putney removed the wooden box from his jacket and smiled as he opened it. Russell and Dawson both smiled back. Putney let the forty-one caliber Remmington derringer fall into his hand. The first bullet split Dawson's skull in the center of his forehead. The second hit Russell in the neck, barely missing his jugular vein. In a second Putney sprung to his feet, plucked Russell's rifle from his hands, and pointed at the villain's head.

"You can't kill me," sputtered Russell. You have disarmed me. It would be against the law for you to kill an unarmed man."

"It would depend on the law," Putney said.

Russell cried, "What law would allow you to kill me like this?"

"Callahan's Law."

THE END